I0628882

AUTHOR OF THE SERIES "A WOMAN OF ENTITLEMENT"

Anne's

WEDDING BARGAIN

BY MARY ANN KERR

THINK WELL BOOKS

thinkwellbooks.com

Anne's Wedding Bargain

Copyright 2017 by Mary Ann Kerr. All rights reserved.

All Scripture is taken verbatim from the King James Version (public domain)

No part of this publication may be reproduced in any form by any electronic or mechanical means, including information storage and retrieval systems, without written permission in writing from the publisher or from the author, except by a reviewer who may quote brief passages in a review.

Published in part by Thinkwell Books, Portland, Oregon. The views or opinions of the author are not necessarily those of Thinkwell Books. Learn more at *thinkwellbooks.com*.

Design and cover illustration by Andrew Morgan Kerr Learn more at andrewmorgankerr.com. Copyediting by Dori Harrell doriharrell.wix.com/breakoutediting

Published and printed in the United States of America ISBN: 978-0-9984894-1-4 Fiction, Historical, Christian

Books by Mary Ann Kerr

DEDICATION

I dedicate this book to
the King of Kings…my Lord and Savior.

I also dedicate this book to
Elida Christine Wagner,
woman of God, warrior for the cause of Christ,
and a most beloved niece.

ACKNOWLEDGMENTS

ANNE'S WEDDING BARGAIN was another one of those stories that simply unfolded day by day. I never know what I'm going to write until I sit down and start typing. The story line had a few things incorporated from my own life that made it easier to write.

I was an orphan by the time I was seven. My brother was a brother like Thad, only he was older, not younger than me. He was the ideal brother and was my hero growing up…he still is! Like one of the characters, my mother couldn't talk. She was also deaf, but the character in the story is not. My eldest sister taught me how to talk, and I also spoke with my hands until I was orphaned.

I was not put into an orphanage, but I did live with an aunt and uncle until I was fourteen and my aunt passed away. I keep wondering if I should write an autobiography, as I have quite a story to tell!

Again, I give all the glory to God for the story. He's given me an ability I never knew I had. Author of creativity, He has bestowed upon me a gifting of which I will never cease being in awe. I look back at some of my books and am amazed that I wrote it. I don't give me credit for it…I give praise to my Father!

I pray that the prayers and Scriptures as well as the godly lives of some of the characters, touches your heart and draws you closer to a God who loves you with a passion.

I thank many of my readers for their encouraging words and wonderful support.

I have made many friends through becoming an author. You know who you are, and I thank you for your friendship and becoming a fan. Judy Maddux and Yvette Mason-Maddux, and Tasha Dunn, who are not quite relatives, but close. I thank you for becoming dedicated readers. Bill and JoAnn Taylor…I've never met you, but thanks for your words of encouragement. Again, Allan and Karen Thomlinson, Earl and Arlene Engle…thanks! Judy Goforth…thanks for spreading the word! Anne Nelson and Anne and Ron Kruger…you bless me!There are just too many of you to name everyone, but you know who you are and I thank you!

Dori Harrell at Breakout Editing, thank you for your amazing ability to edit my stories and even more, for becoming a friend.

Again, I thank Andrew who creates such amazing covers for my books. My undying gratitude goes to you for all your help! If any of you readers have kids or grandkids age seven or older, you should get Andrew's book at PIRATE POND .COM (The spaces are put in because of publisher requirements, so take them out. I guess it messes up their letter print.) It's a great story and will eventually be a trilogy…the illustrations are precious.

Thanks to David, Rosie, Peter, Rebecca, Stephen, Andrew, and Shari Kerr. You are amazing and such a blessing to me. No woman could ask for better relationships than that which we share. I admire your children and their personal relationship to Jesus Christ.

Phil, I cannot express how much I appreciate you and who you are in Christ. You bless me beyond measure and I love you with all my heart.

List of Characters

Thaddeus Parker. . . . . Orphan
Ginger Parker. . . . . Orphan
James Mobrey. . . . . Wealthy philanthropist
Jacob Bates. . . . . James Mobrey's butler
Lucas Falter. . . . . James Mobrey's best friend
Anne Francis Tarkington. . . . . Director San Rafael School of Primary Learning
Jenny Tarkington. . . . . Anne's grandmother
Billy Hargreaves. . . . . Anne's old beau
Herbert B. Herbert. . . . . Lawyer and friend of Jenny Tarkington
Susannah Baxter. . . . . Owner of San Rafael School of Learning
George Baxter. . . . . Chief of San Francisco Police Department
Cadence Cassidy. . . . . Susannah's granddaughter
Donny Miller. Hired hand at Bannisters' Rancho
Josephine Hensley. . . . . Secretary of school
Elijah Humphries. . . . . Lawyer and owner of the mission
Abigail Humphries. . . . . Elijah's wife and director of the mission
Edward Kepler. . . . . A clerk in Elijah's law firm
Matthew Bannister. . . . . Owner of Rancho Bonito Vineyards
Liberty Bannister. . . . . Matthew's wife/mother of twins
Faith and Matty Bannister. . . . . Bannisters' twins
Conchita Rodriguez. . . . . Bannisters' chief cook and housekeeper
Diego Rodriguez. . . . . Conchita's husband/foreman of Rancho Bonito
Constanza Brodie. . . . . Conchita's sister
Timothy Brodie. . . . . Conchita's brother-in-law
Luce and Lupe. . . . . Conchita's nieces/hired help at Rancho Bonito
Dan Hedley. . . . . Owner of property neighboring the Bannisters'
Buck Rawlins . . . . Sheriff of Napa, California
Hattie Rawlins. . . . . Buck Rawlins' wife
Buddy and Rudy Blake. . . . . Outlaws
Chloe Blake (Sweet Pea). . . . . Rudy's daughter
Melody Mackie. . . . . Mobrey's housekeeper
Corabelle (Cora) Meers. . . . . Mobrey's cook
Florence Harris (Flo). Mobrey's main maid
Molly and Alice. . . . . Mobrey's underservants
Abel Murdock (Dock). . . . . Mobrey's head stableman
Harkin. . . . . Bartender of the Napa Saloon
Alex (Johnson) Liberty. . . . . Liberty's twin
Sylvia Cobain. . . . . Constanza Brodie's nurse
Camran Cobain. . . . . Sylvia's father
Dr. William Harrison. . . . . Elderly doctor in San Francisco
Dr. Daniel Gates. . . . . Alex's best friend since childhood
Clint Pierce. . . . . Lawyer from Boston
Tommy Denko. . . . . Young banker

ᴀMAZING ᴳRACE

Help me Jesus my whole life through
To know I'm uniquely made by you.
And though the trials seem hard and tough,
I am your diamond in the rough.

Polish me Lord and let me know
The trials come to make me grow
Illuminate each part of me
That with your Light I'll clearly see

In every test that comes my way
Your Word I'll follow and obey.
May every trial that I endure
I see your love to make me pure.

Each facet cut by your loving hand
To let me shine and know I am
A glorious work in which you place
Your love, your Son, Amazing Grace.

MARY ANN KERR

PROLOGUE

Let those be ashamed and dishonored who seek my life;
Let those be turned back and humiliated who
devise evil against me.

PSALM 35:4

"QUICK, GINGER!" THADDEUS GRABBED HIS sister's hand. "Under here!" He dragged her down, but her skirts tangled as she dropped to her knees. Thad pulled hard on her arm as she tried to scoot in.

Ginger raised up on her elbows, covered her ears with her hands, and stared at the scene unfolding before her. She wanted to see but didn't want to hear the deafening noise. The wagon they'd crawled under wasn't theirs, but the children didn't care.

Just a short time before, Thad had started the fire, and their mother, making dinner, bade Thaddeus and Ginger to get a couple buckets of water. Thaddeus and Ginger Parker had gone down a narrow trail to the river, buckets swinging happily.

Once at the river, both children had quickly divested themselves of stockings and shoes, wading in the shallow stream. The cool water felt good on their hot, tired feet. It had been a long day, but the best one yet. The wagon master said they'd come at least twenty-two miles. Some days they only made nine. The children filled their buckets with cool water before putting on their dusty stockings and shoes.

Trudging back through the woods toward the wagons, they'd heard the wagon master, Mr. Turner, yell for everyone to circle the wagons. The two children dropped their water buckets and ran as fast as they could up the trail. As they emerged from the woods, they stopped dead in their tracks at the skirmish playing out before them. The group of pioneers were already circling the wagons, having practiced the maneuver several times before entering the plains. Word was, Mr. Turner had said, that attacks from the Shoshone had been frequent that summer. As the two children cleared the woods, the sight before them was one of mayhem—everyone running. This wasn't practice.

Men and women grabbed for their rifles and handguns. Thad and Ginger had left their rifles in the wagon. Arrows rained down, and the children couldn't tell which wagon was theirs.

Thaddeus now dropped to his knees and pulled at his sister's hand. She seemed frozen in place, and he yelled again.

"Hurry! Come on, Ginge!"

Ginger shook off her paralyzing fear and dropped down beside Thad, her skirts jumbled up as he pulled on her arm.

The two crawled under the wagon and watched as men and women alike shot their rifles at the oncoming swarm of attackers. A few of the arrows were lit torches, and some of the wagons began to burn. Many attackers jumped over wagon tongues, fighting hand to hand with the men from the wagon train.

The noise was deafening. Ginger screamed when she saw her mother, crouching straight across from them, grab her neck as an arrow struck her. She crumpled to the ground. Ginger started to crawl out, but Thad held her fast, pushing her down with all his might because she was bigger than he was.

Thad sobbed, tears running down his cheeks as everything in him yearned to go rescue his mother, but in his heart, he knew she was beyond help. He wasn't about to let go of Ginger and lose her too.

The children watched in terrified fear as a couple of other children, within the circle of wagons, were scooped up and carried off by the marauders. One Indian dismounted and grabbed at Ginger's dress. She screamed and scooted closer to Thaddeus. The Indian grabbed at her hair, but she bit his hand. He yelped, dropping to his knees to get a better hold so he could drag her out. Thaddeus had his arm around her waist, trying to keep his sister squeezed up next to his body, but he could feel her slipping toward the Indian.

One of the men from the wagon train saw what was happening and fired.

The war-painted face sprawled in front of the terrified children. Thaddeus squeezed his eyes shut to block out the sight of the man, his face forever frozen in a startled grimace.

As quickly as it had started, it was over. With loud whoops of victory, the band left the wagons, mounted bareback on their horses, taking some of the wagon-train horses with them.

Thaddeus waited until he was sure their attackers were gone before he let go of Ginger, who went running across to where their mother lay. The girl made no sound as she dropped to her knees. She pulled her mother into her arms and clasped her tightly, rocking her mother back and forth as tears streamed down, making rivulets on Ginger's dirty face.

Thaddeus walked with measured steps over to his sister, watching as she held their mother. Two months before, the children had lost their father to cholera, the disease raging through the ten wagons traveling together to California. Thaddeus dropped to his knees and wrapped his arms around them, stretching as far as he could reach. His heart felt as if it would burst from sorrow.

Turning his head away from the shocked horror on his sister's face, Thaddeus whispered, "She's gone, isn't she, Ginger? Our mama has gone to be with Pa."

Ginger looked away from him. She held her lips tightly shut, set in a straight line, as tears poured from eyes full of anguish. She made no reply.

CHAPTER I

But where can wisdom be found?
And where is the place of understanding?

JOB 28:12

ANNE FRANCIS TARKINGTON SAT IN a heavy oaken chair made more comfortable by the cushions she'd made for the seat and back. It helped to brighten the room with color. With her forearms lying on the desk, she clasped her hands in front of her—immediately unclasping them. Nerves crawled up and down her spine. She glanced at her calendar. It was Wednesday, the third day in February. The numerals of the year, 1886, were printed in large type above the month.

Mrs. Baxter should be arriving any minute, she thought.

Mrs. Baxter owned the San Rafael School of Primary Learning, and she had approached Anne on the recommendation of a friend of Mrs. Baxter's from Virginia. Anne had been interviewed not only by Mrs. Baxter but by some of the school's staff members. The questions about interaction with children, methods, and goals were most thorough. At the end of the interview, they'd ask her if she had any questions. She had. She asked them to tell her why she should choose to work there. What made this school special to them? It had been enlightening as well as allowing the staff to see how difficult answering questions off the cuff actually was. She'd been hired before the day's end.

This was Anne's first inspection as director since she had taken over as headmistress in December.

She rose from her chair and looked over the room in satisfied contentment. It had been a dull brown with ancient, streaked windows, the caulking cracked and falling apart. Heavy curtains full of dust had choked Anne when she'd removed them. The books on the shelves were good, but they had been dulled with spiderwebs and more dust. She wondered that the man who'd been the previous director could even breathe in the room.

Waiting for her boss, she paced around her office, looking at what she'd done to brighten it. With her first paycheck, she'd replaced the old windows with bigger paned windows that opened easily. She worked tirelessly, after hours, cleaning and painting. She'd replaced the old curtains with white linen ones sporting wide tiebacks. The walls had been painted a suntan yellow, and she'd painted the mantel and dark wooden trim white. Floral cushions of chintz in red, white, and varying shades of yellow graced the love seat under the window, and she'd made matching ones for her desk chair as well as the straight backs that faced her desk. She'd carefully used a leather cleaner for the spines and covers of the books, and they now gleamed on shelves clean of any dirt. It had taken hours of deep cleaning, but she was pleased with her handiwork.

She stopped pacing and returned to her desk. *I hope Mrs. Baxter isn't going to be late. I have a list of things that need doing today.* Flipping open her timepiece, which hung on a chain from her neck, she checked the time.

Mrs. Baxter is late. Anne sighed. She snapped the cover closed over the face of the timepiece, a beautifully engraved gold. It had been a present from the young man she was to marry. She traced her fingers over the smooth etching. It had been a little over six years ago. She held the watch as she let the memories wash over her.

Anne had been raised by a widowed grandmother. Her own parents had perished in a train accident on the East Coast. Anne didn't remember them, not even when she looked at a daguerreotype of them. Her father's widowed mother, Jenny Tarkington, had taken on the task of raising her only grandchild, who was two years old at the time.

Funds had been in short supply, and Anne had been raised having a plethora of chores and knowing frugality. She'd not gone to boarding school but to a day school that had a good reputation. As money allowed, she had plenty of culture in music and museums. Her grandmother had seen to that. She excelled in her studies and from years and years of hard practice was a consummate pianist.

Her best friend had been a next-door neighbor, Billy Hargreaves. Billy and Anne had been inseparable growing up, challenging each other in their schoolwork and everything else they did.

When the two had turned seventeen, Billy asked Anne to marry him. The pledge had been the beautifully engraved gold timepiece. Jenny Tarkington had been ecstatic. She had always liked Billy and had entertained high hopes he'd fall in love with her granddaughter.

Billy's parents were in high dudgeon. Their son had not consulted them about his plans. The Hargreaves had become quite wealthy in recent years and were well connected. They had ambitious goals for their son, and Anne, with no dowry, was not part of them. They severed the relationship, threatening to cut Billy out of his inheritance. At first he railed against it, but in the end, seeing their implacable resolve, he acquiesced. Billy was sent forthwith to England to attend Eton College, an all-boys school.

Anne had been inconsolable and brokenhearted. She couldn't understand how money could be more important to Billy than the love they shared. She'd tried to reason with him, but he was adamant and cut her off. It was over.

For a few years she'd hated the timepiece. She'd wrapped it in a handkerchief and buried it deep in a chiffonier drawer. As the years slipped by, she'd come to see the beautiful piece as part of the good memories she had of growing up. She was thankful she now had no feelings for Billy. He was a friend of her past, nothing more, and no hard feelings remained. She rarely thought of him.

Hearing a tap on her door broke Anne's reverie.

"Yes?"

Josephine, her secretary, poked her head around the door. "Mrs. Baxter to see you, miss."

"Show her in, Josie. Please show her in." Anne rose from her chair, smoothing down her skirts with shaky hands as she walked around the huge desk to greet the owner of the San Rafael School of Primary Learning. She swallowed, her stomach tightening with nerves. *I'm glad my hands don't sweat with nervousness the way some people's do. Mrs. Baxter is a wonderful lady but seems quite exacting. I hope I never disappoint her expectations.*

"Good morning, Mrs. Baxter. It's a pleasure to see you." Anne smiled, reaching out to shake the older woman's hand, already graciously extended.

Mrs. Baxter shook the younger woman's hand with a firm grip and patted the top of it.

"Good morning, Miss Tarkington. I hope I'm not interrupting anything. I'm glad to see you received my message. Sorry you had such short notice. Mr. Baxter and I decided late yesterday to come up from the city for a few days. I wish to talk to you about the letter you sent me a few weeks ago. I'd like to see all the classes, of course, but I especially wish to meet the two new children you wrote about. I must say I am glad you did not turn them away due to physical incapabilities. I understand the San Francisco orphanage wanted to send that traumatized girl to the poorhouse. I am pleased that instead they were sent here. Those children are as in need of love as anyone else. Your letter caused much pathos and made me to want to see this boy and girl. Such a sad story, isn't it?"

Anne murmured a response as Mrs. Baxter continued to talk.

"I looked around a bit before our appointment and must say you certainly have brightened the school with paint and the little extras on the walls. I have received several missives from staff, and all speak highly of your capabilities. I was a bit hesitant to hire you, as you are quite young, but you certainly have not disappointed me."

Mrs. Baxter waved her hand expansively as she continued to talk.

"I like what you have done in here. It doesn't even look like the same room. I see that you've done this throughout the school. More to the point, I would like to raise your salary and provide a spending account for you to be used exactly as you have done. I know you've used your own funds, and I don't want you to do that, young lady. I will reimburse what you've spent. I am proud and pleased with what you have accomplished in the short time you have been running the school. Our last director was not so interested in the children nor their welfare, nor did he care to make the environment a pleasant place."

Anne glowed under her employer's praise.

"Thank you, Mrs. Baxter. Thank you very much." Anne had heard much from the staff about the last director, and none of it complimentary. She had done her best to squelch such talk, but there were several teachers who had difficultly concealing their feelings.

"I feel privileged to be able to run such a fine institution and am grateful for my secretary, Josephine. She is competent and doing an excellent job. The staff have been welcoming and are a credit to your school."

Susannah Baxter smiled and inclined her head in acknowledgment.

"Come—we will take a tour, and you will soon see those two precious children for yourself. For some reason, I feel especially bonded to them. I don't usually allow myself that kind of relationship because it seems I'd like to adopt all of the orphans and take them home with me." Anne laughed a little ruefully. "I've never been a mother, of course, but my maternal instincts must be strong. I want to scoop those two new ones up and soak up all their misery. Things are a bit better for them now than when they were on the trail. I continue to wonder if the girl shouldn't have more medical attention." She opened her office door and led Mrs. Baxter across the foyer and into the hall of learning.

"What do you think, Lucas? Is it insane? I am quite sure it is." James Mobrey was in a quandary and hoped his best friend would have good advice. "Perhaps one day I'll marry, but for now, I believe I'm to go ahead with this. Tell me true—do you think it's temporary insanity?"

"It's not temporary, my friend," Lucas replied with a laugh. "What age bracket are you thinking?"

"What's that got to do with it? I don't know! I simply can't seem to think of anything else." James' reply sounded crotchety even to his own ears.

He and Lucas had met at the Napa Inn for lunch, catching up on news. Lucas had been a guest of James but had left two weeks before, traveling up to the Oregon territory to visit another friend. He'd only just returned from Portland.

Lucas Falter sucked in his upper lip, his lower lip closing over it. It was a sign of contemplation, a habit with which James was quite familiar.

Lucas didn't care to ruffle his friend's feathers, but he had to ask. "Have you made this a subject of prayer? Remember what Reverend

Merill said? He's always saying it—pray first. We seem to rush headlong into things and then pray. He's right, you understand. He's spot on."

"Are you jesting, Lucas? I've been praying about this for nigh unto a year, and so has Reverend Merill. He told me to follow the Lord's leading. He also said to wait a bit and see if this feeling I have passes or if it persists. Yes, of course I've made it a matter of prayer. Let me see…it was February last year, right after Valentine's Day and just before my twenty-fourth birthday. Yes sireee, I'll be twenty-five come the seventeenth. February 17, 1886, is a day I've been looking forward to for quite some time. I have plenty of funds even after building such a huge house, but on this birthday, I'll inherit the rest of the trust set up for me. I have bought a bit of stock in Bell Telephone and the Union Pacific, and both are doing well. Now back to the subject at hand—am I crazy?"

"Certifiable, my friend, certifiable. Where do you think you could go to get a child?"

"It's not simply a child, Lucas. I plan on two, a boy and a girl. I thought perhaps the San Rafael School of Primary Learning. I know those children are well treated, but for some reason my heart seems to be led in that direction. I could travel on down to San Francisco. There's a big orphanage there, but I feel the Lord is pointing me to San Rafael."

"Well, if the good Lord is telling you, then for the sake of your sanity as well as your conscience, you'd better be getting yourself down there." Lucas admired his friend but couldn't fathom his desire to take in children when he should be looking for a wife.

"Why now?" he asked. He took a big bite of roast beef and began to chew, listening to James' answer.

"Well, let me see. My house is finished, Bates and Mackie hired a staff to see to all the needs of a philanthropist's life, and I'm ready to settle down, so to speak. My neighbors, the Bannisters, have been most helpful. I still need a governess, I suppose, if I get the children. I have a question for you, Lucas. Will you return east or stay on here?"

Lucas looked sagely at his bosom companion.

"Now that is something my gut has been talking to me about, my good friend. I feel a tug to go back to what I consider familiar and normal. That to me is *compos mentis*, but my gut is telling me it's time to make a permanent change. So do I obey my mind or my gut?"

He laughed at himself, and James joined in.

"There you are with those Latin words, Lucas. How you lawyers can keep all that information stored in your brains is beyond me. And by the way, quite frankly, it isn't my gut that's been talking to me or my brain either," James said soberly. "It's been during my quiet times that it came to me that I should take on a couple children and make their lives better. I don't just think, Lucas—I *know* I'm to either adopt or become a legal guardian for a couple children. I am quite wealthy, and I'd like to share, improve, and be a part of a couple children's lives."

"I would think the first thing on your agenda should be to get a wife, sir."

"Ye-es...I agree. I've been contemplating a mail-order bride. It's quite—"

"What?" Lucas nearly shouted. "Have you completely lost your senses?" He rose from his chair, making a grab for it before it toppled to the floor. He leaned over, placing his hands flat on the tabletop, and stared into James' calm blue eyes. "I can't believe you'd even consider such a thing. Why, you should just travel back east. You'd have your pick of females. Why would you trouble to write churches and spend the time writing to some woman who probably will send you a daguerreotype of her best friend so as not to put you off? I said you were certifiable in jest. Now I'm not jesting. I know it to be true."

James looked at his friend and laughed.

"You need to go back to collect your things, close up your house, and disperse of your staff. I already know you've bought yourself a nice piece of property here in Napa."

Lucas gaped at James, surprise in his eyes.

"News travels fast in a small community. You should know that." James complacently salted and peppered his mashed potatoes. "What could be easier than while you're there in the East to pick me out a wife?" James laughed at his friend's astonishment. "You should see your face. I'm jesting, Lucas. Seriously, I suppose you've made up your mind to build. Will you build first or return east?"

"I shall continue to be your guest, James, if you'll have me. I decided just this morning, on the train from Portland, to go ahead and build first. That way I'll be able to travel back and collect those things that will be useful in my new home. I had contemplated buying more land in Oregon, but in the two weeks I was there, I didn't see the sun once. It put me off. I need to see the sun on a regular basis. Once it came out, while riding the train, my spirits seemed to soar."

The two men continued to enjoy the luncheon together, conversation flowing easily. They covered many topics, and the time flew by.

The San Rafael School of Primary Learning was not very large. The school's edifice was rectangular and surrounded a huge courtyard in the middle. From the street it was an imposing structure housing fifty-eight students of varying ages. There were also children from the town of San Rafael attending classes, who were day-school students but not orphans. The school had a good reputation. Three full-time teachers lived in the facility. Four more teachers taught during the day but lived elsewhere. Staff included a gardener, a head cook and her helpers, and a head laundress and her helpers, most of whom lived at the school. Three dorm mothers completed the staff.

Anne spoke before opening the door to the arithmetic class in session. "As you know, Mrs. Baxter, we begin with reading, writing, and arithmetic. It doesn't matter how old the child is when entering this institution. They are tested to see at what level they can perform. We have special classes for those who excel, and a large percentage of children take science and history, algebra, Greek, and Latin as well as drawing and singing."

Mrs. Baxter entered the classroom, quietly following Anne's lead. Instruction was in progress. Mr. Hughs was teaching arithmetic. The two women stood quietly observing the class. Finally Susannah motioned Anne that she wanted to leave, and the two women left as quietly as they had entered.

"Is he a good teacher?" Susannah asked.

"Yes, he's excellent and seems to care about the children." Color rose to Anne's cheeks as she replied.

Susannah saw it but said nothing. "Where are the two children from the San Francisco orphanage?"

"Right now—" Anne flipped open her timepiece, glancing at it quickly. A slight frown of irritation at herself creased her brow. *I already knew the time.*

"They are in a history class. We can head that way while I tell you a bit more about the situation. Let's cut across the courtyard."

Anne opened the door and ushered Susannah into the huge courtyard that she and her late husband had designed. It had never looked so cheerful.

"My! You've certainly been a busy woman, haven't you?" She smiled at Anne, her eyes sparkling with pleasure at the transformation Anne had accomplished in less than two months.

Several heavy pots were filled with greenery, spilling over the sides, and lavender just beginning to bloom. Bushes had been pruned and stood neatly waiting for their buds to appear. Everything looked groomed and ready for inspection.

CHAPTER II

With the merciful thou wilt shew thyself merciful;
with an upright man thou wilt shew thyself upright.

PSALM 18:25

ANNE LOOKED AROUND WITH A discerning eye. "I can't take all the credit. The gardener was itching to do something to brighten things up a bit. I have a grandmother who is coming out to visit. She is thinking she may make the move out here if she finds it suits her tastes. She is an exacting woman, and I have worked not only to bring the school up in standards, incorporating a pleasing atmosphere, but I want everything shipshape for the inspection that is sure to come." Anne laughed. "You can be the monitor for how I'm doing."

The two women sat down to chat on a wrought-iron garden bench in the courtyard. It wasn't the most comfortable, and Anne had been looking into weatherproof cushions or wooden benches.

"Where does your grandmother live?"

"She still lives in the house she came to as a bride. I never knew my grandfather. He died before I went to live with her. Sorry…I'm rambling. She lives right on the river in Jamestown, Virginia."

Susannah Baxter was quite taken with her new director. "Well, my dear, I am so pleased with what you have done with the school so far. It's looking better than it has for years. I am wondering, would you be free to come to dinner tonight? I'd like you to meet my George. We've only been married two months." Susannah's face pinked up as she spoke. "My first husband died, you know."

"No, no, I didn't. I'm sorry for that."

"Thank you. I am blessed beyond measure. How about you, Miss Tarkington? Do you have a beau?"

"No." Anne laughed. "And unless the good Lord drops a man into my lap, I don't see one in the offing, either."

"No interest in Mr. Hughs?" Susannah asked archly.

Her cheeks stained red, Anne responded adamantly. "No, no interest there." *But he seems to have a great interest in me*, she thought. She didn't care to share her innermost thoughts with Mrs. Baxter.

"Would it be amenable to you if I ask Mr. Hughs to escort you to our house this evening?"

"Oh, please don't," Anne replied quickly. "I wouldn't care for him to have any added encouragement. He's quite nice but simply a teacher on my staff, nothing more." She changed the subject adroitly. "So what time *is* dinner, and how formal are you?"

"Six thirty please." Susannah eyed Anne, grateful that she was seeing a sparkling personality that had been tamped down during the interview for the position. "And yes, we do dress for dinner." Her cheeks colored up, and she laughed. "Of course we dress! What a humorous word picture that brought to mind!" She laughed, and Anne joined in. "We do have a strange way of saying things at times, don't we?" Her beautiful gray eyes twinkled merrily as she continued to talk.

"Now, about those children. Before I go see them, can you tell me a bit more about them?"

"Yes." Anne folded her hands in her lap as she collected her thoughts that were in a kerfuffle after the discussion about Martin Hughs. He seemed nice, but she simply wasn't interested. Anne knew she was once burned and twice shy. She did not care to get involved with anyone who could break her heart again. Her demeanor changed, and her violet eyes bespoke the seriousness of the children's situation as she spoke to Mrs. Baxter about them.

"The children are brother and sister. The boy, Thaddeus Loren Parker, has just turned seven, and the girl, Ginger Rae Parker, is eight and a half. They arrived here from the San Francisco orphanage before Christmas. That institution had kept them since the first part of October. I was barely settled when they arrived. My understanding is that Ginger almost died in the Forty-Mile Desert. Thaddeus kept her going. It is a horribly arduous trek and is made by night because it is so hot."

Susannah murmured, "I've heard of it."

Anne continued. "Ginger excels in history. She does well in every class, listens, and writes a beautiful hand, but she will not speak. Thaddeus has been her interpreter. From my understanding, until the attack on the wagon train, they were happy, normal children. I wrote the wagon master, a Mr. Turner, and I received a reply just the other day. He filled me in on a few things that Thaddeus left out of his story. I suppose it's taken some time to track Mr. Turner down. He said the children lost their father on the trail, to cholera. Just before reaching the desert, their wagon train was attacked by the Shoshone. Ginger and Thaddeus saw children carried off by the marauders, and both children witnessed their mother killed. Ginger was almost kidnapped. An Indian tried to pull her out from under the wagon. Thaddeus hung on to her. The Indian was shot by one of the men from the wagon train and died right beside them. Trauma doesn't begin to describe what those two children must have endured.

"Thaddeus says Ginger has not spoken a word since the Indian tried to kidnap her. The poor boy has been interpreting what he thinks she is trying to communicate. She doesn't interact much."

"My goodness! Such a lot to bear, and so devastating."

Anne rose and took Susannah's hand. "I'm grateful you don't wish to turn these children out. The girl needs love and attention. I'd like to adopt the pair of them, but I don't have the means, nor am I home enough to be of stable influence."

"Well, let me meet them. Little Thaddeus has had much to bear. He must be a strong character not to break down under such circumstances."

Anne nodded. "I believe he's stuffing everything inside his little heart. He's been extremely brave. Here we are." She opened the heavy door, and the two entered quietly and stood in the back of the room, unnoticed by the class. Miss Judith Jacobs was having a question and answer time.

"Who can tell me the first signer of the Declaration of Independence?" Miss Jacobs asked the class.

Hands were raised, and she called on a girl. "Helen, do you know the answer?"

"Yes, ma'am. It was John Hancock."

"Good...and can you tell me which state John Hancock represented and a little of his background?"

Helen shook her head negatively, and hands went up again.

"Thaddeus, do you know?"

"Yes, ma'am. John Hancock represented Massachusetts."

"Good...and can you tell us what position he held in Congress?"

"Yes, ma'am. He served as president of the Second Continental Congress, was most likely the richest man in the colonies, and he was the first and third governor of the state of Massachusetts."

"Very good, Thaddeus. You have done your homework." She smiled approvingly at him, dimples creasing her cheeks.

The desks were double, and Ginger sat next to him. The two women in the back saw Ginger surreptitiously patting her brother's knee in approval. Both children were towheads, and Ginger's hair was neatly braided into two thick plaits.

Looking at her, Susannah remembered herself at that age with almost identical coloring. Pity for the young girl welled up in her heart, and her eyes misted with tears as she looked at Anne. She nodded toward the door, and they exited the classroom.

"Goodness!" Susannah said. "What darling children. Oh my, I feel so sorry for that poor little girl. No child should have to endure such an experience."

"I know. Every time I look at the two of them, I want to take them into my arms."

Stars twinkled in the inky blackness, and a bright half-moon lit Anne's path. Because it wasn't raining, she'd chosen to walk the few blocks to Mrs. Baxter's residence. She'd worked so hard to get the school into shape that she hadn't time for social outlets. Anne had not met many of the residents of San Rafael besides parents of students. She anticipated an entertaining evening and looked forward to it, pondering what she'd heard about Mr. and Mrs. Baxter, much of it learned from Mrs. Baxter herself.

Susannah Farrow Baxter was a wealthy woman. Two months earlier she had married the chief of detectives of San Francisco, George Baxter, wealthy in his own right. Some residents of San Rafael, upon hearing the news of Susannah's marriage, had been aghast. Susannah didn't care. She was romantically in love for the first time in her life and had dispensed the minimum period of mourning. She'd made the move to San Francisco after a quiet wedding but had returned to San Rafael eager to catch up on a few things, check on the school, and reconnect with some of her friends. George had taken a few days off, something he'd never done prior to meeting Susannah.

Anne was ushered inside by Tess, the housekeeper, who took her coat and led her to the parlor.

The Farrow mansion, built by Mrs. Baxter's former husband, was an imposing edifice in San Rafael. The smallest details had not been neglected. Every room conveyed elegant refinement.

Anne was welcomed by her hostess, Susannah, and introduced to George Baxter, quite a handsome man. Besides an intelligent face and a fascinating groove in his cheek, Anne saw keen eyes that seemed to know her thoughts. She looked at him openly, proffering her hand.

"Good evening, sir. It's a pleasure to meet you."

"It's good to meet you, young lady." George shook her hand. "I've heard about nothing else since Susannah returned from her inspection today. You've captured her heart." He took her arm and led her into the parlor.

She was introduced to Elijah and Abigail Humphries and a single young man, Edward Kepler. She recognized the name. Conversation flowed as the guests partook of apple cider and grape juice.

Anne looked around with pleasure sparkling in her eyes.

The walls were the palest of creamy apricot, and the room's accouterments suggested refinement at its best. Victorian in appearance, the settee and side chairs were a tufted pale apricot, and the frames of the chairs were curved and carved dark mahogany. Two wingbacks, one in cream and one in chartreuse, flanked the fireplace, as well as a pair in the bay window. Splashes of cream, orange, and chartreuse, as well as the apricot color of the settee, blended into a pleasing pattern on the heavy drapes, which framed the windows stretching across the outer wall. A gorgeous painting of George Washington kneeling in prayer hung over the fireplace, and brass candlesticks hugged one corner of the mantel.

Anne made a mental note of the pleasing color combination but was startled out of her contemplations when Edward Kepler spoke to her.

"I believe you've taken over my father's position as director of the school, have you not?" he asked pleasantly.

Anne answered in the affirmative, taking a long look at him.

Edward didn't stay on the subject of his father but abruptly switched to his work with Elijah Humphries. Abigail joined in the conversation, and soon everyone was talking about the law firm and some of the cases taken on by Elijah's partners.

Tess stood in the doorway and announced, "Dinner is served."

Following George and Susannah, Edward took Anne's arm and led her to the dining room, Elijah and Abigail close on their heels.

This room was done in palest mint green. All the woodwork was a dark mahogany and together created an affluent elegance that somehow produced a feeling of contentment.

A huge mirror, mahogany framed and ornately carved, radiated prisms of light from the crystal chandelier. Gilt sconces, lit on either side of the mirror, added to the brilliance. A long marble-topped sideboard with the same color of mint green mixed with cream was gorgeous—an unusual color for marble. The dining chairs were a blend of striped mint, cream, and dark-brown chintz. There were a couple of creamy-colored wingbacks in one corner, with pillows matching the dining chair seats. The effect was elegant yet comfortably warm and inviting.

George opened the meal with a prayer of thanksgiving, and the meal progressed with good conversation and fellowship.

Anne was having a wonderful time. She had dressed in her best for the occasion and knew she was more than passable. The material for the deep-violet dress had been chosen especially because it matched the unusual color of her eyes. She'd made her dress, but it didn't look as if she had. It was beautiful with lace insets above her bosom and in the puffs of her sleeves. Her blonde hair was swept up in a loose chignon held in place by an ornate tortoiseshell comb. A few curls escaped, softening the look around her face. Anne knew she looked her best, and she sparkled with wit and humor.

She looked across the table at Abigail and Elijah Humphries, who were laughing at something George had said. Anne had previously met Abigail at a bazaar in January and had taken a liking to her. She knew Elijah and Abigail owned the mission for women that Abigail ran. It didn't take long for Anne to realize the Baxters and Humphries were good friends.

Susannah Baxter's husband, George, was debonair, and Anne could hardly reconcile that he was chief of San Francisco's detective department. He looked as if he'd just walked out of his tailor's in Savile Row.

Edward Kepler sat on her right, and Anne had the distinction of sitting on George's right, a place of honor. Her host was charming and drew out a few stories about her past. Susannah asked Anne to relate the story about the Parker children, and she did so with unusual pathos.

Abigail pulled her handkerchief out to dab at her eyes as Anne bared her heart to Mr. Humphries.

"I'd love to be able to adopt the children, but directing the school, I feel I wouldn't have enough time to give them the attention they would require." She smiled a bit ruefully.

Mr. Kepler, who'd been fairly quiet, spoke up.

"Wouldn't your hours be about the same as theirs in the school?" he asked. "Surely there would only be a couple hours difference. You could have them stay at the school while you are busy. It'd be a good thing for them to know they are especially loved by you. I should think they are hungry for it."

Edward spoke from personal experience, but only two at the table knew—Elijah, his boss, and George, who was a detective.

"I suppose that's true, but being director of the school takes much of my time. From your perspective, perhaps I could adopt them," Anne replied. "I'd like to have those two children more than anything in the world!"

Elijah Humphries spoke into the silence after Anne's statement. "I would be willing to draw up the paperwork for you at no charge. My heart goes out to those children. As a matter of fact, I know a woman in Napa who signs. She has her hands full right now with twins, but Liberty Bannister could be of great help to the girl, Ginger. It sounds as if there is no physical reason the girl can't talk. You say her brother says she has tried but can't make the words come?"

"Yes, that's correct, Mr. Humphries," Anne said. "Thaddeus says she's tried and tried to talk. She becomes frustrated and angry that she's unable to get the words out."

"Such a shame," Abigail murmured.

"You should see the two of them," Susannah interjected. "They are absolutely darling."

Anne asked Mr. Humphries, "About that woman in Napa, Mrs. Bannister. Do you think if I took Ginger up there on a regular basis, she'd have time to work with her?"

Elijah turned to look at his wife before he answered. He and Abigail could communicate quite well with their eyes. Her eyes told him what he wanted to know, and he replied.

"Frankly, I think she'd be delighted. She worked at the Boston School for the Deaf for years before moving west. She has plenty of help with her babies. I think if you'd be free on Saturdays, you could take the two children with you and she'd be amenable to helping out. You most likely could stay the night and return on Sundays. I'll send her a telegram tomorrow and see if she feels overwhelmed or free enough to help that little girl. I would expect nothing less than the latter."

"Oh, that would be wonderful," Anne said. "I do hope she will. What a boon that would be for Ginger. How far away is Napa? Frankly, I have no idea where anything is except San Rafael and San Francisco."

"It's about thirty-five miles north. Can you ride?"

"Y…yes, but I don't have a horse here. I suppose I could rent one."

"You don't have to do that, ma'am," Edward said. "I have several. You and the children can have your pick any time you choose." His face pinked up at his offer.

"Why, thank you! That's kind of you, sir. I will certainly take you up on your offer if Mrs. Bannister will help Ginger. I certainly am glad I came this evening. A burden on my heart has been lifted because of your kindness. I've been feeling Ginger needs more help than I have the capability to provide."

Later that night, Anne lay in her bed, thinking about the day's events. She wondered at the idea of adopting the children. She wanted those two precious children—for some reason, she wanted those two above all the orphans at the school.

I don't feel at peace to adopt them, Ann thought. *I don't have the money to educate them further than the primary grades. What shall I do, Lord? Please make it clear to me what I should do.*

She lay for some time praying for the school, each of the staff, Grandma Jenny, Mrs. Baxter, and even for Mrs. Bannister, that her heart would be open to teach the brokenhearted Ginger. She was still praying when sleep overtook her.

CHAPTER III

Two are better than one because they have a good return for their labor.
For if either of them falls, the one will lift up his companion.
But woe to the one who falls when there is not another to lift him up.

ECCLESIASTES 4:9–10

LIBERTY BANNISTER STRETCHED AND rolled over. She opened her eyes only to find her husband gone, already up. She reached over to feel his pillow. It was cool. She rolled back over and felt around on her nightstand for her grandfather's watch. Her eyes widened as she looked at the time.

Goodness! I can't believe it! It's eight thirty. She sat up, and as she did so, the bedroom door opened. Matthew came in carrying a baby in the crook of each arm, followed by Boston, their dog. Faith and Matthew, their twins, were four months old. They were happy babies. Faith was a bit chubbier than Matty, but the day before, Matty had gotten up on all fours and rocked back and forth before plopping back down on his tummy.

"Good morning, Mrs. Bannister," Matthew said with a grin as he relieved himself of Faith into Liberty's waiting arms. Before sitting on the side of the bed, he stooped to give Liberty a huge kiss. "Uhmm...you have the sweetest lips. I suppose it's why I call you sweetheart." He sat on the side of the bed as she hurriedly scooted her legs out of the way.

"You'd have to do a great amount of kissing every female to know I have the sweetest lips, Matthew Bannister!" she said with a grin. "I love you too, with my all of my heart." Her green eyes were warm with love for him. "I can't believe I slept so long," she said as she pushed her hair out of her face. "I haven't slept like that since before the twins were born."

"I know. We gave them a bit of sugar water this morning to tide them over. Conchita and I both felt you needed a lie-in. You've been burning the candle at both ends, my girl. What with nursing the twins, training a new horse, and all the other things you do, we felt you needed a catch-up day." He lifted Matty up onto his shoulder, rubbing his back as he continued to talk.

"Conchita is bringing us some coffee and breakfast. I told her I wanted to have a good talk with you."

"You look serious."

"It is serious—not dire, but serious." He smiled as he spoke to let her know everything was all right.

Boston had been wagging his tail, waiting patiently next to the bed. Once Liberty acknowledged him, he went to a corner and curled up to wait.

Conchita came in with a heavy tray loaded with breakfast. Freshly made tortillas stuffed with scrambled eggs, sausage, green peppers, onions, and fried potatoes lent a mouthwatering odor to the room. Dishes of salsa and sour cream as well as orange juice and coffee completed the fare.

"Thees ees hot, an' you muss eat eet now," she ordered. "Eet no taste good eef you wait." Conchita, cook and housekeeper, was a mainstay of the Bannisters' Rancho. When Liberty first arrived at the Rancho, it was Conchita who befriended her and made her feel welcome. Conchita's husband, Diego, was Matthew's foreman, but also one of his best friends.

"I go now. You eet." Conchita reached for the doorknob but turned back to look at the scene in the bedroom. It was a room full of contentment and peace.

Liberty saw her look and grinned up at her as she left the room, closing the door quietly behind her.

Matthew drew back the curtains. "It's going to be a beautiful day. The rains aren't over, but today would be a great day for a ride. What do you say after we're finished here, you and I go for a ride? I'd like to show you what my plan is."

He pulled a side table close to the bed and placed a chair opposite. He sat, prayed for their day, and gave thanks for the food. Liberty munched while she nursed Faith and listened to the plan her husband wanted to share.

"I've been thinking and praying, and it's time to share with you what I've been ruminating upon for the past couple weeks. As you know, we bought Kirk out after harvest last year. He has plenty of income with the gold mine they discovered on his ranch. I felt the burden of responsibility for him after our parents' death, but now he's married. Caitlin's expecting their first baby anytime now, and I no longer feel that burden. So I've been thinking about expansion. Daniel Hedley's selling up. He's lost heart in his winery since he lost Betty. He's moving to San Francisco to be close to his daughter. His land abuts ours to the north, as you well know. I'd like to buy him out. It'll make things a bit tight until after next harvest, but his vines are healthy and producing a great wine. I wanted your opinion on this before I proceed."

Liberty was silent for a minute, thinking about Matthew's idea. "I know how you love to keep busy, and we do have a lot of acreage, but expansion is a good thing. I think it's a wonderful plan, Matthew. I'm grateful you do it honestly."

Matthew looked closely and could still see a bit of the shadows of the past lurking in her green eyes.

"No looking back, Liberty. Keep your eyes focused on what lies ahead and not on what was. Your first husband and your stepfather are memories of a past better forgotten. They didn't know or care about God, and it showed in everything they did. We have a Savior who meets us more than halfway. He is watching over us, my dear, and we need to trust Him with every thought and action." He took Faith from her and placed Matty in her waiting arms. He sat back feeling sated and took a sip of coffee.

"You do think it's a good idea, then?"

"Yes, I do—it's a good plan, except you're going to need more men in managerial positions."

"I know. I've been keeping my eye on Donny. I've been thinking we could upgrade Hedley's house and let him live there. He would be free to marry Cadence and oversee that property. He'd be fairly close to our new neighbor, James Mobrey. Yes, I think that's a good plan, and you're right, I will need some men with experience. The Bannisters' Rancho Bonito is fast becoming a popular wine."

He stood and stretched. "Are you going to nurse all day, or would you care to take that ride?" He leaned over and kissed Liberty's lips, lingering there as he kissed her again.

James Mobrey looked at himself in the full-length mirror and knew his cravat would never pass muster. He'd arisen early, planning to ride south to San Rafael as soon as he dressed. He'd gone to breakfast wearing his usual garb of robe and slippers. Now he was dressed and nearly ready to go.

He decided it was time to put some action to his plan to adopt two children. He was grateful Lucas Falter was again ensconced at Mobrey Manor and wanted to ride south with him. It was a huge undertaking, but he knew Lucas would keep him focused and on the right track. He would have to find another reputable lawyer to draw up the papers. Lucas told him he didn't think he could draw up the legal documents, as he wasn't licensed in the state of California.

James perused himself in the oval mirror to see if he'd pass Bates' approval. Bates had never dressed him—James wouldn't allow it—but sometimes his man would tweak his cravat. His thoughts wandered into the past as he pulled off his cravat and started tying it again.

Melody Mackie was an excellent housekeeper. She'd been with his family since before his parents had died. His butler, Jacob Bates, had been with him since he'd been a boy in knickerbockers. Bates was from England and had been in his late teens when he'd landed a position with the Mobreys in Virginia. He'd tutored James in various subjects. As well, he taught him about wildlife and being a good steward of God's creation.

Bates was loved by the Mobrey family. He'd taken James for trips into the wild and taught him how to shoot both rifle and sidearm and how to hunt. James' father had been happy for his son to learn these skills, having never learned himself.

When James was in his second year at Princeton, his parents had been stricken with diphtheria, their lives snuffed out before James had even been aware of their illness. He'd been beside himself with grief, feeling nothing was important anymore. Coming home for their funerals, he'd felt bereft of his parents and bereft of purpose. He'd thought to quit school. It was Bates who'd got him through the most difficult time of his life. Bates had urged him to continue his schooling, if not for himself, then at least for the sake of his parents' wishes. James did go back and finish and was grateful for the faithful service and friendship of Jacob Bates.

His reverie came to a halt as he finished tying his shoes. Whistling softly to himself, he descended the stairs, looking suave and debonair.

He felt Bates' eyes on him as he entered the kitchen, where Lucas was having another cup of coffee.

"Bates," he said, "I have been a bit remiss. I'd like you to ride with us. You know more about children than either Lucas or myself. Can you pack a bag forthwith? We plan to leave within the hour. I should imagine we'll visit the school first thing tomorrow morning, stay one more night, and be back here the day after tomorrow unless something untoward happens."

Bates looked up with surprise and pleasure filling his eyes. "I'd be happy to do that, sir. I'll have Dock saddle me up and be ready in a trice." He ran lightly down the back steps to the stables.

Jacob Bates and Lucas Falter were James' best friends. Anything that James didn't care to do, Bates did. Bates, with Mackie's help, had hired the entire staff after thorough interviews. No one from the house in Virginia had traveled west with James and Bates except Mackie. An entire retinue had needed to be hired. Bates and Mackie did it all.

First, Bates consulted people in the area, especially Bertha Morrow and Matthew and Liberty Bannister, and also the sheriff, who'd lived in Napa for years. He'd taken their recommendations as well as advertised in the San Francisco Chronicle, which garnered several applicants. He'd told Mr. James, which was what he always called his employer, that until the children were adopted, he didn't think it wise to hire someone to care for them. Bates thought the children might have preferences themselves and should have a choice in the matter.

James was glad for such a thoughtful mentor and friend.

Thaddeus awoke early. Rolling over, he lay for quite a time trying to go back to sleep, but with no success. The boy in the bunk above him was snoring. It was a loud irritant, and Thad was a light sleeper. He curled one arm behind his head and thought about his situation at the orphan school.

I hate sleeping in this big dormitory with twenty-nine other boys. When I lived back east, I had my own room in the attic. On the trip west I either slept on the ground under the wagon or in the wagon if it was raining. Either way, Ginger was always there next to me. I miss hearing her gentle breathing beside me.

As he lay thinking about his circumstances, he began to whisper to God.

"I hate it here, heavenly Father. I've had a hard time controlling my temper. I get angry at those two boys who keep making fun of Ginger. I haven't made any friends here. I feel almost afraid to get close to anyone, and You don't seem to be much help lately either. I'm not too happy with You. What kind of God would take my pa when we needed him the most? And to have Ma die right there in front of us. Couldn't You have done that a bit differently? What about Ginger? Is she always going to walk around being dumb? I don't mean stupid, mind You, but mute— You know, not able to make a sound. It's not that I'm not grateful to You for finding this place for us. The headmistress at that last orphanage didn't like Ginger at all. I think she was going to put her, and maybe me, into the poorhouse in San Francisco. But, Father, am I going to have to live here until we finish what this school has to offer and then be moved on somewhere else?

"I think the headmistress, Miss Tarkington, loves Ginger and me. I can feel it, but I don't want to love her. I'll just end up being hurt again. After all, this is only a primary school. What happens when we finish the grades here? Where do we go then? What if I get adopted and Ginger doesn't? I couldn't bear it if we got separated. I don't think I can bear much of anything right now…no more loss. I'm tired, Father. I feel as if I'm at the end of my rope, and there's nothing else to hang on to. I've tried to be strong and be a help to Ginger, but she isn't the same anymore." Tears seeped out of his eyes, and he wiped them away, impatient with himself. "She used to be the boss of everything, and now she looks at me to be the leader. She gets so mad at me when I don't know what it is she's trying to tell me. It hurts my insides, and she can't even see it—she's so closed up. Father, You're my only father now. I'm asking You for help. Help me bear up so I can help Ginger. I really like Miss Tarkington. She's kind, but I don't want to like her. What if we get taken away? What if I have to leave? I never knew it before, God, but loving people can hurt."

Elijah, usually awake early, had awakened betimes—at the crack of dawn. He'd tried to go back to sleep, but to no avail. He lay in bed a long time thinking and praying. Abigail, beside him, was still sleeping soundly. He made no sudden movements, not wanting to awaken her. He prayed especially for the Parker children, that God would see to it that they were adopted into the best situation possible for them. He thought Anne Tarkington would make a good mother for them, but he didn't like the idea of having no father for the children. Sometimes that was a necessity, but it wasn't the best of circumstances for a child.

As he lay there, he thought about his walk with God and areas of his life upon which he could improve. He took his spiritual pulse every so often to make sure he was still growing and feeding his soul with the things of the Almighty. He also reviewed his interactions with other people, making sure his relationships were open and honest and good.

He thought about the conversation at dinner the evening before. He needed to get a telegram off to Liberty. It'd been quite some time since he and Abby had visited the Bannisters. Elijah loved Liberty as if she were his own daughter. He and Abigail had been childless, and it had been a lifelong sorrow he'd not even shared with Abby, because her own pain was great. Now, the two of them felt fulfilled. God had seen fit to bring this young woman into their lives, and then there was the blessing of her twin, Alex, and his family. They also had recently befriended a young man named Adam Brown, who was now married. He and his wife, Eden, had been added to the list of people close enough to be their own children. Liberty had given birth to twins a few months before, and Elijah felt blessed and praised his God for His love and provision.

He arose, careful not to disturb the bed linens, and tiptoed his way to the commode room to perform his morning ablutions. He hated to shave and felt cheerful every morning after completing the task. He dressed, quietly chose a pair of stockings out the top bureau drawer, picked up his shoes, and made his way down the stairs. Polka Dot, their dog, awaited him, her front paws on the bottom tread.

"Good morning, Polka. Have you been a good girl?"

She wagged so hard her tail seemed a lethal weapon as it beat against the stair spindles. She never went beyond putting her paws on the bottom step. Abigail drew the line at having an animal upstairs. Elijah had been pleasantly surprised she would allow Polka to live in the house.

He eased himself onto the second tread and scooped her head into his lap, lavishly loving on her. He stroked her soft fur and talked softly to her. Her wagging gentled at his touch. He enjoyed putting on his stockings and shoes with her help.

"Well, Polka, do you smell those wonderful odors wafting from the kitchen? I have no doubt you do, my girl. Let's get going. I have much to do today."

CHAPTER IV

For I know the thoughts that I think toward you, saith the LORD,
thoughts of peace, and not of evil,
to give you an expected end.

JEREMIAH 29:11

TWO HORSES RACED NECK AND NECK across the fertile valley. They stopped at a huge oak tree, drawing up sharply. Green eyes met deep blue as both laughed together. Their eyes sparkled with love and enjoyment.

"I can't remember when I've had such a good ride!" Liberty exclaimed. "I don't think poor Pookie has been ridden like that since before I got pregnant."

Matthew watched as she slid off her horse and sat down on the grass, leaning her back against the tree. She wore long leather boots and a split skirt. Her white blouse, open at the neck, showed her lovely throat. She looked feminine and vulnerable.

Matthew was still sitting astride his horse.

He looked down at his wife, and an overwhelming sense of protection and warmth flooded his being. She looked up at him and grinned. *How I do love her,* he thought.

"Piggypie hasn't been ridden like this in a long time either," he replied, "not since Cadence came into our lives and you were unconscious for the second time up at the cave where your stepfather nearly killed you."

He dismounted as Liberty looked up at him. Her eyes widened at his words. He never talked about Jacques and had told her not to think about him or any of the negatives of the past, so his words must have surprised her.

"I forgot about that," she said with a smile, "although I can be excused for forgetting. I wasn't conscious at the time."

"That's true," he replied. "We are so blessed, Liberty. Who ever thought that a few short years ago either one of us could ever be so happy? You in that dark house of Armand's, living with his evilness day in and day out, and me with all the bitterness of a wife who'd left me for the glitz and glitter of a world that can never satisfy."

"I know, Matthew. Believe me—I know. I am grateful to God for His bountiful blessings. I'm grateful for you coming into my life and for you finding a deep faith in God. And look how we're blessed with our babies. We thought we'd never have children, and now we have two. Yes, we have much to be thankful for."

Matthew reached out for Liberty's hands and pulled her to her feet. "I praise God every day for you." He kissed her deeply, and she molded herself to him, giving back in full measure.

He held her back from him and looked steadily into her eyes. "We'll finish this later," he said with a gleam in his eyes. "Let's go. I want to show you the house and grounds before we need to get back to the Rancho."

They mounted up, Matthew giving Liberty his clasped hands to step into and boosting her up.

"I know full well you can do that by yourself, but it gives me pleasure to help you out."

"Thanks," she replied. "I'm grateful that you are so thoughtful of me. I see other men who often leave their wives struggling on their own. Women like to feel cherished even if they are capable of completing a task on their own. I feel cherished by you, Matthew, and believe me—I don't take it for granted. I want to thank you again for Cherry. She's such a beautiful horse and smart too. It won't be long before she will be eating out of my hand." Liberty smiled at the thought of the sweet-tempered horse Matthew had given her as a Christmas present. Her coat was so red she'd named her Cherry.

Matthew smiled at her words, nodded his head, and the two rode off again at a more sedate pace toward Dan Hedley's spread. Matthew pulled up on a steep hill that overlooked the property he'd helped to clear a few years before.

"We've been on Hedley's since coming down that hill," he said. "This is as much as he has into grapes." He waved his hand westward, encompassing the area planted. "It's about an eighth of what we have planted since we have Kirk's land too." He pointed down to the bottom of an escarpment that lay before them. "None of this is plantable land, but once you get to the bottom of this escarpment, there's only that one little hill before getting to the house. All of that"—he waved his hand expansively—"is good, fertile land. The house is not in too bad of shape. I'd hire some workers to do some renovations…put in flush toilets, gut the kitchen and start over there, but I'd like to get a feel for what you think. We could let Donny and Cadence live in it once they're married."

Donny Miller, a young man Matthew had hired about a year before, was an indispensable hired hand and worked hard. He'd fallen in love with Cadence Cassidy, a runaway girl who, it had turned out, was actually Susannah Baxter's granddaughter.

Liberty's face looked thoughtful, listening to Matthew's ideas.

"Thank you for telling me about your plans for it. I know you consult me in so many areas, and yet I still feel a ripple of surprised pleasure when you do. I like being your partner, Matthew." She grinned at him. "I'd like to ride down and see the house. I just may have a few ideas for improvements."

Matthew led the two down toward the house. The escarpment made the way possible for them. It was so wide three horses could have easily ridden abreast.

"Is this man made or natural?" Liberty asked. "It sure makes going down easy."

"It's man made," Matthew replied. "I helped make it. I think I told you I worked for Hedley when Jessica ran off, taking all our money. This is where I met Diego. I pulled him out of the river when the ground beneath him gave way. He couldn't swim. He's been one of my best friends ever since."

"It must be a gratifying thing to save a person's life. You saved our little Matty too. There aren't enough words to express my gratitude for that. God works in you, Matthew, and I can see it and rejoice and give Him the glory for it."

"That's what we're supposed to do, my dear. All our talents and abilities are for His glory. And when you think about it, you saved my life, Liberty Alexandra Corlay Bouvier Bannister!" He grinned, looking over at her as they picked their way carefully down the steep escarpment. They reached the bottom and rode toward Hedley's house, pulling to a stop at the edge of the last short hill. They looked down toward the structure, which lay about a hundred yards away.

Matthew started to head down the hill, when Liberty felt a frisson of angst crawl up her spine.

She pulled up Pookie and said, "Wait, Matthew. Something's not—"

As Matthew turned back to look at her, a window shattered and a shot rang out, the bullet grazing his ear.

"Get down, Libby!" Matthew hissed as he dropped from his horse.

Liberty needed no urging, as she was already sliding off Pookie to lie flat on the ground, thankful for some bushes sheltering them from anyone's view in the house.

"Dan told me a couple days ago that he'd be in Frisco for the next couple weeks. Wonder who's holed up in there? I'm going to circle around to the back."

Liberty nodded. She'd been keeping her eyes fixed on the house. Glancing over at Matthew, she exclaimed, "You're bleeding! You've been shot!"

Blood slowly dripped from his ear onto his shirt.

"Just a graze, sweetie, just a graze, but I'm going to say for the second time today, you saved my life! If I hadn't turned when you spoke…" His voice choked up, but his eyes spoke volumes. "You stay right here with your gun cocked and ready."

He crouched low and made his way to the back of the house, using bushes for cover. He circled around on the left side of the house.

Liberty lay still as she pulled out her gun and cocked it. She stretched out her arm, ready to shoot if need be. Waiting, she peeked through the screen of brush at the house and at Matthew crouched down, moving from the bush to bush, carefully making his way to the side of the house. She prayed silently as she watched.

Matthew gained the side of the house undetected. He slid silently along the wall, ducking down under the only window on that side, and ran lightly to the back. He dashed across to the barn, entering its dimness. He saw only one horse, which made him breathe a little easier, but he noticed a second stall had not been mucked out and held fresh droppings.

There's more than one of them, he thought. He heard a movement behind him but turned too late as a gun butt crashed down on his head.

James, Lucas, and Jacob Bates pulled up in front of the San Rafael School of Primary Learning. Tying their horses at the long railing, James removed his Stetson and smoothed back his light-brown hair in a gesture of nervousness.

"Are you having second thoughts, Boss? Are you nervous?" Bates was surprised but knew James' every nuance. He needn't ask, but he did, trying to put his employer at ease.

"Ah, yes, yes I am. I've never ah…oh, never mind!" James bit his lip, feeling discombobulated. He'd been about to say he'd never picked out children before, as if Bates and Lucas didn't know that fact.

The three men had ridden to San Rafael the day before and spent the night at Three Hawks Inn. They enjoyed a tasty meal served at the inn and stretched their legs afterward, walking through the entire town in deep conversation before going to bed. James awakened early, his stomach a bit in knots over the finality of adopting children. After a leisurely breakfast, they mounted up and rode the short distance to the school.

James spoke to the other two men.

"This is the biggest venture of my life. I want to be sure I'm following the Lord's direction in every detail."

"Perhaps it's the biggest venture so far, but hopefully finding a wife will be the biggest venture," Lucas said. He turned to Bates. "Can you believe your charge told me he was considering sending for a mail-order bride?"

Bates hooted with laughter.

"He's simply having a laugh at your expense. James would never take on a wife sight unseen," Bates replied.

James chuckled. "You know me too well, Bates. Well, let's get on with it." He started up the walk to the front door of the imposing edifice. "The building is attractive, don't you agree?"

Lucas nodded, and Bates, ignoring James' comment, said, "It'll be all right, James. No one is going to bite you. I have every confidence that you are listening to the voice of God, and He will lead you in this right down to the last detail. Chin up, Master James!"

James grinned. "I haven't heard that out of you since I was in knickers." He looked back at the two men behind him and swallowed. "Do I knock, or do we just go in?"

"We go in. No need to knock. No one will be likely to hear you anyway."

James heeded Lucas' words and pushed open the heavy oaken door. He found himself standing in a huge foyer that had several halls exiting from it. The other two men followed him in, and Lucas pointed to the office, motioning the others to follow him. Removing his hat, he led the way into the half-glassed door.

James stood for a couple minutes waiting for the secretary to acknowledge them, but she kept writing and never raised her head. Finally, he cleared his throat.

The woman looked up. She'd clearly been so engrossed in the letter she was scribing she hadn't heard the men enter. She pushed back, still in her chair, but it kept rolling. She looked askance at the three men as she nearly fell out of it when she thumped her feet on the floor to stop it. She rose circumspectly, straightening her skirts as she approached the desk, the color high in her cheeks.

Her eyes met James', who was focused on what he was to say. He knew he looked serious. Her glance swept over to Lucas, whose greenish-hazel eyes sparkled with laughter, and on to Bates, whose light-brown eyes were unreadable. Her gaze came back to rest on Lucas, choking down his laughter. The woman caught his look and began to laugh with abandon.

Startled, James stared for a second and shortly was laughing himself, Bates joining in.

Lucas recovered first, his glance unabashedly interested in this engaging creature with bright-red hair piled high on her head.

"My names is Lucas Falter, and this is Jacob Bates. We are here because my friend," he nodded toward James, "Mr. James Mobrey, is wanting to adopt a couple children."

The woman smiled and said, "I am secretary here, and my name is Josephine Hensley. All approval for adoptions must go through Miss Tarkington. Of course you must pass her test first. She is director of the school." Her cheeks were still flushed, and she kept her eyes averted from the hazel-eyed man, thankful he couldn't read her mind.

James responded to her comment with surprise filling his eyes. "A test?" he asked. "I must pass a test? What kind of test?"

At that moment another young woman entered the office. "It is a test of your character, sir. You must provide references first. After I've checked them, I need to know what kind of home you have and where the child will be reared." She looked around the room at the three men. Her gaze returned to James. "You did not bring your wife with you, sir?" Her voice held an incredulous tone that this man, seeking to take one of the children, would fail to bring the woman who would mother them.

"I'm not married!" James exclaimed, his eyes widening at the thought. "But I can say, with no hesitation, that I'm supposed to be here. I've been wrestling with the whole idea of adopting children for an entire year. I am here today, feeling better than I have in quite some time because I am here in obedience to God's directive. The Lord Almighty Himself led me here."

The woman's look of surprise turned to one of pleasure.

"I'm pleased beyond measure to hear you say that." She held out her hand to him, adding, "I am director of this institution—"

"You're the director!" James' knew his face registered his shock. "You're a bit young and a fem—" He stopped talking midsentence at the look of contempt etching onto her face.

"Sorry. I didn't mean to disparage you. I reckon it's a man's world and tough enough for a female to be able to achieve such a prestigious position. I'm afraid my tongue sometimes runs faster than my brain. Again, I apologize."

He made sure he looked so full of remorse that Anne would take pity on him.

"No harm done, sir. I am Miss Tarkington, Miss Anne Tarkington, and I've only been the head here for a couple of months."

She proffered her hand, and he took it in a gentle clasp as he gazed into her violet eyes.

She quickly withdrew her hand as he spoke.

"I'm James Mobrey, and these are my friends, Lucas Falter and Jacob Bates."

Anne shook their hands and welcomed them to the school as James continued to talk.

"I suppose I'm needing to take that test you're talking about. I've come to adopt two children, a boy and a girl, brother and sister if you have children with that connection. It is without a doubt what the Lord Almighty has impressed upon my heart."

Anne's face blanched at his words.

"I have only one brother and sister living here at the orphanage. You do understand this is an orphanage as well as a day school?"

"Yes, I do know that. I have looked into this very carefully. I also know that the University of California is the sole accrediting organization for this state, and this school is fully accredited."

Anne looked upon this man with a growing respect. This was not some fly-by-night but a man of some means and intelligence, as evidenced by his speech, demeanor, and clothing.

"Yes, it's true. This school is fully accredited. Please, come into my office," she said to him. She nodded to the other two men and turned to her secretary. "Thank you, Josie," she said as she led the men into her private domain.

The three followed her lead, but not before Lucas winked at Josephine, who blushed becomingly.

Entering the office, James looked around in appreciation. Everything was neat, clean, and tidy. He took a long look at Miss Tarkington and felt a kinship with her. She looked tidy and was neatly dressed. He took another long look and was pleased with her appearance. She was tall for a woman, yet he topped her by several inches. He perused her face. She was quite fetching. An idea seeded itself in his mind. It was so clear to him what he needed to do that he almost felt he'd heard a voice.

"Please, gentlemen, be seated." She motioned to the straight backs facing her desk.

"Now, let's get down to business. I deduce from your friends' presence they plan to vouch for your credibility. Am I correct?"

"Yes," Lucas said. "I've known James for fifteen years. He is a man of God and communes with the Almighty every day. He feels deeply impressed to adopt two children."

"And I've known James for seventeen years. I've been his tutor, mentor, and friend. I can vouch for a character unsullied by worldly pursuits. James is a man of integrity and honor. And as Lucas said, he is a man of God. Nothing and no one can surpass that."

"Well," Anne said, "that takes care of your character references, Mr. Mobrey. As to the reason why you are wanting to adopt, I think you've made that quite clear. What is your profession? Have you income enough to be able to support children?"

CHAPTER V

For in thee the fatherless findeth mercy.

HOSEA 14:3

JAMES CLEARED HIS THROAT BEFORE he spoke. "As far as my profession, I am involved in several organizations. I keep account of expenditures and make sure these organizations run smoothly." He smiled at his ability to dodge the question. "As far as income, I live quite comfortably in Napa. I moved west a year ago and am enjoying the milder climate. I have known I need to adopt or become the legal guardian for two children for some time now. Recently, the Lord Almighty has impressed upon my heart to find two children—brother and sister, and He led me to this institution. You say you do have a brother-sister combination living here?"

Anne colored up before she replied, feeling her heart sink at the thought of losing the Parker children.

"Y…yes," she replied. She looked down at her hands lying on the desk and tried to relax the tightly clenched grip. Her eyes filled with tears, and she was horrified that she could so lose control in front of complete strangers. She pulled her handkerchief out of her cuff and dabbed at her eyes.

"I'm sorry, but the children in question have captured my heart. I was hoping to adopt them myself, but as you can see, I am involved with the running of this institution and haven't the time or the means to support them the way they need. Perhaps when you hear of the problem, you won't want to have these children."

"What problem is that?" Lucas asked before James could.

Anne related the events of the two children before coming to the San Rafael School. She did not embellish the story, nor did she omit any of it.

"Whew! What a tragedy for those two." James' eyes misted as he spoke.

Anne's eyes filled with tears when she saw his expression.

"Yes, I…I suppose it would be best for you to adopt them. I believe you when you say you've been led here for this purpose. I cannot stand in the way of the Lord Almighty if He is leading you in this venture. Ginger Parker needs special attention, and living in Napa as you do would make it convenient for her to receive it. There is a lawyer here in San Rafael who knows a woman in Napa, a Mrs. Bannister who ca—"

"Mrs. Bannister! Why, Liberty Bannister is my neighbor!"

Anne knew, by his words, this was the Lord's doing. She tried to pull herself together as emotions welled up within her. Tears coursed unchecked down her face. She put her hand to her heart, as if it physically ached.

"I am so s-sorry! This is s-simply not my n-normal demeanor. I have grown attached to those children. I want to care for them more than anything in the world." She dabbed at her eyes. "What I started to say is that Mrs. Bannister evidently knows sign language and may be able to teach Ginger and her brother so they could c-communicate better."

James glanced at Bates and Lucas.

"Madam, you say you want to care for these children more than anything else in the world. Is that a true statement?"

Anne nodded her head. "Yes. I have no idea why I feel so strongly about those children, but I do."

"Would you be willing to forsake this directorship and come be the children's mother?" James' face blanched at his own words. He felt as if someone else was talking through him.

"What! What are you saying?" Anne's face registered total shock.

"I am asking, madam, would you consider marrying me? You wanted to adopt these children. I know I'm supposed to adopt them. What could be a better solution than for you to marry me?"

Anne was dumbfounded. "I…I don't know what to say! I have employment here! Why, I…I don't even know you!"

She peeked up in time to see Lucas' mouth drop open and Bates trying to contain his laughter.

"We can get to know one another. I'm going to need a mother for the children. If you'd like to have these children yourself, what could be a better proposition than we marry and give these children a stable Christian home?"

Anne's emotions whirled through her being at lightning speed. She stared at this young man as if he'd lost his mind.

"I've never heard of such a proposition. I—"

"Neither have I," James said with a wide smile. "Would you like me to get down on my knees and propose to you? Somehow, I don't think that would make any difference. I tell you we can work this out. Tell you what—let's make a bargain…a wedding bargain. You marry me, and I, ahhh…I won't claim conjugal rights until you're ready and willing."

His face turned beet red at his words, and Anne blanched at his audacity.

"Sir, I—"

"James, madam, please call me James."

"Mr. Mobrey." Anne sat down with a plop onto her chair. "I don't deign to answer this. Even if I did, I would not like to leave Mrs. Baxter in a lurch. She just hired me two months ago, and I—"

"Mrs. Baxter would be happy to see you happy, I'm sure."

"Do you make a habit of interrupting people, sir? That's the fourth time in less than two minutes."

"I see you still have your wits about you," he countered. "I'm sorry for my interruptions. I'm simply trying my best to be persuasive. I can see you need time." He pulled his timepiece out of his fob pocket, glanced at it, and continued. "Let's see. Hmmm, I will give you until tomorrow morning at, uhmm…nine o'clock sharp to make up your mind. That's nearly eighteen hours. Now, I'd like to see the children if I may." He spoke with aplomb, looking cheekily at Anne.

Anne inhaled deeply to calm her breathing. Her heart beat fast. This man irritated her beyond belief. She wondered if he was a feckless mama's boy or if he really was following the Lord's leading on this.

"Really, Mr. Mobrey, that's not a decision I can make hastily."

"No, but you just stated you want to care for them more than anything in the world. This is a perfect solution. God made it easy for me because I know I'm supposed to adopt a brother and sister from this institution, and you only have that combination in the Parker children. You have evidently fallen in love with these two. So what's the problem?"

"I know I said that, sir. It is but a manner of speech. I—"

"Need to pray about it, correct?"

"Yes. Now, please follow me." The color flamed high in her cheeks.

James' was unrepentant as he trailed behind Anne.

Lucas grinned at Bates, who raised one eyebrow in response. The two followed James out of the office.

Anne kept her face impassive as she led the way across the courtyard. Only her brows wrinkled in concentration as she prayed silently, walking with measured steps.

Is this the answer to my prayer, Lord? I told You I would go to any lengths to keep the children. This man claims You sent him here. Please let me know clearly what I'm to do. I feel I could put up with almost anything if I could be the mother of Thaddeus and Ginger. I don't know how they inveigled their way into my heart the way they have. I've worked hard to get a position in a school such as this. Do I throw it all away for the sake of marrying a perfect stranger? What am I to do? Please, please lead me.

They arrived at the far door, and Anne spoke. "You must be quiet, as the class is in progress. The two children are towheads and are unmistakable in appearance. They sit together. Thaddeus translates for Ginger as best he can, although she rarely puts forth an idea."

She started to pull the door open, but James reached the knob first and pulled it open for her, bowing slightly as he gestured her to enter first. Her face flushed slightly as she walked past him.

They stood in the back of the room, and James had no difficulty figuring out who the children were. There were several boy-girl combinations sitting in double desks, but only one set stood out because of their blond hair.

James' heart beat faster as his eyes perused the back of the children's heads. Excitement had filled him all morning, but now an unexpected calm come over his heart. As sure as night turned to day every morning, he knew these two were his. He turned to look at Miss Tarkington, and his eyes must surely glow with a special light.

Anne turned away from him, her eyes misting as she looked back at Thaddeus and Ginger. Her heart clenched, knowing if she didn't accept this man's proposition, she would lose these two children forever. She motioned to the others, and they left the room, filing out as silently as they'd entered.

"I would like the children to meet you and see if they are amenable to the situation, although they haven't much choice, have they?"

"No, not really," James replied. "I know this is what I am supposed to do, and those two are the right children for me."

Anne saw the determined set of Mr. Mobrey's jaw, and confusion filled her.

"I will take you to Mr. Humphries' office. He's the lawyer who knows Mrs. Bannister. He can draw up the papers for us. Let's return to my office. I need to get my shawl and some paperwork to take with us."

Anne led the men back across the courtyard, trying her best to keep her shoulders from sagging.

"Please wait here," she said and pointed to chairs lining the wall of the outer office. She headed into her inner sanctum and closed the door, the latch making an audible click in the quiet office.

James and Bates sat immediately, but Lucas sauntered over to the desk where Josephine was seated and watched as the color climbed up her neck and suffused her cheeks. He leaned his arm on the counter and spoke softly to her.

"We will be spending another night here in San Rafael, and I wonder, would you be amenable to having dinner with me at Three Hawks this evening?" Lucas asked.

"I...I don't know you, sir."

"We met earlier, remember?" he replied.

"I...I would be most happy to accompany you, sir."

She spoke in a rush of words and looked into his hazel eyes.

"Thank you, ma'am."

Lucas continued to talk and make arrangements with Miss Hensley. James and Bates sat in silence, waiting for Anne, each man wrapped in his own thoughts. When Anne finally emerged from her office, she kept her head averted but not before both men saw her reddened eyes and a damp handkerchief in her hand.

James' heart smote him when he saw her distress, and yet he felt his proposition was a fair one and the best solution all around.

"Please, follow me. It's only a couple blocks to Mr. Humphries' office." She led the way, praying she could keep her emotions in check.

Lucas and Bates talked quietly together, walking behind Anne and James.

Anne's emotions swirled in a turmoil, and she wondered that she could even contemplate marrying this man. Without speaking, they arrived at the law office.

It looked more like a hacienda than a business. The building stood alone. Huge recessed arches on either side of the front curved over broad flagstone walkways, which led to an enclosed courtyard behind the edifice. Passing one of the wide arches, James glimpsed a large fountain with the rich colors of clematis and greenery surrounding the pedestal in the middle of the spacious courtyard. Proceeding up the flagstone steps to a wide front porch, James opened the door for the other three.

Anne approached the dark-mahogany reception desk and spoke to one of the clerks.

"Good morning, Mr. Kepler. Is Mr. Humphries available, by any chance?" She smiled at him, and his cheeks reddened.

"Good morning, Miss Tarkington. One moment, and I'll see."

"We"—she waved her hand to the men standing behind her—"need to speak with him about an important matter."

Edward Kepler ran his finger down a ledger and said, "Yes, he's free. Let me make sure he's still here. Sometimes he will slip out the back for a few minutes. It looks as if there are no appointments until after lunchtime."

He walked at a fast pace down the hall and tapped on Elijah's door.

"Enter," Elijah said.

"Miss Tarkington to see you, sir, and three other men with her."

"Thank you, Edward." He rose from his chair and followed Edward back down the hall. As he entered the reception room, Anne walked toward him, proffering her hand.

"Mr. Humphries, thank you for seeing me so readily." She turned to introduce the men with her.

After meeting them, Elijah invited them to his office. He held out his arm and took Anne's hand, wrapping it around his arm. He didn't know the occasion, but he'd seen Anne's reddened eyes and the shadows that lurked there. He pressed her hand to his side to comfort her.

Ushering them into his office, he had them sit on comfortable leather chairs.

James looked around in appreciation.

The walls were done in a light-cream color. Bookshelves, picture frames, and window trim were stained a dark mahogany. The chairs for visitors were dark leather, and Elijah's desk chair, a swivel and tilt model, was oak but stained to match his desk. A huge seascape of a frigate running before a storm dominated the wall behind Elijah's desk. One corner housed a large oaken file cabinet. The office appeared stark, and yet there was an atmosphere of peace, contentment, and joy that seemed to permeate the very walls of the room. The right far corner of Elijah's desk held a thick, worn Bible.

"Can I get you some coffee or tea?" Elijah asked.

"A cup of tea would be just the thing," James replied.

The others nodded in agreement.

"One moment please." Elijah left the room to tell Edward to have the maid bring in some tea.

Reentering his office, he closed the door, went around to sit behind his desk, and clasped his hands.

"Now, what can I do for you?"

Anne, who'd been staring at her clenched hands, was startled out of her thoughts by his voice.

"We have come," she replied, "to have you draw up papers for the Parker children. James Mobrey is neighbor to your Liberty Bannister. He...he wants t-to adopt—"

James stood up. "Sorry to interrupt you, again, Miss Tarkington." He turned to speak to Elijah. "I have been impressed for the past year, by the Lord Almighty, to adopt a child. Recently, I've come to know I'm to adopt two children—a brother-sister combination. This whole venture is nothing short of a miracle. I was led to choose San Rafael over San Francisco. Liberty Bannister is my neighbor, and I have no doubt, being the godly woman she is, that she will tutor the girl, Ginger Parker." He waved at Lucas and Bates. "Lucas is a lawyer but says he can't draw up the papers in California until he is licensed here."

Elijah looked with keener interest at Lucas. He'd been talking with his colleagues just the week before about taking on another lawyer, as their clientele had increased dramatically over the past year. It was becoming difficult to keep up with the workload.

"I had the understanding, Miss Tarkington, that you planned to adopt those children yourself," Elijah said, now understanding the sorrow in her eyes.

Anne nodded but kept silent.

"That can be rectified if she will accept my offer of marriage." James wasn't usually so outspoken, nor was he callous. He simply felt it was the right solution.

Elijah Humphries stared at the audacity of James Mobrey wanting to marry Miss Tarkington. As he gazed at the young man, a peace washed over him, and he knew Mobrey's proposal was made in good faith. Elijah was fortunate in having the gift of discernment. It had helped him many times in straightening out misunderstandings in his practice. It did not always resound within him so clearly as it did right now though.

His gaze swung to Anne Tarkington in time to see the blood rise up and fill her cheeks. Before she could comment, Elijah spoke without hesitation, turning his eyes back on James.

"Mr. Mobrey, saying what I am going to say is not something I say lightly. Was that a confusing sentence?" He smiled at the younger man, seeing in him a desire to please the Almighty. "I don't often comment on things of this nature, but I'm going to make an exception. I believe, young man, you are listening to the Lord on this. I know you, Miss Tarkington, have worked diligently to get yourself into a prestigious position as director of a school. I also believe the Almighty placed you here for this exact purpose. Those children need you to mother them. Last evening you stated that you wanted those children more than anything in the world. Mr. Mobrey living next to Liberty Bannister is a boon, but it's nothing compared to the fact that the little girl and boy will have you to love and care for them. I am without a doubt in favor of Mr. Mobrey's request that you marry him."

Anne raised a trembling hand to her mouth, aghast.

"I...I can scarcely credit your saying that, sir! Why, I don't even know him!"

"Yes, and as you well know, many marriages are arranged with no say in the matter for the girl. Of course in this instance, you have the freedom to make your own choice. It boils down quite simply. Do you want these children or not? How much are you willing to sacrifice to have them in your permanent care?"

"I told the Almighty I'd go to any length to have those two. I must be daft, but I can't seem to think rationally about them."

CHAPTER VI

The integrity of the upright shall guide them:
but the perverseness of transgressors shall destroy them.

PROVERBS 11:3

JACOB BATES STOOD UP, AND all eyes focused on him. "I told Mr. James that the children should have a say in who cares for them. Could you go fetch them, Miss Tarkington, and we'll see what their desires might be?"

Elijah nodded his head in approval. "Excellent suggestion, Mr. Bates."

"Y…yes, yes, I can do that," Anne said. "While I do, here's all the paperwork I have on the children. It's not much, mostly just what the wagon master said and then what I could garner from Thaddeus. He's not even certain whether his parents had siblings. He said he didn't think there was any next of kin. If the parents weren't that close to any relatives, I doubt any of them would want the children anyway." She laid the folder on Elijah's desk. Turning to James, she said, "Mr. Mobrey, should I take you up on your offer, I'd like to ask my grandmother to come live with us. She raised me and has plans to come join me sometime in the future. Would that be amenable to you?" Her cheeks pinked up at her request, and she wondered what kind of home he had and if he even would have enough room for her grandmother.

"Yes, that would be fine with me. I do hope you'll favor the plan. It seems to be the best solution all around. I'm sure Mrs. Baxter will be able to find a replacement for you at the school." His face looked hopeful.

Anne nodded and headed for the door, which Lucas held open for her.

"I'll accompany you," Lucas said.

The two of them walked briskly back to the school while Elijah, James, and Bates sat at the desk to work on the papers for adoption.

"These will be filed with the state and final ones drawn up later." Elijah had drawn up several adoption papers since working in California. "You're sure you don't want a trial period before you adopt?"

"No, no trial period is needed. I know without a doubt this is the Lord's doing. If, perchance, things get difficult, I don't want the option of being able to get out of it rather than work it out. I do want to make sure I am guided by the Almighty—to do His bidding. You seemed as surprised as I was that I asked Miss Tarkington to marry me. I only came to the realization that I should marry her less than a half hour ago. I know we have free will and sometimes we thwart the plans God has for us, but I pray Miss Tarkington marries me, because if she doesn't, I believe she's going to be miserable. I confess—I don't love her, but I will learn to if she will have me."

Elijah nodded. "I've seen stranger things than you asking for Miss Tarkington's hand in marriage. Let's pray together, right now, and ask the Almighty for guidance."

Liberty lay on the grass, her eyes fixed on the scene before her. She wondered what was happening. Surely it had been twenty minutes since Matthew had made his way to the back of the house. She started to get up, when the front door of Hedley's place slammed opened. She flattened herself to the ground and watched through the curtain of bushes. A man raised his gun, aiming in her direction. In a flash of insight, a horrified Libby realized he was going to shoot their horses.

She shut one eye, aimed through her sights, and shot the man in the thigh. He yelled and started shooting wildly in her direction. She shot his right hand, and his gun dropped. Libby felt sick, but the man wouldn't stop. He bent to retrieve his gun using his left hand. He raised it, pointing in her direction. She aimed for his upper arm, but he moved, and the bullet struck his chest. He crumpled to the ground, not moving. She stood up and ran toward the house, keeping her eyes fixed on the man in case he was shamming.

She kicked away the man's gun and realized, with sickening clarity, that he was probably dead. She raised her gun, walking with quiet steps on the front porch. She peered into the dimness of the room. Stepping over the threshold, she entered but still didn't see Matthew. A board creaked under her boot, and immediately she heard a thump come from the kitchen. She held her gun at the ready as she walked warily toward the kitchen. The thumping continued. She peeked cautiously around the doorjamb, shocked at what she saw. Matthew sat tied to a chair, his mouth stuffed with a filthy rag. Dan Hedley sat beside him trussed tightly, eyes closed, head bowed. He wasn't moving. Liberty ran to Matthew, hurriedly taking the rag out of his mouth.

Matthew spat out strings of cotton and said, "He got me in the barn. Where is he, Libby?"

"I...I think he's dead. I...I think I k-killed him." She took a shuddering breath. "I'm not sure. I shot him in the leg, but he kept shooting, s-so I shot his gun hand. Then he t-tried to use his left." She spoke haltingly as her fingers worked at the knots that bound Matthew to the chair. Tears slid down her cheeks, and her hands shook. "He wouldn't stop, Matthew. He just wouldn't stop! So I aimed for his upper arm, but he turned, and I th-think I k-killed him."

The old rope was finally loosened. Matthew went down on one knee in front of Dan, removing the rag from his mouth. He lifted an eyelid and checked his pulse, which was thready, and shook his head.

"He's in a bad way." He stood, taking Liberty into his arms, and held her close, wishing he could infuse comfort. He lifted her chin, gave her a quick kiss, and stood her back, the better to look into her eyes. He spoke quickly, knowing the dead man's accomplice could come back at any time.

"You saved our lives, Libby. It was kill or be killed. There was no other choice." He strode to the front door and onto the porch. Liberty trailed behind him. Matthew rolled the man over but didn't recognize him. The motion of bending over sent hammers into his skull, and he touched the back of his own head, getting blood on his fingers. The place where the man gun-butted him still oozed.

"Oh, Matthew!" Liberty exclaimed.

"I'm all right. Just have a doozy of a headache, is all." Matthew knew the man Liberty had shot was dead but felt for his neck pulse anyway. Picking up the dead man's gun, he tucked it into the small of his back under his vest. Straightening, he looked carefully around at the hills, but he saw no movement. He turned and took Liberty's arm, leading her back inside. He kicked the door closed with his boot.

"There's another man," he said to Liberty. "I don't know when he'll be back. His horse was stabled in one of the stalls, if I'm any judge of horse droppings." He smiled, trying to ease the look in Liberty's eyes. "That's what I was looking at when I got gun-butted."

They went to the kitchen.

"Let's untie Hedley and get him into his bed," Matthew said. He gave Liberty directions as he hurriedly untied Hedley's wrists. "I'm going to ask you to do something, Libby. I need you to ride for Sheriff Rawlins and John. Tell John first, and tell him not to use his buggy. He needs to come as fast as he can. Tell Buck Rawlins to be watchful for any strangers as he rides here. I'll be on the lookout in case the other man comes back. Can you do that?"

"Yes."

Matthew took Dan by the shoulders, and Liberty lifted his feet. They got him into his bedchamber, where Liberty removed his neckerchief and loosened his shirt at the neck and removed his boots. Dan had not regained consciousness.

Matthew went to the pump to get some fresh water. He took a mouthful and swished and spat to rid himself of the taste of the dirty cotton. He took a long drink of the cool water and returned with a bucketful. Liberty lifted Dan's head and tried to get him to drink, but it dribbled out of the corners of his mouth. He moaned and seemed delirious. She went to the bureau and found a clean handkerchief, wetted it, and tried to get it into the man's mouth, but ended up opening his lips and squeezing a little moisture onto his teeth. He didn't swallow.

"I'm leaving, Matthew, but after I go to town, I need to get home. I've got some hungry babies waiting for me."

Matthew set the bucket down and grabbed her. Pulling her to him, he kissed her.

"Okay, off you go. We need John here right away, but frankly, I doubt Dan's going to make..." Pain filled his voice. He looked at his wife with tears in his eyes, but his voice became firm. "Ride like the wind, Libby!" He walked her to the porch.

"Matthew, I love you!"

"I love you too, darling. Now go, sweetheart…get going!"

She ran as fast as she could to Pookie, grabbed the reins, and in one smooth motion, she was up and on her way to Napa.

Conchita was worried. Both babies were crying in earnest, and Liberty wasn't back. It wasn't like her to be late for a feeding. Conchita, her mind on other things, had lost track of time. When the babies started fussing in earnest, she had fretted a bit, thinking Liberty had also lost track of time. Now she felt certain something was wrong. She knew Liberty would be uncomfortable, being way past due for a feeding.

Conchita crossed herself and prayed a quick prayer of protection as she hurried to the barn. Diego was there at a small desk, working out some detail on paper. Most of the time the couple spoke English, but when they were alone together or if there was something important, rapid-fire Spanish was spoken.

"Meester Bannister an' Mees Libby…*Son muy tarde, Diego. Creo que algo está mal.*" (They are very late, Diego. I think something is wrong.)

"*Sí, creo que lo mismo.*" (Yes, I think the same). He got up as Conchita continued to talk and saddled his horse. "*Voy a ir a la casa de Hedley y veo lo que está pasando.*" (I'll ride to Hedley's place and see what's happening.) He led his horse out of the stable, mounted, settled his sombrero on his head, and touching his spurs to his horse, he was off at a gallop.

As soon as Liberty rode off, Matthew whistled for Piggypie. She lifted her beautiful head and trotted down to him. He dragged the dead man by the shoulders around to the back of the house and left him, heading to the barn, but he realized the other man could come riding directly to the barn and not the front of the house. He decided to drag the dead man behind the barn. As he worked, he prayed Liberty would be all right and get back to the Rancho safely. He hauled a couple armloads of straw to cover the dead man, placing several split wood logs on him to hold the straw down. He got a broom from the barn and swept the gouged earth where the man's boots had scored it. Every move was quick and precise. He realized that if the other man came back and knew how to track, he'd readily see the swept dirt all the way around to the front.

As he swept, his mind kept jumping to what needed done. When he reached the side of the front porch, he stepped up, and taking the broom handle, he broke out the rest of the glass from the window. The shards sticking up in the window frame would be more noticeable than no window. He swept the glass off the porch and kicked the larger pieces under it. Sweeping the rest underneath the overhang, he trampled and scuffed up the dirt with his boot. Once finished, he made his way through the house to check on Dan, but the older man was still unconscious.

Matthew went to the barn to replace the broom and whistled for Piggypie, who trotted around to the back. He took her reins and led her through the barn to the farthest stall, where he tied her with a slip knot, not unsaddling her in case he needed to get away in a hurry. He dumped some oats in the manger as a treat.

"You're a good girl," he said and stroked her face. He heard a sound and drew his gun with lightning speed as he spun around.

Diego rode at a gallop rather than his normal relaxed canter. He arrived in short order and observed the scene before him, seeing nothing. He rode down the escarpment he and Matthew, as well as other men, had carved out of the side of the cliff. Getting to the bottom, he stopped his horse and carefully scrutinized the scene before him. There were no horses tied up. He loped down and saw several hoofprints, but only one led to the back of the house. It was a fresh set and had a B stamp. Matthew had a B carved into every shoe of the Bannister horses.

He tied up at the rail and followed the tracks around to the rear of the house. The barn doors were open, so he stepped up to see Matthew turn and draw on him.

"You one fast draw, Meester Bannister," Diego said, his tone admiring.

Air whooshed out of Matthew's lungs in relief as he holstered his gun.

"Dan's nearly dead, Diego. He's been beaten and tied to a chair for God only knows how long. I got bashed over the head and was tied up next to him, but Liberty killed the man and got me loose. She's ridden for John and Buck and will go back to the Rancho once that's done. I'm pretty sure the man she shot has an accomplice. He could come back anytime, so get your ride in here out of sight, and we'll see what happens. I'm praying Liberty doesn't run into him on her way to town."

Matthew's tone was clipped, and Diego saw worry etched on his face.

As Diego strode out of the barn, he said over his shoulder, "God breenged you here, Meester Bannister, to halp Meester Hedley. He weel keep Mees Libby safe."

Liberty loved to ride fast and streaked down the main road toward town. Everything became a blur as she concentrated on what she would say when she saw Dr. John. She prayed he'd be in his office and not off delivering a baby or something.

She didn't pass anyone on her way and slowed to a trot as she approached the main street of Napa. Pulling up in front of John's residence, which was also his office, she slid from Pookie and threw her reins around the rail, not bothering to see if they caught. She hurried up the boarded walk and strode into the front door, turning immediately to her right into John's waiting room.

There were a couple people sitting there, waiting to be seen, and she nodded in acknowledgment but went straight to John's examining room door, which was closed. She tapped on it but got no answer. She rapped harder, and it opened abruptly to an irritated look stamped on the doctor's face, until he saw Liberty.

"John, you need to come quick!" she whispered. "It's an emergency, and Matthew said to ride, not take your buggy. Dan Hedley's been robbed and is nearly dead. We don't know how long he was tied up to a chair. I need to go get Buck. And, John, be careful. There's a man on the loose who's responsible for this."

"I'll go right now," he said.

"All right, people." He spoke to those waiting and the man on his table. "I have an emergency and will be back in this afternoon. Come back if you need to be seen."

He ran up the stairs to talk to his wife, Sally Ann, as Liberty exited, slamming the door shut behind her. Liberty, after talking to Dr. John, strode down the boarded walk to the sheriff's office. She breathed a sigh of relief as she entered, seeing Buck Rawlins, sheriff of Napa, there.

"Good morning, Liberty," he said. "What brings you here this fine morning?" On closer inspection of her face, he strapped on his gun before she could reply.

"It's a beautiful morning, but not a good one, Buck. Matthew and I rode over to Dan Hedley's place this morning. He's been beaten and tied up in a chair for I don't know how long. I...I think he's dying. One of the robbers is dead." Liberty swallowed, holding back the tears. "And...and Matthew thinks there's another robber on the loose. Dan is unconscious. I just talked to Dr. John to make haste and get himself out there. Matthew's alone, and we don't know if..." Tears rolled down her cheeks.

"I'm saddled up, and I'll ride over there first thing. I suggest you get yourself back to the Rancho, pronto. There's no telling where this other outlaw might be." He grabbed his Stetson and settled it on his head, took Liberty by the arm, patted her on the back, and headed her out the door. Both stepped into stirrups and settled themselves on their horses' backs. Buck turned to see if Liberty was ready and nodded at her. The two of them headed out of town, side by side. They reached the edge of town and kicked their rides into a gallop.

CHAPTER VII

Pleasant words are as an honeycomb,
sweet to the soul, and health to the bones.

PROVERBS 16:24

BUCK SLOWED WHEN IT CAME TIME for him to turn up the long lane to Hedley's place. The house was set back about a half mile from the main road.

"You be careful, now, you hear? I'll get the details from Matthew. Don't you worry about him either. He'll be all right."

Liberty nodded. "I'll ride straight for the Rancho, Buck. I have twins that are way past a feeding. As to worrying, I'll try not to. I know he's in God's hands." She kicked Pookie's sides and left with a wave of her hand.

She prayed for Matthew as she rode. Her thoughts swung to Dan Hedley and what might have happened to him before they arrived. He'd looked pretty well beaten. One eye was swollen shut, his face bruised, and his lip cut. She prayed John would be able to help him.

Arriving home, she slid from the saddle and led Pookie toward the stable, but Donny Miller came out of the huge opened doors to help with her horse.

"Diego rode over to Hedley's to see if he could find you," he said. "Conchita is beside herself with worry." His eyes looked questioningly at her.

"Yes, we ran into some real trouble, but I can't explain right now. I'll tell you about it after I take care of the twins." She strode up the flagstone walk, calling over her shoulder, "Thanks, Donny, for taking care of Pookie. She's been ridden hard."

Conchita opened the front door. One look at Liberty's face confirmed her suspicions.

"I know dere ees sometheeng no good, Mees Libby. I tell Diego he muss go to Hedley's an' see what happen. You ees never late for feeding dose babies."

"Your premonition was right, Conchita." Liberty headed straight to the kitchen, where the twins were being held by Luce and Lupe, Conchita's nieces, who also worked for the Bannisters. Both babies were crying at the top of their lungs. Liberty washed her hands and spoke above the din of crying.

"Let me have Faith first," she said to Luce. "Matty doesn't scream as loudly as she does." Liberty spoke with a smile, but her insides roiled in turmoil over the morning's events. She settled into an armchair rocker in the corner of the kitchen, placed there expressly for her to nurse.

Once she relaxed, she related what had happened that morning.

"Matthew and I had a good ride over to Dan's. As we sat on that last little hill above the house, we talked about buying the property and ended up getting shot at. Matthew's ear was grazed. We dropped to the grass, and Matthew decided to go around to the back of the house. He looked into the barn and ended up getting bashed in the head and tied up in a chair next to Dan. The man who hit him came out onto the front porch and aimed for our horses, so I shot him in the leg, but he kept shooting, so I shot his gun hand, but he w-wouldn't s-stop."

Conchita clucked her tongue. "He one bad hombre, Mees Libby."

Tears trailed down Liberty's cheeks. "He p-picked up the gun with his left and st-started to shoot again, so I aimed for his arm, but he turned and caught it in the chest. I killed him. I killed a man." Liberty sobbed.

Luce's and Lupe's eyes were rounded in stunned silence. Neither had ever heard such a story.

"Shush—shush, Mees Libby." Conchita wrapped her arms lightly around her shoulders, not wanting to disturb Faith. "Eet not be good for your milk, you crying like that." Conchita laid her cheek on Liberty's and rubbed her gently on the back to comfort her. "Shush, leetle one. Eet be all right. You halp save Meester Bannister, Meester Hedley, an' dose horses. You do what you haf to do. The good Lord, He know your heart, Mees Libby. *Sí*—eet be a horrible theeng to take a life, but you muss protect your family, an' sometime that ees the only way. Eet not your fault that man turn when you shoot. Ah, *chica*...eet's all right." She rubbed Liberty's back and changed the subject. "What Meester Bannister ees doing now?"

"Matthew is certain there is more than one man. There were fresh droppings in another stall, so he thinks there were probably two men using Dan's house. He had me ride into town for Buck and John. He's going to keep a lookout for the other robber and clean up the mess. I don't know if he's going to bury the man I shot or not, but he's staying with Dan until Dr. John can get out there. Matthew doesn't hold much hope for Dan. I tried to give him water, but he wouldn't swallow. He's unconscious. I feel better knowing Diego rode over there. I hate to think of Matthew facing an outlaw on his own, although he's more than capable."

"*Sí*, you ees right, Mees Libby. Meester Bannister, he take care of himself, that one. He one smart hombre."

Liberty finished nursing the twins, and Lupe and Luce put them down for a nap. They were tuckered out from crying. Still upset, Liberty sat at the kitchen table, and Conchita poured fresh cups of coffee for the two of them. She sat down as Liberty began to speak.

"Matthew would like to buy Dan Hedley's place and have Donny and Cadence live there. Did Cadence tell you how long she would be visiting her grandmother? I forgot to ask her." Liberty had hired a runaway girl just before having the twins. Donny was Diego's right-hand man, and he and Cadence were engaged to be married.

"*Sí*, she stay for the week. Mrs. Baxter, she up from San Franceesco to look over the school een San Rafael. Mr. Baxter, he comed weeth her." She thought about Cadence and Donny living in the Hedley house. "That ees a good plan Meester Bannister haf for dose two lovebirds to live een Meester Hedley's house. I know they ees wanting to marry. Dose two, they ees so een love."

"Yes, they are. I keep wondering if Donny will want to continue working here or end up settling down someplace of his own. Cadence is now a wealthy young woman with more to come, inheriting from Mrs. Baxter."

"I haf wondered about that too." Conchita nodded her head sagely. "Donny, he could start hees own vineyard. He a hard worker like Meester Bannister. I theenk you weel need to find another mans to be working here. Dere ees more an' more works to be done here. I am grateful, Diego an' me, we ees part of thees family. We are loving you so much."

"I am grateful too, Conchita. You made me so welcome from the first night I arrived here from Boston. For some reason this felt like home beginning that very first night. I know I designed and had the house built that Papa and Granny live in, but it never felt like home for the whole year I lived in it. Never like Rancho Bonito does."

Liberty sighed, emotionally drained from the morning's happenings. "You are part of our family, Conchita. God has blessed us richly, and I thank you for your comfort." She eyed Conchita closely, realizing her faithful friend didn't look well. "Are you feeling all right? I know you're not supposed to tell someone they look tired, but you do. You look tired. Is everything all right?"

Conchita looked away from Liberty's perusal and replied, "*Sí*, I ees worried about you. I am fine."

Thaddeus heard the click of the classroom door and swiveled his head to see who had come in. Miss Tarkington stood at the door and gestured to him. He whispered into Ginger's ear and started to leave the double desk he shared with her. He stood, his eyes staring into Miss Tarkington's. He could see distress in hers. She waved at him, signaling for him to bring Ginger too. He whispered again to Ginger, who scooted out of the seat and headed obediently to the back of the room. Thaddeus, following her, felt his stomach curl in on itself with anxiety. He didn't know what this was about, but he had a bad feeling about it. He and Ginger sat near the back of the room, so they made little disturbance as they walked softly toward the headmistress.

Without a word, but with her forefinger to her lips, Miss Tarkington led them into the hall, where a man awaited them. Thaddeus looked questioningly at the director but didn't voice his question. His throat constricted, and he wondered who the man was and what he wanted.

Anne spoke in a quiet voice. "Ginger, Thaddeus, this is Mr. Lucas Falter. Mr. Falter, Ginger and Thaddeus Parker."

Thaddeus sketched a little bow, and Ginger curtsied. "How do you do?" Thaddeus said.

"I do very well, thank you. What nice manners you have."

Lucas Falter spoke with a twinkle in his hazel-colored eyes. He turned expectantly to Anne, who, after glancing at him, and in spite of her skirts, knelt to be on a level with the two children. Love and compassion almost tangibly emanated from her, but when she spoke, her voice trembled.

"Mr. Falter is a good friend of a man named Mr. Mobrey. Mr. Mobrey is waiting in an office down the street. He would like to meet both of you." Without further words, she rose and led them across the courtyard and out of the building.

Ginger, her eyes enormous, was scared. Anything different or out of the normal routine caused her heart to thump so hard she could scarcely hear. Not being able to speak was bad enough, but she had no way of letting anyone know how frightened she was. She grabbed Thaddeus' arm and held on to it with both hands.

He looked at her, his eyes full of misery. Her grasp hurt, but he knew she was frightened. He put one hand over hers and patted it to let her know everything was going to be all right, even though he was sure it wasn't. He had a feeling they would be leaving the school. That fact didn't make much difference to him one way or the other. He wasn't attached to any of the other children. Leaving Miss Tarkington would be devastating though. He barely kept the tears back as he bit the inside of his cheek to keep from crying.

No one spoke as they walked the short distance to the law firm where Mr. Humphries worked.

Anne was caught up in a tumult of emotion.

Whatever shall I do? she wondered. *It's insane to even contemplate marrying a complete stranger. Yet I can't seem to think straight when it comes to these two children. I want them! I suppose I want them at any price. Lord, I've asked You for direction. Please let me be at peace with this decision. I reckon I'm going to marry Mr. Mobrey. I don't want to, but I know in my heart of hearts I will lose the children...lose them forever if I choose not to take this offer. It's frightening and exciting all at the same time.*

Engrossed in her thoughts, she realized they had arrived at the law office, and she'd done nothing to calm the children's fears. She took Ginger's grip off Thaddeus' arm and embraced her.

Thad rubbed his arm to get some circulation going as he watched Miss Tarkington stroke Ginger's hair. She was a kind woman.

"Ginger, it'll be all right, you'll see. Come along now." She led them up the wide flagstone steps as she continued to talk. "I met Mr. Humphries the other night at dinner. He's a lawyer and a fine man who knows a woman up in Napa who can speak with her hands."

Thaddeus drew a deep breath of relief. He'd thought they were to be taken away from the school.

"I thought you said his name was Mr. Mobrey," Thaddeus said.

Anne looked down at the boy, who carried such a heavy load on his thin shoulders, and her eyes teared up. "Yes, yes I did say that. Let's go meet him, shall we?"

Lucas opened the heavy doors and ushered Anne and the children in with an exaggerated bow to make Thaddeus and Ginger smile.

"We'll go straight to Mr. Humphries' office," Lucas Falter said. "Follow me." They headed down the long hall, Ginger's hand firmly clasped in Anne's.

Lucas tapped gently on the door, and it opened immediately, as if Jacob Bates had been standing there, waiting for them to appear.

"Come in. Come right on in," Bates said. He looked at Ginger and Thaddeus with warmth in his eyes, and the two children saw it.

Anne turned to speak to the children as she led them to the desk, where she made the introductions.

"Ginger and Thaddeus Parker…this is Mr. Humphries, who is a lawyer. This is Mr. Mobrey, the man who wants to meet you. Mr. Humphries, Mr. Mobrey, this is Ginger and Thaddeus Parker."

Thaddeus said a polite "how do you do" as he again made a little bow, and Ginger curtsied. James held out his hand to shake Thad's, and the boy felt warmth and concern for his person emanating from this man. He looked up into eyes bluer than his own, startled by the goodness he saw there.

Elijah Humphries cleared his throat. He looked as if he were going to speak, clearing his throat again, but James squatted down eye level with the children.

"As Miss Tarkington said, my name is James Mobrey. Miss Tarkington told me you lost your mother and your father coming west. I am very sorry for your loss. You've had a difficult and harrowing time of it, and I am sorry for that too. I wanted to meet you because the Lord Almighty has spoken to my heart for some time now. If I understand His directions clearly, He wants me to adopt two children, a brother and sister, to come live with me and be my children."

Thaddeus, his eyes now widened by some strong emotion, stared at the man, knowing he was going to be taken away from the school, but more, from Miss Tarkington. He took a couple steps backward and clasped Anne's hand in his, looking up at her beseechingly. His eyes implored her to help him.

She felt his tightened grip, and her heart went out to him; it decided her. She prayed as James Mobrey continued to talk to the children.

"Would you be amenable to come live in my house? I will not try to bribe you with wonderful things or ideas. I will say that I don't want you to come live with me and be little slaves, working for bread and water. You will be my beloved children, and should I ever have any children of my own, you will be equals with them. Do you understand what I am saying?"

Ginger, her eyes filling with tears, nodded. Thaddeus simply stared at Mr. Mobrey, voicing what was on his heart.

"I am thankful for the offer, but I…I…" He looked up at Anne helplessly.

Ginger tugged on his arm and nodded her head. She hated the school and the one girl who made life miserable for her. The girl made fun of her every time the teachers weren't looking. Ginger couldn't understand Thaddeus' hesitation and pulled harder on his arm to get his attention.

"Stop it, Ginger! Just stop it!" Thaddeus pulled his arm away and glared at his sister. "I know what you want, but you're not the only person here needing to make a decision." He turned to James and spoke, sounding as if he were an adult. "I can see you are a kind man. I don't care about leaving this school. It doesn't bother me in the least, and I don't care about leaving the other children either. I do care…" His voice quavered, and tears filled his eyes. He wiped them impatiently on his sleeve and turned to bury his face in Anne's side. With a muffled voice he continued. "I do care about Miss Tarkington. I don't want to leave her.

She loves me, I know she does, and—and I love her!" Thaddeus sobbed into her waist, mortified he was crying in front of other people and that he'd bared his soul.

Anne looked helplessly at James Mobrey.

He returned her stare and said, "What say you, madam?" He pulled the boy away from Anne and scooped him into his arms.

Thaddeus was beside himself and buried his face in James' neck, his shoulders shaking as he cried his heart out. All the pent-up emotions of the past few months made a debut in gut-wrenching grief and sorrow. He missed his mother and father and had never properly mourned them. Ginger was distant and didn't seem to care about anything anymore. She continually hurt his feelings. He was tired of being wrong when he tried to figure out what it was she wanted. He was tired of being strong.

James hugged the boy to himself, wishing he could absorb his pain and infuse love into the little body.

"Will you marry me and be a mother to these children?" he asked.

Anne stared back, knowing in her heart of hearts that this was it. She had no choice but to accept.

"Yes, yes, I will marry you." She spoke the words simply, but her heart was pounding, and her breath shortened. "Under the conditions you stated earlier," she said. Blood suffused her cheeks, but she refused to look away from James.

CHAPTER VIII

God setteth the solitary in families.

PSALM 68:6

JAMES FELT THADDEUS PULL AWAY FROM his neck to join him in staring at Anne. His subconscious took in the fact that the boy's tears had wetted his shirt. James wondered if he'd heard aright as he stared back at Anne.

Her eyes held his steadily as she continued to speak. "I must let Mrs. Baxter know and send a telegram to Grandma Jenny. I also need to know exactly when I'm to marry you."

"When, is now," James replied. "The sooner, the better. We need to be married for Elijah to draw up the adoption papers with both our names as the children's parents."

Anne gasped.

He could see she'd thought there'd be a time of courting, of getting to know each other.

He calmly returned her stare, but his gut churned. He had every confidence he was following the Almighty's leading, but he felt overwhelmed. He'd never thought to ask someone to marry him anytime soon. He only knew a couple unmarried women, and neither were close to his idea of someone he wanted to marry. He knew he was rushing things, but he felt if he waited, Miss Tarkington would turn tail and run. To his way of thinking, she looked scared out of her wits. James felt as if everything around him suddenly came sharply into focus. His hearing became acute. He heard Bates breath expel when Miss Tarkington acquiesced. He glanced at Bates, and seeing that his mentor wanted to say something, James nodded.

"I believe we're forgetting an important element here." All eyes turned Bates' way, and he sat in one of the deep leather chairs before he continued. "Ginger, Thaddeus, please come here."

James put Thad onto the floor, and both children drew near. Bates put his hand on the back of each child, drawing them closer to his bent knees. He kept his hands on them as he spoke.

"This entire situation hinges on one answer from each of you, and you need to think over your answer carefully. This is not a situation you can get out of should you decide you don't like it. Once you are adopted by Mr. Mobrey and Miss Tarkington, soon to be Mrs. Mobrey, it will be the same as if they were your birth parents. They will have the right to discipline you if you're naughty, give you chores, do all the things that normal parents do. Do you understand what I am saying?"

Both children nodded solemnly.

"All right then. Now you must choose if you want this new life with Mr. Mobrey and Miss Tarkington. I don't know Miss Tarkington, but evidently she's made a good impression on you. I do know Mr. James, and he is, without a doubt, the nicest person I have ever known. When people marry, there's a phrase in their vows that says 'for better or for worse.' It's like that for children too. You won't always be happy. There will come times when you are angry or frustrated, but that's the 'worse' part. The 'better' part is that these two people will love you as if you were their own flesh and blood. They will, indeed, be your parents. Think carefully now. Is this your desire?"

Ginger nodded right away. Her eyes slanted sideways, begging Thaddeus, who felt engulfed with emotion. He could scarcely wrap his thoughts around the fact that he could have Miss Tarkington for a mother.

He swallowed, and it seemed a lifetime to Ginger, who waited impatiently for him to speak.

"Yes, I reckon since Miss Tarkington is going to go with us, I'd like very much to be adopted," he said.

Matthew slapped the buttock of the dead man's horse with a light hand. "He's a fine-looking Appaloosa, isn't he?"

"*Sí*, he a *bonito caballo*, that's sure." Diego pushed his sombrero off his head and let it fall onto his back, the leather thongs at his neck keeping it in place.

Matthew pointed to the stall that hadn't been mucked out and asked, "What do you think? Was there another horse besides this one?"

"*Sí*, I theenk you ees right, Meester Bannister. Another horse has been een here. Thees ees fresh."

Matthew agreed. "I don't know where the other man took himself off to, but I'd imagine it was to pick up some food. Dan was supposed to go to Frisco to visit his daughter. He told me he planned to find a small place near her where he could live. Said he was done with ranching. He lost all heart when his Betty died. I know he'd not leave food around to spoil while he was gone." He turned and said, "Follow me." He led Diego around to the back of the barn and showed him where he'd put the dead robber.

"Liberty shot him," he said. "She's mighty upset about killing him. She was trying to be brave when she told me. I'd left her up on the hill and circled round here to the barn, but this man caught me off guard and bashed me on the head." He pulled the straw away from the man's face as he continued to talk. "He tied me up in the kitchen next to Dan and stuffed a rag in my mouth. I was gone so long Liberty didn't know what to think. She started to get up and come down that last rise, but this man"—he toed the pile of straw—"came out of the front door and aimed his gun at the horses. Liberty shot him a couple times, because he persisted in taking aim at our horses. Libby said she shot him in the hand, the leg, and aimed for his upper arm, but he turned and caught it in the chest. I'll not bury him until we see what Buck wants to do with him." Pulling more straw away, he squatted down and went through the man's pockets.

"Mees Libby, she a sharpshooter. She get whatever she aim at. She weel be sorry of keeling thees man, even eef he ees a *bandido*. I weel pray for her." Diego crossed himself as he spoke.

"You're right about him being an outlaw," Matthew said. "It is beyond my ken how a man can treat another human with so little regard.

I know this man was a bad one, but Liberty's going to suffer mightily for shooting him."

The man had a hefty amount of money in a filthy leather money belt tied under his shirt. In one pocket was a small pocketknife, a folded handkerchief that had seen better days, and a thin worn leather case that Matthew opened. It contained a small daguerreotype of a young woman with a baby girl on her lap. The other pocket held a few loose coins and a couple wooden toothpicks. The breast pocket of his shirt contained a small metal case holding tobacco, and a thin packet of papers for rolling cigarettes. There was nothing to indicate who he was or where he was from.

The two men went to the back door and entered the house, going into Dan Hedley's bedchamber.

"It's not looking good for Dan," Matthew said in a low voice. "I hope Liberty found John and he gets here fast. Look—he's black and blue from being beaten. I'm sure he put up a good fight. It doesn't look as if he's had any water. Liberty tried to get him to drink, but he's unconscious and..."

Matthew watched as Diego took the cup Liberty had used. He held it to Dan's lips, but the older man was unconscious.

As he placed the cup on the nightstand, both men knew Daniel Hedley would not be drinking water on this earth anymore. Their faces were etched with sadness for the evil that had befallen this neighbor and previous boss.

"He looking so old, Meester Bannister," Diego said softly. "I never seen heem looking so old. He a good man and doan deserve to die like thees."

Matthew simply nodded as he watched Dan's shallow breathing.

Matthew headed for the kitchen, Diego following, and looked around at the mess.

Dirty dishes filled the sink, and the counter next to the sink bore the remains of several meals. The stove still had a little wood burning in it. A coffeepot sat on its top. Matthew picked it up to find it was still half full.

"May as well drink it up and not let it go to waste." Matthew turned to see Diego's head nod, but he also caught a slight movement out of the corner of his eye through the kitchen window. He set the pot down, and without a word, but putting his forefinger to his lips, he walked softly toward the back door as Diego watched.

Matthew wrenched open the door and ran around to the side of the house, where a little boy balanced himself on a ten-gallon milk can while trying to peer through the window.

He saw Matthew coming and jumped down, running as fast as his little legs could carry him.

Matthew yelled and sprinted after him.

"Stop!" Matthew yelled. "Stop, I said!"

But the little boy dashed toward the hill facing the front of the house.

Matthew tore after him on legs that stretched more than double the boy's stride. As the little guy reached the bottom of the hill, Matthew nabbed him. He yanked the boy around to face him, but the child kicked and screamed at the top of his lungs. Picking him up, Matthew threw him over his shoulder, holding his legs close to his chest so he couldn't kick. He headed back toward the house with the boy pummeling his back, screaming and crying.

"Let me down! You put me down right now, you murdering varmint! You killed my pa! I'm telling you—put me down right now!"

As Matthew entered the front door, the boy quieted, but his shoulders heaved with silent sobs.

Matthew put him down but held his arms so he couldn't run away again. He was filthy. A mop of greasy, curly red hair had been shorn with no thought for appearance. It framed a face full of anger and fear. His clothing was roughly patched, and he stunk. He glared up at Matthew.

"Who are you, and why are you here?"

The little boy, not more than six years old, stared at him, green eyes sparking, but he didn't answer him. He stood quiet under Matthew's hands, staring with eyes full of anger.

Diego came into the room and said, "Meester Bannister..."

Matthew turned suddenly at Diego's tone, but as the boy started to pull away, he held on to him with both hands.

"Meester Bannister, Dan...he ees dead."

Matthew's eyes filled with tears. "Why," he whispered as he turned back to face the boy, "why did your pa do this?"

Tears streamed down his face, and the boy visibly wilted under his hands.

"Who are you?" Matthew asked again. "Where do you hail from?"

With a voice filled with loathing, the boy spoke, his body stiffening under Matthew's hands. "You murderer! You killed my pa! I saw you! You killed 'im."

He spat the words at Matthew and tried to pull away, but Matthew held him fast.

The boy's little shoulders heaved with sobs.

Matthew tried to draw the boy into his arms to comfort him, but the boy kicked him hard in the shinbone.

Matthew ignored the pain in his leg. It was nothing compared to the hammers going off in his head from the gun butt that had creased his skull or the pain in his heart for the needless loss of Dan Hedley. "That your horse in the barn, son?" he asked.

The boy's eyes widened at his question, and Matthew wondered at it.

"N-no. It was my pa's, and you killed him, mister!" He cried again, deep sobs of sorrow.

Ignoring the kicking legs, Matthew lifted the boy up and into his arms, holding him close to comfort but also to prevent any more of his kicking.

"I'm sorry, son, but he was going to kill our horses. And truth to tell, I didn't kill your pa. He bashed me over the head, and I was tied up in the kitchen when that happened."

Diego stood, shoulders bowed in sorrow facing the broken window, and saw riders. He recognized them immediately.

"Here comed the sheriff an' Dr. John," he said. He went out onto the porch to meet them.

Matthew wiped his eyes on his sleeve, but the boy tried to squirm out of his arms.

"You're not going anywhere, young man," Matthew said, his voice stern. "So you may as well stop trying. I'm going to tie you up if I have any more of this behavior. You understand?" He shifted the boy's weight and continued. "Your pa started this whole mess. Now, again, where are you from?"

"I don't know. We lived in some town, an' after my ma died, Uncle Buddy and pa came west. We rode on the train for days. We don't have no house or nothin' anymore. My pa and Uncle Buddy robbed a bank to get some money, and we rode for two days on horseback and ended up here a few days ago. My pa didn't think anyone lived here, but the man who did went crazy when Uncle Buddy walked into the house. He'll come after you. He'll kill you if he gets a chance." The boy closed his lips firmly, as if he'd said enough and wasn't going to divulge any more information.

Matthew strode out onto the porch, carrying the boy, as Dr. John Meeks and Sheriff Buck Rawlins were tying up their rides.

"Who's that?" Sheriff Rawlins asked.

The boy, seeing the sheriff's shiny badge on his chest, squirmed uncomfortably and held on to Matthew's neck in a death hold.

"I don't know who he is," Matthew said. "You want to tell the sheriff who you are?"

"No," the boy said, his voice muffled by Matthew's neckerchief.

"Not another runaway!" Dr. John said with a smile creasing his face.

"This isn't like Cadence Cassidy," Matthew said and grinned at the memory of the girl who had helped to save Liberty after being thrown by her horse. "No, this boy belongs to the robber who was shot."

"Well," Dr. John said, "I need to take a look at Dan." He began to unbuckle his medical kit that was strapped behind his saddle.

"No need, John," Matthew said in a choked voice. "He's gone. Passed just a few minutes ago. I...I can't believe it. I just spoke to him last week. He was looking forward to moving to San Francisco to be near his daughter."

Dr. John turned to gape at Matthew. "He's dead? Dan Hedley's dead?"

Matthew took a deep sorrowing breath. "Yes, and this little guy's pa and uncle are responsible. His pa is dead, and his uncle is out there somewhere."

Sheriff Rawlins walked up to Matthew, and the boy shuddered, turning his head into Matthew's neck to hide his face from the law.

Anne stood waiting as James Mobrey and Elijah Humphries worked out a few details. When there was a lull in the conversation, she spoke up.

"I need to go to Mrs. Baxter's house and talk to her before word reaches her that I am terminating my contract. I feel as if I am leaving her in a lurch." Anne held her head high and shoulders straight as she spoke, hoping she was doing the right thing. Her cheeks reddened as James looked at her. He nodded his head. "I can come with you, if you could wait just a few minutes."

She nodded, feeling completely out of her element. She was going to marry this man and wondered if she were insane. She looked at the children still standing beside Mr. Bates and knew she couldn't part with them.

Elijah Humphries felt as if he'd witnessed an emotional stage play. He drew a deep breath and spoke to Anne.

"Miss Tarkington, Mrs. Baxter is at the mission, spending the day there with my Abigail. I can go down there with you two."

James spoke. "Mr. Humphries, can we impose upon you to introduce us to your minister? I'd prefer a man of the cloth to perform the nuptials."

Elijah, his eyes twinkling, said, "That can be arranged. When are you wanting the ceremony?"

"I think tomorrow morning would suffice. Is that amenable to you, Miss Tarkington?"

"Y-yes, I suppose so. And if we're to be married, sir, I only think it right that you should call me Anne."

"And please call me James," he replied. "I know many couples who continue to call their spouses by their surnames, but I have never been comfortable with that idea."

Ginger and Thaddeus looked at Anne and James and were awestruck by their change in circumstance.

"Where do you live, Mr. Mobrey?" Thad asked.

"I live north of here, in Napa. Perhaps we can borrow or rent a wagon to haul your things up there."

Elijah, ever helpful and generous, offered his prized wagon.

"I have a large wagon, and you are welcome to use it," Elijah offered. "Now, let's all head down to the mission. My cook, Bessie, has surely made something good we can eat."

CHAPTER IX

A good name is better than precious ointment;
and the day of death than the day of one's birth.

ECCLESIASTES 7:1

THADDEUS HAD A SUDDEN THOUGHT and asked worriedly, "Shouldn't we go back to our class? We're missing a lot of school today."

Ginger tugged at his shirt, shaking her head no.

"I agree with Ginger." Anne laughed. "There's no reason to go back to class. You will not be attending our school anymore. We will most likely be traveling north right after the wedding tomorrow morning, and we have a busy day ahead of us." She looked over at James to confirm her statement. "We'll need to get our things packed and ready to go today. I will send a telegram to Grandma Jenny."

She spoke to the children as if they were adults. It was one of the things Thaddeus loved about her.

"Grandma Jenny raised me and will come out to visit, if not to live. I'm hoping she will make the move to come live with us. You'll adore her."

"We don't have that much stuff," Thaddeus said. "After our ma died, people on the wagon train started helping themselves to our belongings when we weren't looking. It wasn't long before there was nothing much left." Thaddeus missed the quilt his mama had made for him.

Ginger's eyes had welled with tears as Thaddeus spoke, and she wiped them away with the back of her hand.

Elijah looked on sympathetically. "I'm sorry those people acted like that. Sometimes it's the unexpected lack of compassion that surprises us the most. We're to help people in their times of need, not make things worse." He opened the door as he spoke, and the entire retinue trooped out.

Lucas asked to be excused, saying he needed to do a few things before the morrow. He tipped his hat to Anne and walked in the opposite direction of the group. He whistled jauntily as he anticipated going back to talk to a certain Josephine Hensley.

The rest made their way toward the mission. There was talk and laughter among the three men. Anne listened with half an ear. She mentally ticked off the many things she would need to accomplish this day.

Ginger gave a little skip every so often, and Thaddeus knew she was happier than she'd been in a long while. So was he.

Elijah walked into the mission with Anne Tarkington on his arm, gestured to the two children to follow him in, and James and Bates brought up the rear.

Anne looked around with pleasure as a warm ambiance enveloped her. The mission exuded peace and modern comfort blended with agelessness and culture. An oaken pew was flanked on one end by a huge plant and on the other by a large round end table. A picture book and a vase of freshly cut flowers lay on it. The effect was one of tasteful charm and old-fashioned cordiality.

Elijah led his party into the kitchen.

Abigail was cutting fresh flowers and arranging them in a beautiful vase. She turned in surprise at the amount of people who gathered into the spacious kitchen, and it pleased her that Elijah had no qualms about bringing in such a large group.

She smiled and welcomed everyone and, to their surprise, stepped over to Elijah and kissed him on the mouth.

Elijah, instead of being embarrassed, beamed with pleasure.

Abigail laughed and said, "I haven't seen my man since breakfast." She turned to look at the Parker children, guessing who they were by the discussion of them the other evening at dinner. Her blue eyes gleamed with delight at the boy and girl.

"How do you do?" she asked. "I'm Mrs. Humphries, Mr. Humphries' wife. And who might you be?"

Thaddeus spoke up right away.

"This is my sister, Ginger, an' I'm Thaddeus Parker. She's eight an' a half, an' I'm seven. It is nice to meet you, Mrs. Humphries. You have a really big house!"

Abigail laughed, delighted by his mistake.

"Oh, this isn't our house, child. This is where I work. This is a mission. It's a place to help women who have run away from home because they have been mistreated. And this is my friend, Mrs. Baxter. She owns the school where you live."

Susannah, who had been sitting at the table conversing with Abigail, stood up at the introduction, but before she could speak, Thaddeus said, "How do you do, ma'am, but we're not living at the school anymore. Ginger and I are moving to Napa tomorrow morning. It's just north of here." Thaddeus was proud of his new circumstance. He gave a little bow to acknowledge the owner of the school.

Susannah was surprised by the boy's statement. She'd thought, after the dinner the other night, Anne would try to adopt the children. She looked inquiringly at Elijah and then at Anne, who flushed mightily under her scrutiny.

"It's nice to see you again, Miss Tarkington," she said, "but I…I don't understand. I was under the impression you were going to adopt these two children yourself."

"Oh, Mrs. Baxter! So many things have changed—suddenly changed this very morning," Anne replied. "I have loved working for you at the school, as you well know, but I am handing in my resignation." She nodded toward James, and her words rushed together. "I'm getting married to Mr. Mobrey. He's been directed by the Almighty to our school with the express purpose of adopting a boy and girl…brother-sister combination. The Parker children are the only brother and sister we have at the school. Oh, Mrs. Baxter, I am mortified that I'm leaving you in a lurch, but it seemingly can't be helped. He—Mr. Mobrey—wants the wedding tomorrow, and Mr. Humphries is amenable to drawing up the adoption papers, and… and…" She beseeched Mrs. Baxter to understand.

"It's all right, Anne. Please don't fash yourself. I must say I am disappointed. You have done a wonderful job in a very short time. The staff was not a cohesive unit before your coming. You've been a healing balm and a voice of encouragement to them after our last director. You can leave knowing you are one of the best. Now, I have to ask, are you telling me that the good Lord dropped that man right into your lap, so to speak? You did say that the other day, did you not?"

She laughed, and Anne joined in, but she felt an incredible burden lift from her shoulders at Mrs. Baxter's kind words. She hadn't expected her to take her resignation so sweetly. Too, the reminder of her earlier conversation made her realize this was the doing of the Almighty. She was going to be able to adopt these children, and the thought thrilled her.

"I did say that, and yes, I suppose you could say it's true. Mr. Mobrey wants to adopt the children and feels led to do so—as do I. This seems to be the best way to satisfy both our wants." She lowered her voice. "I have no idea what Grandma Jenny is going to think about this arrangement. That is my next stop—to get a telegram off to her."

Bessie, the Humphries' cook, was preparing a tasty lunch for the group, sitting at different tables in the mission's huge kitchen. Bessie was in her element and quickly whipped up a pudding for dessert. Anne didn't feel hungry. Since lunch wasn't yet ready, she excused herself, walking to the train station to get a telegram off to her grandmother. Anne had no doubt that she would come.

She walked quickly, her mind fixed on things she needed to accomplish. She would have to have a quick meeting with the staff right after classes and hoped Mrs. Baxter would join her for it. It would make the break a bit easier with the backing of the owner. She didn't have all that much to pack. She'd not bothered unpacking all her things yet, as she'd been too busy making repairs, cleaning, and painting to have much time to herself.

As she walked, she wondered what kind of man would adopt two unknown children but seemingly have direction from the Almighty.

Mr. Mobrey made no bones about wanting a brother-sister combination and seemed to know there'd be one, she thought. *I wonder what kind of house he has. He really didn't elaborate about what kind of work he does. What was it he said? Oh yes, he keeps account of expenditures for several organizations and makes sure they run smoothly. Doesn't sound like a high-paying job to me. He seems to think he has enough to provide for a wife and children. I hope I'm not going to be a drudge. I don't mind hard work. I'd do anything for those two children. I was surprised Mr. Humphries thought this an excellent solution. I trust him though. Wonder what Mr. Mobrey expects of me. He said no intimacy until I'm ready and willing. I don't see that happening, but I suppose we'll see. I've always wanted children of my own.*

She arrived at the station, and Moses Slocum sent her telegram off to Grandma Jenny in short order. She'd talked to the telegraph operator before. He smiled now but didn't mention the circumstances of her message. Anne was grateful for that consideration. She waved a goodbye and headed back to the mission for lunch.

What shall I wear for the wedding? she wondered as she walked. *Well, it certainly won't be a wedding dress, but at least we'll be married by a minister. I've never wanted a huge wedding anyway.*

Anne looked up to see George Baxter coming out of a building just ahead of her.

He heard her step and turned to see her approaching. "Good morning, Miss Tarkington," he said. "Looks like you're heading in the same direction as me. I was invited last evening to have lunch at the mission."

"Well, sir, so am I." Anne smiled up at the chief detective of the San Francisco Police Department.

George crooked his elbow, and Anne slipped her hand into it. She felt safe for some reason, almost as if this man could protect her.

"I have had a complete change in circumstance this morning and am feeling discomposed."

"How so?" he asked.

"Remember I said I wanted to adopt the Parker children?"

"Yes, of course."

Anne went on to tell George Baxter everything that had transpired that morning. When she finished, George had one question.

"What does Elijah think?"

Anne looked at him, a bit startled by the question.

"He seems perfectly fine with it," she replied. "As a matter of fact, it was his opinion that decided me. He is drawing up the adoption papers and will introduce us to his minister today."

George's eyes looked into hers with keen insight. "I can tell you this, young lady. No one and nobody will hoodwink Elijah Humphries. He has the gift of discernment, and the good Lord speaks to his heart and imparts a wisdom that is not of this world. Please believe me—I know. If he seems favorable toward your Mr. Mobrey, then you can rest assured it will be all right. In my line of business, I've met and dealt with all kinds of people. Elijah Humphries is by far the most astute, intelligent man I have ever known, and all of it is attributable to his close personal relationship to the Almighty God."

Anne looked up at George with violet eyes shining. "Thank you for that. It's a comfort to me, and no mistake. I've felt off kilter and wondered if I'm making the biggest mistake or the best decision of my life. If Mr. Humphries is as you say, I suppose I have nothing to worry about."

The two of them entered the mission without knocking. Hearing much laughter and talk, they made their way to the kitchen, where George's eyes went straight to his wife. They were deeply, romantically in love.

Susannah had married her first husband in an arranged marriage. She grew to love him but never thought to be romantically in love. George was everything she could ask for in a husband. They'd been married a little over two months and were still on their honeymoon, so to speak.

George had loved his first wife with a passion, but it had been years since she had passed away. He never thought to love again, but one glance at Susannah had deepened into a gaze, and he was a goner.

Her eyes held his as he made his way to her. She had saved a place for him, and he went straight to her side.

Anne had that initial feeling of intrusion, that uncomfortable feeling of entering a room full of people and not knowing where to sit. She wanted to be anywhere except standing where she was. James Mobrey immediately stood and pulled out a chair for her at his table. Both children sat with him, as well as Jacob Bates and Lucas Falter, who must have returned from his errand. She sat down gratefully and thanked James for his thoughtfulness.

"Did you get your message sent off all right?" he asked.

"Yes, thank you. Grandma Jenny and I made tentative plans before I moved out here. She planned to follow me once I was truly settled. She said she always had a hankering to come west, but the real reason is because she doesn't like to be so far away that the two of us can't visit regularly. She most likely has been giving things away for the past couple months. I'm sure that once she gets my telegram, it will be no time at all before she is here. I'm excited to see her. I do hope you were serious when you said you had room for her." Anne, nervous, continued to talk.

"I met Mr. Baxter on my way back from the station, and we had a good chat. Mrs. Baxter, as you know, owns the school where I've been director, but they don't live here. Mr. Baxter is San Francisco's chief of detectives and has recently married Mrs. Baxter. Her former husband founded the San Rafael School of Primary Learning. Mrs. Baxter still owns a house here and comes up from the city to check on things periodically. I had my first inspection as director the day before yesterday."

James nodded, his eyes fixed on Anne's face, listening to every word.

"I do have room for your grandmother to live in our home. I hope you're not afraid to marry me, Anne," he said. "None of what I've done today is any indication of the type of person I normally am. I have felt compelled to adopt these children." He looked at Ginger and Thaddeus and smiled. "Asking you to marry me is…well, it's one of those things I felt impressed to do. I usually study a situation before I make a move. It took me months to finally obey what I know the Lord was telling me to do about adopting children, but that too was part of His timing, wasn't it?" James smiled at Anne, his eyes warm as he looked at her face. "I know without a shadow of doubt I am doing the right thing. I pray you find this is right for you too."

Anne's face colored a bit at his perusal. "I'll pray thus too. I feel a bit better after talking with Inspector Baxter, but everything has happened so quickly I feel numb. I do hope you know what you're getting yourself into. I am not your insipid, stand-back-and-let-it-all-happen woman. I have a mind of my own and just hope I can fulfill the biblical part about respecting you and being submissive." She smiled at Thaddeus and Ginger. "I really don't know you that well, but I can say that I've fallen in love with the pair of you. I would never try to replace the wonderful mother you must have had, but I can love you as if I were your real mother, and I will care for you the best I know how. Frankly, I don't fully comprehend what I'm getting myself into, and all for the sake of two children I barely know." She smiled at them again.

Thaddeus and Ginger both nodded but didn't know how to respond to what she said, but James did.

"I can identify with you there, one hundred percent. All for the sake of the children."

CHAPTER X

Ah Lord God! behold, thou hast made the heaven
and the earth by thy great power and stretched out arm,
and there is nothing too hard for thee.

JEREMIAH 32:17

JENNY TARKINGTON RECEIVED A CRYPTIC telegram from
her granddaughter. She'd lost count how many times she'd read it. She
perched her glasses on the end of her nose and read it again, even
though by now she knew it by heart.

     DEAR GRANDMA JENNY STOP I AM QUITTING MY JOB
STOP GETTING MARRIED STOP I WANT YOU TO COME
LIVE WITH US STOP MAIL REPLY IN CARE OF SCHOOL STOP
IF REPLYING AFTER TOMORROW SEND TO NAPA
CALIFORNIA IN CARE OF JAMES MOBREY STOP PLEASE
COME! I MISS YOU STOP

"What's a body to think?" she asked herself. "My Anne getting
married. Why, she's only been out west for three months. It's no time at
all to make the decision to marry a man. Land sakes alive, I can scarcely
credit this. My sensible Anne." She muttered to herself a bit more as she
tied her bonnet sashes under her chin, got her reticule off the coatrack,
and checked to see if she had some coins in it. She folded up the message
she'd written in reply and stuffed it into her reticule. Throwing a shawl

around her shoulders, she let herself out the front door, heading for the train station, still talking to herself.

"My Anne, getting herself married. Why, she can't really know a man in such a short few months. Oh my! I so wanted her to marry that Billy Hargreaves. What a disappointment he turned out to be. Broke my Anne's heart, he did. Broke mine too. I had such high hopes. Well, that was six years ago, and here's now. She's gone and done it, hasn't she. Getting married! Land sakes alive, that is a real shock, that! Uhmm-uhmm, married, my Anne! Wonder what kind of man she's decided upon. How can she think she knows a man when she hasn't known him three months? Uhmm-uhmm. That's sure a shock."

She strode down the boarded walk and reached the station without running into anyone she knew. She didn't know if that was disappointing or a good thing. She was in the mood to talk, that was certain.

"Hello there, Sunny Bee. How are you this very fine day?"

"Fit as a fiddle, Missus Tarkington. Yes siree, I'm in the pink, I am!"

Sunny Bee was the telegraph operator and was silent about any work he did—never told a soul about any bit of communication he received or sent. Jenny pumped him once for information, flattering him and giving him cookies and tasty cakes, but he'd never divulged a thing, to her vast disappointment. He was as trustworthy as the day was long.

"I'm needing to send a wire back to my Anne," she said. "Reckon you know she's getting married. Can you fathom that? My Anne getting married."

He made no comment about the wire she'd received. "Do you have the message written down?

"Yes, sir, I do. Wrote everything down I want sent back to her. I'll be moving out there soon's I can get my things together. I'll let Herbert sell the house." She dug into her reticule and handed Sunny Bee the reply message to be sent to Anne.

Sunny Bee knew Herbert was Herbert B. Herbert, her lawyer. He'd always thought it strange the lawyer's parents would give him the name Herbert when his surname was Herbert. He'd secretly thought they should have given him a middle name beginning with an H, Herbert H. Herbert. He chuckled inwardly, but he never said a word about it.

"That'll be thirty cents, Missus Tarkington."

She dug into her reticule again and produced the right coins, muttering to herself over the price.

"You've lived in that house ever since marrying Mr. Tarkington, haven't you?" Sunny Bee asked, to take her mind off the expense of the telegram.

"Yes, yes, I have. Raised Anne up in that old house since she was a toddler. Yes, I have many memories attached to that place, but not every one of them good."

"Are you expecting a reply to this?" Sunny Bee asked as he clicked out the message in Morse code.

"No, I reckon she'll not be replying. She'll just be waiting for me to come, is all. Thanks, Sunny Bee. I need to get myself off to see Herbert. He's always hankered to buy my place. Reckon now he can. Mayhap I'll have it sold afore I get packed!" Laughing, she waved a goodbye.

She pulled her shawl a little closer around her neck. The day was fast fading—the sun disappearing behind a bank of clouds. She headed for Herbert's law office. The sign over his door read *Law Office of H. B. Herbert.*

He worked alone as a lawyer, having only one male clerk, who doubled as his secretary. His office, also his home, was situated a few blocks inland from Jenny's, which sat right on the James River.

She let herself in the front door. A bell tinkled pleasantly when the door opened or closed.

Herbert had bought the bell after a holiday in England, where many of the shops had the little tinkling bell to announce customers.

Jenny breathed in the smell redolent of books, leather, and pipe tobacco. It never ceased to remind her of her father, who'd had an upstairs bedchamber converted into a study. It had the same air of contentment and tranquility. Her mind tripped back to her teen years.

Herbert had been her beau before she'd met and married Marcus Tarkington. She'd thought to marry Herbert, but Marcus had moved into town and had courted her the summer of her coming-out ball. Her parents thought he was the most promising young man. She hadn't married for love but to please her parents. Herbert had never had a chance after that. He'd never married, and she knew he still loved her. Hearing his footsteps in the hall jerked her back to the present. Jenny removed her shawl as he neared the front room.

This is going to be quite a blow to him, she thought. *He's been a faithful friend all these years.* She knew Herbert enjoyed dropping by for tea on an afternoon. Always sure of his welcome, he visited her at least once a week. Her heart beat faster, and she pasted a smile on her lips as he entered the room.

"Ah...Jenny," he said, "what a pleasant surprise!"

She proffered her hand, and he took it into both of his, giving it a gentle squeeze and a pat.

He indicated a chair. "Please, be seated. My clerk left for the day, and when I heard the bell, I came out to see who'd arrived at this late hour for business." He pulled up the legs on his pants a bit and sat opposite Jenny. "What brings you here? It's been ages since you set foot inside my door." He smiled benignly, and she knew no offense was intended.

"I came because I, ah...I came to tell you, Herbert, that I have decided to move." She spoke in a firm tone but looked apprehensively at her lifelong friend.

"Move!" Herbert half rose from his chair and then sat back down with a plop—as if the air had been knocked out of him. "Whyever would you want to move?"

"I've been thinking about this for months. It's not an impulsive decision. I know I've made enough of those in my past to last a lifetime, but my Anne sent me a telegram. She's asked me to move west. I've decided to sell up and move to a place called Napa, California. I know—"

"California! Jenny, that's like another world! That's clear across the United States! Are you sure you want to do this? You were born in this town. All your friends are here."

"I know. I know all that. I've thought about this long and hard, and I've come to know that home for me is wherever my Anne is. I know you've asked me several times if you could buy my house. Well, sir, it's now up for sale, and I'm giving you first opportunity to buy it. I've been asked to put it on the historical registry, but I've not done it yet. It would be something you could do. I want you to sell it if you don't want it."

"Don't you think you should wait? What if you decide you don't wish to live in the West? What if it never becomes home for you?"

"Herbert...for shame! You should know me better than that! Wherever Anne is living will be home to me. I miss her so much. It's like a bitter tonic constantly in my mouth not to have her near me. I could live in Timbuktu if she were there. I just received a telegram from her a few hours ago and have already replied. She wants me to come live with her, and I will do so, fast as I can get myself packed and on the train. I'll leave most of the furniture to go with the house. A few of my treasured pieces I'll take with me. I'm going, Herbert, and nothing and no one is going to stop me, 'ceptin' the good Lord, of course. My mind is made up."

"I know. I know when you make up your mind, Jenny. I've had to live with your decision to marry for the last thirty-five years." Herbert bowed his head in defeat. He looked up into the most beautiful pair of eyes he'd ever seen and said, "I'll buy your house, my dear. And with that statement, I'll wish you all the best."

Jenny Tarkington stood, her shoulders well back and her head held high. "Thank you, Herbert. I do thank you very much." She started to put her shawl around her shoulders, but Herbert took it from her hands and wrapped it around her shoulders, giving them a gentle squeeze.

"I'm going to miss you, Jenny. You have no idea how much."

Jenny Tarkington's cheeks pinked up, and she thanked him again as she started to leave. She turned back and said, "Herbert, you are the dearest friend I have. I thank you for standing by me all these years."

Her eyes looked steadily into his, and he nodded, too choked to say anything. She turned back to open the door, but somehow he was already there opening it for her.

"I'll see you again before you leave. You'll be needing to sign papers. I shall miss you, Jenny. I shall miss you deeply."

Heading back to her home, Jenny thought how she'd always taken Herbert for granted. In the back of her mind, he was always there if she should need anything. *It's easy to take people for granted and not appreciate what we have until we lose it,* she thought. *I shall miss that man more than he'll ever know.*

As she approached the front walk of her own home, Jenny looked up at the old house and spoke to it. "You've served me well all these years. I shall miss your nooks and crannies. I shall miss your creaking floorboards and doors. I shall miss welcoming my friends at your beautifully carved front door." Tears filled her eyes, and she entered with a handkerchief, wiping at them with an impatient hand. "Stuff and nonsense!" she said. "I have much to do." Sadness fled, and excitement bubbled up within her. She began to pack.

Buck Rawlins felt sorry for the little boy Matthew was holding. He'd not yet seen the display of temper Matthew had witnessed. The sheriff stepped up to Matthew, knowing the little boy was scared to death of him.

"Somebody put the fear of the law into you, son?"

The redhead turned and glared at Buck. "I ain't afraid of you! An' I ain't your son! I'm nobody's kid anymore." He put his knuckles to his eyes and cried. All four men felt sorry for him.

Dr. John went into the house, and the others followed him in. John went into Dan's bedchamber.

He stood staring down at Dan for a long minute. He picked up Dan's hand, holding it for a few moments. He was not yet cold, and John gently laid Dan's hand back on the bed. He reached toward the bottom of the bed, pulled a blanket up and over the dead man's face, and left the bedroom with bowed head.

"It's a sad day when a good man dies earlier than he should," he said. "Looks like he's been badly beaten, but looking at him, I wager he died of dehydration. I suppose his captors never thought about giving him anything to drink." As he turned, he noticed Matthew's head.

"Looks like you need some stitching up, Matthew Bannister. You took quite a blow to your head. What happened to your ear?"

"Liberty spoke to me, up on the hill, and if I hadn't turned my head, I'd not be here to tell you about it. The bullet was that close. You can stitch me up in a bit." He turned to the sheriff. "Buck, you need to come with me." Matthew handed the boy to Diego, who sat down and cuddled the little guy in his arms. The boy was nearly asleep from exhaustion.

Matthew took Buck out behind the barn and showed him the dead man. He squatted down as he spoke.

"This man's brother is out on the loose somewhere. I don't know if they split up or if he plans to come back. My guess is that he's out foraging for food and he'll be back. The boy said he'll come back and kill me." He pushed back the straw to show the sheriff. "I laid his belongings out there on his handkerchief." He pushed aside a bit more straw to show the items in the man's pockets. "Couldn't find anything to identify him. His boy said he and the uncle robbed a bank and then spent a couple days riding here. He said they thought the house was empty. Dan must have put up quite a fight."

"This is a tragedy, and no mistake," Buck gritted out. "It makes me so angry when something like this happens, and it's too late to help the victim."

"I know. When I had that amnesia in Sonoma, a good man was killed on McCaully property for no reason at all. The shooter was plain evil through and through." Matthew's eyes clouded with the memory. He nodded his head toward the house. "That little guy in there is a tough one. He won't tell me his name, and you could see he's scared to death of the law. What'll we do with him?"

"I don't know." Buck removed his hat and scratched his head as he thought. Settling his hat back on his head, he said, "I reckon I could take him home. I don't know what Hattie would say. Reckon she'd like the challenge though. Adam and Eden don't want us to move out, but we're almost finished building, and I personally think it's time. Hattie loves your place, and that's the floor design we've chosen to copy. Now, back to the business at hand. This little boy is going to need a place because even if the uncle comes back, he's most likely going to hang for murder."

"Yes, most likely he will. Someone's going to have to notify the daughter in Frisco about Dan. Reckon she's most likely wondering where her pa is. He was going down to stay with her for a while and find a place close to her to live. I was planning on buying this place from him. I don't know what'll happen now. It seemed to me Dan lost all will to farm once Betty died."

"I know. Spoke to him at church just the other day. He was still in good health and looking forward to living close to his daughter." Buck pulled a toothpick out of his breast pocket and stuck it into his mouth. He looked around, wondering where the uncle was holed up. "I'm thinking the uncle is going to come back here. The two men were brothers, after all. I'll get a couple men out here to carry this man back to town. We'll bury him and hope the boy knows his pa's name. I'll see if there's any new wanted posters out. If this man and his brother robbed a bank, someone's sure to be looking for them." He chewed a bit on the toothpick as Matthew stood. "You do need to get that stitched up… you're still oozing blood."

"I've got a wretched headache—that's certain." Matthew felt worn out by the morning's events. His stomach was rumbling with hunger. "If you think about it, pray for Liberty, won't you? She's going to be mightily upset about killing this man—"

"Liberty killed him?"

"Yes, didn't she tell you? If the man hadn't turned, he'd still be alive. When Liberty finds out the man she killed has a little boy…" His voice sounded sorrowful about the situation. "I sure feel sorry for that little tyke. He's going to be a real handful, Buck. He can kick and scream like a girl." Matthew smiled tiredly at the sheriff, and the two made their way back into the house.

Chapter XI

But Jesus said, Suffer little children, and forbid them not,
to come unto me: for of such is the kingdom of heaven.

MATTHEW 19:14

DR. JOHN STOKED THE STOVE, HEATED some water, and was ready to clean Matthew's wound.

"Just you sit yourself down right here, Matthew Bannister. You need a little doctoring, to my way of thinking. I've been told I'm good at stitches. Reckon then we can just hitch a wagon up and take Dan and the other dead man back to town. I can drive, and, Buck, you can take care of things once we get there."

He wetted a clean cloth with carbolic and scrubbed the wound a little too hard. Matthew glared at his friend.

"Take it easy, John! I thought you just said you're good at this—you're not stitching up a horse, you know. You need a gentler hand. My head hurts like the dickens."

"Thought you were tough, Matthew. Here you are whining like a baby." He abruptly changed the subject. "What are you planning to do with the boy?" He jerked his head at Diego, who was still holding the child in his arms. The little guy was fast asleep.

"I am going to take him. Don't reckon Hattie and I will ever have children," Buck said. "We could take him. Hattie has a way with anyone she meets. She sure knocked me off my feet." He grinned. "I know that little boy is afraid of the law. I suppose he's only heard about how bad we are. Living with outlaws, it'd only be natural for him to be scared. At any rate, I'm going to take him home with me, and we'll see what happens."

John, trying to take Matthew's mind off stitching, soaked his catgut in carbolic and began a discourse on the source of catgut.

"Strange they call this stuff catgut when it's made from almost every animal except cats. I read that mostly catgut is made from cows and sheep intestines. My, this cut is pretty deep, but I made sure it was all cleaned out. I'll take these out in about six days, Matthew, and you'll be good as new." He finished stitching and packed up the tools of his trade while he talked. "Diego, you just sit and let that poor boy sleep. We'll load up the robber and then Dan onto the wagon. Matthew, soon as we're loaded, you head for home with Diego. I'd tell you to take it easy, but you know how you're feeling better than me. If your head aches, listen to it and relax. Work will wait till you feel better."

Matthew asked Buck, "Are you going to have some men keep watch on the house? I know the cow needs milking and the chickens are going to need feeding."

"Don't fash yourself, Matthew Bannister! I'll have a couple deputies take care of things. You need to get yourself home and do what John said...at least for the rest of today."

Sheriff Buck Rawlins and Dr. John hitched up Dan's wagon to his horse and loaded the robber onto it. They tied the robber's horse and the doctor's horse to the rear of the wagon.

Buck picked up the contents of the man's pockets and placed them in the hat he'd picked up off the coatrack by the door. He thought the boy might like to have those things when he got a bit older.

Buck mounted his horse, and Diego handed the boy up to him. He stirred some but was still sound asleep.

Matthew looked around the house but couldn't see anything else that needed doing right away. Dirty dishes could wait. He shut the dampers on the stove and departed.

He started for the barn to get Piggypie, but Diego was already leading her out. The two men headed back to Rancho Bonito.

Liberty had waited lunch for Matthew. Conchita wanted her to eat, but her stomach rebelled at the thought of food. She was trying her best not to be upset, but all she could think about was the way the man clutched his chest and went down. She had taken a life. It was frightening to think how quickly he was snuffed out. She paced around the great room, praying for peace, but her mind kept jumping back to the man who had kept trying to shoot their horses.

Finally she heard Matthew and Diego ride in. She went to the barn to find out what happened. Donny came out to take the horses.

"I'll groom them for you," he said. "You look pretty tired, Boss. Is everything all right?"

Matthew, one arm slipping around Liberty's small waist, replied. "No, not really, Donny. Dan Hedley's dead."

Liberty gasped at the news, sorry for a needless death. She hoped the man still on the loose, the one Matthew thought was an accomplice, would soon be caught.

"Poor Dan," she said. "He was such a gentle man. I'm sorry, Matthew, Diego. I know how much you both cared for him. Come on. Lunch is ready, and Conchita made some burritos. Come, Diego. We can dispense with worker-boss relationship for now. I want you to eat with us, please."

"I weel do eet eef my Conchita weel let me." He smiled, his teeth white in his swarthy face. He turned to Donny. "Thank you for taking care of the horses."

Matthew nodded his thanks without voicing it, and the three walked to the house as Donny led their rides into the stable.

Buck and Dr. Meeks rode into town and pulled up in front of the doctor's house. When Buck pulled up his horse, the boy woke up. He reeked, and it almost made Buck, who normally had a cast-iron stomach, gag. It was lunchtime, and the boy had not had breakfast. He was hungry.

"Where're you taking me, mister?" He didn't whine or sound as if he were scared. He sounded belligerent.

"I'm taking you to my home, son." He nodded to John Meeks and said, "See you later, Doc."

The doctor nodded, got down, and said, "Let me know if you need anything."

"Thanks. I will." Buck turned to the boy and said, "We're going to ride out to Sunrise Ranch, located in Sunrise Canyon. It's where I live right now, and I want you to behave, son."

"I'm not a son. I'll never ever be a son!" His voice had risen a pitch higher.

"We'll see about that," Buck said. "My wife and I have no children. We've only been married 'bout half a year, but if I know my wife, she'll take a shine to you. Most everyone I know who knows her loves to be around her."

"I ain't plannin' ta be some sheriff's brat. I'm telling you straight up —I won't be livin' with you, nor any of your friends neither. My uncle'll come gunning for you. He'll not rest once he finds out someone kilt my pa. My pa an' my uncle have always been bestest friends. My uncle's gonna shoot whoever shot my pa. He and Pa were always together."

"How come your uncle wasn't with you and your pa this morning?"

The boy shut his lips and didn't say another word.

Buck rode at a sedate pace but could feel the stiff, rigid line of the boy's body sitting in front of him. He prayed silently as they rode toward Sunrise Canyon.

Lord, I don't know exactly what Your plans are for this little fellow. I do pray we can be of help to him. He's been raised to hate the law and seems to have no thought for what is right and good. I pray Hattie takes to him—that we can help him know Your ways, which are perfect. May we grow to love him and protect him and care for him. I pray this in Your holy name. Amen.

They turned off the main road and into the long lane leading to Chandler House.

Adam Brown had been deeded half of the Chandler Olives estate when Eldon Chandler was murdered. He and Eldon's daughter, Eden, had fallen in love and married within the space of a few weeks. Buck's wife, Hattie, was Adam's aunt and had come west to be close to Adam. She and Buck had met, and it had been one of those immediate, sizzling relationships ending in a swift courtship and marriage. The couple made their home with Adam and Eden but were building a house on a nice property on the outskirts of Napa. For now, Sunrise Ranch was Buck and Hattie's home.

Buck slid the boy down his left side and as he dismounted. Pepe, the Browns' stableboy, came out of the stable to take Buck's horse.

"Thanks, Pepe. This is…ah…what is your name, son?"

"I told you before—I ain't your son!" The boy took a defiant stance and crossed his arms in front of himself, glaring at Buck, not acknowledging Pepe at all.

"Someone sure missed out teaching you some manners, son. And I'm going to keep calling you son until you tell me your name."

Hattie came out onto the porch and looked in surprise at Buck, who was holding a filthy boy by the arm.

"See you have a new friend, Buck," she said.

The boy glared at her and said, "He ain't my friend, missus, an' I ain't his."

Hattie didn't look shocked or disgusted. She merely looked curious and said, "Well, whoever you are, the first thing on your agenda is a bath." She turned to Pepe and asked, "Do you have any clothes that are too small for you?"

"*Sí*, ma'am, I do. They ees clean too. I geet them for you."

"I'm sure they'll be too big, but I can cut the legs off on the trousers. Thanks, Pepe."

Buck was glad he had a firm hold on the boy, because he started to squirm and scream.

"I ain't taking no bath. My pa said I'll catch my death if I get wet all over at the same time. No siree!"

"You'll not catch pneumonia by taking a bath, son. We all take baths around here regularly, and we're not dead yet, but we don't stink to high heaven the way you do."

The boy wriggled, trying to get out of Buck's grasp.

"Hattie, I think we might need to take that washtub out back and fill it. He'll make a mess in the house with his tantrums."

Hattie took another look at the boy and agreed.

"You are most likely right. I'll have Dolly fill it out on the veranda in back." She smiled widely at the boy and added, "You have no idea how nice a bath can feel. Have you ever been swimming?"

"Yes, I have," the boy replied.

"Well, didn't you get wet all over at the same time?"

The boy's eyes widened at this revelation. "Y-yes, I did, an' I didn't catch pomonia. Why did my pa tell me that?"

"It's pneumonia, and I don't know why your pa told you that, but you're going to like the feel of the water all over you." She smiled pleasantly and left to inform Dolly to fill the washtub for the lad.

"I think we'll just make our way around the house to the back." Buck felt in need of changing his own clothes, the boy was that dirty.

When the water was ready, Hattie rolled up her sleeves, donned a thick baize apron, and was ready to bathe the boy. She had several jugs of warm water to rinse his hair.

As she started to take off his clothes, he began to shriek and yell. "My clothes need washing too! I'll just leave 'em on." He kicked and squirmed, and it took Buck, Hattie, and Dolly to hold him down for disrobing.

Buck began to laugh as the boy scowled up at him, for he was no boy at all, but a little girl.

Buck asked her, "Why did you pretend to be a boy?"

"I wasn't pretending nothin'. My pa told me it's better to dress this way when we's traveling. Then, when that other man caught me, he called me son, so I just didn't tell him he'd made a mistake."

"What's your name, child?" Hattie asked.

"It's Chloe. My pa wanted ta call me Sweet Pea, so that's what he called me most of the time, but my ma named me Chloe."

"Chloe is a pretty name. What's your last name?" Hattie asked softly

Chloe looked at Hattie as if she were asking a trick question. Seeing the older woman's face was simply curious, she answered her question.

"It's Chloe Blake—Chloe Ellen Blake, and I'm five years old."

"Well, that's a lovely, name," Hattie said and grinned as she picked up the little girl. "Let's get you into the tub."

Chloe started screaming and kicking, and it so startled Hattie that she almost dropped her.

"I can't take a bath like that! My pa said it'd be the death of me. No! Stop!"

"No, it won't be the death of you. Maybe he said you'll catch a death of cold or something like that, but I take one of these at least three times a week, if not every day, and I'm still alive and kicking, like you. Now let's get you into the water, sweetie."

Chloe stopped kicking at her words, but she shivered, thinking she was going to catch her death of cold. Total wonder filled her face as the warm water enveloped her. It felt like nothing she'd ever experienced.

Their family, none of them, had ever bathed in the altogether that she knew of. She leaned back against the side of the tub, scooting down until she was in up to her neck in warm water.

"This is…ah…I don't know how ta explain it. It feels wonderful." Her rounded greenish eyes closed in ecstasy.

"Do you think you could plug your nose like this?" Hattie held her nostrils closed to demonstrate. "And slide your head under water so your hair gets wet too?"

Chloe eyed the woman, suspicion filling her eyes. "You want me ta drown or something?"

"No, sweetheart, but I can't wait to wash your hair and have you looking spic and spanky clean! Here, first let me check your hair." Hattie parted the girl's hair in several places. She almost gagged from the smell, but gave a sigh of relief, along with a look of surprise, at not finding any lice.

"It's not time ta wash my hair. That only happens in summertime."

"Well, someone has their dates mixed up, because that's supposed to happen every Saturday and sometime during the week if you sweat much. Come on there, little one. Plug your nose now and down you go!"

Chloe came up spluttering but decided she wasn't drowned or dead yet. This was all a novelty, and to her surprise she was enjoying it.

"All right," Hattie said, "what a good girl you are. I'm going to scrub your hair now with shampoo. It's going to take more than one washing to get it clean."

"Wait!" Chloe yelled. "What's shampoo?" She splashed water as she sat up.

Hattie looked startled. "Well, our cook, Berry, shaves bar soap, which is made right here on this ranch, into water and boils it. Then she adds some other stuff to it to make it smell good and vows that it's good for your hair. I use it, and it makes my hair shine and my scalp feel nice."

"All right, you can use it on me." Chloe sank down again into the dirty water.

Hattie washed the little girl's hair and said, "I want you to close your eyes so you don't get shampoo in them when I pour water over your head." She used the jugs sitting beside the tub. "Now we're going to step out of the tub and dump it, and start all over again." Hattie's deep-blue eyes smiled into the greenish ones of this little girl, and with an insight that almost made her gasp, she lost her heart completely to this impish vagabond.

Hattie repeated the entire process, and once Chloe was clean, she wrapped her into a huge towel and took her into the house. She sat down next to the fire in Eden's sitting room and towel dried the little girl's red hair, talking to her the entire time.

Chloe's eyes had widened, seeing the interior of the house for the first time. She had never, in her entire life, seen such a room. Her eyes kept moving from one object to the next in wonder. She'd never been in a room where objects were other than practical. She looked at the pictures and sighed.

"Those are poppies. It's a pretty flower, ain't it?"

Hattie gave her some time to adjust before speaking softly to her.

"Yes, poppies are pretty. They grow wild all over the state of California. Oh, see what we have here? Looks like Pepe found some clothes for you. Let's roll up the legs on these for now, and I'll cut the shirt down to fit a bit better. Do you ever wear dresses?"

"Yes, when Mama was alive, I only wore dresses, but since she died, we've been on the move, and Pa said wearing boy's clothes would make everything easier."

"I can understand that," Hattie said as she helped Chloe to dress. "Are you hungry? Let's go get some lunch, shall we?"

She led the little girl out of the sitting room, across the hall, through the great room, and into the kitchen.

Chapter XII

Wherefore they are no more twain, but one flesh.
What therefore God hath joined together,
let not man put asunder.

MATTHEW 19:6

MATTHEW SAT UP AND LOOKED OVER at Liberty. The light from the moon shone across the bed, and he could see she was tangled in the bedclothes, breathing with a whimpering sound. Boston, their dog, slept in the corner and growled low in his throat at the unaccustomed sound. Liberty was a good sleeper and never had nightmares, but Matthew knew she was in the throes of one. He reached over and gently took her into his arms and rocked her.

"Shush, Libby girl. It's all right. Sh…sh, you're all right."

She awoke in his arms and began to cry.

"Oh, Matthew, I had the most horrible dream. It was awful, and I couldn't wake up. I killed that man all over again, but this time I was trying to." She took a shuddering breath. "He just kept firing back at me, and then his brother came, and he tried to shoot me too and told me I was going to die the way his brother did." Her words were rushed together, and tears seeped out of the corners of her eyes.

"Liberty, he was a bad man. He killed Dan. We don't know anything about him, but if you hadn't shot him, he would have hung. Better this way, honey. He was bad through and through. I didn't tell you earlier because I didn't want to upset you any more than you already are, but the robber had a little boy with him. Buck took him home and wants to raise him as his own. I don't know how all that's going to work out—he's a handful."

Liberty pulled away. She got up and lit a taper and put it to the lamp, turning up the wick. She turned to face her husband.

"I can't believe you didn't tell me that, Matthew Bannister. I've never been one to be molly-coddled, and I don't plan to start now. I know you love me and want to protect me, but please don't withhold information I should know. Yes, I feel horrible that I killed a man, but if I hadn't, our horses would be dead and maybe you and me. That I made a child an orphan is an awful thing, but it couldn't be helped, Matthew. I tried my best to get him to stop shooting, but he wouldn't, that's all. How old is the boy?"

"He's about six years old, I reckon. He wouldn't give us much information. He can kick and scream like a girl though." Matthew smiled at Liberty. "It'd be real entertainment to see Hattie tangle with that little guy."

Liberty smiled back at Matthew. "Sorry for waking you up." She looked at the ormolu clock and saw the time. Two thirty. "We have a few more hours of sleep before we need to get up." She blew out the lamp and crawled back into the bed, cuddling up next to Matthew, who kissed her soundly and spooned his body around hers. They talked softly for a few minutes and soon were sound asleep.

The marriage was a quiet one. Susannah Baxter had insisted on buying Anne a dress for it. It was lovely and white. It wasn't a real wedding dress but was made of a beautiful thin white lawn with lace eyelet threaded by satin ribbons set in the bodice and puffy sleeves. The skirting was gathered and sported matching eyelet and ribbons around the hem. The neckline was high, and tiny delicate rosettes dotted the bodice front. Anne looked lovely and fragile in it. She wore a wide-brimmed hat with ribbon streamers down the back. Her blonde hair was swept up in an intricate French knot, and a few curls escaped and framed her white face.

The wedding took place in the Baxters' mansion. There was a second story, and Anne dressed in one of the upstairs rooms, aided by Abigail and Mrs. Baxter.

Nearly six feet wide, the oak staircase was a grand affair. Halfway up the stairs was an enormous landing. The charming area with long windows across the back wall looked out to a professionally tended garden. In one corner of the landing stood the piano and two wingback chairs with a coffee table between them, faced so a body could view not only the gardens but the piano as well. Beautiful Ming vases, filled with plants whose foliage paid tribute to a talented gardener, spoke of refinement and good taste.

The stairs continued on the left, going opposite the way they'd come up to the landing. The impression was of beauty, elegance, and old-world charm.

When everything was in readiness, Mrs. Baxter sat at the piano and played a lovely prelude. The guests belowstairs quieted as the first strains of music wafted their way. She was an accomplished pianist and switched to Jeremiah Clarke's "The Prince of Denmark's March," a lovely piano piece she'd heard at several weddings recently.

Anne descended the stairs on George's arm. He winked at his wife as they approached the landing.

Anne was nervous and scared. Trying to settle her thoughts, she focused on the music. She'd played that very piece for a friend's wedding two weeks before coming west. As they made the turn to go down the last section of stairs, she glanced to James' face. Her thoughts raced as she stepped down each tread. *I reckon I never thought about it, but he's well-groomed, and his hands are clean and his nails manicured. He must not labor in the out-of-doors at all. Goodness, I didn't realize he was so handsome. Will he keep his part of the wedding bargain? Will he wait before he claims his marital rights? Will I have to share his bed? Wonder how big his house is? His hair looks like a halo with the sunlight through the window resting on it.* Her thoughts came to an abrupt halt as George Baxter handed her off to James.

He felt her quivering next to him and realized behind that composed white face was a woman scared out of her wits. He squeezed her hand next to his ribs and smiled at her reassuringly, hoping to infuse some courage as the minister began the ceremony.

"Dearly beloved, we are gathered here today in the sight of Almighty God to join this man and woman in holy matrimony…" The minister's voice was soothing, but Anne had trouble focusing on what he said. She repeated her vows mechanically in a soft voice.

Her thoughts jumped here and there but suddenly jerked back to the present when the minister said, "I now pronounce you man and wife. You may kiss the bride."

Anne, startled, turned to look into the warm, blue depths of eyes seemingly full of understanding, and yet there lurked a bit of humor. James leaned toward her, and she obediently turned up her face to be kissed. It was quick and sweet and over before she could blink.

James took Anne's hand, and the newlyweds turned around to face the group of witnesses. Anne's eyes widened in surprise—she'd not known there were so many guests. Most all the school staff and a few older students were there, as well as the Baxters, the Humphries, Jacob Bates, and Lucas Falter. Standing between Jacob and Lucas were the Parker children. On the other side of Lucas was Josephine, Anne's secretary. There were a couple girls from the mission, as well as Mrs. Baxter's household staff and Mrs. Humphries' staff. It made quite a showing of people.

Anne looked around in appreciation, trying to memorize the room so she could relate it later to Grandma Jenny. Mrs. Baxter's house was a mansion and a perfect place for a wedding. It was tastefully but elegantly done. The evening she'd come for dinner, she'd thought how lovely it was, and she was grateful for her boss's generosity in inviting her to have the wedding here.

The parlor doors were thrown wide open. Guests were encouraged to eat of the bountiful repast Mrs. Baxter's cook, Opal, and the Humphries' cook, Bessie, had put together on such short notice. It was a veritable feast. An air of laughter and celebration pervaded the room.

Jenny Tarkington sat alone in her Pullman car, gazing out the window at scenery she'd only imagined in her dreams. *In truth, this is beyond anything I've ever imagined.* Her eyes drank in the beauty of earth and sky.

She spoke a prayer of thanksgiving. "I thank Thee, Almighty God, for Thy creation. It is beyond the scope of my imagination that Thou hast created such beauty. These mountains are so beautiful it beggars belief. Snow so deep it looks like fluffy eiderdown. And the mountain streams and waterfalls, Lord, they are gorgeous. The lakes I've seen, looking serene and granting my heart peace, why, the beauty of it all almost makes me cry with joy. I know that Thou art the author of creativity, but the colors and beauty are beyond any experience I've ever known. I thank Thee for this opportunity to have a glimpse of Thy provision for us, for all humanity. Again, I thank Thee."

Her prayer finished, she sat for a while not thinking about anything. It wasn't long before her thoughts shifted to all that had taken place this past week. She was amazed how smoothly everything had come together. Her packing was easy, as she'd been preparing for this event for the past couple months. She'd hired a girl to come in and clean so the furniture would have a spanking-new coat of beeswax, and when she finally closed the door for the last time, she knew the house was in as good a shape as she could possibly make it. She had paid a final visit to Herbert, who had arranged for her many trunks to be transported to the train station. He had all the paperwork ready for her to sign over the sale of the house to him. She was quite sure he'd given her a generous amount, more than the true value, but that was his decision to make, not hers. She wouldn't quibble over money. She carried the entire amount with her, but felt no nervousness about it. She was a self-sufficient woman and enjoyed being on her own. She didn't plan to live in the same house with Anne. They'd need their privacy, and she didn't think the house would be all that big. She'd seen pictures of some of the shacks people lived in out west. She wondered mightily about the man Anne was marrying.

"He'll have to be someone special for Anne to succumb to his wooing in such a short time. Land sakes, I simply can scarcely credit it. My Anne…married."

She watched as the scenery sped by. She was in no hurry.

Jenny had never traveled far from Jamestown. She had numerous friends but only two with whom she felt a special fondness. They'd had a quick tea party for her, inviting only those ladies with whom she had close dealings.

Now here she sat, contemplating God's creation and enjoying a sense of freedom she'd never before experienced. Amazed at the comfortable accommodations, she ate in the dining car with enjoyment. She'd not eaten out many times in her life and reveled in having someone else cook her food. She felt she'd never grow weary of it. "I'm having a delightful time," she said to herself. She picked up her knitting, her needles clicking in rhythm with the train's wheels as she continued to enjoy the scenery. A small town and train station slid from sight. She drew a deep breath of contentment at the tranquil vista coming into view.

"How can I ever thank you, Mrs. Baxter? You have made this day special. I have no idea what the future holds for me, but I will always remember your kindness." Anne stood in only her lace camisole and petticoat, carefully folding her white lawn dress. "This dress is beautiful. Is it linen or cotton?"

Mrs. Baxter took it from her and said, "Linen, and you are welcome, my dear. I wanted you to start out with a day you can look back on with pleasure. I will be praying for you on this venture. Mr. Mobrey seems to be quite a gentleman. I don't know if you've noticed, but I believe him to be quite wealthy."

Anne's face was a study of surprise turning to doubt.

"Why do you say that? I mean, he seems well-groomed, and his nails are clean, but wealthy? Has he said anything?"

"He doesn't *have* to say anything," Susannah Baxter replied. "His jacket is Savile Row and bespoke tailoring, or I'm losing touch with reality."

"What's Savile Row?" Anne asked curiously.

"It's an area in London known specifically for tailoring men's clothing. Bespoke tailoring means that most likely, Mr. Mobrey picked out the fabric himself and it was made specifically to his measurements. My George wears the same kind of jacket—it's why it fits him so well and why he always looks as if he's just left his tailor. Only moneyed people can afford to sail to London and have clothing made to fit."

Anne didn't know what to think. *Have I married someone with money?*

"I asked him what he did for a living because I needed to make sure he had income to care for the children. He said…ah…let me think of his exact words. He said he was involved in several organizations and that he keeps account of expenditures and makes sure those organizations run smoothly. He said nothing about his wealth."

Susannah nodded her head but said nothing more. *Keeps account of expenditures, does he? Indeed!* Her lips turned up into a wide smile.

Ginger and Thaddeus were beside themselves with excitement. As soon as the guests thinned out, Elijah asked Lucas and Jacob, as well as

James, Anne, and the two children, to follow him into the library. The paperwork for the adoption was laid out on the large cherrywood desk.

Lucas Falter looked with appreciation at Elijah.

"I think you have been a busy man since yesterday," he said in a tone of admiration. "That is no mean feat to accomplish in such a short time."

Elijah's eyes gleamed with pleasure at the acknowledgment of his prowess and time spent accomplishing so much in such a short time.

"Thank you, Mr. Falter. Yes, yes, I have been quite busy, but for a good cause, wouldn't you say?"

Lucas nodded as Elijah continued to talk. "I spoke with my colleagues after you left yesterday, and we would like to see if you are amenable to joining our firm. We are shorthanded at the moment, as our clientele is growing faster than we have ability to manage. Are you at all interested?"

Lucas, his mind fixed on a certain secretary, nodded his head slowly as he thought about the offer.

"I think I would like that very much, Mr. Humphries. Let me think it over, pray about it, and give you my decision next week. I recently bought a piece of property in Napa, planning to build, but I can just as easily sell it and build here." He'd had a lovely time the evening before with Miss Josephine Hensley and was smitten.

James cleared his throat, wanting to get the papers signed and be on their way. They had quite a distance to travel, and with a wagon, it'd be slower, but at least the road was well-tended.

Elijah turned from the desk and spoke to James. "It's all here. You both need to sign this, as well as the children." He smiled at Thaddeus and Ginger, thankful to the Almighty for His provision for these two children, who had endured such pain and loss. He prayed Liberty would be able to help the girl.

James picked up the pen and signed with no hesitation. Anne closed her eyes as if in a quick prayer as Elijah handed her the steel-nibbed pen. She took it with no hesitancy and signed her new name with a sure hand. Elijah was glad she'd remembered to write Mobrey and not Tarkington.

Anne retuned Elijah's pen, but he stood watching as she stared at her new husband. He wondered why she scrutinized James' clothing. His shoes were of high-grade leather, and his trousers, matching his vest and jacket, were of good-quality cloth. Her eyes slowly made their way up to his impeccably tied cravat and on up to his face. James' eyes seemed full of humor as he endured her scrutiny.

Elijah, conscious of the quiet atmosphere, saw her blush, and he smiled inwardly.

"You need to sign again, a copy for me and one for you," he said to the adults. "Ginger and Thaddeus, please sign here and here. Now, Mr. Falter and Mr. Bates, could you please sign as witnesses?" He watched carefully to make sure everyone signed in the proper places. He'd already signed where he needed to and had written in the dates. "I now pronounce you a family. Mr. and Mrs. Mobrey and Ginger and Thaddeus Mobrey, may the good Lord bless you and keep you, and may He shine His grace upon you and give you peace."

CHAPTER XIII

Who can find a virtuous woman?
for her price is far above rubies.

PROVERBS 31:10

THE RIDGE ABOVE THE OLD MAN'S HOUSE overlooked the house, barn, and surrounding area. Sitting on his horse out of sight of the house, a lone man stared for a long time looking at the scene before him. Something didn't feel right. Finally he rode quietly up to the man's barn. He dismounted before the big double doors, now shut. That in itself told him something, because he and Rudy never left barn doors shut in case they needed to make a fast getaway. He left his horse and entered the side door of the barn, but the stalls were empty. Rudy's horse and the old man's horse were gone.

He ran softly to the back door and entered on quiet feet, his gun drawn. In the kitchen, where they'd tied up the old man, two chairs sat side by side, and there was rope on the floor beside both chairs. He went through the house, looking into the two bedchambers, and then he spied the living room window broken out. He strode across the floor and opened the front door, trying to figure out what had happened.

There was nothing. The fact that there was no glass alerted him to the certainty that someone had tried to clean up, and it wouldn't have been Rudy. Then he saw it—the porch stained with blood. He knelt down for closer inspection, but it was dry. He went back to the barn feeling within himself that his brother was wounded or perhaps dead. He wondered where Chloe was.

"Sweet Pea," he said into the stillness of the huge barn. "Sweet Pea, it's me, Uncle Buddy." There was no stirring of the hay in the loft. Nothing moved, and he figured she was gone—but to where?

"I'll find you, kid! I'll find you, and I'll get whoever done this ta Rudy. I'll find 'em. For shore I'm gonna find 'em!"

He went back to his horse and started to take the supplies he'd bought off his mare. "Reckon maybe I oughtn't ta stay here," he said. "Someone might come back ta check out this place again, and I don't want ta end up in jail fer robbing the old man. But I'm going ta find out what happened here. Yes siree, you can bet your bottom dollar. I'll find out what happened here and where the blazes Sweet Pea and Rudy is."

The bright day lifted the Mobreys' spirits. It was beautiful and made one think the rainy season was over. Fluffy white clouds puffed their way across a deep-blue expanse. The breeze was gentle, and the sun, although not hot, was a balm to those weary of weeks of rain without end. As the new family neared their destination, the day slowly made its way toward dusk.

"When we going to get there, Mr. Mobrey?" Thaddeus was exhausted. It had been a long, emotional day.

"I should think we have about a half hour more, and we'll be home. It's your home now, and Ginger's home, and"—he turned to glance at Anne—"your home, Anne. Just so you all know, you can call Mr. Bates, Bates. He prefers it. Mr. Falter is my closest friend, and I'll let him decide what you're to call him. He's a guest in our home, at present, and Bates lives with us."

Anne's eyebrows rose at this disclosure. She'd thought Mr. Bates a close neighbor, as he said he'd been James' tutor, mentor, and friend. She then remembered James had said he'd moved west a year ago. *So Bates moved out here too?* She wondered again about Susannah Baxter's words. *Does James have money? I haven't even thought about it, but I wonder if his house will be big enough to live comfortably with a new wife, two children, and Grandma Jenny. He seems considerate, except yesterday morning when he kept interrupting me.*

Yesterday morning I got up and began my day, not realizing I'd be a married woman in a little more than twenty-four hours. She whispered a prayer, which no one would hear over the rumbling noise of the wagon. "Lord, help me be calm. Your word says for me to not be anxious, and I'm trying not to be, but my stomach aches with nerves. I pray for wisdom for me. I don't know how to be a mother, but I love these children to distraction. Let me be attentive to their needs and of those around me. My biggest desire is to be pleasing to you. I pray for a safe trip for Grandma Jenny, and, Lord, open the doors for me to be able to help Ginger, but more than that, I pray you would heal her."

Thaddeus and Ginger sat on the wagon seat behind James and Anne., but Thaddeus had a problem.

They'd been traveling for hours, and he needed to relieve himself. He hoped the half hour went quickly. He sat still, but the bumping of the wagon was agony. He took his mind off himself and thought about how quickly things had changed in just one day.

They'd spent late afternoon yesterday packing all their belongings into the wagon. Thaddeus wondered that there was so little. He'd expected Miss Tarkington to have furniture and everything, but she didn't. She had several trunks, and that was all. Last night they'd had dinner at the Humphries' home. Mr. And Mrs. Humphries were kind, and he liked the way they talked to him, as if he were an adult. He'd fallen in love with their dog, Polka Dot. He wondered if it would be all right to ask for a dog for Christmas, or maybe his birthday since it was coming up fairly soon. The dinner had been one of the best he'd ever eaten, and he thanked Mrs. Humphries profusely until she said she had a cook named Bessie and that Bessie had cooked the dinner, not her. He'd never been in a home where there were servants, and he quietly studied how everyone interacted with one another. He decided servants were like family. Everyone had jobs to do, but servants got paid to do theirs.

He and Ginger had spent their last night in the San Rafael School of Primary Learning. As he had lain there, he'd been thankful it was his last night. He remembered not only to say his prayers but to thank God for answering his so quickly, about getting him out of the dormitory he hated. He had breathed a sigh of relief knowing he wouldn't have to listen to the boy next to him snore anymore.

After the wedding, he'd eaten his fill of food that tasted so good he'd gotten a stomachache from eating too much. That was why he now needed a toilet. His stomach felt rumbly.

They sat on the wagon with Mr. Mobrey and Miss Tar...here he was with his new parents. He wondered what he should call them.

Suddenly, he said, "Mr. Mobrey, I'm sorry, but I need to go behind those bushes, sir—right away, sir. I have a stomachache and can't wait until we get to your house." Thaddeus' face burned red with embarrassment.

James pulled up immediately. Reaching under the seat, he opened a small box and handed Thaddeus some sheets of some Gayetty's Medicated Paper.

"Here, take these and run over there into the bushes. Be careful, son. It's getting dark. We can't see you, and we'll all look the other way anyway."

Thaddeus went at a run while James continued to talk. He turned to Ginger and asked, "Are you all right? Can you wait until we get to my—our house?"

Ginger bobbed her head in the affirmative, and James gave a sigh of relief.

"You and Thaddeus are going to have to teach me how to be a father. I don't know anything about it, but I can learn if you'll teach me." He smiled over at Anne. "If I'd thought about it, we'd have taken a little break earlier."

Thaddeus came back to the wagon and asked, "Wherever did you get such fine paper?"

"Oh, I order it from New York," James replied offhandedly. "We're almost home." He clucked to the horse and slapped the reins lightly, but he felt Anne's quizzical stare.

It wasn't long before they turned off the main road and started up a long lane. Anne looked curiously about but could see nothing because it was too dark. The lane was much smoother than the main road, and soon a house came into view with a large curving drive to its front. It was lit up with lamps lining a sidewalk leading to the double front doors. The illuminated brilliance from the windows cast gleaming halos of light onto the shrubs that grew next to the house. It was a huge stately mansion rising up into the sky, but James did not stop in the front. He drove around to the side of the house, which was dimly lit, and into a large courtyard at the back of the mansion. Light from the porch gleamed across the cobbles separating the house from the stable.

Anne's eyes were enormous. *Mrs. Baxter was right. Oh…my…goodness. I've gone and married myself a wealthy man! It makes no difference to me, but Grandma Jenny will be proud. And I can see why he wasn't worried about room for us. Oh my goodness…my goodness! This place is huge!*

A man came running out of the stable and stood holding the horses still as James threw him the reins and hopped down, coming around to help Anne.

"Anne, I'd like you to meet Abel Murdock, whom we call Dock. He's my stableman, handyman, you-name-it man! Dock, my wife, Anne Mobrey."

Dock's eyes widened, surprise filling their depths, but he said courteously enough, "Welcome to Mobrey Manor, madam. I'm that pleased ta meet cha." He lifted his newsboy hat respectfully.

"It's good to meet you too, Dock." She reached out to shake his hand, which he happily proffered.

"And who might this be?" He bent down to peer into the children's faces.

"This is Ginger and Thaddeus Mobrey. Please meet Dock," James said.

After the introductions, James waited for Dock to take Bates' and Lucas' horses before ushering his new family into the back entry.

They went up a three-step staircase, but before Anne ascended, she looked up and saw that the house was an impressive three stories.

As they entered the back door, she looked around with keen interest. The back entry had lines overhead for drying clothes. The ceiling had to be twelve feet high, and three of the walls, the one they entered and the two sides, were wainscot topped with paned glass all around. The back wall's glassed French doors, covered by stretched lace, were centered between white cupboards that stretched upward and were topped by wicker baskets. One side wall held a washing machine with a place to build a fire under it to keep the water warm while washing. The shelving held wide, flat drawers for linens and tablecloths. Anne was amazed at the size of the room and how conveniently things were stored.

James was waiting for her at the kitchen door, watching her reaction. He had come up with many of the ideas for the house and hoped his new wife would like it as much as he did.

Anne entered with slow step, savoring the feeling of beauty mixed with convenience. She had no time for more perusal because a woman, thin as a stick, her face looking stern until it broke into a wide smile, approached.

James again made introductions. "Anne, this is Corabelle Meers, our cook. Corabelle, meet your new employer, Mrs. Anne Mobrey."

Before Corabelle could say a word, Anne again stuck out her hand to greet the cook.

"I'm so pleased to meet you, Corabelle."

"Just call me Cora, ma'am. I'm happy to meet you, and welcome to Mobrey Manor. You'll be loving it here soon's you get settled in. I've made dinner, so please do excuse me."

Anne nodded, grateful she didn't have to rustle up dinner after the exhausting day she'd had.

Before she could inspect the kitchen, another woman, quite well-rounded with a face made for smiling, walked into the kitchen, her eyes widening with the realization the master was home.

"I didn't hear you come in, Mr. Mobrey." She spoke with an English accent, as did Bates. She walked over to the children and bending low said, "Why, hel-lo there! We've been waiting and waiting and waiting for you to get here. I'm so glad you've come. What are your names?"

"I'm Thaddeus Park...er...Thaddeus Mobrey, and this is my sister, Ginger. I'm seven and she's eight and a half." He favored the lady with a little bow, liking the way she had welcomed them.

Ginger gave a little curtsy.

"I'm delighted to meet you. My name's Melody Mackie, and you may call me Mackie. I am the housekeeper for Mr. Mobrey. My job is to make you comfortable." She beamed at the children, straightened up, and looked at Anne with a question in her warm brown eyes. She held out her hand and said, "Welcome to Mobrey Manor. As I said to the children, I am Melody Mackie."

"And I," Anne said, with humor lurking in her beautiful violet eyes, "am the new Mrs. Anne Mobrey."

The shock in Mackie's eyes was everything Anne could have wished for. She nearly giggled.

"Well, a double-warm welcome for you, madam."

"Thank you, and it's nice to meet you. I know nothing of running such an establishment. I'm sure I will be able to learn much from you."

With that statement, she won Mackie's heart. This wasn't some woman who was going to come in high and mighty and try to change the way everything was done…at least, not yet anyway.

She smiled widely at her new mistress and said, "Please come with me."

James had watched the interchange with interest.

"Mrs. Mobrey will be in the room connecting with mine."

Anne's head lifted swiftly to peruse his face. His left eye winked imperceptibly to let her know it was going to be all right.

"As you wish, sir," Mackie said. She turned to the children and said, "Just you wait until you see your rooms! You're going to like them, and there is a surprise waiting for you there."

She led the way out of the kitchen and through the parlor, into an enormous front entry.

Anne looked around with pleasure. The front entry to the manor house was beautiful, but its crowning feature was a grand staircase much like the one she'd descended for her wedding. It was the second one she'd ever seen built this way, the first being that morning. It split at a huge landing and then ascended to the second story.

Thaddeus spoke to Ginger in a soft voice. "Can you believe it, sis? This is going to be a good adventure, and I don't want to ever lose the feeling of being thankful for it." He looked around and then up. His eyes widened, seeing a huge chandelier suspended from the second story ceiling, the crystals sparkling with prisms of light dancing on the walls.

Mackie heard his comment, her heart warming to the grateful boy. She wondered that she'd not heard a word from the girl.

Going up the first section of stairs, paintings of ancestors lined the wall, and Anne ascended the treads with lagging steps, looking for James' likeness in any of them. When they neared the top, she saw a painting of what must be his mother; the likeness was astounding. She wondered about her new husband. He seemed polite and was obviously well-educated. She felt like Thaddeus, in that this was an adventure for her also. She prayed silently that this decision was a good one. She reached for Ginger's hand and smiled down at the little girl.

"Come on, Ginger," she said. "We'll go up together to see our new accommodations."

They gained the first landing, which, like Mrs. Baxter's, housed a piano. But it wasn't a baby grand—it was a full grand piano. Anne's heart filled with pleasure as the piano beckoned to her. An accomplished pianist, she was delighted she'd be able to play on such a beautiful instrument.

Mackie waited at the top of the second half of the staircase, but Anne dawdled, looking around with gratefulness at the Lord's provision for her. It was lovelier than she could have conjured up in her sweetest dreams.

I can read my Bible right there on that bay window seat. Wonder if this faces east. I hope so. It'd be nice to bask in the morning sunshine.

Some kind of tree grew in an enormous porcelain pot in the left corner. A couple love seats faced the wide bay window overlooking the back area, but it was too dark to see beyond the glass darkened by night.

CHAPTER XIV

Through wisdom is an house builded;
and by understanding it is established.

PROVERBS 24:3

ANNE REACHED THE TOP OF THE STAIRS and said, "Thank you for your patience, Mackie. Who plays the piano?"

"Mr. James is quite accomplished, and Bates can play, but not so well. Bates started Mr. James playing, but Mr. James surpassed him, and his parents got him lessons."

Anne didn't say she played. She simply smiled in contentment.

"Here we are…Master Thaddeus' room," Mackie said. She opened the door, and a scruffy little puppy of indiscriminate heritage bounced across the floor.

It was love at first sight. "I was just thinking of having a puppy not an hour gone!" Thaddeus exclaimed with a little awe in his voice.

Ginger and Thaddeus both dropped to their knees, petting the little pooch.

Thad looked around the room with contentment. It was his. He grinned up at Mackie and said, "Thank you! How I do thank you! Look at those shelves loaded with books! I'm in hog heaven when I have time to read."

"I didn't have much to do with it," she said. "It was Mr. James' doing. He planned all this for the boy he would one day adopt."

"Let's go across the hall to Miss Ginger's room." Mackie was suddenly aware that Ginger couldn't talk. Her throat clogged with sadness at the thought. "This is your room, sweetie." She spoke with tenderness as she opened the door.

Another puppy tumbled across the floor in delightful wags; the twin of Thad's new puppy.

Ginger's eyes filled with tears of happiness, and she looked up at Anne with the most incredible look of thanksgiving. She swung her gaze to Mackie and mouthed a thank-you to her.

"You are very welcome."

Ginger looked around the utterly feminine room, holding a squirming puppy in her arms. Her eyes rounded in wonder. The large wooden bed was painted white. Atop the four posts was a pink lacy canopy. The finials topping the posts were intricately carved crosses, and a pink dust ruffle peeked out beneath a pale-green duvet dotted with pink flowers. The walls were palest pink, and the pale-green trim matched the green in the duvet. A large round braided rug covered the highly polished wood floor, and there were two white nightstands, a desk painted white, and a couple wingbacks covered in the lightest of pink. A white bookshelf spread the length of the windows and housed books, bibelots, and a couple dolls. Ginger felt tears start in her eyes at the thoughtfulness of her new father. She brushed them away, hoping no one saw her display of emotion.

James had been delayed, talking with Cora, and arrived just in time to see the look on Ginger's face. His eyes filled with tears, and he took his handkerchief to wipe them away, glad he'd witnessed her delight. It was easy to overlook someone so quiet, and he said a silent prayer asking that he'd never do that.

He spoke softly, "We haven't named the puppies because we thought you'd want to name them yourselves. I was in Napa, and there was a sign in the mercantile store window about some puppies being free to a good home. I'm sure you both will take good care of them. They're both males. We put those different-colored little bandanas on them so you can tell them apart."

Mackie was glad Mr. James had arrived. She had a few things to do before the family ate. "I'll leave you to it then. Dinner is ready whenever you are." She left on swift feet to make sure all was in readiness in the dining room.

James tousled Ginger's hair and asked, "Would you like to see your new mother's room?" He looked over her head at Anne, who blushed becomingly. "It's right this way." He led them to the last door before his suite of rooms.

Anne laughingly said, "Do I get a puppy, too?"

He opened the door to her room with a smile. "No, I was not expecting to bring a wife home on this trip, only my new son and daughter. The puppies were downstairs until we rode up. I'm sure Mackie had some maid light the lamps in the children's rooms as well as put the puppies in there. I'll light some lamps in here." He picked up a taper on a small side table beside the door and lit it, touching sconces and lamps.

As the first sconce was lit, Anne's eyes widened in surprise at the room she would call her own. It was huge.

She first noticed the bed, a beautiful cherrywood four-poster, but without a canopy. The exquisitely carved heavy columns rose upward in stately grace. She'd never cared for a canopy on a bed and was glad there wasn't one. The duvet cover was a patchwork of colors, but predominantly purple and white with bits of green and lavender. Light, peaceful lavender covered the walls.

As James lit a couple lamps, light brightened the room, and she noticed an enormous watercolor on the wall opposite the bed, over the fireplace. She walked to the foot of the bed, where she stood a few feet away from it and perused it.

James said, "I bought that in Britain. It's—"

"An Alexander Cozens," Anne finished. She smiled and said, "Sorry. I guess *I* interrupted you that time, didn't I? It's beautiful. He's the one that did blot painting, isn't he?"

James was incredibly pleased she knew the painter.

"You have an education in the arts?"

"Some," she replied. She looked around the room, enjoying the fresh beauty and the harmonious blend of colors from the duvet. Purple wingbacks flanked the fireplace, with lavender and white pillows in them. The carpet around the bed was a dark green. Heavy white drapes covered one wall. The room spoke peace to her.

"Thank you for this." She waved her hand to encompass the room. "It's beautiful."

"You are welcome, Anne." James sauntered over to a door in a side wall. It led to a dressing room on the right and a small sitting room on the left. At the end of the little hall was another door, which he opened. "This is the bathing room." He stepped onto the tiled floor. "And this door opens to the water closet." He opened both doors. The space on the left held one of the new flush toilets. The area on the right contained a large bathing room housing a tub, cupboards, and shelves. "This"—he opened the door on the far wall—"leads to my dressing room."

Anne blushed as she realized they would share the bathing room and water closet. She spoke quickly to cover her discomfiture. "It's so modern, isn't it?" she asked. "How long have you lived here?"

"We finished building about a month ago. As you can see, everything is new. Frankly, I like the patina of old wood and the character of an old house, but there were none in the area that fit what I was looking for, so I decided to build. Our neighbors, the Bannisters, were a wonderful help when it came to knowing who to hire for the construction. Evidently, they've only been married a couple years.

"This house is three stories, the third being rooms for servants, with a large storage room as well. There is a basement with a special room for wine, and I have already stocked some of Rancho Bonito's as well as Liberty's Landing, which is where Liberty's father and grandmother live."

He took her by the arm, not venturing into his own rooms, and said, "Let's wash up for dinner, shall we?"

Anne, overwhelmed by her new set of circumstances, answered, "Certainly, I'm famished." She slowly walked back to her room, wondering why this man had chosen to marry her. *He could have his choice of anyone*, she thought. *Why me?*

The next morning was glorious. Sunshine streamed into the kitchen where Buck, Hattie, and Chloe enjoyed breakfast.

Buck and Hattie lived in the big house belonging to Adam and Eden Brown. Buck couldn't wait to move into their new house, which was a lot closer to Napa, where he served as sheriff. Since Hattie was Adam's aunt, they'd been invited by the newlyweds to live at Sunrise Ranch until the house Buck was having built was finished.

Adam and Eden had taken a trip to San Francisco and were lodging in a nice hotel. They needed to meet with some overseas clients. Exporting olives all over the world kept them busy. This time they were meeting with owners of a new company interested in buying their products.

Buck was worried about Chloe's uncle. The man had to be ruthless to treat Dan Hedley the way he had. He'd told Hattie before they came down to breakfast that he was going to ride over to the Bannisters'. He wanted to have a good talk with Liberty and Matthew.

When Chloe found out, she asked, "Can I go with you?"

"No, not this time. I have important business to attend to."

Chloe stuck out her lip in a pout, but it didn't improve her chances.

"Be careful, Chloe. Your lip is out there so far, someone could step on it," Hattie said.

Buck headed out, riding his big blood bay, a beautiful dark-red horse with black mane, tail, and legs. She was a good-sized horse, but he called her Minnie as a jest.

It didn't take long to get to the Bannisters' Rancho Bonito. He dismounted and tied Minnie up to the hitching rail.

Matthew walked out of the barn and saw Buck.

"Well, good morning, Buck. How did everything go with you and that little boy?"

Buck's light-blue eyes twinkled. "Funny thing was, he wasn't a boy. That little firecracker is a girl."

"You're jesting!"

"Nope. She's a little spitfire, she is."

Matthew laughed. "I remember saying to you yesterday, he screamed like a girl. Reckon now it was the truth!" He laughed again, and Buck joined in.

"Let's go inside, Buck. I'm sure Conchita has something we can eat while we talk."

"Used to be, I'd smile for an hour hearing you say that. Now I'm pretty well-fed at Sunrise, and if I'm not careful, I'm going to start a paunch." He grinned and added, "Not that I'm not happy to eat some of Conchita's food. She's quite the cook."

The two men entered the front door, and Boston barked with enthusiasm and joy. He seemed to like most visitors, and Buck was a dog lover.

Liberty sat on the floor of the great room, watching her twins, who lay on their tummies. Matty was able to get up on all fours and rock, quite a feat for a baby so young. Faith, most times, rolled onto her back, kicking and cooing with contentment. Both were used to Boston's occasional barking and were not afraid of it, but they watched as their daddy entered the room, and both smiled and cooed at him.

"Good morning, Liberty. How are you doing today?" Buck was curious as to how she felt after shooting Chloe's dad.

"I'm all right, I suppose. I had some bad dreams last night and still wonder if there was something else I could have done, but I don't think there was. I didn't mean to kill him. I was aiming for his right arm, but he turned quick enough for me to get him in the chest. I am sorrowful for that. How is the little boy Matthew discovered?"

"Well, he's not a boy. Turned out to be a little spitfire of a girl. I lost count of how many tubs of water that child dirtied before she was clean. She's a handful, but I reckon Hattie is up for it. Hattie's determined she's going to make a real polite girl out of her. I told her it wouldn't be easy, but she figures the girl is only five and tamable."

Liberty laughed. "I can see Hattie and that little one having a few brouhahas before that girl is amenable to being taught. Matthew said she has a mind of her own."

"That's true—she certainly does." Buck grinned as he thought about the evening before. "Last night she threw a conniption fit over Hattie saying she needed to wear a nightshirt and not her clothes to bed. Said she hadn't worn a nightdress since her mama died a couple years ago. Hattie told her, 'You are staying here for the time being, and you'll wear this to bed.' She got it on her, but this morning Chloe wasn't wearing anything when she got up. Hattie started laughing, and that made that little girl so mad. She thought it would upset Hattie if she was naked, but it didn't faze my wife one bit. She's going to be a real challenge, and no mistake."

Matthew laughed. "That's the truth. I've got a few bruises on my ribs to prove it."

"How's your head?" Buck asked.

"I've got a headache that won't stop. I keep wondering how my head can stand all the bashing it's had in the last year or so."

"That's right. I forgot about you getting hit on the noggin and left for dead up there in Sonoma. Then getting thrown into that barn post. You must have a hard head, Matthew."

"I think I do in more ways than one. Once I make up my mind, I'm hardheaded about sticking to my guns and going through with whatever it is I've decided on."

Conchita entered the great room smiling her wide smile.

"Good morning, Meester Sheriff. Eet good to see you. You come into my kitchen, and I geeve you some good piece of chocolate cake. Liberty, she make eet, an' I frost eet. Come. I geeve you some coffee, too."

"Thanks, Conchita. I'll take you up on that!"

The men and Conchita headed for the kitchen. Liberty put the twins down for a nap, but it wasn't long before she joined Matthew and Buck.

She poured a cup of coffee and sat down at the large scrubbed-oak table.

"I'm figuring this isn't a social visit, is it?" Matthew said.

"No, frankly speaking, it's not. I wanted to talk to you and Libby about the situation we now have. I don't believe for a minute it's over. You both need to be careful and on the lookout. When we were riding for Sunrise yesterday, Chloe let drop that the man on the loose is her uncle, and he'll come gunning for whoever shot her pa. The two were evidently inseparable."

"I'll be sure to be careful, Buck. You needn't worry about me," Liberty said.

"Does the child know who killed her pa?" Matthew asked.

"She thinks you did it," Buck replied.

"No, not now she doesn't. I told her yesterday I was tied up when her pa was shot, but I didn't tell her it was Liberty either. I'll tell the crew to be sure to be on the lookout for any strangers. One thing for sure, she's a smart enough kid to figure out whoever killed her pa was with me."

Buck nodded grimly. "I'm going to ride into town to talk with Dr. John and make sure he doesn't tell anyone who shot the man. I'm also going to tell Harkin to let me know if anyone comes into the saloon that he doesn't know. That's the most likely place for a stranger to go if he wants to find out information. I plan to keep a tight lid on this."

Anne rolled over onto her back and stretched out full length, holding the position for a few seconds. She then relaxed every muscle in her body. She'd had a wonderful night's sleep once she'd stopped thinking about her new set of circumstances. She'd fallen asleep praying and had slept through the night without waking once.

Anne thought a noise had awakened her but decided it hadn't, when all the sudden the curtains were opened.

"Good morning, ma'am. I'm Florence Harris, but you can call me Flo. I'm head maid here at Mobrey Manor. Sorry I woke you up. I was told to ask you if you want a tray sent up, or are you eating with the family?"

Anne sat up abruptly. "Oh, I suppose I slept in, didn't I? Nice to meet you, Flo. I'll get up right now. I'd like to join the family, but I think I'd be too late. I'm not dressed, and I'd probably hold things up." She swung her legs over the side of the bed and stood. Anne wasn't short, but Flo must have topped her by at least four inches. It wasn't common to see a woman so tall.

Anne proffered her hand, which surprised Flo.

"It's a pleasure to meet you, Flo." Anne spoke with genuine warmth, and Flo's hazel eyes gleamed her pleasure.

"Nice to meet you, ma'am, but you mustn't dress for breakfast. You can just wear your robe. It's what Mr. James does. He's wearing one right now."

"That would be lovely," Anne replied. "You're sure it's proper?"

"Yes, ma'am, purely proper around here."

"That's nice—wearing a robe is what I'm used to," Anne said, "and I'm glad it's the custom here. It makes for a more relaxed breakfast, doesn't it?"

"Yes'm, that it does. That it does," Florence agreed.

"If you'll please tell them I'll just be a minute—I need to wash up first." Anne headed to the bathing room. She took more than a glance at the dressing room as she passed it and thought it huge. Her meager wardrobe would look sparse in it.

She loved the convenience of the flush toilet and wondered how anyone had thought of such an invention. Running back to her room, she grabbed a hairbrush and with swift strokes brushed her blonde hair. She decided she might as well leave it down, as was her custom when breakfasting. Being presentable had never been necessary at breakfast.

She knew many things she was accustomed to were going to have to change. She mentally shrugged her shoulders and donned the deep-violet robe Grandma Jenny had given her. She descended the stairs, wishing she could play a tune or two before eating.

CHAPTER XV

As he saith also in Hosea, I will call them my people,
which were not my people; and her beloved, which was not beloved.

ROMANS 9:25

ANNE ENTERED THE DINING ROOM SURPRISED no one
was there, but she heard voices and laughter emanating from the kitchen.
The wide door to the kitchen was open, and she stood quietly in the
doorway, watching the scene, her lips curving into a smile.

James, Ginger, and Thaddeus were all on their knees playing with the
puppies, only instead of two there were three. Her eyes widened at the
thought that James might have gone into town and found her a puppy too.

He looked up, a wide grin on his face, and said, "Good morning,
Anne. I hope you slept well." His questioning look turned to one of
pleasure as he took in her robe and hair, which curled softly, cascading
down her back.

"I slept the whole night through and didn't awaken once." She
glanced over at the cook and said, "Good morning, Cora."

"Mornin', ma'am," Cora replied. "Breakfast is ready. Please sit, and
you'll have it steaming hot."

James said to the children, "We need to wash up. There's a
washroom right through there." He pointed to a door and added, "Make
haste now. I'll wash up here."

Ginger and Thad scampered to wash up as James washed at the kitchen sink.

Anne now had time to check out the kitchen. Glassed French doors led to a well-lit huge room off one end. The doors were wide open, and it seemed the out-of-doors had invaded the kitchen. She could see a table in it all set for breakfast. A pond nestled in one corner, and a huge fireplace centered itself on a brick wall connected to the house, adding more credence to feeling outdoors. Comfortable chairs circled the fireplace, set in such a way as to invite conversation.

James finished drying his hands, took Anne's arm, and led her to the table, talking pleasantly as they strolled together.

"I'm glad you had a good rest. Yesterday was so full, and I hoped you weren't overtired. Sometimes that hinders sleep for me."

Anne blushed slightly as he took her arm. She tried to relax. She knew he was trying to put her at ease, and she was grateful for it.

The children came in, all puppies trailing behind them.

Cora had two younger girls help with serving. They wore black dresses with white collars and cuffs, plain white pinafores, and dust bonnets. They looked neat and efficient.

James proudly introduced his new wife. "Mrs. Mobrey, this is Molly and Alice. They will be willing to help you with anything you need. I'd like to know if you'd like a personal servant to help you with dressing or such? I think it's customary and would be appropriate."

They each bobbed curtsies to Anne when he said their names.

"I'd like to think about that for a bit. I am quite capable of dressing myself."

She smiled, and a dimple appeared just below the corner of her mouth, which James had not noticed before.

"No doubt. I also dress myself, but Bates always tweaks my cravat. It's never done to his satisfaction. Here at home I dress much more casual. I have a feeling once you meet Liberty Bannister you'll want to adopt her mode of clothing. She's a fine woman and dresses as she pleases.

"Ginger, since you're the oldest, you pick which chair you want to sit in. We will take turns by the week, all four of us."

Ginger took the chair facing the out-of-doors and sat, mouthing a thank-you to James. Thad took the one next to her and spoke excitedly to Anne.

"Papa James took us into town early this morning, and we got the last puppy of the litter at the mercantile store. He said you wanted one too. See the one with the smudge of brown on his nose? That one is yours."

"He's darling. Thank you, James. And I think you just named him for me, Thaddeus. I'm going to call him Smudge."

Cora had fixed omelets, hash browns, and toast. Molly poured coffee as Alice set warmed plates in front of the new family. She poured a glass of milk for the children.

"Let's pray," James said. "Our Father in heaven, how we do thank You for our new family. I pray we will grow to love each other and enjoy each other the way You have created us to love. I pray Ginger will get back her voice and feel secure in this family. I pray Thaddeus will not feel burdened by heavy responsibility but simply enjoy being a boy. I pray Anne and I grow to love each other. Father, I pray You to bless this food, and may it nourish us for this day. In Jesus' peerless name we pray. Amen."

Anne's eyes were warm on James when he finished his prayer, and he could see the blush in her cheeks beginning to fade. She looked down at the plates for the first time, exclaiming over the pattern on the dishes.

"These are beautiful. What pattern is this?"

"It's Limoges 'Pink Roses.' This set belonged to my parents, and I've collected a few more pieces. It never fails to remind me of my halcyon days growing up. Because I was an only child, my parents and I were close. They died of diphtheria when I was away at school, and I was devastated."

"I am sorry for your loss, James. I never knew my parents. They were killed in a train derailment when I was two years old, and Grandma Jenny, my father's mother, raised me. She may arrive in a few days. She's the one I sent a telegram to yesterday. She's not one to let any grass grow under her feet, and she's been itching to come since I arrived in December."

"We've plenty of room, and she'll be welcome here. I know an older lady, Bertha Morrow, who lives in Napa. She's involved in various clubs and organizations and will be happy to introduce your grandmother around." He smiled warmly at Anne and asked, "Do you ride?" He turned to the children, asking them the same question.

"Yes, I do. I have a couple horses in Virginia, but I'm pretty sure Grandma Jenny will sell them if she moves out here," Anne replied with a sigh.

"Ginger and I don't ride," Thad replied as Ginger shook her head negatively. "We had a horse, but our pa wouldn't let us ride him because he was crazy. Sometimes he had fits of temper. It's why we got 'im so cheap. He'd be just a nice normal horse, but sometimes he'd buck my pa off and kick. He wasn't nice."

"Well, that's one thing we'll have to take care of right away. I want us to be able to go riding together. I also want you to be able to shoot."

"Ginger and I can shoot anything with a rifle or handgun," Thad said proudly.

Anne laughed. "I don't know how to shoot, but I'm willing to learn. It sounds fun. I'd bet my bottom dollar my grandma will want to learn too. She wrote me not long ago and told me she was game for anything. You two"—she waggled her finger at Ginger and Thad—"are going to love Grandma Jenny. I hope you do too, James."

"If she's anything like you, I certainly will," he replied unabashedly.

Chloe was madder than hops. Hattie had Gio, the head foreman of Sunrise Ranch, buy her a couple dresses while he was in town. Chloe didn't want to wear a dress, but the denims from Pepe were too big.

"You can just wear a dress for now, and I'll make you some trousers that fit you if you're so set on wearing boy's pants," Hattie said in a soothing voice. She was determined to not raise her voice or get angry at this little girl so in need of love and attention. "I have a stack of material, and you can pick out what you'd like for a pair of trousers, and you can help me make them."

"I don't know how ta sew."

Chloe spoke in a voice a bit higher than her normal tone, but she didn't whine, which was a comfort to Hattie. She'd never been able to abide hearing a child whine.

"I wish I was a boy. I don't *like* being a girl and wearing dresses. I *hate* them!"

"I believe I've already learned that." Hattie's tone was firm. "But for now, that's what we're going to do. Come on now—raise your hands, and I'll just slip this over your head."

After Chloe was dressed, Hattie took her downstairs and into the room that had been Eden's mother's sitting room. The walls were done in a pale apricot. Thick crown molding, stained a dark mahogany, covered the breach between the wall and the ten-foot-high ceiling. All the trim board and casing around the windows and door matched the deep stain of mahogany as well as the mantel over the small fireplace. A huge picture of apricot-colored poppies, blowing in a breeze, graced the wall over the mantel. Each long, narrow picture on either of it was of a single poppy, its delicate pale-green stem bowed to hold the fat bloom. Long chartreuse drapes flanked the huge window looking out to the fields behind the stable. The rest of the room was done in apricot, pale chartreuse, and cream, creating a tranquil and inviting ambiance.

Chloe looked around, awestruck by the beauty.

"I've never been in such a pretty room. It's beautiful, isn't it?" Chloe whispered as she stood still, looking around the room, drinking in the peace that emanated from it.

"Yes, it's probably the prettiest room I've ever been in. Here, I'd like you to take a look at this."

"What is it?" Chloe was curious as she watched Hattie pull a book out of the shelf.

"This used to be Miss Eden's. It's a storybook. Can you read?"

"Nope. Pa said girls don't need ta have book learnin'."

"And you, being such a good girl, believe that folderol? You have got to be jesting, Chloe. Don't you know that is one way for men to keep women as ignorant property? Do you want every boy to be smarter than you? You are a bright girl, and I have no doubt that if you set your mind to it, you could learn to read in a very short time. Being able to read opens doors to all over the world. It takes you places you might never be able to travel."

"You truly think girls can be as smart as boys?"

"Oh goodness, girl, I am smarter than a lot of men I know. You are smarter than most boys, I reckon, but if you had book learning, you can have not only common sense but be educated too. You will find growing up that there will always be someone smarter than you, no matter how hard you try, and some people who will never be as smart as you, no matter how hard they try."

"Well, let me take a look at that there book you got. I want ta be smart. My pa said I would never amount ta much, being a girl and all. Said all I was good for was having babies when I grow up."

"Oh, Chloe, if you only had an inkling of how much the Almighty God loves you, you would never believe that for a minute. You are precious in His sight."

"Who's God?"

"Oh, Chloe!"

Buck Rawlins strolled into the saloon, and all activity seemed to cease. Harkin didn't like the sheriff coming in—it was bad for business. He'd told Buck that very thing more than once.

Buck didn't bother to look around but went straight to the bar.

"Hello there, Harkin. Good to see you."

"It's good to see you, too, Sheriff, but not in here."

"I know. I know. But I have a question for you. Seen any strangers around these parts?"

"Matter of fact, I have," Harkin answered, his eyes widening. He wiped his hands on his baize apron, shifting his considerable weight. He leaned his elbows on the long beer-stained bar. "Man came in the day afore yesterday. He was quiet-like. Said he was just a passin' through, but I seen him out on the street jest yestiday. Had a nag loaded down with supplies, he did. He in some kind of trouble? He seemed right personable. Said he comed from back east somewheres an' he an' his brother were a lookin' ta settle down around here. Say," Harkin said, changing the subject, "heard from Dr. John that ole Hedley kicked the bucket. I was right sorry to hear it. He was plannin' ta go live near Connie and the grandkids. Be a real shock for her, and no mistake, poor girl."

Buck nodded his agreement. "Yes, it'll be a real shock for Constance. The two of them were close. She was a help and comfort to Dan when his Betty died. If you see the stranger again, let me know, will you? I can't bandy about why I need to speak to him, but I can let you know later." Buck didn't care to reveal anything to Harkin. His bar was the center of gossip among men in the town. He had grown up thinking women were the gossips, but after being around men, he'd realized they were sometimes worse when it came to talking. He knew if a body wanted to know something, the bar was the place to go and Harkin was the one to speak to.

James looked across the breakfast table and liked what he saw. Anne could not be considered beautiful, but she was pleasant to look at, having a peaceful demeanor that attracted James more than a pretty face ever could. James had never been one to look at the exterior appearance unless it was so out of the ordinary that he had to take notice. Liberty Bannister was one of those. She was gorgeous inside and out. James liked women tall and short, heavy and skinny. He looked at strength of character. He thought back to two days before and realized what had brought her into focus first was her neatness when he entered her office. It was then that he took real notice of her as something other than the director of the school. Although she was now wearing a robe, she looked prim and proper, and he smiled inwardly.

Anne blushed at his perusal. Her violet-colored robe set off her fair coloring and intensified her violet-blue eyes. James decided right then that she was lovely.

"I understand you play that grand piano on the landing," she said. "I can imagine that landing is a lovely place to sit. I forgot to look outside when I came down the stairs."

"Yes, I do play, and yes, it is a comfortable place to sit and read or simply meditate." He glanced at the children and then back at Anne. "How would you like to go for a drive in the buggy over to our neighbor's house? The Bannisters have a vineyard."

"Oh," Anne said, "I'd like to meet Mrs. Bannister." She spoke to Ginger. "Mrs. Bannister knows sign language. I think it'd be nice if we, as a family, could learn how to speak with our hands. It'd make life much better for you."

Ginger's eyes welled with tears at Anne's thoughtfulness. She nodded yes as Thad spoke.

"That is a good plan. I know Ginger gets frustrated not being able to communicate without a quill and paper." He glanced at his sister. "I get frustrated not understanding what she wants, and then she gets angry at me. She never did that before, and I understand it, but I don't like it. I'm not good at lipreading either."

"Before we get dressed, let's take a real tour of the house, and then we'll dress and go over to the Bannisters'," James said. "Bet they'll ask us for lunch. Their cook is a Mexican woman named Conchita, who can cook the most fantastic-tasting food." He picked up his coffee cup, finishing its contents, and wiping his mouth on his napkin, he sat back, crossing a leg over his knee as he waited in total contentment for the others to finish their breakfast.

Jenny Tarkington had risen early and sat with glasses perched on the end of her nose. Her Bible lay open on her lap, but she was caught up in the beauty outside her window.

The sun was just coming up, and streaks of yellow and orange peeked over the horizon. The heavens lightened as shining fingers of light stretched themselves across the sky. Jenny sat drinking in the glorious new day.

She was having the time of her life. She'd never tasted freedom the way she was experiencing it now. She felt rich with the money Herbert had given her for her house.

She closed the Good Book as she rose to get her shawl off a hook. Picking up her satchel, she made her way to the dining car for a hearty breakfast.

The waiter had taken a shine to Jenny, as she was graciously polite, but also because she asked questions about places the train stopped or about some of the sites they saw. He'd told her about the Great Salt Lake and Devil's Slide and Devil's Peak. She'd wondered at all the names with "Devil," and he had laughed and said he'd heard Devil's Slide was so named because it looked so treacherous The slabs of rock, about twenty feet wide, were forty feet high or more, and the slide length was around two hundred feet. He'd spoken in an almost awestruck voice as he'd related these statistics, and Jenny's exclamations when she'd seen it increased his admiration for her.

CHAPTER XVI

Remember the former things of old: for I am God,
and there is none else; I am God, and there is none like me.

ISAIAH 46:9

LIBERTY WAS IN THE BARN WITH MATTHEW and Buck, showing the sheriff their newest foal. Queenie, one of Matthew's horses, had foaled during the night, and the little filly had the same markings as her mother, a deep brown with black mane and tail, white stockings, and a white blaze from poll to muzzle.

Liberty heard a carriage pull up to the front of the Rancho, and Boston began barking. She shushed him as she left the dimness of the barn.

Liberty saw James and, with a wide smile of welcome, walked over to meet her company. The two men, deep in conversation, followed her out of the stable.

"James!" she called out. "How nice to see you! Welcome. Welcome." She eyed the woman he was handing down from the carriage. Two of the blondest children Liberty had ever seen bounded down behind the woman. Liberty's quick assessment told her the woman wasn't old enough to be their mother, but she could see the same color of blonde hair escaping from the woman's bonnet.

James strode over to Liberty and took her by the arm to lead her back to the carriage.

"Good morning, Liberty. I'd like you to meet my new family...my wife, Anne, and my newly adopted children. Ginger and Thaddeus, this is Mrs. Bannister."

"What a beautiful surprise this is," Liberty said. She held out her hand to greet Anne. "How do you do?"

"I do well, thank you," Anne replied. "It's nice to meet you. I've heard much about you from Mr. Humphries."

Liberty's eyes widened in pleasure. "Elijah Humphries is like a father to me. I am delighted to meet you, and you also," she said to the children.

Ginger curtsied, and Thaddeus made a bow and said, "Ginger and I are pleased to meet you, ma'am." As he looked into her warm green eyes, he knew she was a trustworthy person and added, "Ginger would say it's a pleasure too, but she can't talk."

Liberty's eyes flew to the girl, and she quickly signed a hello with her hands, but Ginger didn't respond. She only looked at Liberty, frustration clearly evident at not understanding what was being said in sign language.

Anne quickly said, "That is something we are hoping you might have time to do. Mr. Humphries suggested that perhaps you could teach our Ginger sign language. She is weary of trying to make herself understood, but being mute is new to her. She's had a traumatizing experience and was left unable to talk, but she can hear you just fine."

"I'm sure we can have you communicating in no time, Ginger." Liberty turned to her other guests. "Please, come on in. Lunch is nearly ready, and we'd love to have you stay."

"Thank you," Anne replied before James could. "We'd be delighted."

James turned to Matthew and Buck, and before they entered the house, once again introduced his wife and children.

Liberty led the way inside, but Anne trailed slowly behind her, admiring not only the beauty but the distinct ambiance of hominess mixed with deep peace. It was almost a feeling of nostalgia...of having been there before and returning to a place of warmth and safety.

"This is lovely," she said.

"Come on into the kitchen," Liberty invited. "This is where we entertain." She walked easily into the large room, and not even Matthew knew the joy she felt in entertaining guests on her own terms. When married to her first husband, she'd entertained guests of renown, formal affairs glittering with heavy silver and crystal and chandeliers. The guests had been sophisticated, dressed in fancy clothes ladened with sparkling gemstones and diamonds.

Liberty had the gift of hospitality and made her guests feel comfortable and welcome in the glitz and glitter of high society or the peaceful, relaxed atmosphere of Rancho Bonito.

But it was here that Liberty had come to find happiness and fulfillment. She loved Matthew with every fiber of her being, and it was returned in full measure. The couple knew the despair of loveless marriages and were grateful to God for this second chance. They held each other's wishes before their own and kept God in the center of all they did. The peace and joy they'd found emanated from the very walls of the Rancho.

Liberty made the introductions. "Conchita, please come meet James' new wife, Anne Mobrey. Anne, this is Conchita." The two women shook hands. Liberty said, "Conchita, this is Ginger and Thaddeus Mobrey. Children, please meet one of the nicest women on earth and without a doubt one of the best cooks!"

"Pleased to meet you," Conchita said.

Again Thaddeus bowed and Ginger curtsied.

Conchita said, "My, you haf the good manners, you two." She turned to Anne and commented, "You haf taught them the nice manners."

"No, not me." Anne corrected with a smile on her lips. "Their mother taught them well, I think."

"Thees ees my nieces, Lupe and Luce. They ees always halping me een the kitchen. Lupe, Luce, thees ees our neighbors, the Mobreys."

The two girls, shy of strangers, simply nodded and giggled as they turned to finish up their work.

Anne smiled at the girls and nodded her head in acknowledgment. Turning to Liberty, she asked, "Where can we wash up?"

Conchita started to answer, but Liberty said, "Let me show you." She nodded at Matthew, who had just entered the kitchen, having seen Buck off. "You and James can wash up at the kitchen sink." She grabbed a full jug of water off the counter and led Anne and the children down the hall to one of the guest rooms.

Matthew expressed his surprise at James' marital status. He said, "I thought you were joshing when you said you were going to mail order a bride."

"I was. I met Anne the day before yesterday, and we got married yesterday." James spoke in a serious tone.

Matthew looked at him with shocked eyes, but he didn't comment.

James continued to speak. "I know it sounds ludicrous, crazy even, but I felt so strongly that the Lord wanted me to marry her. We both wanted to adopt the children. Me, because I felt led to, and her, because she fell in love with them. She didn't have the means nor time to adopt. I did. This seemed the best solution. Elijah Humphries, bless his heart, was all for it."

"You know Elijah?"

"I do now. He drew up the papers for adoption and did some arranging for the wedding. We were married at Mrs. Baxter's San Rafael house yesterday morning and had the reception there as well. After everything was completed, we drove back here."

"You certainly don't let any grass grow under your feet, do you?" Matthew grinned and added, "If Elijah was all for it, then I believe you've made a good choice. I don't think anyone can pull the wool over his eyes."

Conchita had been listening to the conversation, and she added, "I weel pray your marriage, eet ees a good one. She look like a nice girl."

"Thank you, Conchita. I pray that too." James started to say something else, but Liberty, Anne, and the children entered the kitchen. He noticed Anne's red cheeks, and he wondered if she'd heard his comment.

Anne looked around the kitchen, a bit in awe of its gigantic size. Gleaming copper pots hung from a large rack high above a wooden island, serving as a counter and cutting board. Dominating one entire side were windows, with a huge scrubbed-oak table and chairs overlooking a courtyard. Another wall had large glassed French doors wide open to the courtyard that extended past the end of the house. It was spacious, sunny, and cheerful.

"This is beautiful," Anne said. "In a way, it's like the sunroom at James' house."

"Your house too, Anne." James spoke the words softly and watched, with interest, the color climbing back into Anne's cheeks.

Conchita, always aware of undercurrents, spoke into the sudden silence. "Deener ees ready. You can seet and choose what you weel dreenk, and Matthew weel serve the luncheon to you." She glanced at Anne before she bustled over to the stove and opened the oven door.

The smell made mouths water in anticipation.

"I must warn you all," Liberty said. "This dish looks a bit like a tomato salad, but it is not. It's a hot dish called *salsa*, which is Spanish for *sauce*. It is made with tomatillos, onions, tomatoes, and jalapeño peppers, which are very hot. Take a little and see how you like it. We eat it with the tortilla chips and on the *enchiladas*. You don't eat it by itself."

"Please find a chair, and we'll eat luncheon together." She indicated a chair beside her for Ginger. "I taught sign language at the Boston School for the Deaf before moving out here. I can teach you, if you wish. You'll catch on in no time because you already know the words and can hear. Would you like me to do that?"

Ginger nodded vigorously, and Thad said, "She's really tired of not being able to communicate very well unless she writes everything down. Some of the other children at the school in San Rafael made fun of her. It was hard for me not to punch them in the nose!" he exclaimed.

Anne's head jerked up at Thaddeus' comment.

"Why didn't you tell a teacher or come to me? We don't allow that kind of behavior."

"I'm not a tattletale. That's one thing my pa made sure of is that we didn't tell tales even if it would make things easier for us."

"Well," Anne said, "I don't tolerate bullying."

"Neither do I," Liberty said. "It's not tattling when the reason is not trying to get someone into trouble but trying to right a wrong. Nowadays there's too much injustice in this world. Just yesterday we had a neighbor die because someone tied him to a chair in his own house, stuffed a cloth in his mouth, and never gave him any water to drink. I don't know if their intention was to kill the man. They broke into his house, and the result was the same as if they'd planned his death. It's criminal when people treat other people as if they were of no value. We all have value in God's sight."

"Amen to that," James said.

Matthew looked around the table and said, "Let's pray. Conchita has made a mouthwatering lunch, and I want to eat before it gets cold." He smiled and bowed his head, everyone following suit. "Dear Father, how grateful we are for Your love. We thank You that even when others deride us, we have confidence in You to care for us. We thank You for James' new family and that because You are the center of it, the result will be happiness and joy. When an issue arises that could cause disgruntlement, we pray Your hand to be the guiding principle. When no agreement seems possible, we pray that those involved can agree to disagree. Bless the new Mobrey family, Lord, and may the overriding desire be to please You. We thank You now for this food. We thank You for Conchita, Lupe, and Luce, who helped prepare it. Help us never to take Your blessings for granted. We pray these things in and through Jesus, our Savior. Amen."

"Thank you, Matthew. It was a beautiful prayer," James' said.

Conchita, with two hot pads, picked up the large pan full of chicken *enchiladas* and placed them on the table in front of Matthew, whose job it was to dish them out.

"Enjoy thees *enchiladas*. Eet ees my specialty. Liberty, she maked the tortillas the cheecken ees wrapped een. Eet ees her specialty, an' the salsa, my nieces make the salsa. You weel like what your mouth tell you." She bustled out to let her employers and their guests enjoy their dinner.

Matthew dished up, having his guests pass their plates to him.

Liberty sat watching, her hands relaxed and folded in her lap. A smile spread itself across soft lips, and her eyes glowed with pleasure, enjoying the homey, relaxed atmosphere that was her home.

They all began to eat the tasty *enchiladas*, melting cheese dripping from their forks.

A full week had passed, and Buddy Blake stood on a plateau looking over the main road to Napa. He'd ridden up several hills, but this one seemed the most promising view and also had a sheltered place to sleep.

The day was beautiful, with a soft breeze. The temperature was rising, and a few cotton balls of fluff dotted the skies, looking like white dresses dancing softly across the floor of the blue expanse. The valley below him was lush and green with flowers dotting the hillsides.

Buddy didn't notice any of it. He sat down on a log that seemed made for that purpose. He didn't know exactly what to do. Rudy had been the brains behind anything they did. Buddy had never been good at making plans. He had difficulty staying focused.

He'd ridden up into the hills after going through the old man's house. He found a cave that seemed perfect for his needs. It wasn't deep. He'd lit a match to a taper and surveyed it with his gun drawn in case any critters lived in it. His bedroll was tied behind the saddle, and he decided he'd be quite comfortable there until he found out what happened at the house. Having bought enough supplies for three people, he had enough grub to last him for some time.

He wondered where Chloe was. He figured whoever had taken her was the person who shot Rudy. Buddy sat in front of a cave and wondered again what he should do.

Maybe I should ride to another town and see if there's any gossip about what happened. Then again, maybe Rudy ain't dead. Maybe I's too fast to jump to that conclusion. I just saw that there blood and thought it were Rudy's. Maybe he got winged and is sittin' in jail for robbing th' old man's house. That old man weren't looking too good. Maybe what I should do is find the doctor. He probably knows what's happened, and I don't be reckoning that would be hard ta do. I seen his shingle hanging over his house. All I needs ta do is find the doctor in Napa and find out what happened ta Rudy and where they's keepin' Chloe.

A week had passed. Anne sat with her feet curled up underneath her on the love seat located on the stair landing. She had a Bible on her lap, but she was looking out over the lovely garden. It was not too orderly or methodically structured but as she had imagined an English garden to be. Wide arches on either side of the garden led to a grassy area. Wisteria hung from the arches' great height, and the trellis was covered with it. Wisteria trees, planted between the arches, were in full bloom, and flowers of all sorts grew under their overhang. Roses in a variety of colors surrounded the immediate garden, looking like a floral fence. Flowers and shrubs were seemingly planted at random but with eye-pleasing arrangements, and winding paths led to the arches. *It looks like a picture book*, Anne thought. The day before, Anne had sat in one of the swings beyond the arches in the grassy area, playing a word game with the children who seemed to delight in spending time with her.

Now she sat reading her Bible, and noticed, through the window, her husband walking toward the grassy area, with Ginger and Thaddeus leading the way.

Bates was behind James, and she wondered about this amazing man. He'd tutored James and told her he'd love to have a part in the children's education. They'd had a stimulating conversation about teaching strategies and methodologies. His eyes had glowed finding someone he could talk to who wasn't bored by such commentary.

Her thoughts swung to her husband.

He played the piano beautifully. Still, she knew her skill was better than his, and she'd been shy to even acknowledge to him that she played. Years of long practice had rendered her a concert pianist. She'd played many times in Virginia for important events. Once, she'd been invited to the White House and played for the president...President Chester A. Arthur. She'd been a regular player at church and enjoyed sharing her accomplishment with others. It gave them pleasure, and she reveled in that fact. Her grandma had been adamant about practice—she had not wanted to waste her money on good lessons and not make her granddaughter make the best use of them. The urge to play overcame Anne's reticence, and she closed her Bible, laid it on the cushion, and went to the piano.

Opening the fallboard, she slid it back as she sat down on the bench. Running her fingers over the keys, she felt as if she'd come home. Anne had done much praying and thinking in the past week. She was beginning to admire the man she now called husband. Her first impression of the brash interrupter of someone talking had given way to seeing a man who was considerate, thoughtful, and kind. Her fingers slid over the keys, and she slipped into Chopin's *Nocturne Op. 9 No. 2*.

Anne played her heart out, and the music floated throughout the house and into the garden.

Cora paused as she was beating batter for a cake. She knew it wasn't Mr. James on that piano. This was music on a grand scale, like nothing she'd ever heard before.

Florence paused in making a bed. She tiptoed down the hall and was surprised to see the new missus at the piano. She hadn't known she played, but it was beautiful, and she was loathe to go back to making beds. It seemed to lift her beyond the mundane.

CHAPTER XVII

O give thanks unto the LORD; for he is good;
for his mercy endureth for ever.

I CHRONICLES 16:34

MACKIE GASPED IN SURPRISE, KNOWING IT WAS Miss Anne at the piano. Her heart warmed to the new mistress, who was polite and interested in the workings of the house. Mackie knew what was what, and she knew the master of Mobrey Manor had found himself a jewel—a diamond so to speak. But they were not sleeping in the same bed—ever —and it worried her. She sat in the room off the kitchen, mending a crochet tablecloth that had been James' mother's. It was delicate work, but she could think of nothing more enjoyable to accompany her crocheting than listening to someone who could play Chopin the way the new mistress could.

James had been laughing with the children over a bunny rabbit who'd scampered away at their approach, but they could see it hiding under a bush. As soon as the puppies saw it, they scrambled after it, bumping into each other. When the music reached his ears, James plopped down on a bench and watched, unseeing, as the children played with the three puppies.

Anne plays, he thought. *No, she doesn't just play, the way I do—she's an artiste.*

James and Bates sat on a garden swing and let the music pour over them. James laughed at himself and spoke to Bates.

"I played the piano this past week, not for pleasure but to try and impress my new wife. That's a jest on me." He chuckled but prayed silently in his heart. Oh my precious Lord, I give you thanks. You have given me a woman with whom I seem to have much in common. I pray she comes to love me. I pray I can be the man you want me to be and care for my new family. Help me to love Anne and the children.

The waiter saw Jenny standing at the entrance to the dining car, and picking up a pot of coffee, he led her to a midcar table.

She thanked him and ordered, knowing the menu by heart.

"Ma'am, today will be your last day on the train." As he spoke, he poured her a cup of strong coffee.

"Thank you," she replied and added, "Oh my! I'm so excited to see my granddaughter. I want to thank you for all your explanations and taking time to answer my questions."

"You are welcome, ma'am. It's been my pleasure. Although this route is beautiful summer and winter, sometimes it begins to pall. Having you ask questions has made this trip enjoyable for me."

Jenny smiled a thank-you at him. She hadn't looked out the window, being engrossed in conversation, but when she did, she gasped in wonder.

"What is that mountain range? Goodness me, it's so close I feel I could reach out and touch it."

The waiter beamed.

"That, ma'am, is the Sierra Nevada Mountain Range. It begins in Canada and extends all the way into Mexico. We're heading straight for it. Colfax, California, is our next stop. It's a hundred miles from Reno, and it's incredibly steep going. You'll almost want to get off the train and help push it up the grade, it's so steep. Once we reach the summit, we have just one hundred five miles all downhill to Sacramento. We'll most likely be there by early afternoon."

"I have to say, I've enjoyed every single day riding on this train. None of it has bored me in the slightest, but I'll be glad to arrive at my destination too. I understand I will be transferring to another train—is that correct?"

"Yes, and I've talked to a porter who will be happy to help you make that connection."

"Thank you, sir." A niggling worry lifted from her shoulders.

The waiter left, and she sat enjoying the scenery while she ate bacon, eggs, hash browns, and toast. She drank a second cup of coffee and made her way back to her berth. The waiter had told her that as soon as she finished, she needed to get back to her compartment, as the train would start the arduous climb to Colfax. He'd said sixty-two miles of the hundred-mile run to Colfax was all tunnels and she'd experience pitch darkness and needed to be seated. Upon entering the first tunnel, she was glad to be safely seated. It felt eerie to be enclosed in such darkness…she couldn't even see her hand in front of her face.

Like heavy shutters flung open to the sun, sudden light at the end of each tunnel was startling. The snow deepened as the train climbed. It lay in deep drifts. Jenny felt it was a perfect time to travel up the Sierra Nevada Mountains.

As she sat in the darkness, she thought back over the years and at how tied down she'd always been.

She'd had her coming-out ball and all the frills that went with it the summer of her sixteenth year. Marcus Tarkington had moved to Jamestown that summer, and her parents thought him a promising match for their daughter. She's always thought she'd marry Herbert and was surprised when her parents chose Marcus. She'd just turned seventeen when she was married Marcus, not for love but out of obedience.

Six months before her marriage, her father had invested in a new product coming out on the market, but it never brought in any money. Within a few months of her wedding, he had liquidated all his assets, pouring money into the product. He'd taken a gamble but lost everything. Not able to bear the scorn of friends or the deep sense of shame, he'd said farewell to his wife and daughter and departed for parts south, never to be seen again. Jenny's mother was alone and with no income.

Jenny had asked, then pleaded, with her new husband to take in her mother, but Marcus refused. He was involved in money schemes, gambling, and drinking too much. He was found dead one night in a hotel room. The coroner ruled it was from natural causes, never knowing what had killed the young man. No mark was found on him. Gossip raged through the small town, but Jenny went about her daily business, holding her head high through it all. She was expecting a baby.

Her mother moved in with her, and the two of them had earned a meager income from tailoring clothing, taking in laundry, and selling baked goods to make ends meet.

Herbert had waited a decent time and then asked for her hand in marriage, but she'd turned him down. Looking back, she realized it was pride that kept her from accepting him. He was a good, kind, and gentle man, but she'd wanted no handouts, not considering that he might actually love her. He'd never asked her again.

She and her mother raised her son, Justin, trying to give him the best of everything. He'd married a sweet young girl who loved him deeply. Jenny's mother passed away shortly after Justin's marriage, and Jenny was left with half the income she'd previously made. Justin helped out as he could, but what had been a saving factor in the finances of Jenny had been Marcus' father, who'd died suddenly. He'd left Jenny all his worldly goods. She sold his house, which had provided plenty to live on if she was careful, and she was.

When Justin and his wife were killed in a train derailment, Jenny had been nearly inconsolable. It'd been Anne, Justin's two-year-old-girl, who got her through that horrible time. She'd poured herself into Anne's upbringing, seeing her education was supplemented with arts and scraping money together for piano lessons. She'd been delighted when the neighbor's son, Billy Hargreaves, had fallen in love with her Anne. What a blow to Anne when Billy's parents squashed that connection. Jenny had secretly mourned but had been a tower of strength for Anne.

Now, here she was on her way west, and Anne was married. Jenny prayed the man was a good one. She wondered why Anne hadn't asked her to the wedding or even let her know she had a beau. She spoke aloud to herself as the train entered another dark-as-pitch tunnel.

"Well, she's a grown woman and has taken her time marrying. Afraid of men, after that Billy, I imagine," she said to herself. "Hope he's good to her. Wonder if I'll live with them. Mayhap, he won't want me living there with them, same as Marcus didn't want my mother. Well, time will tell. I like being on my own anyway. Didn't think I would, but I'm feeling my oats, so to speak." She grinned at her reflection in the large window.

The train left the tunnel and climbed the steep incline, chugging away at an incredibly slow pace. Jenny sat gazing at cliffs piled with snow. An eagle circled lazily in the distance. Her view was suddenly cut off, and it was black as night, again. The train was slow but sure. It took a long time, seemingly endless in the dark, but eventually the train made the summit. Finally leveling, the locomotive rolled into Colfax. It felt good to be back in the sunlight. Jenny stood and stretched.

"Another hundred miles, and all downhill!"

She gathered her things and was amazed she could get by on so little. While they were stopped, she took a quick sponge bath and changed into a clean traveling dress. It was wrinkled, but she felt better cleaned up. The porter said her next train would be without Pullman cars, so she'd be sitting with other people. He also told her not to worry about getting off in a hurry, as the train would have a long stop because it had to take on more fuel for the steam engine. There'd be no immediate rush.

It seemed no time at all between Colfax and Sacramento, as the train seemed to make up for its previous slowness climbing to the summit. The big locomotive streaked down the mountain toward Sacramento.

Snow drifts grew smaller and smaller, and soon the landscape was a sea of green. Fields dotted with all sorts of wildflowers and scrub oak quickly made an appearance, and it was almost a shock to see after days of snow.

It wasn't long before Jenny heard the call. "Next stop...Sacramento, California. Next stop...Sacramento, California."

She put her hat on, threw her shawl around her thin shoulders, and gathered up her satchels. She said a goodbye to the room as she closed the door to her compartment for the last time. She strolled slowly down the aisle toward an exit and stood behind several people with whom she had a polite nodding acquaintance. Others lined up behind her.

The train slowed and finally came to a complete halt. She alighted, and a porter took her by the arm to lead her toward the back of the train, where they were off-loading. The cobblestone platform was solid under her feet, and the lack of a swaying floor seemed strange. It reminded her of when she'd changed trains in Chicago. The transfer of belongings had gone smoothly, and she'd had time to send a telegram to Anne to give her the specific time of her arrival, barring any mishaps along the way.

Jenny had several trunks and pieces of furniture wrapped in blankets. As she arrived to the back of the train to collect her things, she heard a cry, and turning her head, she saw Anne running toward her, arms outstretched.

"The train's coming! The train is coming!" Thaddeus ran across the station platform, yelling the information everyone within hearing distance already knew. Looking back over his shoulder at the train in the distance, he tripped and fell. Before Anne could even react, James was lifting him to his feet.

"You all right, Thad?" he asked.

"Yes, just scraped a knee. I didn't see that ring poking up on the platform. What's it for anyway?"

James started to reply, but the train rumbled closer, and he couldn't be heard, so he stopped talking.

Blood dripped down Thad's leg, and Anne took her handkerchief, dabbing at the boy's knee.

Ginger had plugged her ears against the noise. The earsplitting whistle pierced the air again as the train, blowing smoke, chugged its huge weight slowly into the train depot of Sacramento. Brakes had been applied, and the train slowed. Metal on metal, it screeched to a halt.

Anne's heart beat faster in anticipation of seeing Grandma Jenny.

For some reason the telegram had been delayed for several days. It had arrived only yesterday, and plans had quickly been laid to leave for Sacramento. The newly formed family, along with Lucas and Bates, had taken the buckboard, with its long flatbed, and the large carriage as far as Vallejo, where they'd spent the night. They had taken the early train from there to Sacramento, where they ate a quick luncheon at a waterfront restaurant.

Anne was tired. She'd barely slept a wink. She'd shared a bed with Ginger, and James had slept with Thaddeus. She was excited to see her grandma as she stood watching the porters opening the train's doors. People began to stream out. She wondered what her grandma would think of her hasty marriage and adoption of these two children. They stood back against the wall of the station, the better to see where Grandma Jenny would exit the train.

James, his blue eyes shining into her violet ones, spoke to Anne over the heads of the children standing between them. "Don't worry about us. We"—he nodded his head toward Lucas and Bates, who were deep in conversation—"will watch the children."

She smiled at him in a quick glance of understanding, not wanting to miss her grandma coming out. "Thank you. I appreciate—oh! There she is! Grandma!" She walked with quick steps to Grandma Jenny as she made her way down the last step. "Oh, Grandma Jenny! How I've missed you!" She didn't know why the tears came even as they streamed down her cheeks. She knew her grandmother didn't have patience with what she called "public displays of emotion," but at this point, Anne didn't care.

She hugged her grandma, and Jenny, who didn't have time for such folderol, dropped her satchels right there on the platform and hugged right back.

Anne pulled away, the better to see into her grandma's eyes. Grandma Jenny, too, had tears. They kissed each other and hugged again as James and the children drew up behind them.

A man started to pick up a satchel, and Grandma Jenny was ready to hit him with her umbrella for stealing it.

Anne lifted her hand to stop her grandma. "It's all right, Grandma Jenny. That's Lucas. He's with us." She laughed through her tears, and her grandma did too.

"Sorry, young man. I reckon I'm not thinking too straight right now. And who is this?" she asked as she looked at James holding the hands of two children. Her instantaneous thought was that Anne had gotten herself married to a widower. *He looks awfully young to have children this old*, she thought.

"Grandma Jenny, er, Jenny Tarkington, please meet my husband, James Mobrey, and our children, Ginger Rae Parker, I mean Mobrey, and Thaddeus Loren Mobrey. We three"—she pointed at the children—"are new to being Mobreys. James, please meet my best friend and grandmother, Jenny Rae Tarkington. Oh my goodness, I never thought of it until just now, but you, Ginger, could have been named after my grandma. You both have the same middle names."

"I'm right pleased to meet you, James...I may call you James, mayn't I?"

"Of course, and I'm pleased to meet you, and I also welcome you to come live with us."

They took a long look at each other and smiled in recognition of a common love...for in that moment, James realized he loved Anne, deeply and forever.

Jenny turned to the children and said, "I'm Grandma Jenny, and I'm pleased to meet you, Ginger and Thaddeus."

"We're pleased to meet you too," Thaddeus said. He sketched a bow, and Ginger bobbed her head in acknowledgment and also gave her new grandmother a sweet curtsey.

She slipped her hand into this woman's hand, who looked as if she would care about everyone around her.

It surprised Jenny, and she squeezed the girl's hand lightly, as if to say they were now related. She wondered that the boy had spoken for his older sister, but Jenny didn't look curious or voice her question.

Anne said, "Oh, Grandma Jenny, I have so much to tell you!"

"Well," her grandmother said in a dry tone, "I expect it'll have to wait until we collect my things." She started down the platform with Ginger in tow, almost having to run to keep up.

Anne, right behind them, glanced back at the startled men and laughed. Her grandmother never let any grass grow under her feet. The men, along with Thaddeus, hurried toward the back of the train.

Chapter XVIII

*A word fitly spoken is like apples of
gold in pictures of silver.*

PROVERBS 25:11

HATTI WAS AMAZED HOW QUICKLY CHLOE was learning to read. The two had only spent a week together, and yet Chloe was learning to read out of the 1805 edition of the *New England Primer*.

Chloe, having been led to believe girls couldn't achieve or amount to much, applied herself heartily to learn all she could. It made her angry that both her dad and uncle had caused her to feel she was not worth teaching.

Her heart was sad when she thought about her father. He hadn't cared for her physical needs much, but she had always been with him, and she missed him terribly. She was surprised that she enjoyed being around Buck, but she adored Hattie. Hattie was everything she thought a woman should be.

"Is this all there is to learn?" she asked. "What I mean is, if I was to go to school, would this be all the book learning I would get?"

"No, child," Hattie replied. "You would begin to learn to count and begin learning Latin, Greek, and history."

"What's Latin?"

"It's another language."

"I don't know anyone who talks in another language, so why would I want to learn it?"

"Because the language you speak has many words that come from Latin, and Greek as well. By learning those languages, you could become a doctor or teacher or whatever you'd like to be when you grow up."

"Can I go to school?"

"Well..." Hattie said, "I don't know if you can go until you learn to read." She thought about the consequences of Chloe going out in public. "What's going to happen when your uncle finds out where you are?"

"I don't want to live with him no more."

"Anymore," Hattie corrected.

"Anymore. I don't want to live with someone who told me I'd never amount to nothing."

"Anything."

"He told me I'd never amount to anything. That because I was a girl...oh, never mind. I reckon it was why I was trying so hard to be a boy. I like being a girl, but I don't like wearing dresses. They're not very comfortable, are they?"

"Well, honey, I don't rightly know. I've never worn anything in my life but dresses. I know someone who does wear something close to trousers yet still looks very, ah, very womanly."

"Can I meet her?"

"I suppose you can. She's a wonderful person. She's married to the man who, uh, to the man who was tied up in the kitchen where Buck found you."

"I heared he was dead."

"Heard."

"I heard he was dead."

"Not that man—the other man. Your pa tied him up after he bashed him over the head."

"Yeah, I saw him do it. I was up in the loft of the barn, playing. I saw that man what caught me."

"Who."

"I saw the man who caught me come into the barn, and my pa was right behind him." Chloe wiped at her eyes with the skirting on her dress. "I miss my pa. I miss him somethun horrible."

"I'm sorry, sweetheart." Hattie wrapped her arms around the young girl and picked her up, sitting her on her lap in a rocking chair. "I am so sorry. It's hard to lose someone you love."

Chloe slipped her arms up and around Hattie's neck. She closed her eyes, loving the closeness and the good clean smell of her.

Buddy Blake stretched, lifting his arms up high. He took a big breath of the fresh air, coughing a bit. He felt sore from sleeping on the ground and chilled from the early-morning breeze. He started a fire, laying it so little smoke rose. Taking a tin pot, he filled it half full from the nearby stream, thinking where he'd holed out was a perfect place to hide. He dumped some coffee into the pot and waited for it to boil.

While he waited, he fed his horse and then sat down on a short log near the fire. He pulled out a pouch of tobacco from his breast pocket and a packet of thin papers to roll a cigarette. He curled the paper around his left index finger and poured some baccy into the little tunnel. He expertly rolled the paper back and forth a bit before the final roll, and licking the edge, he sealed it. He stuck it into his mouth but took it out and spit out the loose tobacco on his tongue. He didn't waste another match to light it. He took a thin little stick and held it to the fire until it glowed, lifted it to his cigarette, and drew on it. Once it was lit, he threw the stick onto the fire.

He sat figuring out a plan of action. He wondered if he should ride back into Napa and see if the barkeep knew anything. *Maybe Rudy ain't dead. I feel in my gut he is, but iffen he is, what's happened to Sweet Pea? I cain't see anyone shootin' a little kid. She's got ta be around here somewheres, an' I'm gonna find 'er.*

He enjoyed his smoke. The air was cold, but a fine day was on its way. He was thankful it wasn't raining. He stood and placed a cast-iron griddle on the fire to heat. He let the pan get hot as he dug into a pouch to get some bacon out of the newsprint it was wrapped in. He plunked it onto the griddle, and it sizzled, a pleasing sound. Once it was nearly done, he added eggs. He sat on the log, and Buddy's mouth watered in anticipation of a hot breakfast. Once finished, he picked up the pan, his fork, and plate and went to the stream to clean them, using sand and gravel as a scraper for the utensils and pan. He put his things into the cave and straightened his bedroll. Going back to the log to have another cup of coffee and a smoke, he sat thinking about riding into Napa, but he couldn't think of what to do beyond that. He rinsed out his cup, kicked dirt onto the fire, and saddled up his horse.

Buddy rode leisurely, with no hurry, into Napa. He headed straight to the saloon and tied up his horse. Stepping on the boardwalk, he pushed through the double doors. No one took much notice of him, and he strode to the bar.

"Shot of whiskey," he said.

Harkin nodded and turned to get a shot glass. "Here ya go, sir. Have ya found your brother yet?"

Buddy stared at him, wondering if he should say anything. He decided if he wanted any information, he'd most likely get it here.

"No. I'm supposed to be meetin' up with my brother and his kid. You seen 'em?"

"Naw. We get a lot of strangers in here ever' week, but I ain't seen one with no kid."

Buddy nodded his head. "No one come lookin' fer me, huh?"

"Waal now," Harkin replied, "I wasn't sayin' that. Sheriff comed in here th' other day lookin' fer some stranger. Don't rightly know iffen it be you or not."

"Nah, he ain't lookin' fer me." Buddy didn't bat an eye. "Did he say what he wanted?"

"Nope, jest said he wanted ta talk ta you iffen you came in here." Harkin smoothed back his hair in a nervous gesture, seeing the glitter in the man's eyes.

"No lawman's a lookin' fer me. I can tell you that straight up. Anybody die around here lately?"

"Matter of fact, someone did turn up his toes. Ole man Hedley died a few days ago. Never heard what happened. He was fixin' ta move ta San Francisco ta be close ta his daughter. Poor girl. It'll be in a real shock ta her, an' no mistake. Dan hadn't seemed all that sick afore. Jest saw 'im a couple weeks ago, an' he seemed right fit. Iffen ya want ta know about yer brother, the sheriff'll most likely know. His office is right across the street and down a few doors ta the left."

Buddy upended his shot of whiskey and plunked the glass on the counter. "Thanks fer the information. Maybe I'll go talk ta 'im."

He strolled unhurriedly out the door, and looked both ways. Because he knew the bartender's eyes were on him, he walked across the dusty street. He turned left, and when he was out of sight, he circled back to get his horse, untied it, and led it down the street a bit before he climbed on and cantered out of town.

"I'm gonna stick around here till I find out what happened ta Rudy." He spoke aloud to himself in a determined voice. "Come hell or high water, I'm gonna find out what happened to 'im."

Jenny Tarkington gave directions to Lucas and Bates as well as James. They were grabbing her trunks, being off-loaded by the train crew, and setting them on a wide wheeled cart. Thaddeus was trying to help, but most things were too heavy.

"I'll go get another cart," he said. Several long carts were lined up against the station for the purpose of hauling things from the train to waiting wagons or, as in this case, to the next train. He scampered off and was soon back with another huge flatbed cart.

There were several pieces of furniture wrapped in blankets and tied with ropes, and quite a few trunks, large and small.

Jenny looked at her granddaughter and said a little smugly, "I brought Piano Keys and Fortissimo."

Anne gasped, putting her hand to her mouth in astonishment. "Oh, Grandma Jenny! Oh my. Oh, I am so thankful!" She grabbed her grandma by the shoulders and hugged her, tears starting in her eyes at her grandmother's generosity.

"Who's Piano Keys and Fortissimo?" Thaddeus was curious.

Ginger and James stopped loading, and James asked, "Yes, who are they?"

"My horses. Oh, Grandma Jenny, I can't believe you spent that much money, but I'm more grateful than I can say."

"I know, child. I know. Sold my house to Herbert, and he paid me outright. I know how much you love your horses. They're back there in the boxcar near the end. We'll need to get them out. Is there a cattle car or boxcar for animals on the train to Valley Joe?"

"It's pronounced Va-lay-ho, Mrs. Tarkington." Thaddeus spoke seriously. "Almost all the *j*'s in California are pronounced like an *h* because they are Spanish names."

With a twinkle in her eye, Grandma Jenny said, "So in a couple months it'll be Hune and then Huly?" She smiled at her jest, while Thaddeus laughed heartily.

Ginger's lips curved up into laughter, but she made no noise. Jenny was still not certain but suspected the girl couldn't talk.

"No! The months are still called June and July." Thaddeus was still laughing.

"You all"—she included James in her look—"are to call me Grandma Jenny. We are all family. We'd best be getting those horses out and onto the next train."

"Oh my, he's simply gorgeous!" James said. He was impressed as well as astounded.

Anne led Piano Keys down the ramp. James took the rope harness from her and held it while Anne went back up the ramp and into the boxcar to get Fortissimo. She started to lead him down the ramp, but he was skittish and wouldn't step onto it. Anne halted him before going down. Stroking his neck and speaking love words in his ear, she said, "Come on, boy. You can do this. Come on now." She tugged on the rope, but he wouldn't budge, pulling back against her. She let him shake his head and spoke calmly to him for a couple minutes. But before trying to lead him down again, she took her shawl and wrapped it around his head to blindfold him. He went down the ramp with no problem. Anne walked down, close beside him. As she unwrapped her shawl, James spoke again.

"Oh, Anne, they're gorgeous! So striking! They're tobianos, aren't they? Just look at those blue eyes."

Anne's face expressed her amazement that James would know what kind of paint horse she had. "Yes, they are tobianos, and I love them!" She stroked Fortissimo's side as she spoke.

The two horses were geldings. Both stood proudly, their necks arched as they pranced a bit. They were black-and-white paints—hence their names were taken from *music* and *piano*.

"Reckon we'd best be heading down to the other train," Jenny said.

Lucas pushed one cart heavily ladened with trunks, and Thaddeus and Ginger pushed the other one that wasn't loaded quite as much. They walked ahead of the horses. James strolled along beside Anne, who was leading Fortissimo, while Bates led Piano Keys behind them. The luggage was loaded in short order by the train workers, and James gave them a healthy gratuity. Anne had to lead Fortissimo up the ramp, as he seemed to want to bolt.

Anne said with a laugh, "For sure he doesn't like ramps!" Once the horses were in the boxcar, she and James headed to the passenger car, where the rest of the group were already seated.

James helped Anne onto the train, his hand lingering on her waist. Ginger wanted to sit with Jenny, so Thaddeus sat on the other side of Ginger, next to the window. Anne, whose cheeks were rosy, sat next to James on the bench seat facing Jenny and the children.

James, with his sudden self-acknowledged awareness of his love for Anne, wanted to drape his arm around his wife but contented himself with the occasional brush of her arm next to his. He knew without a doubt that this woman was someone he would hold precious. He could only hope Anne would come to love him. He listened as she and her grandma talked, catching up on news from Virginia. He was glad Anne didn't talk about the children in front of them. It showed sensitivity, and he was grateful for it.

"So, when I received your telegram," Jenny said. "I had little to do, as I've been nearly packed up for a month. Walked over to Herbert's and sold my house to him in less than two shakes of a lamb's tail. Well, it took a half hour, and next day he went to the bank and withdrew the entire amount and paid me outright. I felt pretty flush, so I decided your horses should come too. Truth to tell, I didn't have the heart to sell either one of them."

"I can't thank you enough for doing that for me. I…I…"

"Oh, don't fash yourself, child. I had the means to do it, and it pleased me to do so. Now, tell me how you two met."

Anne colored up and spoke in a hesitant voice. "Can we talk about that a little later, please?"

Jenny's eyebrows rose, and she looked sharply at James, who sat looking content and a bit smug. He looked at Jenny with humor and love clearly shining forth from his eyes. Jenny chuckled and knew there was quite a story here; she looked forward to hearing it.

The train started slowly but soon gained momentum, and Thaddeus leaned forward and bounced a little on his seat, trying to help the locomotive on its way.

He glanced over to see James' eyes on him and stopped bouncing, but then he realized James' eyes were warm and full of love. They were not censuring him for bouncing. Thad smiled back but turned to look out the window. *I've been loved all my life. My ma and pa loved me, and Ginger loves me, but this man, James, barely knows me, and yet I can see the love he has for me. It's not only in his eyes but in the way he treats me…as if I were something precious. It makes me want to mind him and please him in every way I can. I know him to be a man of God, righteous in all he does.*

Thad listened with half an ear to Anne and Grandma Jenny talking. He felt sorry that Ginger could not enter into the conversation. He remembered his ma saying Ginger was like a parrot she'd seen at a circus. It never stopped talking. Ginger used to be able to sing too. She had a pretty voice, and now it was silent. He turned his head to look at her, wondering how awful it must be to not be able to talk. He thought it strange that she hadn't been hurt by the Indian, and yet she'd been so scared it took her voice right out of her.

Ginger felt his eyes on her and turned to stare at her brother. She saw love and concern for her, and he squeezed her hand to let her know he loved her. She smiled and turned back to listen to Grandma Jenny talk about a going away party some friends had given her. Ginger wanted to tell her that some friends of theirs had a party for them, wishing her ma and pa well and a good journey to California. Ginger looked down at her lap, thinking of the hardships they'd endured on the trail. She'd not prayed since the day her ma was killed. She had decided there was no God. If there was, and He let such bad things happen, then she didn't want to have any part of Him.

They got off the train in Vallejo, and because the day was fast fading, James decided they would stay at the inn for the night.

Once again Anne covered Fortissimo's eyes with her shawl, and he came out of the boxcar with no problem. Anne and James led the horses to a stable. Lucas, along with Bates, loaded up the long flatbed wagon with Jenny Tarkington's belongings, covering the trunks with a tarp and crisscrossing a rope to hold everything in place. James had the wagon moved to the stable, and after checking to make sure all was in order, he went back to the inn.

Jenny, always aware of her surroundings, realized Thad had put his things in James' room. He was sleeping in the same room as James, and

Anne was sharing a room with Ginger. She had her own room and was glad, as she knew she snored some but would deny it with her dying breath.

CHAPTER XIX

Hast thou commanded the morning since thy days;
and caused the dayspring to know his place?

JOB 38:12

THE STAFF OF SUNRISE RANCH HAD BEEN let off to have a few days to themselves while Eden and Adam Brown attended another meeting in San Francisco. It was a rarity for Hattie to enjoy the kitchen without Berry, the Browns' cook. She was grateful to her nephew, Adam, for allowing Buck and her to stay with them while their house was being built. Hattie was excited that the house was almost finished. She, like Buck, was getting antsy to settle into their own home.

She pulled a loaf of zucchini nut bread out of the cooler as she hummed to herself. The week before, she'd shredded up the last of the zucchini she'd stored over the winter and had made the last four loaves. It'd be a few months before there was more. She thought it was nice that the Browns had some acreage in nut trees. Most of Sunrise Ranch was in olives. Nuts always came in handy for cooking. She took out a sheet of paraffin paper and wrapped the loaf, tucking in the ends. She found a jar of raspberry jam she'd put up herself and carefully put it and the bread into a satchel.

Going over to the stairs, she called out. "Chloe darling, are you ready? I've had Pepe saddle up our horses. We'll probably stay for lunch. Come on, now. It's time to go."

Chloe came running down the hall and down the steps, jumping the last three to land on the floor.

"Are you related to a kangaroo?"

"What's a kangaroo? That's a funny name…kangaroo."

"A kangaroo is an animal that hops around on its hind legs. They have a large tail that helps them balance, and they have short front legs compared with their big, muscly back legs. Remind me when we get back from the Bannisters' Rancho, and I'll dig out a picture of a kangaroo so you can see what they look like." Hattie looked carefully at Chloe. There were dark circles under her eyes, as if she hadn't slept well.

"Hattie…I bin thinking." Chloe could feel Hattie's eyes on her, and she thought it was time to divert her attention.

"I have been, or I was thinking," Hattie said to Chloe with a smile.

"I have been thinking. I don't ever want to go back to live with Uncle Buddy. Can I just start calling you Mama and live here forever?"

Hattie almost crumpled with relief but tried to speak calmly. Her voice trembled a little. She wondered if that was what had caused the smudges under Chloe's eyes. Maybe the girl was worrying she'd have to go back to her uncle Buddy.

"Chloe, there's nothing I'd like better. I love you as if you really were my own daughter, and you can be that for me. I'm afraid I fell for you like a ton of bricks the first moment I laid eyes on you." She scooped Chloe up into her arms and danced around and around until they were both laughing uncontrollably, when Buck walked in.

"Hello, darlin'," he said.

He hugged Hattie right around Chloe's little body, and she liked the feeling of love she felt emanating from this couple. She'd never, in her life, seen her pa kiss her ma the way Buck kissed Hattie. He bent her backward sometimes, and the room seemed to sizzle like bacon when it hit the pan. Chloe loved the feeling. Buck kissed her on the cheek, and she grabbed his neck and gave him a squeeze.

"I'm your daughter now," she said proudly. "I'm gonna call Hattie Mama and I'm gonna call you Papa. I called my own pa, just that…Pa. So don't worry none about me getting anything mixed up. I just don't ever want to go live with Uncle Buddy again."

Buck kissed her other cheek and said, "I'll like having you for a daughter. The only thing is, you have to mind us. You're not an adult yet, but we'll treat you well. Have you ever had a spanking?"

"Are you jesting? What kid hasn't had a spanking? I've had lots of them."

"We don't spank unless it's necessary, young lady. I hope I don't have to spank you. It will make me sad in my heart," Hattie said.

Chloe just stared at Hattie, surprise sparking from her eyes.

Hattie set her down easily back onto the floor.

"Where're you two going anyway?" Buck asked. "I see your satchel here, and Pepe's saddled up your horses."

"We're riding over to Bannisters'. Want to come with us?"

"Be happy to. You're going to be there for lunch, aren't you?" he asked with a smile. "I love that Mexican food Conchita makes, don't you?"

"Yes, I do." Hattie smiled, a little dimple appearing by the corner of her mouth. Her eyes sparkled with love for her husband. They'd been married less than a year.

Chloe didn't know that. She simply saw the love and care for each other like nothing she'd ever seen before. She knew she had a long way to go because her temper could fly at the drop of a hat, but she wanted to stay here and be with these people who seemed so full of love and concern for her. She'd never had attention the way she had it now. Her ma had always been too busy working from sunup to sundown to show her much of anything. She hadn't been a demonstrative woman, and Chloe couldn't remember having flesh-on-flesh contact with anyone unless it was riding with someone on a horse. No one had ever taken much time with her.

"I'm all ready to go," she said as she picked up her own satchel. "I want to try some of that Mexican food you bin talking about."

"You have been talking about," Hattie said, smiling at Chloe. She added, "Let's be on our way then."

Chloe couldn't believe she had her own horse. She had gone with Buck two days earlier and picked out a horse from a stable down the road. At first she thought he was going to give her the horse that belonged to Dan Hedley, the man who'd died because her pa hadn't given him any water. Her pa had stuffed his mouth with a dirty kerchief. She didn't want that horse, not that he wasn't a pretty one. He was, but she wanted to forget all the horribleness of taking over that poor man's house and making him die. She'd started to give him some water when they were eating dinner the second night they'd been there. She hadn't wanted to eat in front of him and thought perhaps he'd like a drink. She'd taken the kerchief out of his mouth and had the ladle full of water in her hand, but her pa had knocked it away, spilling it all over the floor. He'd told her if she didn't sit down and eat, she'd go without supper. She'd glared at him and said she'd gladly go without supper, but the man needed a drink. Even Uncle Buddy said, "Aw, Rudy, let 'er give the old man a drink." But her pa had cuffed her on the cheek and yanked her by the arm over to a chair at the table, yelling at her all the while. "You sit yerself down, Chloe, an' eat, right now!" he'd yelled. "I won't have you makin' friends with no stranger. You hear me, girl? And you, Buddy, you keep yer trap shut, you hear?"

She had wanted to yell back and say, "How can I help but hear you with you yelling at me?" but she didn't. It would get her a beating, and she knew it. She'd looked mournfully at the man as her pa stuffed the kerchief back into his mouth. Uncle Buddy hadn't said anything more either.

Last night she'd had a bad dream about it. She'd gotten up in the middle of the night, crying. Then she'd had to use the toilet because she couldn't go back to sleep without getting up. Hattie had asked her this morning if anything was wrong, but she didn't want to tell Hattie what had happened or that her pa was the reason Mr. Hedley was dead.

"I love my horse," she said. "I thank you again fer gettin' me such a pretty one."

"For getting me," Hattie said.

"For getting me such a beautiful horse," Chloe said. "I love her already, and I think she's going to love me." She carefully enunciated her words, and Hattie smiled down at her in approval.

Chloe smiled back. She patted Buck's arm and said again, "I mean it, Papa. I love this horse, and I think she loves me already."

"What are you going to name her?" he asked.

"I bin thinking and thinking about that."

"I have been thinking about that," Hattie corrected.

"I have been thinking and thinking about that." Chloe grinned. "I haven't made up my mind yet."

"Well, let me help you up, and we'll be on our way." He turned to Pepe and said, "Thanks, young man, for saddling up the horses. We won't be back for several hours, so if you want to go fishing or do something on your own, you're welcome to. If you're not here, we can take care of our rides when we return. See you later." He squeezed his knees, and his horse set off down the road.

James awoke early. He'd had a good, deep sleep, but not enough of it. He lay quietly, one arm curled under his head, and thought about his new life.

I can't believe I have fallen so completely in love with Anne. I never thought that could happen. I now have a wife, children, and am responsible for their welfare. I'm grateful I don't have to drudge at some job to keep bread on the table. His thoughts shifted back to Anne. *That was an amazing moment, yesterday, talking with Grandma Jenny. All the sudden I realized I love Anne. I am thankful she is a part of my life. I pray she comes to find she loves me too.*

He arose quietly, so as not to awaken Thaddeus, who slept in the other narrow bed. It was still dark. He slipped on his trousers and shirt, tucking his tails in before buttoning up his fly. He slipped on his vest and sat on the bed. It creaked noisily. He couldn't see Thad, but the boy didn't stir and was still in a deep sleep.

James pulled on the stockings he'd worn the day before. Standing, he groped around the bedpost for his gun belt and slipped it over his shoulder. He picked up his boots, grabbed his Stetson off the dresser, and settled it on his head as he quietly let himself out the door. He sat on the top stair and pulled on his boots. He stood but didn't strap on his gun. He'd wait until he'd taken care of his business. He walked down the hall on the worn red carpeting to the water closet. Funny word, that. He called it a water closet because of Bates, but most Americans called it the toilet. There was a jug beside the wash basin, and he splashed water onto his face, washing away the remains of sleep. He peered at the towel and decided he could air dry. He smelled coffee as he descended the stairs and thought it was early for anyone to be up.

Pushing through the double swinging doors to the inn's dining room, he saw it was empty, and the only light came from a single sconce on the bar. He headed toward what must be the kitchen and heard a pan being banged onto the stove.

"Good morning," he said to a heavyset man's back.

"What's good about it?" the man growled as he turned to look at who was interrupting his thoughts and priorities for breakfast.

"I suppose it's because I'm alive this morning, and the Almighty has dictated in His word that we are to rejoice in the Lord. I could be six feet under, or poor and destitute, or have no legs to walk on. I guess it's all a matter of perspective. And I don't suppose you need nor want to hear a long monologue this early in the morning. I simply came in here because I followed my nose. I'm in search of a cup of coffee. I'm going to go out to watch the sun come up and wondered if I might take a mug of your brew with me. I'll return it when I come in for breakfast. Would that be all right?"

"Hmmph! I reckon...long's I get my mug back. Pot's on the stove." The cook jerked his head toward the huge cooking stove. He was holding a heavy cast-iron skillet, which he plunked down on the stove next to another one just like it.

"Thanks," James said as he poured himself a cup of the wonderful-smelling brew. "I'll get out of your hair and let you carry on. I look forward to eating your breakfast later." He exited before he irritated the man any more than he already had.

The coffee was too hot to drink, which made James happy. He climbed the steep hill behind the inn, and he was winded by the time he reached the top. He'd been careful not to spill his coffee. He sat down on a log facing east overlooking San Pablo Bay. He couldn't see the bay yet, but a thin line of silver stretched itself over the horizon. He sat and drank the coffee, now, little better than lukewarm, but it tasted good, and he enjoyed his solitary state. He again thought of his newly acquired family. He knew he'd have a good relationship with Grandma Jenny. She was a no-nonsense, get-it-done kind of woman.

The sun broke over the horizon, and his thoughts turned to the beauty before him. The gleam of the sun's rays on the water transfixed him. Streaks of light stretched out across the bay in varying shades of yellow, orange, and red. His heart felt full of thanksgiving. He remembered a verse in Job where God spoke to Job about creating the morning. "Hast thou commanded the morning since thy days; and caused the dayspring to know his place?" James smiled as he reflected on the verse. Only God could command the morning to come or the dawn to know its place. Birds began chirping, breaking his reverie, and he heard the mournful call of a quail behind him. The brisk air refreshed him, and the sweat from his climb had cooled, making him shiver in the early-morning light. He upended his mug, drinking down the last bit of coffee.

"Time to get on with the day," he said aloud. He walked down the hill, and careful of his footing, he whistled a happy tune.

Thaddeus awoke to an empty room. It didn't bother him. He was thankful not to hear the snoring from the boy in the open dormitory at school. He'd heard people say when you get tired enough, you'll sleep despite the snoring, but he didn't believe it. If he awoke during the night or didn't get to sleep before the snoring boy did, that was it. Many times he'd gone into the hall with a blanket and slept there so he could get away from the noise.

He'd awakened during the night, but James didn't snore, and Thad had been able to roll over and go back to sleep.

Thad could tell it was morning. The thin organdy curtain might block out prying eyes but, being almost transparent, did little to block the light. He lay with his eyes still closed and thanked God for his new family. Had that curmudgeon at the orphanage in San Francisco had his way, he and Ginger would most likely be separated and living in the poorhouse, laboring for their sustenance.

He prayed that Ginger would find her voice. It was beyond his comprehension that she couldn't talk. It wasn't that she wouldn't...she'd tried and tried. He prayed God would heal her. He knew she'd taken a real shine to Grandma Jenny, who seemed wonderfully nice. He prayed Grandma Jenny would be able to help Ginger. After a quick prayer, he got up and stretched. He opened the door and peeked into the hall, but no one was there. He ran down the hall to the toilet, and after getting back to the room, he dressed quickly. He liked his new clothes. James had taken him into town and bought him some good clothes and some to wear for every day. He had on his good duds right now and loved the feel of the sturdy but soft material.

He started down the stairs, but James was at the bottom, coming up. James beckoned him down and turned, going back down the few steps to wait for him.

"Good morning, Thaddeus," he said, and he bent down and hugged the boy. "I couldn't sleep anymore, so I hiked up a hill and watched the sun come up. It was beautiful. How are you doing this fine morning?"

"I'm doing quite well. I'm hungry, but I don't suppose we'll eat until the women get up."

"Well, I'm sure we can get you something to tide you over. Would you like a blueberry muffin? I'm pretty sure I saw a batch of them sitting on a sideboard in the kitchen when I went to get some coffee earlier. C'mon, and we'll see if we can buy one."

CHAPTER XX

But the stranger that dwelleth with you shall be unto you
as one born among you, and thou shalt love him as thyself.

LEVITICUS 19:34

BUCK, **HATTIE AND CHLOE PULLED UP** in front of the Bannisters' Rancho. Chloe looked around with pleasure, excited to see someplace new.

The drive had swept around in front of a beautiful house. The Rancho was all on one level, and the roof was rounded red tile. The wide front was creamy stucco and had arches all across, which were painted a pale orange on their underside. A large flagstone walk spread itself between the arches and the actual front wall of the house, like a breezeway front porch, only it was level with the ground. Growing on either side of the entrance, orange trees with fruit in every stage of ripeness hung on neatly trimmed branches.

Chloe's mouth watered as she looked at the oranges. She'd only ever had one in her entire life, and it had been delicious. She climbed off her horse, having to slide a bit to hit the ground, and tied the reins carefully to the hitching post.

Hattie spoke down to the tousled redhead. "Chloe, you're going to love the woman who lives here, as well as the cook and…well, everyone. You're going to love everyone."

Donny came out of the stable and welcomed them.

"Who's this?" he asked as he looked down at Chloe.

She turned her greenish eyes to his and saw the clearest, most honest-looking blue eyes she'd ever seen.

"I'm Chloe. I'm their new girl," she said as she jerked her thumb back at Hattie and Buck. "What's your name?"

"I'm Donny Miller, and right pleased to meet you, Miss Chloe." He smiled widely at the cheeky little girl.

Chloe grinned up at him. "No one's ever called me Miss Chloe before, but I likes it."

"I like it," Hattie supplied.

"I like it. I really really like it." Chloe stuck out her hand. "Put 'er there, pardner!"

Donny shook her hand, laughing, and Hattie joined in with no corrections.

A lovely woman came out to greet them.

"Welcome to Rancho Bonito," she said. "Who is this?"

"I'm Miss Chloe Blake, soon to be Rawlins, at your service, an' I'm pleased as punch ta meet cha!"

Hattie put a hand to her mouth to cover her laughter, swallowed, and said, "To meet you."

"Pleased as punch to meet you." She stuck out her hand again.

"I'm delighted to meet you, Miss Chloe." The woman shook her hand. "I'm Liberty Bannister, and you are welcome here. Please come on in. We were just sitting down to lunch and would love for you to join us." She turned to Donny. "Thanks, Donny. Perhaps you wouldn't mind watering their horses?"

"No, I'd be pleased as punch to do it." Donny winked at Chloe, who laughed at his reply.

Chloe followed the woman into the house, thinking Liberty had the smallest waist she'd ever seen on a woman. She was beautiful and seemed like an angel.

They entered the house, and Chloe looked around with pleasure but didn't say anything. She was too absorbed, feeling in her heart a peace that seemed to permeate the very walls of the house.

"Come. Please come in, wash up, and we'll eat," Liberty said, "It's ready. Conchita has made chicken *enchiladas*, which are my favorite, I think. Well, unless she makes something else!" She laughed and pointed to the huge sink in the kitchen. "You can wash up there."

Liberty grabbed Chloe's shoulder, which startled the little girl momentarily as Liberty spun her around to look into warm chocolate eyes.

"Conchita, I'd like you to meet Miss Chloe Blake, soon to be Rawlins." She squeezed the little girl's shoulder, knowing it was this girl's father she had killed.

"Ah," Conchita said, "you ees the leetle girl Matthew, he theenk ees leetle boy." She smiled, and her teeth looked startling white in her swarthy face. "You ees welcome here, Mees Chloe, an' you look nothing like a leetle boy."

Matthew entered the kitchen. He'd been cleaning up and hadn't heard the company arrive.

"Well hello there!" He smiled over at Buck and Hattie and then squatted down to Chloe's level. "You sure had me fooled, little girl. I thought you were a boy. You look really nice cleaned up."

"I'm Miss Chloe Blake, soon to be Rawlins, and it's nice to see you again, sir."

Matthew's eyebrows raised up over Chloe's polite speech. He looked over at Hattie, who was washing her hands, his eyes bright with laughter, but he kept a straight face all the while. He glanced back at Chloe and said, "I like your nice manners, Miss Chloe."

"My new mama is teaching me. I am learning to read and write and everything."

"And she's learning amazingly fast," Hattie said. "She is one smart girl. Here, sweetie, let me wash your hands." She had a wet cloth and washed Chloe's hands.

"I never in all my borned days have had so much cleaning up," Chloe said.

"Born days," Hattie said.

"Born days," Chloe repeated.

"Let's sit down," Liberty said. "Conchita has made a wonderful meal, and we are happy to share it with you. Sit anywhere you like."

She gestured toward the table, and everyone found a place to sit except Matthew, who went to get another chair.

The table was a huge round oak, and there was still room for more people to sit if more chairs had been pulled up to it.

"Let's pray," Matthew said.

He bowed his head as Chloe watched furtively while everyone else bowed their heads and closed their eyes. She squeezed her eyes shut, and all the sudden realized he was praying for her. Her eyes flew open, and she stared at him as he continued to pray.

"And, Lord, we are thankful for Chloe and that Buck and Hattie could make a home for her. Lord, we pray she comes to know You as her Savior, protector, and friend. Help heal her heart of any mourning, and bless the relationship that is growing between her and Buck and Hattie. Lord, we are grateful for this day, this food, and most of all for Your love. We pray in the peerless name of Jesus. Amen."

"Thanks, Mr. Bannister. I never had no one pray for me before like that at dinner."

"I've never had anyone pray for me…" Hattie said.

"I've never had anyone pray for me when we're going to eat," Chloe said. She grinned at Hattie. "An' I didn't say ain't once!"

Conchita, along with Lupe and Luce's help, served up the *enchiladas*. There were *totopos* to dip in salsa along with the *enchiladas*. "*Totopos*," Conchita said, "Eet comed from Zapotec peoples from Oaxaca een Mehico. They baked thees one in clay ovens with salt mixed in the corn masa. Eet ees broken up tortilla. I can use eet een the *tostados*, so we ees dipping the salted ones een the salsa. Ees very good."

Liberty silently perused Conchita. Her accent was heavier than normal, and eyeing her carefully, Liberty realized Conchita was not well. She said a quick prayer for her and got up from the table, excusing herself.

"Conchita, could you please come with me?" she asked. "I have something I want…" She led Conchita down the hall. She hadn't wanted to embarrass Conchita in front of their guests, but she was concerned. Conchita was never ill.

"Conchita, you are not well, are you? Lupe and Luce can take over. I'm sorry about the unexpected company, but in this house, we do not pretend to be well when we are not. I can see you are sick or something. What is wrong?"

"Nuhsing ees wrong, Mees Libbee. I just tired, ees all. Thank you for seeing eet, and I weel lie down now. Thank you." She entered her room and closed the door on Liberty, who was surprised at her acquiescence but also surprised she would close the door on her. Liberty stood for a moment, staring at the door.

She went swiftly down the hall and let herself out the door. She ran to the stable and called out. "Diego! Diego, are you in here?"

Diego came out of the tack room, and Liberty guessed he'd been lying down.

"What's wrong, Diego? Conchita is looking tired and ill, and you don't look so well either."

"Eet be her seester. Lupe and Luce's mama. She ees dying. We no tell the girls, an' they doan know. Her seester, she have something een her tummy, an' the doctor, he say there ees nothing they can do."

The Mobreys were nearly home, the journey long because the heavy-ladened wagons slowed them down.

Anne hadn't said anything to Grandma Jenny about her new home. She wanted to surprise her. Anne knew her grandmother had been sorely disappointed, so many years ago, about Billy Hargreaves not marrying Anne. Grandma Jenny had been happy he'd had money and would be able to provide for her granddaughter. Her hopes had been dashed when he'd broken the engagement. Anne never talked about that time, but its insignificance now made her smile. She hadn't known when she'd married James that he was wealthy, and she was glad in her heart she could honestly say it hadn't influenced her decision. She glanced at him, his smooth hands easily holding the reins. She grinned to herself, thinking, *I don't even know how old he is.*

Her thoughts continued at a rapid pace. *I can scarcely wait until Grandma Jenny sees the house. She's going to swoon with excitement.* Her glance slid sideways to look at her grandmother without being observed. Her thick gray hair was swept up into a fat bun, which was covered by her bonnet. Laugh lines fanned themselves out from her deep-blue eyes, which were examining everything around her. Her clothing was plain but good material, the cuffs and collar white and spotless. Anne wondered how, when traveling on a sooty train, she could still look so fresh and clean.

As if she could hear Anne's thoughts, Jenny turned to her granddaughter. "I declare I do need a bath. I know many people don't bathe much or often, but I enjoy a good hot tub. I feel almost gritty from being on that train, not that it wasn't clean. We can heat some water soon as we get to your place, can't we?" She went on talking without waiting for an answer. "I had such a delightful time traveling." She poked James on the arm and said, "You realize, young man, I won't be a burden on you and your new marriage. I'm sure I'll be able to find a nice little cottage or some house for me to live in. I won't want to cramp up your house having me underfoot all the time, so to speak."

"Oh, I think you should live with us," James replied. "At least until you decide what you want to do. You won't be underfoot, and I'm sure you'll be a great help to Anne." He winked at Anne, who smiled back as if the two of them shared a sweet secret.

"Well, I'll just have to see what's what afore I make up my mind. I'm not one to want to cause anyone more work or undue stress. If I can be of help, well, we'll just see—that's all." Jenny set her lips in a straight line.

Anne nearly laughed with sheer delight in anticipation of arriving home. She hadn't been paying much attention and suddenly realized they'd be turning off the main road within a short time. She looked at Thaddeus and felt like bouncing in her own excitement.

He returned her look and said, "We're almost home."

"Yes," Anne replied, "we're almost home."

They were in the lead wagon. Tied to the back were Piano Keys and Fortissimo. Lucas and Bates trailed behind them in the larger wagon. Jenny hoped she'd find a place deserving of the fine pieces of furniture she'd brought.

James slowed and made the turn off the main road and started up the long lane, which was much smoother than the rutted road. The lane had trees lining it, but they were not yet full grown. The path curved, and the house came into view for the first time.

Jenny gasped audibly. "Oh my!" she said. "Oh my goodness!" She put her hand to her breast as if to quiet her heart as she gazed at the stately mansion.

"Welcome to Mobrey Manor," James said.

Anne giggled. "I think, Grandma Jenny, that we have plenty of room for you to live with us. That is my desire, and I hope you'll feel the same."

"Well, I must say, Anne, you're certainly one to play your cards close to your chest. I've been wondering if you lived in some cabin in the West with marauding Indians, and here you are living in style in a glorious mansion."

When Jenny said "marauding Indians," Ginger looked around with fear in her eyes and sidled closer to Jenny.

Anne saw it and patted Ginger's leg.

"It's all right, Ginger. You don't have to worry about that here. You are safe, and no one is going to hurt you or us. Do you understand me?"

Ginger nodded, but her eyes were like saucers, and she had squeezed herself as close to Jenny as she could get. Jenny, looking surprised, responded by scooping the girl into her lap and holding her close.

Jenny looked up, her attention caught up with the size of the house and the beautiful aggregate walk leading up to the double front doors. Huge windows lined themselves in two stories across the front of the mansion.

James had slowed but didn't stop, driving around to the side of the house and into the back area where a large cobbled courtyard separated the house from the stable.

Dock came out of the stable and stood holding the horses.

"Welcome home, Mr. and Mrs. Mobrey. Welcome home."

"Thanks, Dock. It's good to be home," James responded. "Jenny, I'd like you to meet Abel Murdock, my stableman and handyman. Dock, this is my wife's grandmother, Jenny Tarkington."

"Pleased ta meet you, I'm sure," Dock said as he looked into Jenny's deep-blue eyes.

"And I am glad to make your acquaintance, sir."

"Whoa! Look at those tobianos! Those yours, ma'am?"

"No. They belong to Anne—uh, Mrs. Mobrey."

"Anne's fine. I'm just Anne," she said. "Mrs. Mobrey sounds so formal, doesn't it?"

"They're gorgeous!" Dock said, and added, "Mrs. Mobrey is pleasin' ta me ears, ma'am. I'll stable them before I help with unloading these wagons."

Jenny craned her head up to look at the back of the house, which rose three stories. *It's impressive*, she thought. She was tickled pink that Anne was mistress of this mansion.

James helped the women down, and once on solid ground, Ginger slipped her hand into the crook of Jenny's arm.

Jenny realized Ginger was insecure and wrapped her arm around the girl, hugging her close to her side in a protective manner.

"This is beautiful, young man," she said to James. "What was it you said you did for a living?"

"I don't believe I said." James laughed. "Frankly, I'm a philanthropist and watch how monies are spent in organizations I donate to."

"I think his exact words to me were that he keeps account of expenditures and makes sure the organizations run smoothly. Wasn't that what you told me, James?" Anne asked.

"Yes, I suppose it was." He grinned and added, "Let's show Grandma Jenny her new home."

They went up three steps and entered the back door. Jenny looked around curiously. She nodded in appreciation of the storage and the lines overhead for drying clothes. The ceiling was high, and the long paned glass gave the workplace a cheerful look. The entry to the kitchen was lace-covered glass French doors, centered between long white cupboards for storage. The enclosed back porch sported a modern washing machine like nothing she'd seen before. There was shelving and places for linens and tablecloths in wide, flat drawers. She was amazed that a place for laundry and ironing could conveniently store a multitude of items.

Once inside, Ginger seemed to settle down, and both children ran ahead of the pokey adults, eager to see their puppies and to see if their rooms were the same as when they left.

Jenny was slow entering the kitchen, still surveying the back entry.

Cora bustled in the kitchen, and as the children ran up the stairs, Melody Mackie was coming down.

"Welcome back, children. We missed you! Did your grandma Jenny arrive?" Her voice was always agreeably modulated and her English accent pleasant to the ear.

Thaddeus answered, "Thank you, Mackie. It's good to be back, and yes she did. Ginger really likes her, don't you, Ginge?"

Ginger's head bobbed a quick yes, and she smiled widely at Mackie.

"You're a sweet girl, Ginger, and I'm glad you like your new grandma. You run along up, now. Your dogs have just come in from a romp. I'll go greet the rest of the family." She squeezed Thad's shoulder as she passed him on the steps.

The children went to their rooms, and Mackie headed toward the kitchen, shaking her head, a smile on her lips at the master of this mansion who always brought everyone in by the back door.

CHAPTER XXI

It is a good thing to give thanks unto the LORD,
and to sing praises unto thy name, O Most High:
To shew forth thy lovingkindness in the morning,
and thy faithfulness every night.

PSALM 92:1–2

JENNY WAS BOWLED OVER BY THE gracious grandeur of her granddaughter's new home. She couldn't have imagined such a kitchen. She saw the cook turn as they entered.

"Welcome to Mobrey Manor," she said. "I'm Corabelle Meers, head cook. I don't have a monopoly on this kitchen, and you are welcome to use it any time you wish."

"Thank you," Jenny replied, holding out her hand to shake the hired help's. "I'm Jenny Tarkington and pleased to be here. Thanks, too, for your kind invitation. I'll be sure to clean up after myself if I make use of these beautiful facilities."

The two women looked at each other with complete understanding and mutual respect.

Mackie entered with a gracious air of refinement, and Jenny unconsciously straightened her back.

"Welcome. Welcome to Mobrey Manor," Mackie said as she held out her hand.

Jenny took it unhesitatingly and said, "Thank you. It's nice to feel not only the beauty of the house but the warmth of welcome."

Mackie nodded and said, "I'm Melody Mackie, the housekeeper, and I serve at your pleasure."

Jenny's smile was one of delight as her ears relished the English accent.

"My name is Jenny Francine Tarkington, and I am pleased to make your acquaintance."

The two women eyed each other with some inner knowledge that they would soon be friends.

James observed the interaction with a satisfied look of contentment and the knowledge that because his staff all served God with a whole heart, there were less personality clashes or self-aggrandizing among them.

"Anne, I'd like you to show Grandma Jenny her new home. I need to help get her things unloaded. Could you please show her where her rooms are first? Maybe see if we need to move some of the furniture out of there?"

Anne nodded. "I'd be happy to."

Jenny, meanwhile, took a good look at the kitchen. *It is more than a body could dream up. It looks like a restaurant kitchen. Just look at that,* Jenny thought, *two stoves, a huge fireplace at one end, and look at all those cupboards and drawers. My oh my!*

"Come on. We'll follow James' advice and see if we need to get rid of any furniture before the men start hauling things upstairs."

Anne led Jenny through the dining room and to the front entry, where the flooring was huge black and white tiles set in diamond shapes instead of squares. It was grand, and Jenny's eyes darted here and there trying to take it all in.

Anne led her up the stairs, and Jenny gasped when they stopped on the landing.

"I know, Grandma Jenny. I know. It's gorgeous, isn't it? I love sitting here and reading my Bible and looking out the window at such a beautiful sight."

"But look at that piano! Did James buy it for you?"

"No, he didn't know I played. He plays quite well, and I'm sure sometime we'll play together. There are some nice duets for two piano players, and I think it'd be fun. Come. I want to show you your rooms."

"Rooms?"

"Yes, rooms." Anne grinned at her grandmother with sparkling violet eyes full of laughter as she led her up to the second-floor landing.

Jenny stared in awe.

"I'm laughing at myself. When I was in Jamestown, I thought of coming out to the old rustic West, and here I stand in a house the Hargreaves would envy."

"Oh, Grandma Jenny! You don't still harbor any regret that Billy never married me, do you? That was six long years ago, and I've certainly grown up since then. Billy was a childhood friend, nothing more. I don't know if I ever really loved him romantically. I believe I was in love with the idea of being married to him more than loving him for himself. He was incredibly shortsighted and immature. No, I don't believe if I'd stopped to really think about marrying him and all it entailed, that I would have."

Jenny looked at her granddaughter with the revelation that she was a woman, not a child, her mind bright and uncluttered by past might-have-beens.

"You're right, you know. He was immature, but I thought you loved him. You certainly moped for a long time after the broken engagement. I'm thankful to know you aren't holding on to memories that gloss over reality. So often I think we humans look back on situations with rose-colored glasses. It's important to live our fullest in the here and now. Yes, we may have wonderful memories, but we are never too old to make more wonderful ones."

The two women had stopped in the wide hall. Anne hugged her grandma, who hugged her right back.

"I'm so glad you're here. I praise the Almighty for His bountiful provision and for your safe and wondrous trip west. I am grateful He watches over us and we are never alone. I've missed our talks. We're going to have such great times together! Look at this," she said as she threw open the door to the rooms her grandmother would inhabit. "It's a bit sparse on furniture, and we can take out more if you want more room for your things."

Jenny gasped at the beauty of the room.

It was painted a pale salmon with honey-colored trim. This room wasn't the bedroom but a private sitting room with a fireplace on one end. But what was surprising was the light. Long windows along the back wall let in an incredible amount of light. Each window didn't stop at the ceiling but extended inward about two feet, a part of the roof. Glass French doors, in the middle of the glass wall, led out to a balcony. Jenny opened the doors and stepped out onto the wide balcony with wicker chairs and a table looking like an inviting place to sit. The ends of the balcony were walled so it was completely private.

"This is gorgeous. Look at that view," Jenny said.

"I know. I've always loved wisteria, and I think those arches are impressive, aren't they?"

"It's all impressive!" Jenny exclaimed as she gazed out over the landscape and beyond to wooded fields.

They moseyed back inside, and Jenny realized on either side of the door to the hall housed a staggered-shelved bookcase. The bottom half was glassed in a crisscross pattern, and the rest, all the way to the high ceiling, was open. A wooden rolling ladder stood in one corner was, and all was done in the honey oak.

Anne opened another French door of solid oak leading to the bedroom. It too was spacious with many windows. On the far side another door led to the commode room, only there was no commode with chamber pots. Rather, a flush toilet and sink graced the room.

Jenny looked at it in awe. "I've heard about these contraptions, but I've never seen one. My oh my, what will they think up next?"

They both laughed with joy at being together as they went back to the sitting room.

"I think all my things will fit in here just fine."

"Let me show you through the house then," Anne replied.

She led her first into her own rooms and the connecting area to James' rooms, but she didn't open his door. She knocked on both Ginger's and Thad's doors before entering, and Grandma Jenny took time to make friends with the puppies.

"Let's go back to the kitchen, and we'll start from there," Anne said.

They descended the stairs, and Anne showed her grandmother through the beautiful house.

"It's lovely, my dear, just lovely."

"Follow me, Grandma Jenny. There's a lot more to see."

Jenny was amazed at the size of the rooms and all the appurtenances of wealth found in the most minute details. She loved the library and knew she would spend many a happy hour reading. She'd always treated herself to reading at the day's end, but now she would be a woman who didn't need to make her own candles or clothes. Her eyes gleamed with pleasure that Anne had landed on her feet, and no mistake. She was eager to find out the story of how Anne and James met.

Chloe was listening closely to the adults talk. She looked around and wondered where Conchita had gone. As she looked, she liked what she saw of the Bannisters' house. It had a feeling of peace she'd never felt before. She ate quietly, gazing around the spacious, homey kitchen. She'd never known people could live like this. It wasn't just that they had money and nice things. It was this feeling of kinship, of unity. Her pa and ma had argued all the time before her ma died. She would go out to the woodshed and hide so she wouldn't have to hear all the mean things they said to each other. It was as if they'd made each other the enemy. Her pa and uncle Buddy had horrible rows, so awful it scared her. They'd even had fistfights and not spoken to each other for days on end. She wondered at this feeling of harmony.

Chloe sat in pure contentment, enjoying the meal. It was like nothing she'd ever tasted before. She hoped they'd come here again. She liked the salsa and the cheese dripping down the sides of the *enchilada*.

The adults were engrossed in their conversation. Piecing a few things together, Chloe came to the realization that Liberty had shot her pa. She stared at this beautiful woman who could shoot a man. She stared and stared and felt a bit sick to her stomach. She quietly left the table, slipping into the hall. Walking almost the length of it, she noticed one door on the right was closed. She opened it to see the woman who'd cooked the meal sobbing on her bed. Chloe could hear the heart-wrenching sobs and crept into the room. There was space on the edge of the bed, and she crawled up and lay down on the bed, holding the woman's head in her arms.

Conchita was surprised, but undone by her grief. She continued to cry as if her heart was broken. She and her sister were very close. Her sister was several years older, but because of their deep faith as well as being sisters, they were bonded twice over. She was the only one in the world who shared memories of growing up and experiences of joys as well as unbelievable poverty. Conchita, undone by grief, was already mourning her sister.

Chloe just continued to hold this woman who suddenly had become precious to her. She didn't know what was wrong with her, but tears began to slip down her own cheeks as she entered into this woman's grief.

It was some time later that Chloe was missed at the table. Hattie was annoyed she hadn't paid more attention, and Liberty told her that she hadn't heard the front door, so Chloe must be in the house somewhere.

Liberty found her in bed with Conchita, and both were fast asleep.

After quietly closing the bedroom door, Liberty ran back to the great room to let Buck and Hattie know Chloe was all right.

She spoke to them in almost a whisper, not wanting Lupe or Luce to hear. "I didn't say anything while we were eating, but Conchita has found out her sister, Lupe and Luce's mother, has a tumor or something. Diego told me she is dying. I think, Matthew, that you and I should go to San Francisco tomorrow. We could see if Alex's best friend, Danny, would know what to do or if anything can be done for her. We could leave in the morning and take Conchita with us so she can be with her sister. She feels such responsibility for us, and I'm sure she didn't want to cause us concern. Perhaps, when she gets up, we could pray with her and then pack up for a trip to San Francisco."

Matthew nodded. "I'll write out a note and have Donny take it to the telegraph office. We need to let Alex and Emily know we are coming. Maybe we could spend tomorrow night with Elijah and Abigail."

"That's a good idea," Libby agreed.

Hattie said, "Chloe never takes naps. I do hope she's not getting ill or something."

"The way they were sleeping, I think Chloe was trying to console Conchita," Liberty responded. "She's a darling little girl."

"Yes, she is that. It's fun having her around, listening to her views on things. She's smart as a whip and determined to learn. She was told only boys were smart enough to have book learning. I think part of her effort is to prove that theory wrong."

"Well," Matthew said, grinning at his wife, "we all know that's not true. Liberty's had a lot more book learning than me."

Buck said, "If you write up that note to Alex before we leave, we'd be happy to drop it off at the telegraph office for you. I'm sure Chloe would enjoy the extra-long ride."

Buddy had been scouting out the area, and so far he didn't think anyone had seen him. He knew the location of the houses closest to the one he, Chloe, and Rudy had holed up in. They were large ranches, huge spreads, and he didn't know how he was ever going to figure out where Chloe was or what had happened to Rudy.

He sat on top of a ridge astride his horse, looking down over the main road. He saw three riders in the distance and pulled his horse back between two huge boulders, keeping his eyes on the riders. He pulled a spyglass out of his saddlebag and spent a minute focusing. Suddenly, Chloe came into view as plain as day, riding with two adults. He fastened his eye on the man and saw the star pinned to his chest.

"Aha," he said. "Our handsome sheriff has my niece. Fine kettle of fish, but I'll make him pay. Bet he shot Rudy or he's got him in jail. I'm going to find out where he lives and get Chloe back. Poor little Chloe. She'll be happy to see me, I reckon."

The three riders rode abreast, clearly not noticing anyone behind them. When they got to town, the sheriff took the lead and headed for the telegraph office, with the woman and Chloe trailing behind.

Buddy Blake, who had followed them, pulled up by the bank and waited to see what would happen next. He couldn't hear what the sheriff said but could see him speaking.

"I'll only be a minute," the sheriff said as he dismounted.

He strode into the building as Buddy watched, biding his time. He was in no hurry. He heard Chloe laugh at something the woman said, and it angered him that she could be so disloyal. He wondered if Rudy was in jail or dead. The bartender didn't seem to know anyone died except the old man. *Well, I'm gonna find out where Chloe's stayin', and then I'm gonna somehow make a plan. I know Rudy was the planner, but I gots ta figure this'n out on my own.*

When the sheriff came out of the telegraph office, he mounted his horse, and they rode out of town. Buddy trailed far behind. He'd let them get a good start; there was only one main road out of town. When they turned into a wide lane, he saw the spacious sign over the generous entrance. The lane could have fit three wagons abreast it was so wide. He pulled up and walked his horse slowly when he was at the middle of the sign. The lane was long, but he could see a huge house and several outbuildings. Maybe he could get a job there and stay out of Chloe's vision. He'd have to think on it.

It was early morning, and the Mobrey family were all gathered in the lovely sunroom for breakfast. Fluffy clouds lay low on the horizon, but the sky was pure azure. The sun, although not warm, streamed in through the long windows. It lifted spirits, and the atmosphere was saturated with contentment.

Jenny was thankful for her decision to come west. It wasn't that she was a snob. It was simply that she'd thought she was to live in a log cabin and work till the end of her days. What a blessing to be able to live in comfort and enjoy her granddaughter and her new great-grandchildren. She'd thought Anne would never marry after Billy Hargreaves. Her heart overflowed in thankfulness to God for His bountiful blessings. She chuckled when she thought of how she figured things were thus and thus, but reality never seemed to coincide with what she thought would be or would happen.

God surprises me so many times, she ruminated. *It's not often that what I worry about comes to fruition. I reckon it's why the good Lord ask us not to be anxious. It's not healthy to stew over things, especially when I have no control over it anyway. Lord, help me to trust that Your ways are higher than my ways and Your thoughts are higher than my thoughts, like your Word says in Isaiah. Help me not be such a worrywart.*

Her prayer ended, but not her thoughts.

Today, we're supposed to ride to the Bannisters' Rancho. Anne told me she was looking forward to introducing me to Mrs. Bannister. Yesterday she'd said she also had plans to set up a regular schedule to learn sign language for Ginger, as well as the rest of the Mobreys. I sure surprised her when I said I wanted to learn sign language as well. I want to be able to talk to Ginger. She's taken a liking to me, and the feeling is mutual.

CHAPTER XXII

Bear ye one another's burdens,
and so fulfil the law of Christ.

GALATIANS 6:2

THEY WERE STILL SITTING AROUND THE table in the sunroom. Jenny, admiring the beauty of the room, enjoyed the feeling of being out-of-doors to eat.

"I declare I don't believe I'm ever going to get used to eating is such style. It's lovely and peaceful in here. How did you come up with such an idea, young man?" Jenny asked.

"It isn't an original idea," James replied. "I was visiting a friend outside of London, whose parents had a solarium. It was gorgeous. I thought then that if I ever built a house, I would incorporate that idea into it. Because it rains so much in London, they wanted a room that felt as if they were outdoors. Theirs was solely for rare trees, plants, and entertaining, but I thought since it rains here from November through February, it'd be ideal to incorporate a place that feels like the out-of-doors. So, *voila!*" He smiled, and his eyes fastened on Anne.

Her cheeks warmed under his perusal, and she quickly looked away.

"I supposed we'd better get around if we plan to visit the Bannisters," Anne said. "We'll need to take the wagon for the children. They've not

yet mastered riding. I suppose that will be the next thing on our agenda."
She looked at James to see if he agreed.

"Yes, Bates and I plan to go look at some horses this next week.
We can all go if you're interested." James grinned at the children at their
gasps of surprise. "Today we'll take the carriage, but it won't be long
before the two of you will be galloping across the countryside as if you
were born in a saddle."

It was early morning, and the sun was beginning to make its way over
the horizon when Liberty awoke. She lay, feeling almost drugged from a
night of fitful sleep. Exhausted, she started to snuggle up next to Matthew's
back but realized what had awakened her was one of the twins.

She got up and padded into the nursery. Faith was crying. She'd been
fussy the night before and hadn't nursed much. Liberty picked her up
and sat down to nurse her. Matty started moving around and was soon
awake too. It was far too early for them to be up, so after nursing Faith,
Liberty nursed Matty. When she finished, she saw Faith was asleep, and
as she lay Matty back into his crib, she hoped both would sleep in late
this morning.

She crawled back to bed, hoping to go back to sleep. She tried to
keep her mind free of niggling thoughts, but contemplation of Conchita
and her sorrow kept her awake. She thought about the day ahead and
realized she didn't feel like going to San Francisco. She was tired, and it
was something of an ordeal to get the twins' clothing, diapers, and
bedding readied. She would have to hold one of the babies the entire trip
unless they slept. She wondered if her twin, Alex, could get Danny, who
was an excellent doctor, to take a look at Conchita's sister. Libby scooted
carefully away from Matthew and rolled onto her back. She yawned and
began to pray for a long list of people, falling into a deep sleep.

Matthew awoke a short time later and rolled over to see his wife
sound asleep. The sun was up and showed him the shadows that lay
under Liberty's eyes. He rose stealthily and closed the door to the bathing
room with care. He shaved, dressed, and exited through the door to their
private sitting room.

Conchita was up, and breakfast was ready.

"Conchita, do you mind if we don't take Liberty with us?" he asked. "She looks exhausted, and although she could visit with Alex and Emily, she isn't needed for anything in particular. I've noticed since the debacle over at Hedley's that she is looking tired.""*Sí*, I see eet too, Meester Bannister. Weeth Cadence een San Rafael, I am theenking she ees too busy weeth steel nursing dose tweens an' training that horse an' all tings she do around here. I theenk she still feeling bad about keeling Chloe's papa. She doan say, but I theenking eet ees true. Eet be good eef she weel stay here. I am fine weeth that. An', Meester Bannister, I am grateful you take me to see my seester, Constanza. She write me she ees dying. It sound like notheeng can be done for her. She ees very seek."

Conchita's eyes filled with tears, and Matthew pulled her into his arms. She cried from deep within, and her sobs tore at Matthew's heart.

"I want to go because I doan theenk her husband, Timothy, he weel geet a doctor for her. He haf money, but he ees not the nice man. Her first husband, Fernando, he dies eight years ago, and then Constanza, she marry thees man weeth lots of money. Lupe an' Luce, they no like heem. They tell me stories."

"Don't give up yet, Conchita. We never know what the Lord has in store for us. Just pray. It's the best thing, and God can comfort your heart."

She pulled back from him, wiping her eyes on her apron. "*Sí*, Meester Bannister, I haf been praying. God ees een control after all ees said and done."

He nodded and said, "I know some people won't go to the doctor because they feel they are to rely only upon God. I can respect their wishes, but I believe God has given knowledge and wisdom to doctors to be able to help us too. It's a matter of prayer and seeking what the Lord would have us do." He shook his head and added, "It's not always easy to discern the will of God, but it draws us closer to His heart when we spend the time talking to Him. By the way, does Diego plan to come with us?"

Conchita nodded. "Ees eet okay weeth you, Meester Bannister?"

"Of course. Donny is a good worker and can take care of things here. I don't suppose we'll be gone long. At least I won't. Have you told Lupe and Luce about their mother?"

"No…I can no do eet. I weel wait an' see what can be done for her first."

"Don't you think it would be good for them to know?"

"No, I theenk ees best to wait. I weel get no work out of dose girls eef they are theenking about their mother."

Matthew shrugged his shoulders and went out to the barn to talk to Diego before he ate.

"Conchita says you're going with us. I think that's a good idea. If things don't look good for her sister, you can stay in Frisco and be a support to Conchita. I've decided Liberty should stay here. She's tired, and if you need to stay with Conchita, I don't want you to worry about things here. I'll come home and keep things going."

Diego simply nodded. It wasn't often in his marriage that Conchita was down emotionally, but when she was, it took its toll on Diego. He adored his wife and hated to see her so sad.

Matthew went back to the kitchen to eat his breakfast. It wasn't long before Liberty, a green silk robe sashed around her tiny waist, entered the kitchen. Boston had waited in the bedroom for her to get up and padded in at her heels. She looked tired, but Matthew didn't tell her his concerns. He wondered if she was still feeling bad about shooting Chloe's father. He didn't ask her that either. He stood and drew his wife into his arms. She looked fragile, but growing up with an evil father and married to a man who was worse than a scoundrel, Liberty had grown into a woman of resilience and fortitude. Being a totally dedicated Christian, she was a tower of strength spiritually. He seated her but not before giving her a tender, lingering kiss on her full lips.

"Thank you, Matthew. I'm hungry this morning and look forward to a good breakfast, but first I'm going to drink my cup of coffee and think about the day ahead. I have much to do this morning before we leave," Liberty said.

She no sooner got the words out of her mouth than Conchita sat a mug of coffee in front of her. She looked up in surprise, as everyone generally served themselves for breakfast.

"You seet, Mees Libbee…you seet, an' I weel deesh you up thees morning."

"Why thank you, Conchita. I can get it. I need to get around though, as I still have a bit of packing to do."

"No, darling, in truth you don't," Matthew replied.

"What do you mean?"

"I think you should stay here and keep the home fires burning, so to speak. There's no reason for you to go to San Francisco. Conchita knows you love her and support her, but for now I'd like you to take it easy. You're burning the candle at both ends, my dear, and without Cadence here to help you, it's a bit much. When is she coming back anyway?"

"She's planning to come back next week. Susannah and George were in San Rafael, and Cadence wanted to visit her for a bit. They are planning her wedding."

Matthew nodded. "I'll talk to Alex and see if his friend, Danny, can either treat Conchita's sister or if he knows of a doctor who can. Conchita hasn't told Lupe or Luce about their mother yet. She wants to wait until there's a more definitive diagnosis. They will both be here to do the cooking and whatever else you need done."

Liberty's shoulders, always so straight, prim, and proper, sagged a bit in relief. Her eyes misted, and she blinked away the tears, overcome with emotion.

"You are the most thoughtful man! I love you!"

"I love you back." He smiled, the warmth of his love filling his deep-blue eyes. "Just relax as much as you can, although with the twins always demanding attention, I doubt you'll get much rest. Lupe and Luce can watch them if you wish to train that horse of yours today. I'll be back in a day or so."

Outside, Diego climbed up to the seat of the wagon. He hated wagons, but Conchita had never learned to ride, and although she wasn't afraid of horses, she wasn't comfortable being around them. He had his own horse tied to the back of the wagon in case he did any riding in the city without Conchita.

Matthew stood, holding Piggypie's reins. She was a gorgeous piebald mare. He shaded his eyes and then turned to Liberty, who looked at him questioningly.

"What is it, Matthew?"

He responded by waving toward the main road, a goodly distance from the house. "We have company, my dear," he said. "I don't think you will be able to rest this morning after all. Sorry we can't stay, but we need to catch that ferry. I'm hoping Danny will be around and able to see Constanza or at least know of another doctor who can find the problem."

He swung his leg over Piggypie's back and settled comfortably in the saddle while Diego looked on with envy clearly stamped on his face.

Matthew saw his look and grinned widely, knowing Diego's disdain for wagons.

Short trips around the ranch or into town didn't bother Diego at all, but long rides were tedious.

They sat waiting for the Mobreys to arrive. Boston started barking, but Matthew stopped him with one word. "Hush!"

He decided he should climb down off his horse to shake hands. He tried not to be impatient, but he didn't want to miss the ferry either. When the wagon came around the sweep of the drive and pulled abreast of Matthew, he spoke quickly, wanting to be on his way.

"Welcome! Sorry I can't be here, but we're headed for San Francisco, and if we want to make the ferry, we're going to have to be on our way." He turned and gestured to Liberty. "My better half isn't going, so you're in luck." He turned, grabbed his wife, and planted a huge kiss on her mouth. He grinned down into her green eyes as the color rose into her cheeks. "I love you," he whispered into her ear before mounting Piggypie. He didn't wish to be rude, but he turned Piggypie and gestured to Diego.

With reddened cheeks, Liberty said to her guests, "You're welcome to come on in."

Matthew saw her color deepen as Liberty realized the amusement sparking from James' eyes.

She turned to Matthew, whose eyes laughed into hers.

"We'd better be on our way," he said.

Liberty nodded and stroked Piggypie's face.

"See you later then." He clucked his tongue, and Piggypie responded by taking the lead as Diego followed behind in the wagon. Conchita waved and blew a kiss. Matthew, with a squeeze of his knees, set Piggypie into an easy lope.

After waving goodbye, Anne hopped down, helped by James. He turned to Grandma Jenny and grasped her hand to help her down.

Jenny smiled and said, "Thank you, James." She turned to Liberty, who was waiting to greet her.

The bloom was still in Liberty's cheeks, and she witnessed the amused light in Jenny's eyes.

"My name is Liberty Bannister," she said graciously, proffering her hand. "Welcome to Rancho Bonito."

Jenny took her hand in a firm clasp and replied, "I'm Jennifer Tarkington, but my friends call me Jenny. I'd like you to do so too."

"Thank you, and you may call me Liberty. We're not so formal here in the West. I came to California a little over three years ago. Anne told me you're from Williamsburg. I hope you had a pleasant trip out. Isn't it a marvel to travel such a distance so comfortably on the train?" Liberty talked, hoping to put their new guest at ease.

"This is quite an acreage you have here," Jenny replied. "And yes, it is marvelous to travel on a train across country. It was a refresher course for me, in praising the Almighty for the beauty I often take for granted. He's created such a breathtaking universe for us to enjoy."

Liberty nodded and then welcomed the children with a hug to each.

"Hello there! I'm glad you came to visit me. Come on in. Look at Boston…he's happy to see you, and the twins will be too. I don't know what it is about children, but babies love kids, don't they?"

The children skipped happily in before Liberty who, by now, had regained some of her composure. She smiled inwardly as she reflected that Armand, her first husband, was not able to discompose her with all his sneering and outright degrading behavior the way Matthew could set her off balance with a single kiss. She led the Mobreys into the great room and excused herself to go to the kitchen and tell Luce and Lupe they had guests.

Only Luce was there, cleaning up the remains of breakfast.

"Lupe ees with the babies," she said. "They ees awake."

"Ah," Libby replied. "I wanted to tell you we have company, as I'm sure you've guessed. I'd better go feed—" Her voice stopped abruptly as she heard a commotion by the front door. She turned and saw Buck, Hattie, and Chloe entering. She hadn't seen them coming down the lane, as she'd been too discombobulated by Matthew's kiss in front of the Mobreys and too engrossed in meeting Jenny.

Liberty entered the great room and said, "Welcome, welcome! Looks as if we're having a party! You are just in time to entertain the Mobreys. I'll let you introduce yourselves," she said with a laugh. "I'm afraid I'm needed in the bedroom." She left hurriedly as she heard her hungry twins crying.

In the great room, Chloe eyed the two children, who were older than she was.

"My name's Chloe Blake—ahh, well, not anymore. I mean I'm going to be Chloe Rawlins." She jerked her thumb back toward Buck and Hattie. "They're going to adopt me…leastways, I hope they are." Chloe spoke with collectedness, the words rolling off her tongue.

"I'm Thaddeus Park—ahh, Thaddeus Mobrey." Thad spoke with hesitance, not sure how Chloe would react to his sister not being able to talk. "This is my sister, Ginger."

"Hello, Ginger," Chloe said.

Ginger bobbed her head in acknowledgment, but Thaddeus spoke up for her. "She can't talk. She used to, but…" His face reddened as Chloe looked with inquisitive eyes at Ginger.

"That's all right if you can't talk." Chloe said, linking arms with the older girl as if to support her. "We can figure out some other way for us to talk to each other." She squeezed the older girl's arm to comfort her. "I'd like us to be friends. I know you're older and mightn't like to be friends with a little girl like me."

Hattie looked on with relief. *Chloe's a compassionate child*, she thought, *not only with this girl, but the other day with Conchita.*

CHAPTER XXIII

Why art thou cast down, O my soul?
and why art thou disquieted within me?
hope in God: for I shall yet praise him,
who is the health of my countenance, and my God.

PSALMS 43:5

INTRODUCTIONS WERE MADE. JAMES already knew Buck but had never met Hattie. Jenny and Anne were pleased to meet someone else who lived in the area.

Luce had stacked cookies onto a tray and headed to the great room in time to hear Hattie's comment.

"I'm not sure if you know, but Matthew is taking Conchita to see her sister, who is very ill." She spoke in a quiet voice. "He's hoping a friend of Liberty's brother can take a look at her or get another doctor who can see if there's anything to be done. Evidently she wrote Conchita that she is dying."

Luce let go of the tray, which crashed to the floor with a loud popping of porcelain on the tile. Putting her hands to her face, she spoke in anguish. *"Mi madre se está muriendo?"* With shocked eyes, she stared at Hattie while the words echoed around her brain…*My mother is dying.*

"Oh dear, me and my big mouth," Hattie said as Luce ran down the hallway. "Lupe and Luce are Conchita's nieces," she explained to James, Anne, and Jenny. "It's their mother who is ill. I had no idea the girls didn't know about their own mother." She picked up the tray and some shattered porcelain from the broken cups. Jenny and Anne stooped to help her. As Hattie stood up, Buck put an arm around her waist to comfort her. The three women headed to the kitchen.

When Luce burst into Liberty's bedroom, where Lupe was comforting baby Matty while Liberty fed Faith, both Lupe and Liberty were startled.

"Our *madre*…" Luce said and began to cry. "*Nuestra madre se está muriendo*. Why not Conchita tell us?"

Her accent deepened in her distress, and her eyes swung to Liberty, who could see the accusation written in them. Luce began to cry as Lupe looked on in shock. Liberty's shoulders sagged. This was something she'd been anticipating, but not when Conchita wasn't here to answer their questions. She'd been encouraging Conchita to tell her nieces about their mother, but Conchita had been adamant that she wouldn't tell them until they had a definite diagnosis.

Both crying girls turned to Liberty, who looked at them with great compassion in her green eyes. *Oh Lord*, she prayed, *please help me to have wisdom for this moment*. She consciously eased her grip on Faith, trying to relax after Lupe's abrupt entry.

"Girls, it is true. Your mother is quite ill. There's been no diagnosis, but she evidently wrote Conchita and told her she was dying. Perhaps she told Conchita not to tell you. I don't know. It's important for you to remember your mother is a person who has lived her entire life to be pleasing to God. There's a verse in the fifty-seventh chapter of Isaiah that says sometimes God takes out the young man so he doesn't have to endure the wicked day. We don't know His plans for your mother, but you can rest assured that she is in His gracious hands. He is an all-knowing, all-caring, compassionate, loving God. He values your mother. You can sorrow in your heart about your mother, but please remember that God loves you and knows all things. He loves your mother and knows what is best for her. Lean on Him, talk to Him…He can comfort your heart."

Matty started crying. He was hungry and must have felt the tension in Lupe. Liberty had finished feeding Faith, so she handed Faith to Luce and asked her to burp her.

Luce rubbed Faith's little back. She rocked the baby back and forth, feeling some comfort from the contented state of Faith as Liberty took Matty from Lupe's arms. He stopped crying immediately. Luce blew her nose, beginning to recover from her bout of crying, but tears continued to slip down Lupe's cheeks.

"Would you like to go to San Francisco?" Liberty asked the girls. "I can get along just fine without you. Cadence is due back from San Rafael by next week. She can help me. And as you know, Conchita made some food before she left."

"*Sí*, eef eet is all right with you, we would like to do that." Luce's voice quavered.

Lupe nodded in agreement.

"All right," Liberty said. "I'll finish nursing Matty, but I want you to tell Donny to get your horses saddled. You need to gather up the things you'll need for a visit. I know you're used to traveling down there without anyone else, so I won't start worrying about that, unless you'd like Donny to go with you as far as the ferry."

"Noh, we ees fine to go by ourselfs," Luce said, her accent thickening.

Liberty spoke with sincerity, but a smile of encouragement spread across her face. "I think it's good for you to see your mother. You take as long as you need to visit with her, and be sure to tell Conchita the same. She is to stay as long as she needs or wants."

"*Gracias, señora. Muchas gracias.*" Both girls left immediately to prepare.

Liberty breathed a big sigh of tiredness. She felt as if she'd been in a race. She finished feeding Matty and saw that Faith had gone back to sleep. She carried Matty into the great room, and Ginger quickly sat down, holding out her arms. Liberty saw her action and placed Matty into her waiting arms. The girl drew Matty into a quick hug, releasing him to hold him lightly but firmly on her lap. She bounced him gently and smiled as he cooed.

"Ginger likes babies," Thaddeus said. "On the wagon train, she helped some of the women with little children. Our mother said she was a little mama..." He realized it was the first time he'd spoken out loud about his mother. He glanced quickly at Anne, who walked over and squeezed his shoulder. He looked at Ginger, who'd stopped bouncing the baby, tears misting her eyes.

Chloe sat down next to Ginger and looked at the baby in awe. "I've never been around a baby. Nope, not in my entire life!"

Ginger looked at her new friend with surprise in her eyes, but Liberty spoke to Chloe.

"I hadn't either, until I had these two. I think mothering is something that comes fairly natural. You learn as you go. In truth, Matthew is better at knowing what to do than me. I think it's because he's taken care of calves, sheep, and other animals."

"Ginger seems to know how to hold a baby—that's for sure," Anne said. "She could probably give me lessons. I've not been around babies much either."

Ginger looked up at Anne and smiled at her comment.

Liberty said, "One thing for sure, you'll have good help when you and James have a baby, with someone like Ginger around."

Color flooded into Anne's face.

But James took the comment with his natural aplomb. He drew a deep, silent breath as he realized that Thaddeus was healing. It wasn't that the boy would ever forget his parents, but the deep pain in his heart was easing for him, to be able to speak about his mother.

"Thanks for being patient," Liberty said. "Things are in a bit of an upheaval, but I think we have it sorted out. Lupe and Luce are going to San Francisco to be with their mother. Conchita was up early this morning making a tray of *enchiladas,* so I am hoping all of you can stay for lunch. There's not much to do other than make salsa and toss a salad. Yesterday, Conchita made a cake."

Jenny smiled and said, "If you need me, I'm willing to stay for a couple days and help you out. Having twins can't be easy. Perhaps Ginger would like to stay and help too."

Liberty replied with surprise in her eyes. "I'd like that. I'd like that very much. If you're sure you would like to stay, I could use your help. I normally have a girl here who helps out, but she's in San Rafael visiting her grandmother. I think she's supposed to come back from San Rafael sometime next week, but I'd appreciate your help." She turned to Ginger. "Would you like to stay and help take care of the twins?"

Ginger's head bobbed in the affirmative, and a wide grin split her face.

"Is that all right with you, Anne?" Liberty asked. "She'd be a big help to me, I'm sure. We also could get started on some sign language. Ginger is going to be a lot happier girl when she can communicate with you."

"Certainly. Grandma Jenny can do as she pleases, and Ginger has my permission to stay and help," Anne said. "The only thing is, we all want to learn to sign."

"Can I stay too?" Chloe asked Liberty. "I promise I won't be any trouble, and I'd like to help out. I know how to do dishes and everything!" Her eyes pleaded with Hattie, whose eyes flew to Liberty's to see what she thought.

Liberty's head nodded slightly, and Hattie breathed a sigh of relief.

"Let's see what Papa thinks."

"Papa thinks it's just fine," Buck responded. He winked at Chloe and added, "Chloe will be a good babysitter. Don't hesitate to tell her how to do things. She's one of the fastest learners I've ever been around."

Chloe's eyes glowed under his praise, and she straightened her back to stand taller.

Liberty excused herself to go outside and see Lupe and Luce off.

Donny had saddled their horses, and both girls' saddlebags looked fat. Normally, there would be gaiety on their faces. It was a rare treat when Conchita gave them a break, letting them off to go home, but there was no laughter or chatter today.

"Godspeed," Liberty said, "and tell Conchita I am praying for Constanza." She gave Luce's horse a slap on the hip, and Lupe, with a nod of acknowledgment, kicked her horse into a gallop.

Liberty stood watching, shading her eyes with her hand, until the girls reached the curve in the lane. She drew a deep breath. Exhausted, she turned back to the house and thought how grateful she was for the extra help these new friends offered.

I've been too proud in the past, not wanting to be an inconvenience to anyone, but in a way, that's a form of pride, she thought. *When I struggle, not wanting to be a bother to anyone, I am denying someone the joy of service and help.* Her thoughts turned into a prayer. *We all need each other, don't we, Father.* She entered the house with another deep sigh.

Buck, Hattie, and Chloe were getting to know the Mobreys. Chloe made it her personal ambition in life to be good friends with this girl who couldn't talk. Ginger, who'd been hungry for friendship, took to Chloe like a duck to water. Even though Chloe was only five, she was a precocious five. If she weren't so little, people would think her much older by her voice intonation and conversation. She had an awareness of others most five year olds didn't have. Chloe knew what was what, and this girl needed her help.

Jenny was in the kitchen, putting Conchita's tray of *enchiladas* into the oven, and Anne was putting a salad together. Buck, Chloe, and the rest of the Mobreys were at the huge scrubbed-oak table, chatting away as if they were old friends.

Thaddeus, grateful for Chloe's complete acceptance of Ginger, spoke. "You don't act like five years old," he said.

Chloe glared at him, deciding to give Thad a piece of her mind, but when he finished talking, she instead smiled complacently.

"What I mean is, most people would think you're older by the way you talk and act."

"Thank you," she replied demurely. She'd thought he meant she acted younger than five. "You act older than seven. You have quite a large vocabulary for a seven-year-old."

Thad's eyebrows rose as he contemplated a five-year-old complimenting his vocabulary. Right then he decided Chloe was all right...for a girl. He wanted to stay at the Bannisters' and spend the night too but felt too shy to ask.

Seated comfortably on his horse, Buddy Blake settled himself under a tree on a high mesa overlooking a large vineyard—the vineyard he'd seen Chloe ride into.

The morning was fair with high fluffy white clouds and a warmth to the sun, which felt good on his back after a cold morning. There was a slight breeze with a coolness in it that made a body realize spring had not yet fully arrived.

Every morning he'd been up early. Not having any light or anything to do after sunset, he'd been going to bed betimes. Normally he'd go right to sleep, but if sleep was elusive, he'd lay watching the heavens lit with stars. Buddy hadn't wanted to make any fires at night, as someone might spot the light. He made fires, for a very short time, early in the morning when he heated water for coffee and made a hot breakfast. He'd been keeping watch over the huge olive-grove house, observing closely everyone who rode in or out. Whenever he saw Chloe ride out, he'd follow at a far distance.

Sometimes he wondered if he should just leave Chloe with the sheriff and head on out. His money wouldn't hold out forever. He was pretty sure Rudy was dead, but he hadn't any proof. He could be in jail since it was the sheriff who was caring for Chloe.

This morning Chloe had ridden out with the sheriff and his woman, riding to this large vineyard. It wasn't far from where he was camped out. He didn't know how long he'd have to wait, but it didn't trouble him any. He was a patient man. He wondered what he'd do if he ever got hold of Chloe.

Beat the pants right offa her is what I oughta do, he thought. *Little runt, runnin' off like that an' actin' like butter wouldn't melt in 'er mouth. Needs a good thrashin', by my reckonin'.*

He spat a long stream of tobacco at a rock, watching the chaw slide down the gray stone. *I needs ta think of a plan. I need ta figure out how ta get holt of Chloe.*

He dismounted and tied his horse to a branch. Climbing a huge rock, he thought he'd sit in the sun for a spell and keep a watch on the road to the vineyard, waiting to see when Chloe came out.

Napa had been clear and sunny, but San Francisco was overcast, the heavens promising rain. Wind whipped around and rollicked, blowing up from the bay and then coming in from the west.

Matthew, Diego, and Conchita arrived in the big city, having caught the ferry just before it left Sausalito. The trip seemed short, but it was nearly lunchtime when they arrived at Constanza's house.

Conchita hopped down from the wagon, with no help from Diego, and strode up the walk, making a beeline for the front door. She pulled her brightly colored shawl closer around her shoulders, feeling chilled, not only from the dampness of San Francisco but also with a deep foreboding.

The Brodies' house was a beautiful Queen Anne row house with mullioned windows and a transom window over the ornately carved front door. The entire edifice was painted a sage green with creamy trim. Constanza's husband, who was an engineer and had studied at Cambridge, held an excellent position with the city planning commission.

Conchita didn't knock but let herself into the house, leaving the door open for Diego and Matthew to follow. With light steps she went up the first flight of stairs and tapped on her sister's bedroom door before letting herself in.

A nurse sitting next to the bed had surprise clearly stamped on her face at Conchita's entrance.

"Who are you?" she asked in an authoritative tone. Her face registered incredulity that someone would enter the sickroom without having permission.

"I am Constanza's seester, an' I have comed to veesit weeth her or to halp her eef I can." Conchita's accent became heavy, as she was clearly upset. Her sister did not stir in her bed. Conchita went over and laid a hand on Constanza's brow, but she didn't awaken. "I know Timothy, he get a good doctor for her, but I would like another doctor to take a look at her, *sí.*"

"I believe you'll need permission from Mr. Brodie. He's her husband, after all." The nurse was young. She sensed the love Conchita had for her sister and hoped Mr. Brodie would allow another doctor to look at her. She didn't think much of the doctor taking care of Constanza now. He was older and not at all up-to-date on the newest techniques and information. He was respectable, of course, a man of some repute, but set in his ways. The nurse's thoughts swung to Conchita, and she made a quick decision to voice her fears. Perhaps this woman could get Mr. Brodie to have someone else look at Constanza.

"The doctor Mr. Brodie hired for Mrs. Brodie is using out-of-date practices. I told him she needs to be in a hospital and perhaps have surgery, but Dr. William Harrison thinks he knows best, and your brother-in-law trusts him."

"I need no permeession. I luf my seester and weel get her the best halp." She nodded at the open doorway, where Matthew and Diego now stood, and spoke to Matthew. "You go talk to Meester Alex, an' I weel stay here."

CHAPTER XXIV

Blessed are the merciful:
for they shall obtain mercy.

MATTHEW 5:7

"I'M ON MY WAY," MATTHEW REPLIED. "You coming with me or staying with Conchita?"

"I not needed here," Diego replied. "I come weeth you, Meester Bannister. I am happy I brought my horse." He walked into the room and gave Conchita a quick buss on the cheek. "You weel be all right, *mi corazón*. Remember, Constanza, she ees een God's hands. You can halp, but try not to worry."

Conchita stroked Diego's cheek and said, "Gracias, *mi amor.*"

The nurse cleared her throat, clearly unsettled by this open display of affection, but Conchita and Diego were oblivious. Matthew grinned at the nurse, who was looking at him. She blushed to the roots of her thick auburn hair. Matthew, still grinning, shrugged his shoulders and turned to head down the stairs, his spurs jingling. Diego, with light steps, followed.

Conchita pulled up a chair and sat down on the other side of the bed. She reached under the coverlet to hold her sister's hand.

"What ees your name?" she asked the nurse softly.

"It's Sylvia Cobain, and frankly speaking, I'm grateful you have come." She spoke in a quiet, gentle voice. Her eyes were a light topaz color of brown and gleamed in the darkened room.

Conchita was thankful they had come too. She would see to it her sister had the best care available.

Diego untied his horse from the wagon, and both men mounted their horses, heading into the business section of the city. Alex's office was located on Battery Street in the heart of the business district. Diego had never been there, but he knew Alex, Liberty's twin, well.

Arriving in short order, they climbed off their rides and tied up at the hitching post. Matthew scratched Piggypie's forehead before leaving her. They entered the office, and Matthew realized a few things had changed. Before, the office had been one small room with a potbellied stove occupying a corner. It looked as if Alex must have purchased the building behind his office and expanded. Now spacious, what had once been his office was the reception area.

The clerk rose and greeted the two men.

"My name is Adrian Wagner, and I clerk for Mr. Liberty. May I help you?"

"Yes, I'm Matthew Bannister, Mr. Liberty's brother-in-law." Matthew smiled inwardly, knowing Alex had recently dropped his last name of Johnson. He was now Alexander Liberty II. It was quite a story how Liberty and Alex had been separated at birth, but legally, Alex's name had never been Johnson. "I'd like to see Alex, if I may."

"Certainly, Mr. Bannister. I'll let him know you're here. Mr. Liberty has an appointment in twenty minutes but presently is free." The clerk spoke formally but seemed friendly. He left, walking down a glassed hall from which light poured into the area. It evidently connected the two buildings. Matthew was impressed with the new office layout. He walked around and stopped to look at a wall hanging, a pencil-and-ink map of Marin County.

The clerk returned, but Alex was right behind him.

"Matthew! Diego, good to see you!" He gave Matthew a bear hug and shook hands with Diego.

"Nice setup you have here, Alex," Matthew said. "I like what you've done."

"Come look at the corridor that connects the two buildings," Alex said proudly. He led the way into the naturally lit hall, both men following him.

"I saw the light coming out of here, but this is amazing." Matthew spoke with admiration in his voice. "I've never seen anything like this. It's beautiful."

The hall was made of stained oaken beams and supports, but the walls and ceiling were all glass. On either side was a beautifully groomed garden. Hostas, a couple ninebark, hydrangeas, rhododendrons, and roses, as well as shrubs, colored the areas open to the skies above but walled on three sides by the other brick buildings. A couple of wrought-iron benches hugged the corner of the garden on the left.

"This is where I often eat lunch," Alex said. "It was Emily's idea, and Nana picked out some of the shrubs."

"It's peaceful," Matthew said, "and a great way to lighten up what would have been a dark hall. I can see why you enjoy sitting out there."

Alex searched Matthew's face and asked, "All right, what's brought you down to the big city?"

"We need your help, Alex," Matthew replied. "Conchita's sister lives here in the city and is very ill. We wanted Danny to take a look at her or get someone who is a specialist to do so. She's still at home but evidently has a full-time nurse."

"Let me point you in the right direction. Danny has his own practice now. It's located just down the street from St. Luke's Hospital, which reopened last year. It's on Valencia, near Army Street."

Liberty checked on Faith, but she was still sleeping. She put a hand to her baby's forehead and thought she felt a little warm, but no real cause for alarm. She headed back to the kitchen, where Matty was still seated on Ginger's lap, cooing and having a great time. Quickly donning an apron, she made some fresh salsa to go with the *enchiladas*.

There was much laughter and talk as Chloe entertained them all with some anecdotes of learning to read. She hadn't liked anyone laughing at her when she first went to live with Buck and Hattie, but she was learning that when they laughed at her, it was full of love, not ridicule. She enjoyed being the center of attention.

Jenny sat, while conversation swirled around her, contemplating what to collect when she got home. It'd only be a few days, but Jenny was nothing if not organized. *I must bring a few clothes, a nightgown, and my toothbrush. As well, I should gather up a few things besides clothes for the next few days. I must have my knitting, cross stitch, my Bible, and that book I'm reading. Now, what else?* She spoke into the conversation. "May Chloe ride with us to Mobrey Manor? Ginger and I need to collect our things, but perhaps Chloe would enjoy seeing Ginger's and Thad's new puppies. I will drive us back in the carriage. If that is all right with you, James."

"Of course," he replied.

Chloe bounced a bit in her chair but didn't say anything until she heard Hattie's reply.

Hattie turned to Liberty. "We will be putting Chloe in your charge. Is that all right with you?"

"Of course. I'm sure Chloe will be delighted to see the children's puppies," Liberty replied.

"It's not just their puppies." Anne laughed. "James got one for me too. We have three puppies at our house."

Liberty smiled. "It's a good thing you have servants to help, especially when you're away from home."

Ginger's eyes gleamed at Liberty, who smiled back. Ginger was seated next to Chloe and reached over to squeeze her arm, her lips curled up in a delighted smile.

Chloe grinned back, happy for this new adventure.

The *enchiladas* were a huge success. Jenny exclaimed at the different-tasting flavors bursting in her mouth.

"I need to learn how to make this," she said. "It is delicious!"

Liberty grinned and said, "*Enchiladas* was the first dinner I had after arriving at the Rancho. I fell in love with western living right then!"

"I can certainly understand that." Jenny turned to James. "Does your cook know how to make these?"

"No, I don't think so, but we could send her over here to learn from Conchita," he replied.

When the meal was over, they sat discussing plans. Buck and Hattie would go home, and Buck would return later in the day with some of Chloe's clothes.

Chloe didn't quite know how she felt about Liberty. Her feelings were mixed, knowing this woman killed her pa.

She sat staring at Liberty, who felt her perusal.

Liberty returned Chloe's long look, her eyes mirroring Chloe's sorrow.

On the ride back to Sunrise Canyon, Hattie slowed her horse to a walk and ruminated out loud.

"I already miss that little girl. She's certainly wiggled her way into my heart."

"I know what you mean, darling. She's a character, and no mistake. I keep praying she will have such an intimate relationship with the Lord that she can let go of her past. I read somewhere that those first five or six years of a child's life can determine their character and who they are as a person. Course, I know the Almighty can change us if we're willing to let him."

Both were silent for a bit, thinking of Chloe and how important she'd become to them is such a short time.

"Her mind is like a sponge. She's soaking up every bit of information she hears or reads. She's a bright little thing. It's criminal the way she's been brought up to think she's worthless because she's a girl. I love her, Buck. I love her so much. I also have something I've been waiting to tell you. I waited and have seen Dr. John to make sure."

She pulled up, and Buck looked at her, tugging gently on his horse's reins.

A sudden dread came upon him, as he thought she might be very ill.

She grinned at him. "You and I are going to have a baby. We're going to have a baby, Buck!"

Buck's breath expelled in a sudden rush. He hadn't known he'd been holding it.

He got off his horse faster than Hattie had ever seen anyone dismount.

He grabbed her off her horse and began to dance with her around and around until the two of them were breathless and laughing. He took her face into his hands and kissed her, long and deep. Gazing into her eyes, his were filled with love and wonder.

"Should you be riding a horse? Oh, Hattie, I never thought to have a child of my own. I've just turned forty! Did Dr. John say you'd be all right? You're not so young yourself to be having a first baby!"

Hattie laughed. "Dr. John said it might be a little rough, but I'm fit as a fiddle and should be fine. I'm to use common sense, of course."

She laughed again, her lips curving up, and a dimple appeared in the corner of her mouth.

Buck gave her a hug and said, "I love you so much, Hattie, it almost hurts!"

"I thank the Lord I came west to be with Adam. I'd never have met you if I hadn't."

"Well, he's a wonderful young man, that nephew of yours, but I sure am thankful you came out to be with him. I never saw love coming to me again, until I set eyes on you. Love at first sight! I never believed in it before."

He helped Hattie back onto her horse and stepped into the stirrup of his, swinging his long leg over. They continued on their way to Sunrise Ranch, each silent, thinking their own thoughts.

Buck broke the silence by voicing his. "Hattie, I don't want to alarm you, but you do realize that Chloe's uncle is most likely looking for her, don't you? I went into the saloon in Napa to see if Harkin had seen any strangers. He's the owner and barkeep. I've probably never told you, but he's the biggest gossip this side of the Mississippi. Right after I brought Chloe home, I thought I'd better talk to him. He told me there was a stranger who'd come into town for supplies…that he and his brother were looking for a place to settle down. I went back the other day, and Harkin said the man had come back into town looking for his brother and his brother's kid. Harkin said he pointed the stranger in my direction, but of course the man isn't going to come looking for me. I also noticed someone following us this morning when we rode to Bannisters' Rancho. He hung way back. It could be a coincidence, but I don't think so. It's the first time I've consciously been keeping a lookout. He could have followed us before, but I haven't been watchful of that until this morning. I didn't want to say anything earlier, as I didn't want to alarm Chloe."

"If he's caught, he'll hang for what he's done, won't he? Oh, I just pray Chloe can be spared any more heartache. She doesn't say so, but I know she's heartsick about her pa. Even though her life was pretty rough, she loved him."

"I know, sweetheart. I know. And yes, if he had anything to do with not giving Hedley any water, he'll hang. If he didn't, he'll most likely be placed in a chain gang or prison for robbing a bank. I just pray he doesn't come to a bad end. Chloe's had enough sorrow. She doesn't need any more."

Matthew and Diego rode toward St. Luke's, hoping it wouldn't be difficult to find Danny. Matthew had taken a liking to Alex's best friend. Daniel Gates had grown up in Alex's home; they were like brothers. Matthew had met him at a wedding and several times since at Alex's house.

As they rode toward the hospital, something kept niggling at the back of Matthew's mind. *That nurse said Dr. William Harrison. Why does that name ring some kind of bell in my mind?* Matthew tried to think why the name should, somehow, be one he'd heard before. He couldn't remember, but he knew he'd never met the man.

When they arrived at St. Luke's Hospital, they dismounted, looked around, and saw Daniel's shingle hanging by brass chains. It was gray with light-red raised lettering: *Dr. Daniel Gates*. The two men walked their horses down the front cobblestone street and tied up at a long hitching post in front of the edifice.

They went inside, and a secretary sat at the desk. He didn't even look up when they entered. There was only one man sitting against the wall in a straight-back chair. His arm was bleeding through a torn petticoat used as a bandage.

After the secretary finished writing on a ledger, he looked up.

"Yes, may I help you?"

"We're not here because we're ill," Matthew said to the younger man. "Just in need of talking to the doctor."

"Well, I'm sure he can see you, but of course this other gentleman is first. I'd like you to fill out this form."

"There's no need," Matthew said agreeably. "We'll wait, no problem."

Diego picked a chair, and Matthew sat next to him. They talked quietly, but Diego was not used to sitting. He kept bobbing his knee up and down and shifting his weight in the straight-back chair. Matthew turned the subject from Constanza to grapes, and Diego forgot about being uncomfortable. They didn't have long to wait.

Danny came out with his patient, who had burns on his face.

"I want to see you next week, sir. Please come in at your convenience."

The man nodded and left as Danny said something to his secretary. As he turned to welcome his next patient, he saw Matthew and Diego sitting patiently.

"Well, look who's here! Matthew Bannister! It's good to see you!" Danny strode over to them as he spoke to the patient, "I'll be with you in just a minute." He turned back to Matthew and asked, "What brings you here? You hurt or sick?"

"No, go ahead with your patient, but can we take you out to luncheon?"

"Certainly." Danny grinned. "I never pass up a free meal!" He led his patient into the adjacent room as he asked him what had happened.

Matthew and Diego sat back down to wait.

Buddy Blake, sitting on a huge rock, spied someone riding out of the lane from the vineyard onto the main road. He raced to his horse, grabbed his spyglass, and ran back to the rock. Adjusting the lens and with one eye shut, he stared at the couple riding out of the grape vineyard.

"Well, well, well, looky here…looky here. What d'ya know! Chloe's not with 'em. Wonder why?" He watched as they rode down the main road. All the sudden, they pulled up, and the sheriff lifted the woman off her horse.

"What the blazes is he a doin'?" he asked himself. "Dancin'! They're a dancin' an' look happy." He zoomed in on them, making their features come clearly into view. "Wonder if they's glad to get rid of Chloe? She's a regular handful, and no mistake. Look at that! That's some kiss. Look at that! He's a hangin' a lip on that gal, that's certain!"

He watched as the couple remounted. It was some time before they rode out of sight.

"Wonder why they left Chloe?" He started to walk back to his horse to put the spyglass away, when he saw a wagon loaded with people come onto the main road. "Ahh," he said as he trained the lens on the occupants in the wagon. "There she is, a ridin' with a family. Reckon I'd best be a following 'em. No tellin' where they might be headed."

He carefully returned his spyglass to its leather case, knowing he had plenty of time to get down to the main road. He didn't want to ride too close and give himself away.

CHAPTER XXV

He that refuseth instruction despiseth his own soul:
but he that heareth reproof getteth understanding.

PROVERBS 15:32

DOCTOR **DANIEL GATES USHERED MATTHEW** and Diego out of his office. He liked his best friend's brother-in-law and was curious as to why he wanted to talk to him.

"There's a good eatery just down the hill." He pulled a timepiece out of his fob pocket, the gold chain glinting in the sunlight. "I have until one thirty," he said. "I'll need to be back by then. Is that all right with you?"

"It's fine," Matthew said. He glanced at Diego, who nodded.

The three men headed toward the small restaurant while Diego explained in detail why they'd come to San Francisco.

Danny spoke in a serious tone in reply to Diego's explanation.

"I professionally cannot take over another doctor's patient without the patient or family's approval. Is Mrs. Brodie's husband aware of you looking for another doctor? And who's the doctor that's treating her?"

"No, Mr. Brodie wasn't home when we got there," Matthew replied, "but Constanza's in a bad way, and the nurse doesn't think Dr. William Harrison is doing the correct thing for her."

Danny's head jerked up. "Wonder if that name's a coincidence?"

"What is it about that name? I've been brooding over it since I heard it. I know I've never met the man, but I've heard the name before.""It's the same name as the doctor Madam Violet Corlay had. He's the one who delivered Alex and Liberty—the one who took Alex home to be Sarah's son."

"Ah, that's right!" Matthew exclaimed. "He was the philanderer."

"Yes," Danny replied. "He was the doctor who took Alex to raise him as his own son. When Sarah discovered Harrison's infidelity, she left him, taking Alex with her. It's an amazing story. I don't know if you've heard all of it, but nonetheless it's amazing." He turned to Diego. "I'll have a look at Mrs. Brodie. Dr. Harrison must be getting up there, and if he's not keeping up-to-date with the advancements in medicine…well…let's just leave it at that. I'd like to see her. I have that one thirty appointment I can't dismiss, but after that, I kept my calendar clear to go visit some patients who aren't able to get out. I'll skip those today and come see Mrs. Brodie."

Diego breathed a sigh of relief. He didn't care to go back and tell Conchita that Dr. Gates wouldn't see Constanza. He offered a quick prayer of thanksgiving.

The three men had a delicious luncheon. Danny, full of various funny stories and jests, shared one Matthew would be sure to remember to repeat to Liberty.

"We had a woman who had her baby on the second landing of the stairs at St. Luke's," Danny said. "She started crying and said to the nurse, 'I can't do anything right. Why can't I have my baby in a bed like other women?' The nurse tried to soothe her and said, 'It's all right, honey. Not all women have their babies in a bed.' But the woman just kept crying and said, 'No, I just can't do anything right.' The nurse, trying to console her said, 'Really, it's all right, dear. Women have their babies in all kinds of places. Why, two years ago we had a woman who had her baby right out there on the front lawn.' The woman started crying harder and said, 'That was me!'"

Matthew and Diego laughed, and Danny joined in. They finished their lunch and walked back up the hill with Danny.

"We'll just wait around until you're ready to go. Is that your ride?" Matthew pointed to a horse tied at the rail but with no saddle.

"Yes, it is. My saddle's in my office. If you'd like to saddle her up for me, I'd appreciate it. I don't think this appointment will be a long one."

"Sure, I'll come get it now."

The Mobreys arrived at the lane leading to Mobrey Mansion. As the house came into view, Chloe gasped, her eyes enormous. The look she turned onto Ginger was of unbelief. She'd never seen or known such a house existed, let alone housed someone she knew. James guided the horses around the front sweep of the driveway, the horses' hooves clattering a pleasant sound on the cobbles. He drove along the side of the mansion and pulled up at the rear. The three children hopped down, Thad holding Chloe's hand for the big jump off the wagon.

Dock came out of the stable and took the reins from James.

"Have a good luncheon?" he asked.

"Wonderful," James replied. "Dock, meet our new friend, Chloe Rawlins. Chloe, meet our stableman, Dock."

Chloe stuck out her hand and said, "Put 'er there, Dock. I'm right pleased ta meet you."

Dock laughed and took Chloe's hand "I'm right pleased ta meet you, too, Miss Chloe. Welcome to Mobrey Manor."

Chloe looked up at the house and counted three stories.

"This is the biggest house I ever seed in my entire life! It's not only the biggest house, it's the biggest building I ever seed."

"Seen," Thaddeus said. "I hope you don't mind me correcting you, but seed is only a little thing you plant in the ground. It's *I see, I saw*, and *I have seen*. I see it now. I saw it a while ago, and I have seen it in the past." He smiled down at the little girl. "*Have* is a helping verb for *seen*. You can never use seen without a helping verb."

"Thank you. I am working on being better at speaking, but I was not taught correctly." Chloe enunciated clearly and distinctly and hoped she was saying it right.

"I'm glad you're not ashamed to have someone correct you. Lots of people have too much pride, and they keep doing things the wrong way. I don't mean just their speech either." He changed the subject abruptly. "You sure have pretty red hair. It glints like gold in the sunlight."

Right then, he won Chloe's heart. He was her hero.

Ginger tugged on Chloe's arm and pointed to the house.

"I see it. I saw it when we drove up, and I have never seen it before." Chloe spoke cheekily.

Ginger's lips turned up as if she were laughing, but she made no sound. Thad laughed too. The children entered the house noisily, and Mackie welcomed them home.

"Hello there. What's your name?" she asked Chloe.

"My name's Chloe Rawlins, and Ginger, Thaddeus, and me are friends."

"Why, you must be Sheriff Rawlins' little girl. I didn't know he had any children."

"He didn't. I'm new. Well, I'm not new. I'm just new to being his child."

"Same as we're new to being Mobreys," Thad said.

Mackie looked down at the little girl and said, "Welcome to Mobrey Manor. I'm Mackie, and if you need anything, just let me know."

"Thanks, Mackie," Thad said. He turned to Chloe. "Let's go upstairs. Ginger is wanting you to see her room and her puppy."

The children scampered off as James ushered Jenny and Anne into the kitchen.

Dr. Daniel Gates finished with his last appointment, followed Diego and Matthew toward the beautiful Queen Anne house belonging to the Brodies.

When they arrived, they tied up at a long hitching post. Diego strode up the walk, Matthew and Danny right behind. Diego pushed open the door without knocking. Two men were sitting in the parlor, and one stood up immediately.

"Why, I guess you're making yourself right at home, aren't you, Diego." Timothy Brodie's greeting wasn't very welcoming. They were brothers-in-law, but not friends

The other man stood as Matthew and Danny stepped over the threshold.

"Ye-es. Constanza, wheen she ees well, she always making me feel at home." Diego was clearly nervous, his accent heavy.

He didn't like Timothy Brodie, not one whit. It looked to Matthew as if the feeling was mutual. Brodie's eyes were hooded, and he held his lips in a taut line.

"You brought company, Diego?" he asked. "I'm sorry, but we have illness here and are not in the mood for guests." "*Sí es verdad*. That is true, and so I breeng Conchita to halp her seester."

"She doesn't need help. I've hired a nurse, and I have Dr. Harrison here. He has assured me it's nothing more than influenza. Isn't that so, Dr. Harrison?"

"Yes. In a few days I expect her to be feelin' much better." Harrison was still sitting. Although he was not fat, he had more weight on him than was wise.

He had blue eyes and a florid complexion but was one of those kinds of men Matthew thought of as oily. He sat fingering his silk cravat.

"Thees man here is D—"

"We are friends of Diego and Conchita." Matthew cut Diego off before he could voice that Danny was a doctor, afraid that with the tenor of the atmosphere, Brodie would deny him access to Constanza.

"I'm Matthew Bannister, and this is Daniel Gates." Matthew wondered how he was going to get Daniel up to Constanza's room, but he needn't have worried. Conchita, hearing their voices, came down the stairs on swift feet.

"You come here weeth me." She beckoned to Danny.

"Now just you wait here a minute," Timothy Brodie blustered.

"No, you weel wait just a minute." Conchita spoke with a voice of authority. "I weel take thees man to see my seester. You know she is ver' ill, Timothy, an' eef she get no halp, she ees going to die. She wrote me eet."

Timothy looked at Conchita, his mouth dropping open in total surprise and anger.

Dr. Harrison stared at Danny and seemed to look as if he recognized him.

"Daniel Gates?" he asked. "Dr. Daniel Gates, is it not?"

"Yes, I'm Dr. Daniel Gates," he replied. "Are you Dr. Harrison, originally from Boston?" Danny asked.

William Harrison, totally taken aback with surprise, replied, "Why yes, yes, I lived in Boston for quite some time. I grew up and started my practice there. Why do you ask?"

"Oh, nothing in particular. Just thought I'd heard the name, is all." Danny wished he'd held his tongue. It was not his story, and he knew neither his friend Alex, nor Alex's supposed mother, Sarah, would thank him for talking out of turn or interfering. Dr. Harrison looked on the younger man with suspicion in his light-colored eyes, but curiosity reigned. He didn't want the younger man to leave, hoping to get a bit more information from him, so he said, "I would not mind having a second opinion if you care to look at the patient."

Timothy Brodie looked indignant.

"I don't think that's necessary," he said and turned to Dr. Harrison. "I thought you said she had influenza and would be all right in a few days, that you have everything under control."

"I did, but it never hurts to have another doctor's opinion."

Timothy Brodie shrugged his shoulders. Dr. Harrison pointed to the stairs and said, "First door on the right."

Danny mounted the stairs and tapped gently on the door.

"Enter," called a voice in a gentle tone.

Danny pushed open the door, and Sylvia, clearly startled, stood up. He looked at her nurse's uniform. The afternoon sun streamed in the window, and the nurse stood facing him in its path. He couldn't see her features for the brightness of light.

"I am Dr. Gates," he said. "I've come to take a look at Mrs. Brodie." He looked over at the bed and saw a woman who did not move at their voices.

Sylvia walked over to Danny and spoke in a low tone.

"I don't think Mrs. Brodie has influenza, sir. She is very ill and should be in a hospital." She blushed to the roots of her hair as Danny's eyes swung from the bed to the nurse. "I know I'm speaking out of turn, but Dr. Harrison is using outdated practices. Mrs. Brodie hasn't even had a thorough examination. I did speak to Mr. Brodie, but he wouldn't listen to me after he spoke to Dr. Harrison. Mr. Brodie has not been in the sick room for the past four weeks."

Conchita was standing behind Danny and gasped at her statement, but Danny didn't hear it.

He was listening, but it was as if what the nurse said was spoken through a long tunnel. He looked at this petite young woman and lost his heart. He nodded but continued to stare, completely flummoxed. *I never thought to fall in love. I thought I'd never marry. I can't believe this is happening. Oh Lord, please don't let her be married.* He glanced at her hand and thought, *It's ringless, but most people don't wear wedding rings. You're mine, darling. I don't even know your name, but you're mine.* He suddenly realized she was finished talking and blushing even more at his continued perusal.

"I'm sorry if what I said upset you, Dr. Gates, but it's the truth nonetheless." Sylvia felt frustrated, as if she was talking to someone who wasn't paying attention to her words.

"I will take a look at her. What's your name?"

"Nurse Cobain, nurse Sylvia Cobain," she replied, a bit mollified by his tone.

"I'm pleased to meet you, Nurse Sylvia Cobain." He held out his hand to shake hers.

It startled her. It simply wasn't done. Men never proffered a hand first, and certainly not a doctor to a lowly nurse. She lifted her eyes to his as she took his hand, which was warm and seemed, somehow, comforting. His eyes sparkled, their blueness deepening as he gazed into her tawny ones.

Danny, loathe to let her hand go, smiled and said, "All right, Nurse Cobain, let's take a look at our patient."

He began to examine Constanza, who didn't even awaken. Conchita took her place in the straight-back chair by the bed but said nothing, sitting back to give Danny access to the blankets covering her sister.

Danny's lips thinned as he performed his examination. Angry, a scowl marred his face, which was usually cheerful. Personal thoughts were pushed aside as he listened to Constanza's heart. When he finished a most thorough examination, he spoke in a clipped voice to Conchita.

"I am sorry, Conchita, but your sister is gravely ill. I believe she is bleeding internally—somewhere in the abdominal cavity." He saw Conchita's questioning look and explained. "Somewhere in her stomach. She needs an operation—immediately. And I'm not sure, but it may already be too late. Her heart is working too hard, trying to get more blood."

Danny, his eyes on Conchita, bit his tongue. Professionally, he would not speak out against Dr. Harrison, but he was grateful the nurse had been honest in her assessment.

"I will get a stretcher and some orderlies to help get her transferred to St. Luke's. The problem will be Mr. Brodie and Dr. Harrison. Normally, I wouldn't recommend even moving her, but she is in need of surgery now. I wouldn't even wait until morning."

"I take care of eet, Dr. Danny. You leave that to me."

Danny turned to the nurse.

Sylvia was breathing easier, knowing Mrs. Brodie was in capable hands. This doctor knew what he was doing, and he did it well.

"I will need your help," Danny said. "While I send Mr. Bannister to round up a couple orderlies, I will need to scrub Mrs. Brodie down to prepare for surgery. I'll need hot water, clean sheets, and a clean gown for the patient."

"I can halp with that too. I go now and send Matthew for dose orderlies." Conchita took a deep breath but waited to hear what else Danny had to say.

"Thank you," Danny said. "I don't wish to get into a quarrel with another doctor, but your sister needs surgery. She should have had it weeks ago. I don't want to get your hopes up, Conchita. She's in a very bad way. How long has Dr. Harrison been seeing her?" He turned to Sylvia for the answer.

"She's been ill for over a month but, of course, not this bad. I wondered if I should have reported this to someone at the hospital, but with Dr. Harrison looking after her..."

"It's not your fault, nurse. It is criminal neglige...never mind. Just know, please—it's not your fault."

Sylvia began to fold the covers that had been on Constanza, who still had not awakened.

Conchita delivered her message to Constanza's husband and Dr. Harrison. She brooked no opposition, but Dr. Harrison took the stairs at a rapid pace and was huffing and puffing as he reached the top, his face an alarming red. Timothy Brodie followed at a more sedate pace.

"What do you think you're doing?" Harrison gasped. "This is my patient. I only said you could examine her, not take over."

"Dr. Harrison, I know you wouldn't intentionally harm this woman, but she's bleeding internally and needs surgery right away. She's nearing a heart attack. Her heart is pumping far too hard, laboring to get more blood, which isn't available because, as I said before, she's bleeding internally."

A shocked looked replaced the anger. "N-no, of course not. I thought she, I thought she ah…" His bluster suddenly deflated as if the flame in a hot-air balloon had been extinguished. He'd never thought of taking her to the hospital or getting a second opinion.

Timothy Brodie stood in the doorway. He'd not come near his wife in weeks for fear of catching what she might have. As he heard the conversation, he went over and realized Constanza was oblivious to all that was going on around her. She'd lost a tremendous amount of weight, her face thin, gaunt, and emaciated. He looked with shocked eyes at Dr. Harrison.

"What have you done?" he whispered. "What have you done to my wife? I can see, even without your knowledge, that she is dying." He went to his knees next to the bed, took Constanza's hand, and kissed it. He crossed himself and began to pray.

Conchita, meanwhile, after telling Diego and Matthew what was needed, was directing the cook and housekeeper.

"You heat plenty o' hot water," she said to the cook. "An' you," she said to the housekeeper, "right away, you geet the clean sheets an' nightgown for my seester. She very seeck and weel go to the hospital, but she need bath first. She not contagious, so doan you worry."

The women, knowing Conchita well, hurried to do her bidding.

CHAPTER XXVI

Is there no limit to windy words?

JOB 16:3

JENNY STOOD ON THE THRESHOLD OF GINGER'S room, listening to Chloe chatter a hundred words a minute. She smiled, thankful Ginger had found a friend.

"Are you girls ready to go?" she asked. "I packed some oatmeal cookies Cora made this morning, and I have a pie in the hamper and some cold cuts, a loaf of fresh bread, and some salad too. Cora has also given us a bunch of pasties, which are delicious. They're a pastry folded over but filled with meat and vegetables. I have no doubt there's enough food to last for a couple days.

"What have you packed, Ginger?" she asked. "Besides food, I've packed the clothes I'll need, my Bible, my knitting, cross stitch, and a book."

Ginger beckoned her to look into her satchel. She opened the top and pointed while Chloe answered the question.

"She has her toothbrush, hairbrush, and the aloe cream your cook made for her. She has lots of clothes, her nightie, and two books along with the Bible Mrs. Mobrey gave her."

"Oh, thank you for reminding me. I forgot my hairbrush. I'll just be a moment, and then I reckon we'll head back over to Liberty's house. I'll just be two shakes of a lamb's tail," Jenny said. "And thanks, Chloe, for helping Ginger."

"You're welcome, ma'am," Chloe replied.

Jenny left to get her hairbrush, a few hairpins, and a shawl. When she returned, she had Ginger take her puppy out to wee before they left.

Ginger and Chloe took the puppy downstairs and outside, going through the kitchen. Ginger wanted to show Chloe the garden and see her reaction to it.

Chloe felt as if she'd died and gone to the heaven, it was so beautiful. Hattie had told her about heaven and some about hell too, but Chloe didn't want to think about that. She was quite certain her pa was there. She danced around and grabbed Ginger's hands and had her dancing around too. The puppy barked and barked and tried to jump on the two girls, who fell to the ground breathless.

"It's so beautiful, Ginger," Chloe said. "Thanks for showing it to me."

Ginger nodded, satisfied that Chloe appreciated the beauty around them. Ginger showed her some tiny flowers almost hidden under a bigger bush. She pointed, and Chloe dropped to her knees to smell them. She couldn't smell anything, but the white and purple flowers were almost like lanterns.

"Those are so pretty," Chloe said. "Thanks for showing me all this." She waved her arm to encompass the entire area. "It's amazing, and my new mama said God made all of it."

Ginger merely stared at Chloe a second and scooped up her puppy. The two girls went back inside the house. Chloe knew she'd made Ginger angry, but she didn't know how.

Mackie left some paper and a pencil on the secretary in the front foyer for Ginger to use when she wanted to communicate in a specific way.

Ginger wrote on a piece of paper, making it known to Jenny that she wanted to take the puppy with them.

"No, sweetheart," Jenny replied, "I don't think that's wise. We don't know how Boston would react to a puppy, and your puppy would miss the other puppies and likely cry at night. Then the twins would most likely wake and start crying. No, I don't think we should impose any more than we are on Mrs. Bannister's hospitality."

"I could take care of the puppy. That could be my main job," Chloe said. She looked hopefully at Jenny, not wanting Ginger to be disappointed about anything.

Jenny smiled down at the girl, who wanted to please Ginger.

"Thank you for your offer, Chloe, but no. We're not taking the puppy with us," Jenny said firmly. She turned to Ginger and said, "You can put Thad in charge of your puppy. Have you named it yet?"

Ginger nodded and wrote *Jolly* on a piece of paper.

"His name is Jolly? What a nice name. He is a happy dog, isn't he."

It was a statement rather than a question, and Ginger smiled.

"Well, children, I think it's time we headed back to Rancho Bonito. Let's go find Anne and James, shall we?"

Anne and James were talking in the sunroom, and Thad was playing there with his and Anne's puppy.

"Reckon we're ready to go back to the Bannisters'," Jenny said. "Your Cora gave us enough food to last for a couple days, I'm sure. I thanked her for her generosity, and I thank you too."

The family gathered to see them off, Thad secretly wishing he could go too.

James looked over at the boy, whose face looked a bit forlorn.

"I reckon we could go fishing," James said, "that is, if you'd like to. We could go to a lake or to the river…your choice."

Ginger heard the offer James made, knowing he was trying to comfort her brother. She bobbed her head and grinned at Thaddeus. She turned and hugged him, giving him an extra big squeeze. Bending down, she stroked her puppy, who was sniffing her shoe. She was amazed she felt so connected to James and Anne already. She hugged her new mother goodbye.

Anne hugged her back, smoothing the top of her head and kissed her cheek. She straightened one of Ginger's bright blonde pigtails.

"I hope you have a wonderful time at the Bannisters. You will be a big help to Miss Liberty, I'm sure. I know I don't have to tell you to mind your manners. Your manners are probably better than mine" She smiled and hugged Ginger again.

Ginger bobbed her head, and James held out his hand to beckon her closer, drawing her into his arms.

"I'm going to miss you, Ginger. I'll take you fishing with us next time if you'd like to go." He picked her up, gave her a big hug, and kissed her cheek. "I love you sweetheart. I'm looking forward to the day you'll be able to talk again. Thad told me you have a lovely voice and can sing like a bird, and I want to hear it!" He put her down but took her chin in his hand. Looking deeply into her eyes, he said, "I am praying your voice will be restored to you. I don't know why you can't talk, but the good Lord can heal you. Don't lose hope, and don't, whatever you do, stop believing He can help you."

Ginger looked into James' eyes, so clear and honest, and tears misted her own. She *had* lost hope that God cared about her. She was angry at God. He'd given her a wonderful new family and new friends, and she felt she should be grateful, but she was still angry. When James let go of her, she hugged him around the waist and looked up at him with eyes full of love.

"I know. I love you, too," he said. "Have a good time." He turned to Chloe and spoke to her as if she were an adult. "Thank you for being a friend to my children. I hope you have a good time. Don't stay up all night, or you'll be no use to Miss Liberty." He grinned at the tousle-haired little redhead, ruffling her short curls.

Chloe grinned back at him. "You don't have ta worry about that, Mr. Mobrey. When my head hits the pillow, I'm asleep. Mama says it's 'cause I'm so full of energy during the day. I'll take care of Ginger—don't you worry about her." Chloe spoke as if it were her sole duty in life to care for Ginger.

Jenny climbed to the seat of the wagon, and Dock, who'd been holding the horse's harness, handed her the reins.

"She's a sweet horse. Name's Stockings, an' I have no doubt you know why." He smiled at Jenny and stepped back.

James grabbed Chloe to put her into the wagon, but she spoke to Dock as James lifted her up.

"It's 'cause she's got four white legs. I'd've called 'er that too!" She plunked herself down next to Jenny as James lifted Ginger to the wagon seat.

"See you in a few days," Anne said. "We'll miss you!"

"Reckon when Mrs. Bannister's husband comes back, we'll come home," Jenny said. "Bye now." She clucked to the horse, slapping her back lightly with the reins, and they set off for Rancho Bonito.

Danny and Sylvia prepared Constanza for surgery. The housekeeper came in with clean sheets and a nightgown. Danny's face was grim as he looked at the woman's emaciated body.

Constanza wasn't much older than he was, he guessed, but her body looked eighty.

"I can't believe any doctor would allow his patient to get in such a deteriorated state and not know she needed something. Has he checked on her dietary needs, water, anything?"

"No," Sylvia replied. "I tried to tell him, but he ignored me. I've gotten a bit of fluid down, but not nearly enough. She's dehydrated. I told Dr. Harrison I was quitting the case, and he told me he'd be sure to smear my name if I did." Sylvia was almost in tears, looking at Constanza's body. She'd not seen her completely uncovered.

It wasn't long before three orderlies came up the stairs with a stretcher. Danny, when he'd first moved to California and began working at the hospital, had required his orderlies to learn how to be stretcher-bearers. He required them to read the *Manual of Exercises for Training Stretcher-Bearers and Bearer-Companies*, by Sandford Moore, BA, RSS, out of London. It had been published in 1877, and it wasn't long before everyone in the medical profession was using it.

The men came in and gently shifted Constanza to the stretcher, carrying her down the stairs and out the door.

Danny turned to Sylvia and said, "No one is going to smear your name. Are you married?"

Sylvia blushed to the roots of her hair and replied, "N-no, I'm not."

"May I have the privilege of courting you with that intent?"

Sylvia gasped, her eyes widening with shock. "What are you saying? You don't even know me!"

"No, that's true—I don't, but I'd like to take a lifetime to." He spoke seriously, but his eyes sparkled with laughter. "Don't ask me how this happened. I'm the think-everything-out-beforehand kind of guy. Look at my great age. I'm thirty-two, for goodness sakes, and I've had plenty of opportunity to find a wife. I've had women throw themselves at me, but none of them ever came even close to where you already are in my heart. I took one look at you, and I was lost."

Sylvia looked at Danny as if he were crazy. "I am not a spontaneous person, so to speak. I-I will have to ponder this…uh this…proposal? Is that what this is?"

"Not a formal one, of course, but I would like to court you. Do you live with your parents? For that matter, where do you live?" he asked. "We can work out the details later, but I certainly don't wish to lose track of you."

"Well, Dr. Gates," she said.

"Danny,"

"Well, Dr. Gates, I…I suppose until I know you better, I will meet you at a designated spot. I don't plan to give you my address until I know more about you, and no, I don't live with my parents. I have a roommate, and we share a flat in the city."

Danny's eyebrows rose in surprise.

"I can assure you, Nurse Cobain, I am certifiably sane. I need to get to the hospital. Would you care to accompany me? There are many questions I'm sure you'll be able to answer." Danny knew he was pushing, but this was the girl for him.

Sylvia couldn't decide if Danny was normal or not, but she did need a ride. She'd been riding in a hansom cab to and from work and thought riding in Dr. Gates' carriage would save time.

"Yes, I'd appreciate a ride."

"Let's go," he said.

They descended the stairs to see that Conchita and Diego had gone with Constanza. Matthew was waiting for Danny, and Timothy Brodie and Dr. Harrison were talking to each other. Brodie's voice was full of anger.

"I ought to have you horsewhipped. If my wife dies, you'd better find a good place to hide!" Timothy Brodie was incensed by Dr. Harrison's cavalier attitude, and a good measure of self-guilt for not checking on his wife added to his anger.

"I'm sorry, Mr. Brodie. I truly am. I will waive any amount owed me by you." Dr. Harrison knew he was in deep waters with Mr. Brodie. He was an influential businessman in the city.

Danny, ignoring their conversation, spoke to Matthew who'd been listening unashamedly to the two men haranguing in the parlor.

"Nurse Cobain is going with us."

Matthew nodded and replied, "Let's get going then."

They headed out the door where Constanza was being loaded onto a special wagon that had thick cords tied to the corners of the stretcher to keep it steady. Diego was on his horse, and Conchita was in the wagon beside her sister. The wagon was already moving, and Diego nodded to Matthew and headed out with it.

It wasn't until they got to the horses that Sylvia realized Danny didn't have a carriage. Her eyes widened, and she swallowed down her astonishment.

Matthew, already climbing onto Piggypie, asked, "By the way, I didn't have time to get a telegram off to Alex. Are you still eating there?"

"Most times, unless I'm swamped, I do." Danny added, "I'm hoping Nurse Cobain can join us this evening. They always have plenty to eat." He reached down for Sylvia's arm, and she leaped as he swung her up behind him.

Matthew grinned at the look on Sylvia's face.

She saw it and felt the blood climb from her neck to her cheeks, which were stained red. She couldn't remember being this close to a man since sitting on her papa's knee years ago. She sat primly.

Matthew, grinning widely, spoke to Danny.

"You'd better get her to hang on to you, or she'll slide right off the back of your horse." He laughed and gave Piggypie a little kick.

Without saying a word to Sylvia, Danny felt her hands timidly creep around his waist, and as he clucked to his horse, her hands tightened. He marveled at his reaction to this woman. Without a word, she had stolen his heart. He prayed she would feel the same way about him.

The two horses, side by side, headed for the hospital.

Buddy Blake followed the wagon loaded with a family, but more importantly Chloe, at a distance. He wondered how to proceed. He wished like anything Rudy was with him. He'd been the brains, the one who'd been the planner of everything they did. Robberies had been his specialty. When they'd come upon the house where they'd tied up the old man, Rudy had said it was abandoned. It'd been a real shock when the old man came after them, telling them to get out. Rudy had beaten the old guy to a pulp before tying him up in the chair. Rudy planned everything, and when they'd run out of food, Rudy had sent Buddy to get some.

Yes, I miss 'im, he thought. *Now, iffen that sheriff is a heading home with that woman he kissed on the road, then the jail will be all right to visit. I kin make sure Rudy's not there. I kin drop by and not be questioned since the sheriff ain't there.*

After he saw the wagonload of people turn into the lane of the vineyard, he spurred his horse to a gallop and headed to town. He didn't care to miss something if Chloe came out of that lane and headed somewhere else. He concentrated on the path but made plans as he rode.

I'm thinking I'd best be getting a few more blankets and grub while I'm in town. Mayhap I'll get holt of Chloe. I reckon I don't have a blanket nor nothin' fer her ta sleep in. I kin bide my time till I get holt of 'er. I'm thinkin' when I catch 'er, I'm gonna beat that stinkin' kid within an inch of 'er life, or I'm not Buddy Blake. She could a made herself scarce and hid from the sheriff 'stead a gettin' herself caught. She could a tol' me what happened an' iffen 'er pa is dead…waal…we could a been headed outta here and not stick around here where we kin get caught. Yep, when I get holt a 'er, I'm gonna beat the tarnation outta 'er.

He rode hard and pulled up in front of the sheriff's office. Throwing his reins around the hitching rail, he stepped carefully to the boarded walk and up to the door. He looked furtively around, and seeing no one paying him any attention, he tried turning the knob.

It's locked, by golly. Think I'll mosey to the back window an' see iffen Rudy's there.

He went around to the back of the office and saw the barred window.

"Rudy," he said. "Rudy, ya'll in there?" He raised his voice a few notches and called out again. "Rudy, you in there?"

No one answered. His eyes teared up, and he took a deep, shuddering breath. He felt like crying. He might have had his quarrels with Rudy, but he was his brother, and he loved him just the same. He sniffed and wiped his eyes on his shirtsleeve.

Circling back to the front of the building, he untied his horse and walked across the street to the saloon. He tied up in front and wiped his eyes and nose on his sleeve again, and pushed his way in, cringing in his gut when all eyes seemed trained on him, but he strode up to the bar as if he owned it.

Harkin was sitting on a stool behind the bar and saw Buddy push through the swinging half doors. He grunted, shifted his weight, and stood up on sore feet. He waddled to the bar.

CHAPTER XXVII

And he said, Behold, I make a covenant:
before all thy people I will do marvels, such as have
not been done in all the earth, nor in any nation.

EXODUS 34:10

"**H**ELLO THERE, STRANGER. AIN'T SEEN YOU fer a few days. You ever find your brother?"

"Yes, yes, I done found 'im," Buddy lied. "We're on our way to Frisco. Mayhap we'll be back this way, but I doubt it. I heard tell they's got a prisoner over at the jail that's gonna be hanged. Did I hear that right?"

"Nope," Harkin answered with authority. "I know all the happenin's around this here town, an' there ain't no one in that there jail. It's been a long spell since we had any hangin's around here. Sheriff don't like 'em. He'd rather put a man on a chain gang, or if the crime ain't all that bad, he has them doin' what he calls community service."

"Waal, gimme a shot a whiskey, will ya? I'm feelin' right parched." Buddy flipped a couple coins onto the bar, sliding them with two dirty fingers toward Harkin.

"He put anyone on that chain gang recent?" Buddy looked Harkin squarely in the eye. It was something he'd always had trouble doing. His eyes slid away after he asked the question.

Harkin plunked down his shot of whiskey and replied.

"Naw, we ain't had no one in that jail fer over three months now. Ever' one around these here parts is scared of the sheriff. He don't take no guff from no one. Now, we do get the occasional stranger what don't know about our sheriff. Them's the most likely ta get strung up. We did have a case last summer. A right nice couple got murdered on th' main road. Went ta a party, they did, an' lo and behold someone comes out and shoots them dead afore they got home. They shot Sheriff Rawlins too, only they didn't kill 'im. He never did catch 'em neither. Made a lot of people talk about whether he was fit ta be sheriff. I always figured he knew who done it, but he wasn't tellin' nobody. He's a closed-mouth one fer sure. Keeps his cards close to his chest, so to speak."

"Yeah, I know the type," Buddy said. "Some of those sheriffs think they're the onliest ones what should know all the facts."

"Got that right," Harkin replied.

Buddy upended his glass in one large swallow.

"Waal, I best be goin'," he said. "I'm s'posed ta meet up with my brother an' his kid down San Rafael way. Don't know iffen I'll be seein' you again, but it was downright nice ta talk ta you." He lifted his hat respectfully to Harkin and made his way out the door.

He stood outside the saloon, gazing around himself thoroughly, looking to see if the sheriff had come to town. Buddy didn't see him. He untied his horse and walked over to the mercantile, tying his ride up once again.

He picked out a couple cheaper blankets, more matches, some lamp oil, and a few other things he felt were necessities, cursing under his breath, all the while, about the amount of money Rudy had been carrying. He was going to have to be careful, as Rudy hadn't given him nearly as much as he'd put in that money belt of his.

He bought more bacon, beans, beef jerky, and another pan for cooking. The proprietor kept trying to make conversation, but Buddy only grunted in reply. He wanted the merchant to think he was panning for gold, not holed up in a cave, waiting for an opportunity to get hold of

Chloe. He picked up a few more items, paid his bill and began packing everything into saddlebags.

He climbed onto his ride and headed out of town. First he rode to his little camp, unloading all his new purchases. He wanted to get back to a hillock where he could spy on the lane where the wagonful of people had headed down. He took a bite of the beef jerky and began to chew, hoping he wouldn't be too late to see Chloe riding back out of the lane.

When Jenny reached the main road, she looked to her left but turned right. There wasn't a soul to be seen. She slapped the reins a bit, and they set off at a trot.

Chloe chattered, making up for Ginger's silence.

"I bin learning to ride a horse," she said.

Ginger patted her on the leg and shook her head no.

"I have been learning to ride a horse." Chloe grinned at Ginger, who grinned back. "I don't like to trot. It's too bumpy. I love to canter though. It's so smooth and steady. Ginger took me out to the garden, and we played a little with Jolly. It is a magnificent garden, ain't it, Miss Jenny?"

"Isn't it," Jenny replied and added, "Yes, it is gorgeous. James planned almost all of it."

Chloe continued to chatter nonstop, and Jenny and Ginger grinned at each other over her head.

"I'll say one thing," Jenny said. "You're never at a loss for words, are you?"

Chloe looked up at her and grinned. "Nope, and now I get to talk for two of us."

The ride to the hospital didn't take long. Matthew and Sylvia stood aside as Danny directed the stretcher-bearers where he wanted the patient. Conchita didn't leave Constanza's side. Diego, who'd stayed with Conchita, came out of a curtained room. He told Matthew and Sylvia that Danny wanted another opinion as to whether they should even operate.

"Eet's not looking too good for Constanza," he said. "Dr. Danny, he say even healthy patients, they geet infection after surgery, and about half them die. He say he make sure anyone who touch Constanza, they muss be very clean. He's worried eet ees too late for her to haf surgery."

They saw Danny come out of the room. "I need to confer with a couple other doctors," he said, his brow creased with worry. He strode down a long hall and disappeared into a room.

"Constanza, she not wake up," Diego said. "Dr. Danny, he theenk she no make eet." He sat down, pulling a large red bandana from his hip pocket to dab his eyes.

Danny came back with two other doctors following him into the room.

Matthew turned to Sylvia and spoke. "Did Danny invite you to dinner this evening?"

"I think he did. What do you think, Mr. Bannister? Is he normal…I know he's a doctor, but what I mean is, as a person, is he, uh…" Sylvia's cheeks pinked up, but her eyes held a question that needed an answer.

Matthew smiled and replied, "In truth, I don't know Danny very well. I've only been around him a few times, but what I do know is, he is my brother-in-law's best friend. They have a deep friendship going back for years, beginning in Boston when they were schoolboys together. Danny is a committed Christian and holds honor and integrity as values he must follow to the letter of the law. He's never been married, and according to my brother-in-law, Alex, women are continually chasing him. Alex says Danny is one of the nicest men he knows. And yes, he's normal if you're talking about his credentials, but he's a cut above most men I know. Now, I have a question for you. Why do you ask?"

Sylvia looked at him with surprise clearly marked on her face. "I ask because, although he seemed competent in his examination of Mrs. Brodie, he…uh…he doesn't know me, but"—her words became rushed —"he asked to court me with the intention of marrying me." The blood rose from her neck to suffuse her cheeks.

Matthew looked down at her in amazement.

"Nurse Cobain, if Danny said it, he means it. It's certainly not his normal behavior. Alex says it drives him crazy sometimes, the way Danny has to look at every angle before making a decision. If you are at all attracted to him, you need to give him a chance. He's a fine man."

Sylvia started to speak but stopped. She looked away, trying to digest what Mr. Bannister had said.

Danny came out of the room, walking over to them slowly. He took hold of Diego's shoulder and spoke in a gentle voice.

"I'm sorry," he said. "She passed away just a few moments ago." He squeezed Diego's shoulder. "I don't think we could have—"

A scream rent the air. Danny turned and sprinted back to the room.

"She not dead!" Conchita shouted. "She not dead!" Conchita had stood without knowing it and then plopped back down as if all the air had been knocked out of her.

Constanza was thin as a rail, but with a radiance to her face that brought astonishment to all three doctors who gazed at her.

Matthew, Diego, and Sylvia were on Danny's heels as he entered the room.

Constanza turned her head to see Conchita, tears running down her cheeks for joy. Conchita rose from her chair and, leaning over the bed, hugged Constanza, stroking her cheek and then her hair. She hugged her again.

"Oh my seester, how I do love you." The tears continued down Conchita's cheeks unabated. She stood back, and her sister sat upright in the bed.

"*¡Alabado sea el Señor! ¡Alabado sea por su regalo de sanidad!*" (Praise the Lord! Praise Him for His gift of healing!)

"I was dead," Constanza said. "I saw Jesus…I'm not crazy…I'm telling you, I saw Jesus! Oh, He was glorious! Oh my, I didn't want to come back! He spoke to me, and He told me I wasn't finished here…that I had to come back. I didn't want to come back…oh my, the peace I felt is unexplainable." She pulled the pillow behind her up and leaned back. "Where's Timothy? Where's my husband?"

Matthew replied, "I'm sure he's on his way. He was talking to the doctor who's been treating you. Firing him, I should think."

Constanza smiled and nodded her head as if she agreed with that assessment. Suddenly, she said, "*Tengo hambre.*"

Conchita began to laugh through her tears of joy. "She ees hungry. My seester, she ees hungry."

Diego said, "I'll go find something to eat. You wanna eat too, Conchita?"

"Yes, I am hungry too. But before you leave, I want to say something. Dr. Danny, he pray for you, Constanza. Thees doctors, they all theenk eet be too late to operate. Dr. Danny, he pray for God to heal you. And when he feenish, you quit breathing. You died, Constanza. Eet be why you see Jesus. I glad for you to steel have job to do here. Every one of us here, we see God's miracle. He geets all our praise and devotion. Praise God for your life."

The late afternoon sky was a glorious blue. Wisps of silk threaded their way across the heavens with a light breeze pushing the white strands into a crazy pattern.

Buddy Blake, chewing on a piece of the jerky he'd bought, rode down from his camp. He traveled for about fifteen minutes, reining his horse to turn off the main road opposite of where the wagon, with Chloe in it, had turned in. He rode at a walk over the uneven ground, climbing steadily up a hill with a few scrub oaks and foliage. He tied his horse to one of the branches behind a screen of bushes, rounded it, and sat down to roll a smoke, looking forward to it.

Buddy had a clear view from his perch atop the hill. He was able to see the main road for miles in both directions. He sat down on a flat rock and pulled his tobacco pouch out of his breast pocket. All the sudden he spied a wagon some distance down the road. He dropped his pouch of tobacco and ran to his horse, pulling out his spyglass. He dashed back and peered through the spyglass, adjusting the lens.

"Aha," he said. "There she is. I reckon she's a headin' back to that vineyard where she comed from a few hours afore. I best be gettin' myself down there an' watch fer when she comes out later. Mayhap she's gonna eat there afore she goes home."

He picked up his tobacco pouch, stored his spyglass, and climbed back onto his horse. He started to ride to the main road faster than when he'd left it, but he realized the wagon would be out of sight whether he rode hard or not. He slowed, not caring to have his horse hit a gopher hole or something. He pulled onto the main road. After arriving in a leisurely fashion at the place opposite the turn-in, he rode across the flat area and up a hill where he could watch. Thinking that maybe when it got darker he might spy out the house, he sat down to wait and smoke.

Jenny arrived at Rancho Bonito safely with the two girls.

Liberty came out to welcome them back. She was thankful that Lupe and Luce had the bedrooms spick and span before they left for San Francisco. She needn't do anything except enjoy her guests and feed them.

Donny came out of the stable to take their horse. He held out his hand for Jenny to step down, and the two girls hopped down unassisted.

"I'm glad I have the girls to help me." Jenny laughed. "I'd have forgotten my hairbrush and pins. You'll be glad to know, Liberty, Cora gave us enough food to last for a couple days, if not longer."

Liberty started to pick up the hamper of food, but Jenny said, "Careful! It's really heavy."

"Goodness," Liberty said. "It is really heavy! Oh, I am glad you've come! It's been so quiet for the last couple hours. Usually I enjoy the alone time, but I always know someone is near at hand. The twins are down for a nap, and most afternoons Conchita and I have an afternoon tea. Without Matthew, Luce, Lupe, and Conchita, the house feels empty. I laid down right after you left and slept for an hour, at least. I feel more rested."

Boston, with only a couple barks, had come out to greet them. He gave Chloe a lick on the face, something he wasn't supposed to do. She giggled and hugged the big dog's neck.

"Come on inside," Liberty said. She turned to Donny, "Thanks for taking care of their horse, Donny. Do you know when Cady is coming back from San Rafael?"

"Yes, ma'am, I do," he replied. "Four more days. She'll be back in exactly four more days. I sure miss her, but I'm glad I'm here to be able to help." He grinned, led the horse closer to the barn, and started unhitching the wagon.

"I'm glad you're here to help too." She glanced at Chloe and didn't say anything to him about her worry. Buck had told Matthew about Chloe's uncle out looking for her. She didn't know if Matthew had passed that information on to Donny or not.

Liberty led her guests into the spacious great room, setting the heavy hamper on the floor.

"Before I show you your rooms, I have a question for you girls. Do you want to share a room, or would you like to sleep separately?"

Ginger took Chloe's arm, poked her in the chest, thumbed her own chest, and poked Chloe again in the chest.

"I think that means we're sharing a room," Chloe said, and Ginger nodded vigorously.

"All right, but Ginger, this is the sign for yes. Can you do that?" She signed, and Chloe and Jenny repeated the sign along with Ginger.

"Good! Now, please follow me."

She led the two girls to the room Maggie, her maid, had stayed in when they'd come west three years before. It was a beautiful bedroom done in different shades of apricot. White organdy-lined silk curtains hung in the two windows, and all the trim was stark white. A white mantel stretched itself over the fireplace, which looked as if it hadn't been used much. A large picture graced the wall above the mantel, a painting of a terrace with delicate chairs, lacy tablecloth, and an ocean in the background.

"This is where you girls will sleep. You can unpack your satchels, but first I want to show you where Jenny will sleep. Her room is right through here. You will share the *salle de bains*, sorry…that's French for bathroom."

The bathroom between the bedrooms was pretty, but Liberty led them through it to the room Jenny would occupy.

"This is the room I stayed in when I first came west." Liberty waved her arm expansively to encompass the room. "My coming west is a long story, and perhaps I'll tell it to you one of these days."

"It's a beautiful room, isn't it," Jenny stated. "I feel as if the sun just came out."

Liberty nodded. "I felt the same way when I first walked in here."

The room was painted an airy yellow, making the entire room look sunny. French doors—all glass—led to the outside. A curtain on the door was pulled to one side, with matching curtains at the large windows. It was fresh and warm. The four-poster bed looked inviting. There was a fireplace in this room too, but the mantel was a dark-mahogany. Above the mantel was a painting of a field of daisies.

"I'll leave you to settle your things. I put a couple jugs of water by the sink. We're soon to put in the flush toilets and running water. I can't wait! I'll be in the kitchen when you're ready. And again, I do thank you all for coming. Taking care of twins can be quite a chore besides doing all the other things that need done. I'm grateful you're all here." She left, going out Jenny's door that opened to the wide hall.

"Okay, girls," Jenny said, "let's get our duds put away. Perhaps we could have tea with Liberty and have some of those cookies Cora made for us."

CHAPTER XXVIII

And be ye kind one to another, tenderhearted,
forgiving one another,
even as God for Christ's sake hath forgiven you.

EPHESIANS 4:32

IT ONLY TOOK A FEW MINUTES TO PUT AWAY their few belongings. They headed to the kitchen, where Liberty was laying out the food stuffs from the hamper.

"Goodness!" she exclaimed. "What a blessing! Cora was generous. Look at all this!"

Besides all the things Jenny had told the girls, Cora had added fried chicken and a potato salad as well as an apple pie.

"No wonder that hamper was so heavy." Jenny laughed. "I thought it felt heavier than when I first picked it up."

"This will make a fine dinner for us," Liberty said. She was delighted she didn't have to cook. She felt bone-tired, as she was sleeping fitfully. She kept having dreams of shooting Chloe's father, and every time there was a different outcome. She knew there'd been no option. As Matthew had told her, it was kill or be killed, only she hadn't meant to kill him, just disarm him. She glanced over at Chloe, whose eyes were watching her.

"I put some water on to boil. Would you join me in having a cup of tea and some of those cookies?"

"Yes. Grandma Jenny said we just might have tea with you." Chloe spoke solemnly, still not knowing how she felt about Liberty.

After the teapot had tea steeping, they sat down, and Liberty spoke to all of them.

"I know we plan to have a good time together, but I need to clear the air, so to speak, with Chloe." She looked at the other two, who clearly had no idea what she was talking about.

"Chloe," she said, "that day Matthew found you, we were riding over to visit Dan Hedley. He was a healthy man, looking forward to living close to his daughter. His wife had died a month or so before, and he didn't want to farm anymore. We were planning to buy his property, because it abuts ours, and Matthew was a close friend of Dan's.

"Matthew said you were hiding in the loft and couldn't see what was happening, but you did see your pa bash Matthew on the head. After tying up Matthew to a chair, he came out onto the porch and aimed at our horses. I was lying down in the grass, because your pa had already shot at us and almost killed Matthew. If I hadn't spoken to him just as your pa fired, I don't think he'd be alive. The bullet caught a little of his ear as it passed by.

"I realized your pa intended to shoot our horses, so I shot him in the thigh. He continued to shoot, so I shot him in his gun hand. He bent down, picked up the gun in his left, and started to shoot my horse, so I aimed for his upper arm, but he turned suddenly, and I caught him in the chest." Tears ran down Liberty's cheeks. "I'm so sorry, Chloe. It was not intentional, but I didn't know what else to do. I haven't been sleeping well because of it. I never intended to kill him, but he wouldn't stop...he simply wouldn't stop shooting at our horses."

Jenny said nothing, and Ginger's eyes had widened.

Chloe went to Liberty's side.

She slipped her hands around Libby's waist and said softly, "I'm sorry, Miss Liberty. I'm sorry for it all. I miss my pa, but he was a bad man. I knew he was bad even afore my ma died. And it's the truth that I'm happier being the Rawlins' kid than I ever bin...than I have ever been, in my whole life. I know you didn't mean to kill him. My new mama said bad things happen, an' it's because this world isn't like the one we were supposed to live in. I hope you sleep better. I'm sleeping better. I asked Jesus to come into my heart and take away all the bad thoughts and things I've done. He forgave me, and I forgive you for shooting my pa."

Liberty scooped the little girl into her arms.

"You are such a sweet girl, and you are wise for only being five. Thank you for your words. I've been so sorry about all this, and I accept your forgiveness." She hugged Chloe, who hugged her right back.

"Now, can we have some of those cookies?" Chloe asked.

Everyone laughed as the atmosphere lightened.

Jenny said, "I'll pour."

Timothy arrived at the hospital while arrangements were being made for Constanza to be sent home. When he was taken into her room, his eyes nearly popped out of his head. He ran to her side and began to weep.

"Oh, my darling! I thought I'd lost you! Oh, Constanza, when I saw how ill you were, I fell to my knees and asked the Almighty God if I could have another chance. I asked Him to forgive me for the cavalier way I've treated you. I promise to be the husband you thought you married. I'm sorry for the way I've ignored you and pray I can make it up to you." He looked into her eyes and asked, "What did they do to you? You look as if you're well—thin, but well. What did they give you?"

Between Conchita and Constanza, the explanation was made to him, and he looked in awe at his wife.

"I think you are an angel, my darling."

"Eets about time!" Conchita said under her breath.

"Yes," Timothy said. "It *is* about time."

Dr. Danny had witnessed the interchange and thanked God silently that some good would come out of Harrison's folly.

"Mr. Brodie, you can take your wife home. She needs to eat soups and light food, but more often. Please don't upset your system by eating a regular meal, at least for a couple days." Danny smiled and added, "What a miracle we have witnessed this day. I praise God I was here to see it."

Constanza replied, "Yes, I too am thankful."

All the sudden there was a commotion outside the room, and Lupe and Luce rushed in.

"Oh, mama," they said in unison.

"Conchita, she never tell us you are seeck," Lupe said, her voice sounding petulant. She looked accusingly at Conchita. Both girls went to their mother and hugged her.

"That ees true. I doan know how seeck she ees, an' I know I geet no work from you eef you worrying about your mother."

Timothy said, "I vote we move this discussion to our house." He turned to Danny and held out his hand. "I cannot thank you enough for coming to the rescue. I had no idea Harrison was so negligent." He took a wad of folded bills and pressed them into Danny's hand.

"I don't need your money, Mr. Brodie. I went to your house on request from Diego. Frankly, I did nothing. It was God who healed your wife."

"I know. I know, but just the same I'd feel better if you'd take it."

Danny pressed his lips together and said, "Put it into the offering at church." He ignored Timothy's handful of money and turned toward Conchita. "Would you please lend Constanza your shawl to cover the nightgown?"

"Yes," Timothy said, "I think it's time we headed home."

They exited the hospital quietly.

Diego hung back and spoke to Matthew.

"I stay weeth Conchita," he said. "I theenk we be coming home een a few days."

"It's all right. You take as long as you need. I think Conchita is in need of your support. This has been a huge emotional time for her."

Diego nodded and walked slowly out of the building. Only Matthew, Sylvia, and Danny were left.

"Shall we make our way to Liberty House?" Danny asked.

Matthew nodded, and Sylvia looked at him with a question in her eyes.

"Liberty House is where my best friend, Alex Liberty, lives," Danny said. "You will enjoy meeting them, I think. They have six children, but they eat in the nursery if there's company. Let me sign these papers, and we'll be on our way."

Within a short time, Sylvia was once again ensconced behind Danny. This time she felt a bit more comfortable.

Darkness was beginning to fall, and stars twinkled in the great expanse.

Danny looked up at the heavens, stars multiplying, and his heart was warmed by the fact that the woman sitting behind him would assuredly one day be his wife. He waxed eloquent.

"'Canst thou bind the sweet influences of Pleiades, or loose the bands of Orion?'"

"What are you talking about, Dr. Gates?" Sylvia asked.

"Danny, it's just Danny to you. And what I'm quoting is from the book of Job…when God is answering Job out of the whirlwind. Sorry. I'm quite sure you think I'm insane enough without me talking aloud. It's just that my heart is overflowing with gratitude to the Almighty. I witnessed a miraculous healing, not an hour past, and found my girl on the same day, which in and of itself is a miracle too. I hope you don't mind me being so forward. I know I am, but I can't seem to help myself. I am so full of joy right now, I feel nigh unto bursting with it!"

Sylvia laughed. "I hope you know what you're getting yourself into. I'm not a witless female with nothing more to think of than what dress I'm going to wear or what soirée I plan to attend. I've been accused of being strong minded, hardheaded, opinionated, I have quite a list and could go on and on. What's sad is, I'm afraid it's true."

She laughed again, and Danny enjoyed the sound of it. He hoped he'd be able to hear it for the rest of his life.

When they arrived at Liberty House, it was pitch dark. Matthew and Danny, having never brought guests before, rode to the back where the stable was.

Renny, the stableman and handy all-around man for the Libertys, came out with a surprised look on his face.

"Welcome, welcome to Liberty House. Mr. Bannister, haven't seen you for quite some time. Dr. Danny, it's good to see you too. You've been here scarcely once this week."

Matthew tipped his hat and said, "Hello, Renny, always good to see you too."

"Good evening, Renny," Danny replied. "I've had a busy schedule this week." As Renny reached for Sylvia's waist, Danny said, "This is Nurse Sylvia Cobain. I invited her to dinner. Are we too late?"

Renny swung Sylvia down with ease.

"Nope, family is in the parlor. They have some lawyer from back east in there wantin' ta talk to Mr. Alex, so dinner is later tonight. Nice ta meet you, Nurse Cobain. Welcome to Liberty House. May you find peace and joy as you enter the door."

"Why, thank you for such a sweet blessing. And thank you for making me feel so welcome."

"Any friend of Dr. Danny's is welcome here. This was his home until the place became overrun with children. He moved out to give the Libertys more room, but he'd be welcome to move back in, in a minute, if he chose to do so. You're special, Nurse Cobain. He's never brought a female here yet."

"Come on, folks," Danny said. "It's time for dinner, and Renny'll talk all night if you let him." He slapped Renny on the shoulder good naturedly, and added, "Thanks, sir, for taking care of our horses."

"My pleasure, lad, my pleasure." Renny was already leading the horses into the stable.

Only Gussie, the Libertys' cook, was there to greet them at the back door.

"Why, hello there, Dr. Danny. Well look who's here. Mr. Bannister, it's good to see you too!"

Danny took Sylvia over to the cook, who was stirring a pudding and hadn't left the stove.

"Gussie, meet a friend of mine, Nurse Sylvia Cobain. I asked her if she'd have dinner here with me, and she accepted."

"Happy to meet you, Nurse Cobain. Any friend of Danny's is more than welcome here. I fixed plenty of vittles, and the family is in the parlor. Please make yourself at home. We don't stand on a lot of formality around here."

"Thank you, Gussie. I feel welcome already." Sylvia smiled sweetly at the cook, but she could feel her stomach tighten with nerves. It was always difficult for her to meet new people. Once she knew them, she didn't have a bit of trouble, but meeting people wasn't her forte.

Matthew headed for the parlor, and Danny stepped aside to let Sylvia precede him.

Nana saw them standing in the doorway. Penelope Weaver had helped raise Alex from the time he was an infant, and Danny had lived in their home since he was twelve.

"Welcome, what a wonderful surprise! Emily, Alex, look who's here!" Penelope exclaimed.

Emily, Alex, and their guest turned to see Danny, Matthew, and Sylvia enter the parlor.

Emily walked over, trying to hide the curiosity in her violet-blue eyes.

"Welcome to Liberty House," she said graciously. "Please do feel welcome. We have plenty to eat, and it's a perfect night. The children are in the nursery with Nanny Jane, and it's nice to have a quiet evening."

Danny took Sylvia's arm and brought her up to his side, as she'd hung back with Matthew.

"This is a friend of mine, Sylvia Cobain. She's a nurse, and I hope it's all right to have her come for dinner. I didn't have time to warn you, as it was a spur-of-the-moment thing." He grinned, knowing he could have brought a dozen people and the Libertys would make them welcome. They were his family.

"Sylvia, this is Emily and Alex Liberty, and my nana, Penelope Weaver."

Introductions made, Alex brought a man forward. He was probably in his late fifties, looking suave and fit. He had distinguished gray hair, a thin mustache and warm hazel eyes.

"This is our guest for the evening, Clint Pierce," Alex said. "Clint, this is Dr. Daniel Gates, his friend, Sylvia Cobain, and this is my brother-in-law, Matthew Bannister."

They greeted each other, but Clint Pierce seemed to stare at Danny. Danny felt the man's eyes on him several times and wondered why.

Emily had grape, apple, and marionberry juice on the sideboard. The parlor was full of conversation and small talk, and laughter ensued.

Matthew left the little group to wash up. He came back with combed, wetted hair.

"Is there somewhere I can wash up?" Sylvia asked Danny in a whisper.

"Yes, follow me. It's right through there." He pointed to a room off the kitchen.

It was fitted with the new flush toilet and had running water in the sink. Sylvia was glad, as it was so convenient. She splashed a little water on her face and straightened her dark hair, pinching her cheeks for a little color. She stared for a moment at her reflection and then grinned. *I am having a wonderful time*, she thought. *When's the last time I had an enjoyable evening besides being with family? I can't remember, but this is like an adventure. Danny is…ah…I don't even know what to think.* She returned to find Danny was waiting. He, too, used the little room and came back looking as if he'd just combed his hair.

She smiled warmly, and he took her arm possessively as they returned to the parlor.

Jamison, the Libertys' butler, pulled himself up to his full height, stood in the double doorway and announced, "Dinner is served."

The family and their guests entered the dining room which, though formal enough for gala occasions, seemed much friendlier than most dining rooms. The walls were done in a sunshine yellow, and the oak wood trim was stained a warm brown sugar. Ten-foot ceilings were of the same oak as the trim boards, and huge beams crossed the expanse of the room. An enormous oak-framed mirror hung over the fireplace on the far end wall and cast the reflected glow of the sconces and chandeliers. A large ship's steering wheel made of beautiful teak hung on the opposing end wall. Pictures of famous lighthouses as well as brass sconces graced the walls. Three antique brass-and-glass chandeliers hung over the long table. Long windows lined the entire wall facing the ocean. Although it was dark, the night was clear, and a couple ships' lights could be seen through the windows. The dining room's fireplace glowed with a small fire, lending the room an air of warmth and hominess.

Sylvia was surprised that the table had been set to include them. That was quick, she thought. Good organization and well trained staff.

"What a beautiful room," Sylvia said. "It's elegant yet welcoming too."

"Nana bought this house," Emily said, "and most of what you see in it was by her design. She's been gracious to let me do whatever I want, making me mistress of this domain, but I can see no reason to change what I consider perfect."

"Goodness, child," Penelope said, "you make me out to be some angel." She laughed and said to Danny's guest, "Believe me, Sylvia—I am not."

"Maybe not an angel, Nana, but you are a saint," Alex said with a grin. He turned to his guest and added, "Clint, we like to thank the Lord before we eat. Shall we bow our heads?" He gave a quick glance around the table, and every head was bowed.

"Lord, we pause to recognize You and Your faithfulness to us. What a miracle You have given us to enjoy. We pray for the Brodie family and for continued good health for Constanza. What a blessing You have bestowed upon her. We are in awe of Your majesty and power. Bless now our guests at this table. Thank you for this food and for the hands that prepared it. We praise Your holy name through the name of Your son, Jesus. Amen."

Gussie, Renny, and Jamison served a delicious dinner. Dispensing with the hors-d'oeuvres, the starter was a delicious French onion soup. The second course was poached salmon with sauce mousseline and cucumbers. The main course was filet mignon smothered in a mushroom and onion sauce with peppercorns and capers. The side was buttered carrots and mashed potatoes drowning in the mushroom sauce.

A cheese was served, small portions after the main course, and then a sorbet to clear the palate. Served with the coffee, a chocolate ganache cake was the dessert—so rich, a small slice was filling.

CHAPTER XXIX

The Lord is their strength,
and he is the saving strength of his anointed.

PSALM 28:8

EMILY ROSE AND SAID, "LADIES, SHALL WE?" She led the way out of the dining room in the time-honored custom of allowing the men to drink, smoke cigars, and discuss whatever they wished without women present. Emily led Penelope and Sylvia to the parlor, hoping she would hear from Sylvia how she'd met Danny. She'd been quite aware of Danny's eyes continually returning to his guest.

Once the women left the room, Alex said, "I'm so glad you came this evening, Danny. If you hadn't, I'd have come looking for you tomorrow. Clint is a lawyer from Malden, Massachusetts."

"Just north of Boston, isn't it?" Danny asked.

"Yes, it is," Clint replied. "I combed records but couldn't seem to find you, Dr. Gates. I happened to stumble upon your name because I was looking up something for a client and came across a file on Penelope Weaver. Your having lived with Penelope Weaver made you easy to trace. Penelope still supports several large organizations as well as several schools of learning back east. Her address is publicly listed."

"Why would you be searching for me?" Daniel asked. "I have no relatives that I know of, no family except what I have living with Alex and Penelope."

"I'm sorry your mother never had that conversation with you—about her family, you understand. Your mother was Margaret Marie Monroe Gates, was she not?"

"Yes, she was."

"You never had a relationship with your grandparents, did you?"

"Grandparents? I don't have any grandparents save Nana."

"Your mother came from a tragic home. She'd had a brother, Daniel, who was two years older than she. He and your grandfather, whose name, by the way, was also Daniel, were out hunting. Your grandfather tripped and accidentally shot your uncle Daniel in the back. It took him a month to die, and your mother's home was turned upside down. Your grandmother and grandfather stopped speaking to each other. Your grandmother's grief was so great, she took her own life. Margaret was basically left on her own to cope with the two tragedies as your grandfather became a recluse."

Daniel sat spellbound listening to a story he'd never heard.

Clint took a drink of water. "Margaret met Henry Gates at a party. He swept her off her feet, and they married within two months of meeting. When Daniel, her father, heard about it, it was too late—she was married. He cut Margaret off and told her he never wanted to see her again. Much to her vast disappointment, she found Henry had married her knowing her father had money, and she his only child. Henry took to drinking, and you know the rest of the story."

"Is my grandfather still alive?"

"No, he passed just two months ago. It's taken me that long to find you." Clint smiled at the younger man. "It's a tragedy your grandfather never made amends with your mother. It surprises me she never told you any of it."

"No, she never did," Danny replied in a quiet tone. "Maybe she was afraid my grandfather would reject me, and what with having a father who beat me on a regular basis, she most likely thought it was better to let sleeping dogs lie."

"That may be so," Clint said, "but your grandfather evidently knew about you and knew your mother had passed away. His will leaves his entire estate to you."

"What do you mean, entire estate?" Danny swallowed wondering what was coming next. He didn't plan to move back to Massachusetts and become a farmer.

"There are no restrictions, no encumbrances. It's all yours from your grandfather. The estate, after taxes, is seven point two million dollars free and clear."

Danny felt as if someone had tied a noose around his neck. His throat felt constricted, and he drew a deep breath.

Alex slapped him on the back. "My rich brother," he said exaggeratedly. "Now you will find all kinds of relatives you never knew you had." He laughed and turned back to Clint. "I didn't want to interrupt you, but Nana, I mean Penelope, has never disclosed her wealth to us. We all know she has money, but you said organizations and schools? Is she a philanthropist?"

"I shouldn't, professionally, answer that question, but your nana is richer than Croesus."

Alex's eyes widened. "Surely you jest, sir."

"No, no jesting. Frankly speaking, I don't know anyone richer than your Penelope Weaver. I was anticipating a ton of servants and a mansion on Nob Hill. Instead, she has a comfortable house, homey, warm, and inviting. I like her. I like her very much. She's a vibrant, intelligent woman, even at her age. You must be very proud of her."

"I am proud of her," Alex replied. "Discounting the fact that she's wealthy, I've always been proud of her. She's been more like a mother to me than Sarah."

While Clint and Alex talked, Danny held his head in his hands, trying to soak into his brain that he was a multimillionaire, and moreover, his nana was too.

"I have a favor to ask," Danny said. "It's a big favor. I don't want you to say anything to anyone, not even Emily, Alex." Danny took out a handkerchief and wiped his forehead. "I need to assimilate this. I met Sylvia today, and I asked permission to court her."

Alex's eyes widened with disbelief. "You just met her and wish to marry her?"

"Oh, and you're the one to talk, Alex. One look at Emily, if I remember correctly, and you were sunk." Danny grinned at his friend.

"Well, yes, I guess that's true."

"That's the way it was with me too," Matthew said. He'd been sitting quietly listening to the conversation and praying that money would make no difference to these two men who were so devoted to helping others. "I took one look at Liberty, and although I tried to deny it, thinking she was married, I admit, I was sunk." He grinned at the other three men.

"We've taken quite some time here. Shall we let the women back in?" Alex looked at the other two.

"I do have a question." Danny looked at Clint. "Do I have to go to Malden to collect?"

"It would make things a whole lot easier," the lawyer replied.

"Perhaps it could serve two purposes. I could take Sylvia with me on our honeymoon. Wonder how long she's going to make me wait."

"Danny, you just met her! At least I courted Emily for six months or more before I married her."

The evening was a great success. Matthew stayed at Alex's house, planning to return home first thing in the morning.

Danny and Sylvia said their goodbyes, and Danny, with Sylvia once again behind him, headed for town.

"Where am I taking you?" he asked.

"You can take me back to St. Luke's, and I'll find my way home from there."

"Nothing doing, my girl. Not at this time of night. I'm taking you home. Now where do you live?"

"I accept that you would like to court me, Dr. ah…Danny, but my father will have to approve of you. He's quite strict and unhappy that I've chosen nursing as a profession. He'd like me to be one of those witless females you were talking about. As to where I live…I live with a roommate while I'm working and on my days off, I live with my family on Snob Hill."

Danny chuckled at her comment. "It's a bit late to meet your family tonight, but if I may, I'd like to meet your father tomorrow."

"I'm sure that would be fine. Come for dinner, six o'clock sharp." Sylvia was exhausted and leaned her head on Danny's back, closing her eyes.

Danny headed for Nob Hill. "Is this it?" he asked as Sylvia had directed him.

"Yes, the house, grounds, and outbuildings take up the entire four corners of the block."

He helped her down and watched as she entered one of those mansions Clint Pierce had spoken about after dinner.

Matthew awoke early. He decided to do a bit of needed shopping while in the city. *Reckon I'll get some supplies and ride as far as San Rafael. I'll spend tonight with Elijah and Abigail.*

After a noisy but delicious breakfast with Penelope, Alex, Emily, and their six children, Matthew headed to the business district with Alex. When they arrived at Alex's office on Battery Street, Matthew said goodbye and headed for a mercantile close by.

He made a few purchases, including a big jar of honey for Conchita, a pocketknife for Donny, buckles for harnesses, several lengths of leather, rope, and of course several pieces of peppermint twists for Libby's sweet tooth. He also bought some cotton tatting thread, as his wife liked to make doilies and lace tablecloths. He started to leave the store, when he thought of Abigail. He looked around a bit, trying to think what he could get her. He snapped his fingers as he thought of it. Abby was learning to shoot a gun. She and Elijah were both learning, and Elijah had bought both of them the same type of gun Libby carried. It was a **Smith & Wesson New Model Number Three revolver.**

He walked over to a glassed case and saw a beautiful tooled leather belt and holster. "I want that." Matthew pointed to the glassed case, and the proprietor hurried over. He retrieved the holster and handed it to Matthew, who nodded. "Do you have a matching one?" he asked.

The proprietor turned and yelled at a clerk. "Jerrold, see if we have another one of these." He held up the holster. His clerk went behind a curtain and came back with an identical one.

"Thanks," Matthew said. He paid for his supplies and left, whistling under his breath as he loaded his purchases into saddlebags. He gave Piggypie a slap on the rump and climbed on. He headed toward the Presidio and the ferry.

Jenny was having a good time getting to know Liberty. Impressed with Liberty's knowledge, Jenny was glad she'd come. Liberty was vivacious, intelligent, and clearly devoted to Christ. Jenny felt herself drawn to her and hoped she was being a help. Just being around this younger woman made Jenny feel as if she had value. Chloe and Ginger were both a huge help with the twins.

"I slept like a baby last night." Jenny was astonished she could sleep so soundly in a strange room. "Wonder why they say that?" she asked. "Many times a baby can be awake half the night. Perhaps I should say I slept like a log." Jenny laughed again. She was sitting beside Liberty on the sofa, learning how to tat. She could knit and crochet but had always wanted to learn how to make lace.

"When I went to bed last night, Boston kept growling in his throat. I wondered if someone was poking around outside." Liberty had thought to sleep the night before but had spent a restless night due to Boston's growling. "He doesn't usually bark or growl unless there's something strange going on. It was a bit unnerving."

Jenny looked closely at Liberty's face and realized the rested look of the day before was gone. Besides not sleeping well, nursing the twins obviously took a lot out of Liberty's energy.

"Have you had any problems before with someone poking around?"

"No, not that I've ever noticed." Liberty glanced at the two girls and asked, "Chloe, could you and Ginger go out to the barn and ask Donny if he'd like to eat in here for lunch instead of getting his own? We have those pasties Cora made with meat and potatoes inside and leftover *enchiladas*."

The two rose to go, and Liberty said, "Thanks, girls!"

Liberty spoke solemnly to Jenny. "Matthew told me that Sheriff Rawlins said Chloe's uncle is looking for her. I wish he'd just move on. What good can he do for Chloe when he told her women were unable to learn anything and only good for having babies? At any rate, without Matthew here, I was unnerved last night, thinking he could be outside looking in. He was, evidently, very close to his brother, and I killed him." She took a deep sigh. "We're in the Lord's hands, after all. No sense worrying about it, is there?"

Jenny looked at the younger woman and spoke sagely. "It's easy to say we shouldn't worry. It's much more difficult not to. After a crisis I've endured is over, I realize most of it was taken out of my hands anyway. Besides the fact that getting through difficult times makes me a stronger person."

"Wise words, Jenny."

Ginger and Chloe came back in to say Donny was going to town and would eat while he was there. The day seemed to hurry by. In the evening, Liberty made popcorn, and after the twins were put to bed, the four of them played Parcheesi. Ginger knew how to play and helped Chloe, who caught on quickly.

"You are a bright girl, Chloe," Liberty said. "I can see you becoming famous someday."

Chloe beamed under the compliment. "I'm doing my best to learn. I'd like to learn how to sign too, so I can understand Ginger better. Do you think I'd be allowed to have lessons too?"

"I don't see why not," Liberty said. She yawned, covering her mouth. "Well, everyone, you may stay up if you care too, but I'm for bed. I can scarcely keep my eyes open."

Matthew arrived at Elijah and Abigail's in the late afternoon.

Elijah had no more clients that day and had come home early. Abigail and Bessie had left the mission when he dropped by there to tell them he was heading home. Bessie already had a stuffed chicken roasting for dinner, and the smell, filling the house, was tantalizing.

Matthew handed Elijah and Abigail each a wrapped package.

"What's this?" Abby asked. "Oh, I do enjoy surprises!"

They unwrapped the new holsters.

"Thanks, Matthew! This is fine leather, and neither Abby nor I have holsters for our new guns." Elijah's eyes gleamed with pleasure.

Abby stroked her holster and said, "Thanks, Matthew. These are beautiful as well as needful." She hugged him and added, "Please excuse me a minute while I get my gun."

She came back and slipped the gun into the new holster, and both she and Elijah put on their new gun belts. "I'm going to have to wear split skirts the way Liberty does if I want to tie those leg thongs on. I suppose I can just let them hang loose. Thank you again."

Elijah and Matthew talked about guns while she went to the kitchen to get some coffee.

"Oh, Matthew, we're delighted you've come," Abigail said after she'd served him coffee and a piece of cake. "You can catch us up on all the news. How are the Mobreys doing?"

"They seem to be settling in well. Anne's grandmother came west. I couldn't stay to meet her. They arrived at our place just before Diego, Conchita, and I left for Frisco. We didn't stay to meet her, because we didn't want to miss the ferry."

Matthew related to them all that had transpired concerning Constanza. "It was a miracle."

"Praise the Lord!" Elijah said. "I praise God every day for Abby's miraculous healing. To have someone pronounced dead and then they come back alive! Well, there are no words, are there?"

"The Lord is good." Abigail smiled. "Matthew, you do know the Bible story of Jesus raising Lazarus from the dead, don't you?"

"Why yes, I do. I always wondered why He tarried when He got the news that Lazarus was dying."

"That's exactly why I asked you. I was reading about that and came across an article. In Jewish tradition, they believed only Messiah Himself could raise a person from the dead after three days. Jesus tarried because He raised Lazarus from the dead four days after his death, thus proving Himself to be Messiah! Isn't that a wonderful explanation?"

"Yes, it is. I know the Scripture says He tarried, and I thought it was because Lazarus, Mary, and Martha lived in Judea and the disciples didn't want Jesus to go there, knowing the religious rulers were wanting to kill Jesus."

Abigail smiled. "It is amazing. Now, do you have any more news?"

"Have you seen Alex's remodeled office?" Matthew asked. He wanted to share about Danny's inheritance, but it wasn't his story. He did tell them Danny had met someone. Conversation flowed the entire evening, and Matthew was glad he'd stopped for the night.

He left early the next morning, right after breakfast. Matthew thought now of Lupe and Luce arriving at the hospital. He'd been surprised to see them. As the realization that Liberty had no help at all hit him, he felt like kicking himself that he'd not gone home the day before instead of staying with the Humphries for the night. He didn't like the idea of Liberty being home alone with no help and only Donny for protection. He kicked Piggypie into a steady canter, heading for home and Liberty.

The girls were having a delightful time with Matty and Faith. Matty, the thinner of the two, was trying to crawl. Faith was a chubby little baby with many smiles and coos, but she had never gotten up on all fours.

"Look," Chloe said. "He's up on his hands and knees and then flops on his belly." She laughed, and Ginger smiled. Chloe looked at her new friend quickly, sorry she just couldn't make any noise at all. Sitting back on her heels, she thought how she'd feel if she couldn't talk. *I'd hate it*, she thought. *I'd hate it like anything. I talk all the time. Thad said Ginger used to sing really pretty. Okay, Lord, I'm gonna pray to You right now. My new mama said You care. I asked You to be my Savior last week, and I know I'm not smart about how all this works, but I'm gonna pray right now for You to give Ginger her voice back. You made her with a voice. I'm gonna ask You, whatever it takes, could You please make her able to talk again? Please?*

Chapter XXX

Let him kiss me with the kisses of his mouth:
for thy love is better than wine.

SONG OF SOLOMON 1:2

JENNY WIPED HER HANDS ON A TOWEL. She'd been helping Liberty make lunch, which was nearly ready.

"Those girls sure are a big help, aren't they?" Jenny asked.

"I cannot begin to thank you for coming to help me," Liberty replied. "Yes, they've been a wonderful help. I had another sleepless night last night. I don't know if you heard Boston, but he barked just as I was going to bed and then about a half hour later. I'm pretty sure there's someone spying out our house. I know"—she lowered her voice—"Chloe's uncle is going to be out to get her back and take down whoever shot his brother. That would be me, but he may think it's Matthew or the sheriff. I lay there last night wondering what kind of man could tie up an old man, stuff a cloth in his mouth, and never care about food or water for him. Someone with no conscience, that's for sure."

"It's amazing what mankind is capable of, and most all the evil is for selfish gain," Jenny said. "There's no care as to how it affects another person or how it can ruin the future of that person…sad but true."

"I know what you mean," Liberty said. "My first husband and the man I was raised with, thinking he was my father, were both incredibly evil. I would never have been able to claim myself as a whole person without the knowledge that God was with me through it all. I know there are people who think if you're a Christian, you won't have trials, or if you just work to be more Christlike, you won't have to suffer what other people suffer. That is so wrong. It's not that we won't suffer. It's that we have someone who enters into our suffering with us and helps us to get through it. Living in a fallen world the way we do predicates the fact that there is evil in it. It's like the psalmist who saw the wicked prosper and wondered at it until he saw their end. We think a lifetime here can be long, but it's just a drop in the bucket compared to all eternity. What we invest in here determines where we'll be for all time."

Jenny nodded sagely. "You're right about that. If we have Jesus as our Savior and invest in heaven, our time, talent, and treasure, we won't have to worry about where we will spend all eternity."

"That's true, Jenny. It's sad most people never find that out."

They heard a commotion at the door, and Liberty left the kitchen to see what it was.

"Matthew!" she cried. "I didn't expect you for at least another day!"

He took off his hat and took her into his arms.

Chloe and Ginger watched them kiss, but the couple were oblivious to their perusal.

"How is Constanza? Why are you home already? Is Conchita all right?"

Questions bubbled from Liberty's lips, and Matthew laughed, picked her up, and swung her around before he replied.

"Yes to number one. Number two, because I wasn't needed anymore, and yes to question number three. Let me wash up, and I'll be with you. I'm glad to see you're not alone. Looks like some professional help here," he said as he saw the two girls with the twins.

"Yes, and Jenny Tarkington is here too. She's Anne Mobrey's grandmother. I am so grateful to them for helping me. Go wash up…it's time for lunch."

Danny finished seeing patients for the day. He hoped no one had a baby or that there'd be no emergency this evening. He was excited to see Sylvia again, yet apprehensive about meeting her father. He went to the back of his office, opening a door to a narrow stairway. It led up to his apartment. It wasn't very big, but because he had a paucity of furniture and was neat as a pin, it looked spacious.

He heated water and took a bath, dressed in his best suit, and tied his cravat carefully. He combed his hair, looking at himself in the small mirror in the bathroom. He decided he looked as good as he ever would. His stomach rumbled, and he didn't know if it was nerves or hunger. *Probably both*, he thought.

Whistling, he descended the stairs. Going to his desk, he slipped a large piece of paper out of the drawer and wrote a note informing anyone that if there was an emergency, to go to St. Luke's or ride to the address on Nob Hill. He locked his front door, hung the note on it, and looked at his fob watch. He knew he was a bit early, so he strolled in an unhurried manner, his hands in his pockets. He headed down the street to the stable where he boarded his horse, whistling a little tune. His horse wasn't saddled, because he hadn't made any house calls, nor had he been out of the office the entire day.

The air freshened as it blew in off the bay. Puffy white clouds scudded themselves across the skies, and the sun neared the horizon.

Danny saddled up and snugged his frock coat a bit. He rode to the Cobains' house on Nob Hill and tied up his horse, praying he'd get along with Sylvia's father. He wondered about her mother, as she hadn't said anything about her. He knocked on the door and waited.

A maid in a cap and black dress with white cuffs and collar answered the door.

"Dr. Gates?" she asked.

"Yes, and your name?" he asked.

Her smooth eyebrows rose in surprise, but she curtsied, smiled, and said, "Ella, sir, thank you for asking." She took his top hat and frock coat, hanging them up on a coat tree, and said, "Please, sir, follow me. The family is gathered in the parlor."

Danny followed her into the hall leading out of the foyer and into a wide room that emitted a first impression of hugeness.

All movement seemed to stop as the maid announced, "Dr. Daniel Gates."

Sylvia walked smoothly over to him, her tawny eyes warm and inviting.

She stretched out both hands and smiling into his blue eyes said, "Welcome, Danny. Welcome to Cobains' Corner."

She linked her arm in his and took him immediately to a man who, he figured, was her father. He was several inches shorter than Danny, had a receding hairline, and lifted hooded hazel eyes to peruse Danny. His appearance was benign until one looked into the depths of his eyes. There lurked humor and great intellect.

"Papa, I'd like you to meet Dr. Daniel Gates. Danny, this is my father, Camran Cobain."

The two men shook hands, in appearance a friendly gesture, but at the same time, they seemed to take measure of each other.

Camran Cobain spoke first. "Welcome to our humble abode, young man."

Danny heard the soft Gaelic accent and guessed the man was originally from Scotland.

"Thank you, sir. It's a pleasure to be here, and begging your pardon, sir, far and away from humble. Your daughter assured me I was welcome, and I thank you for opening your home to me."

Sylvia took his arm again and said, "Let me introduce you to a couple cousins, uncles, and aunts."

"Before you do, I'd like to say I'm glad you met my daughter the way you did."

"Papa." Sylvia blushed to the roots of her hair.

"Let me speak my mind, Sylvie." Camran Cobain could mask his feelings as well as the best, but when it came to his daughter, most times he was quite blunt. "I'm glad because she is an only child and stands to inherit all I have accrued during my lifetime. When she had her coming-out party, at just sixteen, she had so many offers of marriage, even from mere acquaintances, that she didn't wish to go to anymore parties. She has assured me that you didn't even know where she lived until last evening."

Danny grinned at the older man and said, "That is true. I actually know little about her. I wonder, since you're being so candid, if I may be also. Did Sylvia happen to tell you we just met yesterday?"

Cobain's jaw dropped, and his eyes swiveled to his daughter in disbelief.

"Please don't blame her. As far as I know, she is a model of propriety. I would like to court your daughter, sir, with the intent to marry her within a short period of time."

Now, Cobain's eyebrows rose in disbelief. "You want to marry her, but you just met yesterday?"

"Yes, sir, if she'll have me, I do. I can take a lifetime to get to know her. I didn't plan on this happening. I have been married to my work, so to speak. I do get to a concert now and then, but for the most part, I have been too busy for the social amenities. I don't have blood relatives anymore, but I was raised by Penelope Weaver and—"

"Aha!" Camran interrupted. "Yes, yes, you have my permission to court my daughter and marry her if she'll have you. That decision I now leave to her. She does have a mind of her own, that one." He smiled benevolently upon Sylvia and clapped Danny on the back. "I had no idea you were *that* Danny."

"I'm sorry, sir. I think you lost me a couple sentences back." Danny looked a bit flummoxed.

Camran smiled at Danny and said, "I've known Penelope Weaver for years. We serve on several boards together. If she wasn't old enough to be my mother, I'd ask that woman to marry me in a snap!" He snapped his fingers. "Go ahead, Sylvie. Take him around to meet your extended family."

The couple walked a few steps, and Danny asked, "Will you have me, Sylvia? Will you marry me to have and to hold?"

She squeezed his arm to her side and said, "I've thought of nothing else for the past twenty or so hours."

"Just a minute," Danny said, and he led her back into the foyer. He took her face between his hands and kissed her gently.

Sylvia did not seem surprised or indignant. She kissed him back, and passion built between them. When they drew apart, they stared into each other's eyes with wonderment and love shining through both.

"That's my very first kiss, Dr. Daniel Gates."

"Well," he replied smiling, "it's not mine." He kissed her quickly again and chuckled. "I kissed a girl once, when I was eight, and she slapped me."

He laughed, and Sylvia joined in. They both entered the parlor with smiles on their faces.

It was time for Jenny and the girls to leave the Bannisters' Rancho. They'd stayed a couple more nights, even though Matthew had returned and Diego and Conchita had arrived the following day. Breakfast had been a leisurely affair with much talk and laughter. Conchita was happy to be home and grateful her sister would have a husband who would now treat her well. Lupe and Luce stayed in San Francisco to help out in any way and visit a bit with their mother.

Jenny decided after lunch, she and the girls would head home. They gathered up their few things. Once Chloe was ready, she headed to the kitchen, where she knew she'd find Conchita. Since lying in Conchita's bed and comforting the woman, Chloe had taken a shine to her.

Conchita gave the girl an extra hug. "You come back any time you wheesh to veesit. Maybe you come weeth Ginger an' learn to talk weeth your hands too."

"Thank you. I want to learn so I can talk easily with my friend." Chloe spoke solemnly, her heart tender and sorry for Ginger.

Matthew assured them they were welcome anytime.

"You girls were such a big help with the twins. I'm glad you stayed on here the extra couple days. Now that Conchita is home, we should be all right."

Jenny, too, thought it best for them to be on their way. "We thank you for the hospitality and were glad to be of help. It's what neighbors do, isn't it?"

The girls and Jenny put their things into the back of the Mobreys' wagon while Matthew had Donny hitched it up.

They were all standing outside, and Liberty picked a carnation and tucked it into Jenny's breast pocket. "Again, I cannot begin to thank you enough for coming to the rescue," she stated. "It's comforting to know I have neighbors who care. Jenny, it's been a delight to get to know you. Don't stop tatting. You've made a good start on that—you simply need to practice. Whenever Ginger has a signing lesson, please come. Your hands move a lot when you're talking anyway, so I think signing will come easily to you.

"Chloe and Ginger"—she hugged the two girls—"I don't think I could have made it without your help. Goodness, you both are going to make wonderful mothers! I'd never been around a baby when I was growing up, so I had to learn by having one." She laughed and added, "By having two."

"Let's pray for you before you leave," Matthew said.

They joined hands, and before Matthew could say a word, Chloe began to pray.

"Our Father, who art in heaven, I want to thank You for the wonderful time Ginger and I had visiting the Bannisters and helping with Matty and Faith, and I thank you for friends, and I pray You make Ginger's voice come back, and I'm not gonna stop praying for that until I hear her voice! Amen!"

Matthew smiled, but not in a disparaging way. He knew children were a gift from the good Lord, but the smile was in thinking of the big change in this girl in just a few short weeks. "Father, we thank You and pray Your blessings and protection for Jenny, Ginger, and Chloe. Thank You most of all for sending Your son to die on the cross to save us from our sins. Help us to live in a manner that brings You delight. Amen."

Chloe's eyes were shining, but Ginger's eyes were clouded with confusion as she climbed up to the seat on the wagon. Jenny saw it and wondered if she might be able to help the girl.

"Thanks again, Liberty, for being such a sweet hostess. We had a good time. Come by Mobrey Manor anytime. You are both welcome. Bye now." She clucked to the horse and slapped the reins gently.

"Bye, and hope to see you soon," Liberty replied. She and Matthew linked arms and watched until the turning lane hid the wagon from sight.

Matthew pulled Liberty into his arms, giving her a tender kiss on her upturned lips. She smiled into his eyes, but all the sudden she gasped.

"Matthew! I was so glad you'd come home, and in all the excitement of hearing about Alex's office renovation and about Danny and the incredible story of Constanza's miraculous comeback, it totally slipped my mind to tell you about Boston growling and barking the two nights you were away. He doesn't usually bark unless something's going on. I don't think it was an animal prowling around. I kept thinking it was a person lurking outside."

Matthew's eyes, warm from their kiss, turned serious. He started walking toward the back of the house, Liberty trailing after him.

"I didn't even think to look for boot prints." Liberty knew what he was about, and she was irritated, disgusted with herself for not even thinking to check. She could have had Buck stay, if indeed there were signs of someone having been by the windows.

Matthew pointed. "See there? The branch on that bush is broken, and there are prints of a boot right there under that window. He moved along the back side of the house to their room." They walked right along the wall, and Matthew showed Liberty the prints of one pair of boots along the way. "They must have been very quiet, or Boston would have gone wild. Bet my bottom dollar it was Chloe's uncle. I'll ride over this afternoon and tell Buck."

It was early afternoon, but the sky was overcast. Lowering clouds gave fair warning that rain was on its way. With no sun, the air felt chilly but not terribly cold.

Jenny turned onto the main road and headed to Sunrise Canyon. She pulled at her shawl a bit to ward off the air hitting her neck. Ginger hunched over a little and snuggled up to Chloe, wrapping her arm around the younger girl as she shivered.

"Are you cold?" Chloe asked Ginger.

"I am," Jenny replied, while Ginger nodded yes and squeezed Chloe's arm.

"I'm not cold." Chloe spoke as if she were fifteen instead of five. "I have ridden in snowstorms and rain and lots of hot, hot weather. I'm tough."

"Being cold doesn't make a body weak, nor does not being cold make a body tough. We are all different. As long as I'm saying that, I'm going to say a bit more. I don't know too much about either of you girls. I know you've both been through hard times—very hard times. Times many people will never know or have to endure. One thing I've come to understand at my great age"—she smiled down at the two girls and then looked back at the road—"is that every single one of us has a story. We can look at others and think their life is so easy. Or…we may wonder why ours seems so tough. Chloe, you've had a rough life losing your ma and then your pa, and being told you're not worth anything. Ginger, you've lost your pa and then your ma in a tragic way, and to top that off, you've lost your ability to speak. A body can get angry with God. I think He understands that. You can read the Psalms in the Bible, which are called the laments, and see how people of old did just that. They wondered why the wicked prosper or why such and such happened, but they always come around to the fact that God is there, knowing and comforting. People blame God for all kinds of things He hasn't done. God is good... not just some of the time like we are, but always and ever...eternally good. The problem is that He made a perfect world, and mankind failed it. We live in a world that's now full of sin and depravity of all kind. It's not God's will. It is the result of the evil that is here. When bad things happen, we blame God, but the fault lies with man. God didn't make us puppets so that we do everything according to what He'd like. No, He gave us free will, and how that must hurt His beautiful heart to see what we, as people, have done with that freedom. Sometimes He does intervene in a situation and poke His oar in, so to speak. When we see that, we call it a miracle. Most times He just lets us do what we want, even though it's not good or right. Yes, our circumstances can be horrible, but our attitude toward that circumstance can change. The Good Book says that God can take what Satan meant for evil and turn it to good if we let Him.

"I reckon that's enough for you to chew on for a while, but one thing you should remember is that God is ever present and ever knowing, and He loves you more than anyone on this earth ever could."

Jenny had no sooner finished talking, when a man with a gun in his hand rode past and grabbed the reins of the horse, bringing the carriage to a swift halt.

"Uncle Buddy!" Chloe cried. "What are you doing?"

Buddy didn't answer the question. "Get out!" He waved the gun in their direction. "Chloe, I'm telling you right now—I'm so angry with you I could flay you alive. You'd best be doin' what I say, or th' old lady here's gonna get a bullet in her elbow. You hear me? Now y'all get offa that wagon!"

CHAPTER XXXI

He that is our God is the God of salvation;
and unto God the Lord belong the issues from death.

PSALM 68:20

BUDDY WAVED THE GUN AT THE OLDER woman as if to shoot, but Chloe ran up to him, grabbing his arm. Not meaning to, he pulled the trigger, and the bullet cut through Ginger's arm. Buddy's eyes went wild, fearing he'd killed the girl.

The other little girl opened her mouth as if to scream but made no sound.

Buddy looked at her in amazement, understanding at once the girl couldn't talk.

Chloe started beating Buddy with her fists. "You shot her! You shot Ginger! She's my best friend, and you shot her! You're a horrible man, Uncle Buddy! I hate you! I hate you!"

He punched Chloe hard in the stomach and said, "Shut your trap!"

The air whooshed out of Chloe, and she fell to the ground with the blow. She struggled for air, gasping from the pain. She felt her ribs and thought one might be broken. It hurt to breathe. She lay panting from the pain.

Jenny, who'd taken a bit more time to get off the wagon, ran to Ginger.

"Stop! You stop right where you are, woman!" Buddy shouted at her, feeling like he was losing control.

Jenny paid him little attention.

"You shot this little girl, and I'm going to tend to her. Shoot me if you must. I don't really care!" Jenny ripped a piece of her petticoat and bandaged Ginger's arm, glad to see the bullet had passed through and must have exited.

Buddy was startled by her spunk. While the old woman was occupied, he quickly unhitched the wagon.

When Jenny finished wrapping her arm, Ginger put her head down, feeling faint and scared but angry too.

Buddy said, "Gather up your satchels, unless you don't need them." He waited until their things were out of the wagon. Taking the satchels away from them, he hooked them over his saddle horn. He took a length of rope and tied the woman's wrists together. With another piece, he tied Chloe's wrists, who'd not said a word since he hit her. He didn't tie Ginger. He didn't have any more rope, and he was afraid he might cause more bleeding.

Keeping an eye on his prisoners, he said to the woman, "Step on the wagon, and get up on the horse."

She looked at him gauging his temper, but his eyes looked wild, so she complied.

"You, girl, get up behind 'er," he said to Ginger. "I said get moving!" Buddy spoke sharply, as Ginger was slow to obey. He waved the gun at her, and she climbed up behind the woman. He grabbed Chloe by one arm, threw her onto his horse, and climbed up himself.

Chloe gasped with pain and held on to her side.

"We're going for a little ride." Buddy spoke gruffly and led the way, holding the reins of the Mobreys' horse. He looked back to see his prisoners and started down the road at a fast trot, heading for his camp.

Chloe felt like she couldn't breathe, as the bouncing trot was painful.

Ginger squeezed Jenny's waist to get her attention and slipped off the back of the horse. Jenny turned quickly and saw her run to the wagon and disappear behind the inside wheel, hiding from sight.

Ginger watched for a long time until the riders were out of sight. The man glanced back a couple times but must have assumed Ginger was still behind Jenny. He kept riding straight down the road.

Ginger's arm had bled through the petticoat and hurt like the dickens. She ignored her pain and started running back to the Bannisters'

Rancho. She'd get a stitch in her side and slow to a walk and then start running again. Her mind churned with what Jenny had said.

I'm going to pray to You, God Almighty. I'm going to pray for Jenny and Chloe's protection. I know I've been angry with You, but I do think You've taken care of me since my parents died. I'm in a good home, and people seem to love me. Help me love You the way I should. I'm sorry for blaming You for the evil that was done to my family, but I do ask you to save Grandma Jenny and Chloe. Please, please help them. Tears ran down her cheeks, and blood ran down her arm. It seemed like forever before she saw the lane belonging to the vineyard. She felt faint and giddy, her legs sluggish, but she kept running.

Matthew, crossing from the barn to the house, stopped when he saw someone running toward him on the lane. He shaded his eyes to see better, but he couldn't make out who it was. He saw her wave her arm, and he starting running toward her.

Ginger was in such a state, she forgot about everything but to get the message out to Matthew.

"They…they've been kidnapped," she shouted. Her eyes rounded in total surprise. She put a hand to her mouth in shocked astonishment. "I can talk. I can talk!" She started crying and stumbled just as Matthew got to her.

He swooped her up into his arms, and Ginger spoke again.

"Chlo—Chloe's uncle Buddy got us. I…I don't know where he was taking us, b-but he's got Grandma Jenny and Chloe. Oh, please find them. Please find them!" Ginger fainted in his arms.

She was a lightweight. Matthew ran with her in his arms, noting the blood and bandaged arm.

He yelled, "Diego! Donny!"

The two men came running out of the barn. Matthew, out of breath from running with Ginger, panted, "Donny, get Dr. John…and hurry! Use Piggypie—she's saddled. Diego, you tell Sheriff Rawlins to meet me at the Mobreys'. If he's not in town, ride for Sunrise Ranch as fast as you can. It'll save time. I want both of you at Mobreys' place once you deliver your messages. I'm forming a posse to go find Jenny and Chloe."

Donny, with hardly a glance at Ginger, replied, "Yes, sir."

Diego and Donny rode down the lane at a gallop.

Matthew carried Ginger into the house, going straight to the guest room she'd slept in.

Liberty heard his shout outside and came out of the kitchen in time to see him carrying Ginger. She ran to the kitchen doorway.

"Conchita, hot water!" She turned and ran down the long hall. "Oh my goodness...what happened?"

Matthew replied in a curt voice. "She can talk, Liberty! She can talk. Before she fainted, she told me they'd been kidnapped by Chloe's uncle Buddy." He gently unwrapped the soaked piece of petticoat. "Looks like she's been shot. You take over from here. I need to saddle up Pookie. I lent Piggypie to Donny, who's going to get Dr. John, and told Diego to get Buck. Hope he's there in Napa. Otherwise it'll take him some time to ride out to Sunrise. I told Diego we'd meet at the Mobreys'. I'll ride over there now. I know James and Bates are good shots."

"Go, Matthew! Get going. I'll take care of things here, and I'll pray."

Matthew gave Liberty a quick kiss and headed out the bedroom door. He strode down the long hall and to the kitchen.

"I see you're heating water," he said to Conchita. "Jenny and Chloe have been kidnapped." He nodded his head, sure in the knowledge that Conchita would have things ready in case there were any more injuries. "I may bring a posse back here to eat if everything turns out all right."

She waved her hand. "Go weeth God, Meester Bannister." She crossed herself and turned away, already planning what to cook and to pray.

Matthew made it to the Mobreys' in short order. He stood at the bottom of the staircase and didn't say anything until he had Anne, James, and Bates together. Explaining what had happened, he saw Anne blanch. He glanced up to see Thaddeus at the top of the stairs.

"Ginger told us. She's been shot in the arm, but praise be to God, she can talk! She fainted, and I sent Donny for Dr. John. Diego's riding to town to get the sheriff. I told them to meet us here."

"I want to see Ginger," Thad said, running down the stairs.

Anne scooped him into her arms. "We'll go right now, Thaddeus. We can't help here anyway." Her eyes met James' over Thaddeus' head, and James nodded his agreement.

Anne realized in that moment that she loved him. She loved his quiet, comforting presence. She loved his sharp mind and gentle ways with the children. She stared at him.

James nodded again, seeing her startled look of comprehension. He wanted to take her into his arms but restrained himself.

"I'll have Dock saddle up a couple horses. Thad, you can ride behind Anne." He turned and strode toward the kitchen and back door.

After some time, Buddy turned off the main road and headed up to his camp. He was proud of himself, having the forethought to lay in supplies. He hadn't planned beyond getting Chloe back and wondered what he'd do with the old lady. *Maybe I'll kill the woman or just tie her to a tree and let the varmits get 'er. Sure wish Rudy was here*, he thought. *He always thought of ever'thing. What am I gonna do with that old lady and the dumb girl?*

Chloe was doing some planning of her own. It hurt to turn, but she glanced back. Her eyes widened as she realized Ginger wasn't behind Jenny.

Jenny was holding on to the pommel, but it was difficult, as Buddy had tied her wrists tightly.

When they finally arrived at the camp, Buddy realized that Ginger wasn't behind Jenny.

"When did you lose the girl?" he asked as he hauled Jenny off her horse.

Jenny didn't reply, and he hit her hard in the chin. She fell backward, and the air whooshed out of her lungs. She struggled for a moment, trying to breathe.

"Stop, Uncle Buddy. Stop it!" Chloe cried. He backhanded her, and she landed on the ground, her ribs screaming out at her, her face quickly bruising up where he'd hit her.

"You shut your mouth, Chloe, right now! Truth ta tell, I'd just as soon kill you as look at you. I want to know what happened to Rudy, you little tramp. I know you know what happened to 'im, and I want to hear it. He's dead, ain't he? Your pa's dead!"

Chloe got up, feeling as if she didn't have enough air and trying to take a deep breath. She nodded her head yes to his question. Her face felt stiff and tight where he'd hit her.

"I don't want to live with you, Uncle Buddy," she said. "I don't want to ever live with you again. I have a family now who love me and care for me, and I love them. I've learned how to read and do sums. You and Pa always told me I was worthless, but I've learned none of us is worthless."

"I don't care whether you live with me or not, you little tramp. I ain't got time ta care about the worthless little weasel you've become. I just want to know what happened ta your pa an' who shot 'im, an' I want ta know now!"

Chloe's lower lip came out, and Buddy knew that was a bad sign. He thought he'd better back off. When that lower lip came out, he'd get nothing out of her, no matter what he did to her.

"We're gonna eat first, an' then you're gonna tell me," he said.

Jenny got up, albeit unsteadily, having her hands tied. She stood with her shoulders back and her head held high.

"Does it please you to bully an old woman and a little girl?" she asked. "Does that really give you a feeling of satisfaction?"

"Shut your trap, you ole hag." Buddy didn't like the feelings this old lady stirred in him, feelings his mother had tried to instill in him and Rudy. He rustled around in his sheltered cave for some jerky.

Chloe decided to run for help. While Buddy was digging around for grub, she put her hands up to her chin, her forefinger at her lips. She walked on silent feet, heading down the hill. At a distance she considered safe, she started running, but her ribs kept her from her normal speed. She heard Buddy behind her and ducked behind some bushes, crawling on her hands and knees to get away from where she'd gone in. Peeking through the undergrowth, she saw his legs run right past where she was hiding. She lay still, waiting and waiting for him to return, but he didn't. Her eyelids felt heavy as she waited, and exhaustion overtook her.

Buddy searched and searched but could not find Chloe. He backtracked and hiked back up the hill the way he'd come down, his lungs wheezing for air. Buddy commenced to curse his lack of foresight. *I shoulda tied 'er ta a tree*, he reflected. A sudden thought hit him, and he climbed up the hill faster, his breath coming in gasps. He reached the opening where his camp was, but the old lady was gone too.

She can't have gone far, he thought, *but I lost 'em. I lost both of 'em. Rudy would be so mad. He'd give me a tongue lashin' fer sure.* Buddy ran into the cave. *What'll I do? What'll I do?* He tossed his things into his satchel and saddlebags. He knelt and rolled his bedding as fast as he'd ever done. Packing his things onto his horse, he started to step into the stirrup but thought he should take the other horse. He untied the other horse, stepped into the saddle, and headed down for the main road.

"I'm done. I'm clearing out," he said aloud. "I don't want that brat anyways, an' Rudy's dead. Iffen I stay around here, I'll be dead too." He rode at a trot down the hill, the ground was steep.

Jenny had been hiding behind bushes, thinking he'd find her. She was relieved to see he didn't have Chloe in tow. *I do hope the girl has sense enough to go straight downhill and head for the road. Surely someone will be looking for us and find her.* Another thought hit her. *Anne doesn't know we're heading home, and the Bannisters won't know we didn't make it back to Mobrey Manor unless someone sees that wagon. Ah…if Ginger makes it back to the Bannisters, she can write a note and tell them what happened. Oh, Lord, Thou knowest all things. I pray Thy hand of protection upon us. Mayest Thy will be done.*

Jenny watched Buddy ride down the hill, with their horse in tow.

Donny first went to Dr. John's office, but his wife, Sally Ann, said he'd gone to Bertha Morrow's house. She helped out with several charities, and Dr. John was on the board of a couple of them.

Donny was glad Bertha lived on the edge of town and not way out in the country someplace. He delivered his message to the doctor, and without waiting for him, he headed for the Mobreys'.

Diego found Buck with no problem. He was in his office catching up on paperwork.

"We haf emergency." Diego spoke quickly and tried to slow down so Buck could understand.

Buck started strapping on his guns as Diego spoke.

"Chloe's uncle, he kidnap Chloe, Mrs. Tarkington, an' Ginger. Ginger, she get shot but runned away and tell Meester Bannister. He forming posse. We meet at Mobreys'."

"Got a wanted poster of the Blake brothers today. They're wanted for murder in Sonoma. Any way you look at it, Buddy Blake is going to hang," Buck said grimly. "I'm glad I'm here and not out at Sunrise. Hattie would be wild with worry. Let me get a couple more men, and I'll be there as quickly as possible." He strode down the boardwalk and spoke to one of the bankers. Tommy Denko was young but had landed a position at the bank. Buck knew he was a bit of a hothead, but he was a good tracker. A few doors farther down, Buck solicited the owner of the mercantile for help. Trayne Alastair had ridden with Buck many times. He was levelheaded and reliable.

Diego didn't wait for Buck but rode straight for Mobreys' as fast as he could. Donny wasn't there yet, but Matthew, James, Bates, and Dock were ready to ride.

The men talked while they waited for the sheriff.

"Lucas is in San Rafael," James said. "He's been offered a place at the law office where Elijah works. He's taken a real shine to Anne's old secretary, Josephine. Reckon it won't be long before they're married."

Matthew grinned. "Love must be in the air," he said. "Danny, my brother-in-law's best friend, was a confirmed bachelor. He fell for a nurse he met just a few days ago."

James grinned back and said, "Love is most definitely in the air!" He felt elated and wished he could go back into the house, take Anne into his arms, and tell her how much he loved her. He hoped he was not mistaken as to what he'd seen in her eyes.

Thaddeus came out to the stable yard ahead of Anne. Dock had saddled Anne's horse. They were going to the Bannisters' to be with Ginger. Anne walked up to James and spoke to him in a quiet voice.

"I'd ride with you, but I think my place is with Ginger. Find Grandma Jenny." She grabbed his lapels and said again, "Oh, please find her! And do be careful, James. I'll be praying for you."

James drew Anne into his arms, giving her a quick hug. "I'll ride to the Bannisters' before I come home, to make sure you're not still there."

"I will be," Anne said. "Thad and I have packed a few things for overnight. I'm sure Ginger is not going to want to ride if she's been shot. She's a brave little girl. I long to hear her voice. We'll be spending the night if we're invited." Anne turned her face up to James and gave him a quick kiss on the lips. She blushed and turned away, walking to her horse, Piano Keys. She stepped into the stirrup, and Dock swung Thad up behind her.

"There ye be, laddy. I'm glad to hear your sister can talk. Say hello to her for me, will you?"

Thad nodded, anxious to get going.

Anne kicked her horse, and they were off.

It wasn't ten minutes after her departure that the waiting men could see four men riding toward them. It was Buck, Donny and two others.

CHAPTER XXXII

There is a way that seemeth right unto a man,
but the end thereof are the ways of death.

PROVERBS 16:25

BUCK DIDN'T WASTE TIME DOING much talking. He rode up to the waiting men and spoke, his tone clipped, his face grim. "Our job is to find Jenny Tarkington and my daughter, Chloe. Let's get to it." He turned his horse and raised his hand for everyone to follow. They rode out, no one chatting or making light of the task ahead.

They rode for some time on the main road, but Buck pulled up when he saw the wagon. It was pulled a little off the road. The wagon was empty and the horse gone.

Buck turned back and yelled, "Trackers!"

Matthew and Tommy rode up front. They both climbed off their rides, and as Tommy started to talk to Buck, Matthew walked a bit farther and knelt on one knee.

He turned back to the posse and said, "James!"

James rode up, passing the rest of the men.

"Yes?"

"Your horses—they have an *M* on the shoe?"

"Yes, yes they do. When Dock brought the idea to me, I thought it a good one. All our shoes have an *M* stamped into the metal."

"This look like it?"

James got down and looked at the clearly marked print in the dirt of the road.

"Yes, that's my horse's shoe," he said.

Tommy elbowed James aside and squatted down next to Matthew.

"I think we should go cross country. Our man most likely headed up the hill there."

"No, no, he didn't." Matthew spoke with authority. "He's gone down the road. Reckon we can track 'em if we keep a good watch and don't 'muddy the waters,' so to speak."

"I'm with you if you're sure he traveled down the road. I'd have cut off the road to make sure no one could follow me," Tommy said.

"Yes, but I think our man is a few cups shy of a quart," Matthew said. "There's no telling what he might do.

"Ah, well maybe you're right, and he headed down the road a bit. Let's see if we can find more prints."

Buck told Matthew to take the lead. They headed down the road quite a distance, when Matthew suddenly held up his hand to stop.

"Here," he said, "they turned off here."

Buck looked across the flat and up to a hill that overlooked the road in both directions. Trees sheltered the foot of the hill and most of the climb up.

"If he's up there, he's already seen us. Been up there a few times myself. It's a perfect view."

Buddy, who didn't even look to see if anyone was on the road, came out of the woods and onto the road, still holding the reins of the other horse.

Tommy Denko spied him several hundred yards ahead. He spurred his horse and let out a bloodcurdling yell. Buck, Dock, Bates, and Trayne followed close behind Tommy.

Figuring there were enough men going after Buddy Blake, Matthew, Diego, Donny, and James turned toward the woods to look for Jenny and Chloe.

Buddy, seeing a man charging, dropped the reins of the other horse and galloped down the road, kicking his horse repeatedly. He turned in the saddle to see the man gaining on him. Abruptly he left the road and headed toward the wooded area, but he suddenly realized the man was going to catch him. He turned his horse and taking aim, shot at his pursuer but grazed his horse.

Tommy's horse bucked, and a surprised Tommy flew from the saddle, hitting the ground at an awkward angle.

Buddy slipped from his horse, and crouching on one knee, he took aim to fire on the posse, knowing he didn't stand a chance.

Trayne lifted his gun and fired, missing the hunched figure.

The outlaw fired back, the bullet whizzing past the merchant's ear. Trayne didn't miss the second time and hit Buddy full in the chest.

Buddy went down, face forward, not moving. As the men neared him, they saw that Buddy Blake would never move again.

Bates stopped where Tommy lay with one leg twisted beneath him.

"'Fraid I broke my leg," he gasped.

"Looks like it," Bates replied, "a real sockdolager."

Tommy groaned. "A what?"

With his English accent, Bates explained, "Sockdolager means *exceptionally*. You understand there's no doubt you've really done it, sir."

Tommy groaned again. The other men came, and they lifted him to straighten his leg out, but it was bleeding profusely. Tommy bit his lip to keep from screaming out his pain, and it was a mercy that he fainted from it.

Bates took Tommy's cravat and his own, wrapping them around where bone protruded the skin.

"Bates, you and Dock take Tommy to the Bannisters'," Buck said. "I'm pretty sure Dr. John is there with Ginger. Let's get him up on Blake's horse while he's unconscious. You can ride back as far as the wagon and hitch this horse to it. Hopefully you can haul him onto it before he regains consciousness. He's got a really bad break. We'll find Tommy's horse later. Maybe he'll head for home on his own. Trayne, you ride with me. We need to find Mrs. Tarkington and my Chloe."

Buck had climbed off his horse to help load Tommy onto Buddy's horse. He took the reins of what must be the Mobreys' horse and handed them to Trayne.

"We'll need this horse," he said. Without another word, Buck mounted his own animal and headed for a trail he knew led up to the top of the cliff. Trayne followed him.

Anne and Thaddeus turned into the long lane of the Bannisters' Rancho, neither of them talking much. Riding up and around the sweep of driveway, Anne pulled Piano Keys to a stop. Thad slid off her horse, giving him a pat on his flank. Anne dismounted, tying him up at the railing next to Dr. John's mount. They walked up the flagstone path, and Anne rang the cowbell.

Conchita answered the door and ushered them inside.

"Eet good you come," she said in a low voice. "Ginger, she een much pain, an' she be asking for you." She looked at Thaddeus. "She say her brother always make her happy."

Thaddeus' heart swelled with love for his sister. They'd been through much together, and he hoped he could take her mind off her pain.

Conchita led them down the hall to one of the bedrooms. Liberty was sitting beside the bed, but Ginger was lying with her eyes closed.

Her hands were folded, and at first it scared Thaddeus, as she looked as if she were dead.

Liberty whispered, "I'll go to the kitchen and keep Dr. John company and let you have some privacy." She left on quiet feet.

Ginger knew her brother had come. She opened her eyes, smiling at Thaddeus.

"I can talk, Thaddy. I can talk. You'll never shut me up now."

Thad walked over to the bed and took her hand.

"I'll never want to shut you up again, Ginge. It's been way too long since I heard your voice. I'm thankful you've got it back. How's your arm?"

"It hurts like I've burned it on a frypan, but I'll be all right. I'm praying Chloe and Grandma Jenny are okay. Chloe's uncle is a scary man, but in truth, he just made me mad. After what happened to us last year, it's going to take a lot for me to be really frightened again... worried maybe, but frightened, no."

Anne leaned over the bed and kissed Ginger on the cheek, looking deeply into the girl's blue eyes. "What a brave girl you are. I'm so proud of you. Your actions will most likely save Grandma Jenny and Chloe. No one would have known you all were missing. And oh, Ginger, what a beautiful voice you have, darling. I'm so thankful." Tears flooded Anne's eyes. "I'm so very, very thankful you got it back."

Liberty was having a cup of tea with Dr. John, when there was a commotion at the door. She ran to open it, but it flew inward before she reached it.

Bates and Dock were carrying Tommy Denko.

The injured man floated in and out of consciousness, the pain excruciating.

"Sorry. The sheriff told us to bring him here." Bates gasped from the effort of carrying dead weight.

"Follow me." Liberty led them to a bedroom on the opposite side of the hall from Ginger. She grabbed a couple towels to protect the bed linen. "Lay him here," she directed.

Dr. John had followed Liberty to the door.

"What's happened to him?" he asked as he unwrapped the bloodied cravats.

"His horse got grazed by a bullet and threw Mr. Denko off," Bates replied. "It's a dreadful break, I'm afraid."

Dock added, "He's bin in and out, talkin' a lot of nonsense, fer sure."

Dr. John went first to the kitchen to ask Conchita to heat some water and then to the stable to see what he could use for splints.

Dock and Bates headed for home.

Matthew, along with Donny, Diego, and James, had ridden steadily upward. They reached the mesa and saw signs of a camp, but no one there.

Jenny, who'd heard the horses, had hidden behind a tree, not knowing who was coming. When she saw who it was, she entered the clearing, exhausted and her chin swollen blue from Buddy's fist.

"Praise the Lord!" she said. "Do you have Chloe?"

"No, we haven't seen her," Matthew replied. "Are you all right?" He slid from his horse, and taking his Bowie knife out of a scabbard, he cut the rope on Jenny's wrists.

"Yes, I'm all right." She rubbed her wrists. "I'm tuckered out from all the excitement, I reckon, but I'm fine."

"Where's Chloe?"

"I don't know. She ran away when that wretched man was digging about in the cave. I thought she might head down to the main road. When her uncle came out of the cave, he tried to catch her, but he came back without her and cleared camp. Oh my...what if he hurt her? We've got to find her. It'll be dark soon, and I'm sure she'll be frightened out of her wits!"

"We'll find her. You just sit tight, and we'll find her. Which way did she head out?"

"Through there." She pointed to the spot where Chloe had begun to run away.

"I'll ride that way," Matthew said. "You all fan out, and we'll see if we can find her. If you do, shoot your gun once. If you need help, shoot your gun twice. If it's once only, everyone can head home from where they are." Matthew rode Piggypie down the steep grade, and the other men fanned out, riding down in different directions. Diego, riding down, ran into Buck coming up.

"We find Mees Tarkington, but Chloe, she not be there. She runned away from her uncle. Mees Tarkington, she ees waiting up there." Diego jerked his thumb upward.

Buck's face tightened with worry.

"Thanks, Diego. I'll go talk to Mrs. Tarkington and see if she knows anything more."

Trayne tipped his hat respectfully at Diego but said nothing, following Buck's lead.

Diego nodded and continued down in a zigzag fashion.

Buck and Trayne gained the clearing at the top.

Jenny was sitting on a log, her head bowed in prayer. She watched the two a bit warily, as dusk was setting in and she couldn't see them clearly. Her shoulders sagged in relief as she saw it was the sheriff she'd met at the Bannisters'.

She took a deep breath and pointed toward the spot that Matthew had gone down.

"She ran down, right there." Jenny spoke before Buck even asked a question. "I forgot to ask Matthew, but did you catch Chloe's uncle?"

"He's dead, ma'am. He tried a shootout rather than surrender." Buck turned to Trayne. "I want to thank you. I wouldn't have liked shooting Chloe's uncle, albeit the man deserved it."

Trayne nodded. For a businessman, he was a man of few words.

Buck asked, "Are you up to riding, Mrs. Tarkington?"

"Yes. I've never ridden astride before, but I'm sure I can."

"Trayne, would you mind taking Mrs. Tarkington to the Bannisters' on the Mobreys' horse? She needs that chin looked at. And by the way, Mrs. Tarkington, your Ginger can now talk."

He turned away to go hunt for his Chloe and missed seeing the tears that filled Jenny's eyes, tears of thanksgiving and exhaustion. Blindly, she mounted James' horse, her high-topped shoes and part of her legs exposed, but she didn't care. She nodded to Trayne, and the two started down the hill.

Matthew had gone down the trail, seeing the broken branches, but spotted nothing. He turned his horse and started back up, looking more carefully than when he'd gone down. He had a feeling she'd gone off the trail somewhere and didn't want to miss it a second time. It was getting dark, and the air was cooling.

"Chloe!" he called out, "Chloe, it's me, Matthew. Chloe!"

Buck heard his call and called out himself. "Chloe! It's Papa! Chloe, are you hiding? It's all right—come out!"

Matthew got off his horse. He peered at the branches on his left and followed the trail to find Chloe curled up deep in the bush. His heart stopped when he first saw her, thinking the worst, but as he gazed, he saw her deep breathing. His breath expelled in a whoosh of relief.

"Here she is, Buck!" He lifted her gently, and she awoke. Matthew handed her up to Buck, looking up into his eyes, which were misted over.

Buck held out his arms, and the transfer was made as Chloe came fully awake.

"Papa! Oh, Papa, I knew you'd find me!" Chloe, who rarely cried, sobbed her heart out, her little arms clinging around his neck.

"There, there now," he said. "It's all right, sweetheart. It's all right." He hugged her little body, but she cried out in pain.

"Uncle B-Buddy fisted me, and I think my r-ribs are broken." She tried to stop crying, but tears ran down her cheeks.

Buck wiped them away with a big kerchief and said, "Oh, sweetie, I'm sorry. I'd never hurt you on purpose." He held her carefully in his arms, his eyes full of love and thanksgiving as he spoke to Matthew. "Plug your ears, sweetheart. We need to let the other men know you've been found."

Matthew drew his pistol and shot into the air.

Buck said, "All right, let's get out of here while we can still see."

While Dr. John was finishing up with Tommy Denko, who had regained consciousness, Jenny and Trayne Alastair walked into the Rancho. Jenny was so exhausted, she hadn't even thought to knock.

Trayne wondered what he should do, but Conchita entered the room just then, taking the decision out of his hands.

"Oh, Mees Tarkington, we ees so worried about you. You seet here. Dr. John, he fixing up the man weeth the broken leg. I geet you some ice from the icehouse. You haf a bad chin." She looked up at Trayne, knowing he owned the mercantile in Napa. "Meester Alastair, you want something to dreenk? Coffee, tea, or something stronger?"

"Coffee's fine." He smiled at Conchita, and it lit up his usual solemn features. Conchita blinked and realized she'd never seen him smile before.

"You seet. I geet eet for you. Mees Tarkington, what you like to haf?"

"Tea, please. Is Ginger all right? I saw Anne's horse is here. Is Thaddeus here too?"

Conchita answered her questions and bustled to the kitchen to pour hot water into a teapot, adding a couple teabags to steep. She poured hot water into a coffee mug to heat the ceramic. Next, she took a small bowl and the ice pick out to the icehouse. Stabbing at the big block, she chunked some thick pieces of ice into the bowl and went back to the house.

She wrapped the ice in a soft cloth and took it to Jenny.

"Here, thees weel make eet feel better. I get your tea now." She bustled back to the kitchen and sliced two thick pieces of yellow cake with chocolate frosting, dumped the hot water out of the cup, and poured hot coffee into it. She piled everything on a tray, carrying it back to the tired guests.

"Thees make you restored," she said. "Now, I tell Dr. John you ees here."

Just then James, Diego, and Donny entered.

Conchita crossed herself and said, "I thank the Lord you ees safe. Where ees Matthew?"

"We ees all safe," Diego answered. "Matthew, he and the sheriff, they ees looking for Chloe, but they find her, but we doan know how Chloe ees. We just ride for home. Chloe's uncle, he ees dead."

James asked Conchita, "Sorry, but where is Anne?"

Conchita led him down the hall and left him in the doorway.

Dr. John joined the others in the great room. While Conchita was telling him about Jenny's chin, Matthew and Buck walked in. The sheriff carried Chloe to the sofa and laid her gently on it.

"Broken ribs," he said succinctly. It angered him mightily that Buddy had so abused Chloe and Jenny. Emotionally drained, he would wait for Dr. John to wrap Chloe's ribs before heading for home and Hattie.

Liberty felt exhausted but knew there'd be no rest until bedtime. As she walked down the hall, she saw Matthew had returned safely. Thanking the good Lord under her breath, she went to see if any more help was needed.

EPILOGUE

God is our refuge and strength,
a very present help in trouble.

PSALM 46:1

BUCK LEFT WITH CHLOE RIGHT AFTER Dr. John wrapped her ribs. It was dark, and Hattie, who knew nothing about today's affairs, would be worrying.

Trayne, having been invited to dinner, declined, knowing the house was already overflowing with guests.

Dr. John left before dinner, leaving some laudanum for Tommy Denko, who was sedated and sleeping.

The twins had been up for several hours, and dinner was late. Liberty had fed them, and they were now asleep.

The Mobreys, Matthew, and Liberty finished Conchita's famous *sopapillas*, a dessert filled with honey, and were relaxing in the great room.

Ginger was up and sitting on the sofa, snuggled between Thaddeus and Jenny. James and Anne were sitting together on a love seat, and Liberty, at last relaxed, squeezed in next to Matthew in a wide leather chair.

Conversation flowed as Ginger and Jenny gave their accounts of the ordeal now behind them. Matthew gave his version, and all were quiet when he told of how Buddy had died.

"If he'd simply surrendered, he wouldn't have been shot."

"That's true," James said, "but if I'd have been him, I'd have chosen the same option. He'd have hung for what he did. Better to go that way than to have to wait, knowing he was going to be strung up anyway."

Liberty turned to Matthew.

"Do you think that's why Chloe's father kept shooting at me? Buck told me they were wanted for murder in Sonoma. He got a wanted poster today about the Blake brothers. I still feel badly about shooting that man, but I feel better, somehow, knowing he'd have died anyway if he were caught." She breathed a deep sigh.

"I have no doubt about it." Matthew hoped his wife could let this issue go. "He was an evil man, and besides, whoever it was he killed in Sonoma, he killed one of my best friends—maybe not with a gun, but the result was the same. He'd have killed us if he got the chance. Yes, he'd have hung anyway. We can be so grateful that God is our refuge and strength, a very present help in times of trouble. Chloe knows that. I think Thaddeus and Ginger know that, don't you?"

Ginger answered candidly. "I was so hurt and angry at God for letting my parents die. Then I was really angry about not being able to talk. I tried and tried but couldn't. Today, as I ran here, I thought of how God had provided for me. Grandma Jenny talked to Chloe and me on our way home, before that evil man got us." Ginger slipped her hand into Jenny's and kept talking. "She said a lot of things to us, but what stuck in my mind is that we live in a world full of evil. God made us a perfect world, but people have gone against what His desire is for us. He didn't make us puppets. It wasn't His fault my father died or my mother was killed. Grandma Jenny said what Satan has meant for evil, God can turn to good. I told God I was sorry for blaming Him for things that were not His fault."

Jenny squeezed her hand. "You are so precious, child. I'm glad I can be your grandma."

Liberty was quiet and then thought about her guests and where they would sleep.

"I should tell you where you're sleeping," she said. "Jenny, I'm putting you in the room next to Tommy Denko's. He'll not be using the bathing room." Her cheeks pinked up, but she didn't say he'd be using a bedpan. "Thaddeus, you'll be in with Ginger, and James, I'm putting you and Anne in the connecting bedroom."

James smiled inwardly. Anne's cheeks pinked up from Liberty's directions, but her hand sought James' under the cover of her dress. He grasped it and gave hers a gentle squeeze as he turned to look into her violet eyes.

Love, warmth, and laughter shone from Anne's eyes.

The wedding bargain had been fulfilled. This was their wedding night.

Books can be purchased on Amazon

Website: mary ann kerr .com (delete the spaces) (signed copy)

Inklings Bookshop, Yakima, WA

Songs of Praise in Yakima, WA

Or by writing me at:

Mary Ann Kerr

10502 Estes Road

Yakima, WA (I charge no tax, sign the book, and the cost of shipping priority mail is $6.49) (Media rate is ($4.00)

My public e-mail is: hello at maryann kerr .com (delete spaces and add @) where you can also order a book.

You may message me on Facebook page: Mary Ann Kerr (comments are welcome!)

When readers take the time to write or e-mail me their experience reading my stories, I sometimes put their comments on my blog if they don't mind.

Liberty's Inheritance	(sale price. . . . .$14.99)
Liberty's Land	(sale price. . . . .$14.99)
Liberty's Heritage	(sale price. . . . .$14.99)
Caitlin's Fire	(sale price. . . . .$14.99)
Tory's Father	(full price. . . . . $14.99)
Eden's Portion	(full price. . . . . $14.99)
Cady's Legacy	(full price. . . . . $14.99)
Anne's Wedding Bargain	(full price. . . . . $14.99)

Books by Peter A. Kerr (my author son)

Adam Meets Eve (nonfiction)—$10.00 + 5.65 shipping and handling

The Ark of Time (science fiction)—$12.00 + $5.65 shipping and handling

Book by Andrew Kerr (my author son and my cover and design guy)

Ants on Pirate Pond (children's black-and-white chapter book with darling illustrations)—12.95 + $5.65 shipping and handling

Prologue

Maggie's Redemption

Unto the woman he said, I will greatly multiply thy sorrow
and thy conception; in sorrow thou shalt bring forth children;
and thy desire shall be to thy husband, and he shall rule over thee.

GENESIS 3:16

"**MEGDN, MY DEAR SWEET MEGDN.** How I do love you my precious girl. It won't be long now, me darlin'. I know you to be in a good deal of pain. Hold fast my sweetheart—me love—hold fast. McDermish says I must leave you to it, but you ken I love you me darlin'." Shamus' hand had been holding her steady.

The labor was intense, and Shamus hoped his voice sounded reassuring to the woman's ears in a room filled with pain. He, in truth, was worried. He wasn't sure how much strength his dear wife had left. She'd been in labor for hours and hours. Shamus kissed her—shamelessly in front of the doctor.

He saw the surprised look of disgust that came over the face of the man of medicine. He grinned inwardly and kissed her again. Kissing in front of any onlooker simply wasn't done. Shamus O'Neill knew he struggled to conform to the standards set by society. Most of it was an absurdity to him.

Shamus looked at the doctor, Taghd McDermish.

"I will leave you now, but I will brook no departure of my orders. You will be clean or clear out. Your choice."

Taghd McDermish, angered by O'Neill's stipulation that he must scrub his hands or that anything else that touched his wife must first be boiled, waggled his forefinger at Shamus angrily.

"Yer edgiecation, Shamus, it's gone to yer head, man!" The doctor seemed incensed by Shamus standing over him making sure all was clean, but Shamus didn't care.

With a tender squeeze of Megdn's hand and another kiss on her forehead, Shamus made no reply to the doctor as he headed toward the door.

As Megdn groaned with her next pain the father to be left the small room with reluctance, closing the door quietly behind him.

Descending the steep narrow stairs, he went to the kitchen to make sure everything was in readiness for a newborn baby. He didn't care that McDermish was unhappy with him. If Megdn hadn't wanted the doctor so badly, he would have had the midwife in. He knew and liked the the woman. She was clean, and she'd delivered many babies in the valley in which they lived. Shamus cringed inwardly when he thought of McDermish's fingernails. They were filthy.

Shamus Barra O'Neill, professor at Trinity College, Dublin University, specialized in mathematics, but he was interested in all the sciences and had, in the past, talked to Ignaz Semmelweis, a physician from Hungary. The two had met at a conference in Vienna and had taken an instant liking to each other. With their shared passion for research, they stimulated each other's minds, enjoying the camaraderie that comes from likemindedness. Semmelweis told Shamus he'd reduced the death rate of new mothers dying from puerperal fever in half, simply by having doctors scrub their hands vigorously with soap before delivering babies.

Shamus nearly winced, as he thought of the doctor upstairs. His hygiene left much to be desired. At least McDermish had washed his hands. Shamus had stood there and watched him, handing him the bar of soap. He'd insisted the doctor scrub them well. The father-to-be wasn't a religious man, but he said a quick prayer for God to please spare his wife and the new baby.

Because the O'Neill household had enough money, Shamus had hired a woman, a live-in maid, to help his wife. They lived modestly in a nice section of Dublin within walking distance to stores and Trinity College where he taught.

As Shamus entered the kitchen Magda, their maid, nodded to him.

"She'll be havin' the babe soon, I ken," Magda said sagaciously.

"Yes, and I see you have everything in readiness. Are you cooking that flannel?" Shamus' eyes expressed his surprise seeing the small blanket folded on top of the cooler section of the wood stove.

"Aye, that I am. The wee one'll be needin' the warmth after leavin' the shelter of its mam."

"You're a good woman, Magda Shaunessy, and we are grateful to have you. Megdn sings your praises nearly every day. We are thankful for your unstinting loyalty and help in our home."

Magda's face reddened under the praise, and she turned back to the stove. Shamus could tell she was not used to anyone voicing a compliment. Quite young, she worked hard and was wholly capable. Her curly jet black hair was scraped back into a bun, but curls escaped and softened her face under the mobcap. She picked up another piece of wood and fed the old stove to keep the heat at a temperature to cook the stew which simmered on its top.

It was unusually warm this day of May 12, 1864. The cold and damp of early spring had given way to a beautiful feeling of summer. Flowers lifted their heads to the warmth of the sun, bursting forth in a riot of color. Lilacs, usually blooming in April, were in full bloom. Seemingly overnight, trees had clothed themselves in velvet leaves, soft and new.

Shamus opened the back door and left it open to the warmth of the day. He stood on the back porch, glad he'd had it partially enclosed. When it rained, his stack of wood at the end of the porch stayed dry. The price of wood was expensive, but he thought it burned hotter than the popular peat. He gathered an armful of wood and dumped it into the woodbox near the stove.

"Thank ye, sir. Air ye hungry?"

Before he could answer, a scream ripped through the house.

"Aye, sir. She'll be havin' that babe afore long," Magda said.

Shamus nodded his head, wondering how anyone could bear such agony overlong.

"She's been at it for far too long, Magda," he replied. "How can she endure it?"

Another scream rent the air and a lusty cry followed. Without waiting for an answer, Shamus tore up the stairs two at a time. He threw open the door. The doctor was in the process of cutting the cord on the crying baby, but Shamus could see Megdn had lost consciousness.

"You can't be in here!" McDermish said angrily. The anger dropped away, and his shoulders slumped as he added, "She's lost too much blood. Don't know if she'll make it but for certain she won't be havin' anymore bairns." He looked at Shamus' shocked face. "I'm sorry." He packed up his bag and started to leave, "I'll collect payment, later, sir." He clumped down the stairs and banged the front door shut behind him.

Shamus ran back down the stairs and yelled for Magda to come help. He wet a cloth from an ewer and wrung it out over the basin. Magda grabbed the warmed flannel and sheets. Gaining the stairs, she quickly took the baby from the bed and wrapped her tightly in it, seeing it was a girl. Shamus bathed Megdn's face.

Her eyes opened and looked huge in her pallid face. She whispered, "What is it, Shammy; is it a boy?"

Surprise spread itself over Shamus' face. He didn't know and looked across the bed at Magda for an answer.

"It's a girl," she said softly, "it's a beautiful baby girl."

Shamus asked, "What do you want to name her, Megdn me luv?"

"Oh Shammy, I want to name her Margaret—Margaret after your mother. I loved your mam so much," Megdn replied in a whisper. Tears formed at the corners of her eyes.

"Aye, Margaret's a fine name. I think Regan will do for the middle name. I always did like your maiden name." Shamus said.

Megdn smiled weakly, "Margaret Regan O'Neill it is." Tears began to seep from her eyes. Emotional and physical exhaustion claimed her. She seemed almost shrunken in the huge bed. Closing her lids, sleep overtook her.

Magda tucked the little baby next to her mam and set about to clean things up.

www.ingramcontent.com/pod-product-compliance
Lightning Source LLC
Chambersburg PA
CBHW021209250626
47155CB00008B/2740